PATRI(

Vantage Point

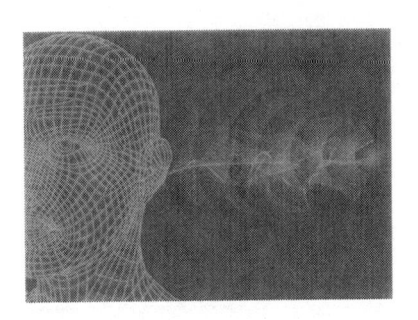

— A KATE ROARTY, P.I. NOVEL —

Vantage Point
Copyright © 2016 by Patricia Filteau

This book is a work of fiction set in the future. Any reference to historical events, real people, or real places are used fictitiously. Other names, characters, places and events are products of the author's imagination, and any resemblance to actual events or places or persons, living or dead is entirely coincidental.

All rights reserved. No part of this book may be used or reproduced in any matter without prior written permission.

Soundwave by Leinad Lehmko from the Noun Project

ISBNs
Softcover: 978-1-77302-068-6
eBook: 978-1-77302-069-3

To my friend, Karan Maguire, who knocked on the door thirty-eight years ago, stepped across the threshold, and continued into the future. Thank you.

1

Kate swam in the evening, traversing the lake then making her way along the shore, as far as inclination and imagination took her. Open-water swimming released an accumulation of stresses and woes. The day became ordered — its vagaries slipped away with each rhythmic stroke. She swam alone and loved it that way. The inhabitants of the lake, the loon, the fox, the bear, and the beaver, seemed to accept her solitary intrusion as part of the landscape of their watery and shoreline domain. She gave neither heed nor concern to the people of the lake. Most often, they were simply not there at all.

Kate preferred swimming the breaststroke in open water. However, after twenty years of pounding the pavement while running and jogging, her middle-aged knees required greater care, forcing her to adopt the front crawl, the accompanying flutter kick of which was more efficient and strong yet gentle, although the overall experience was less aesthetic. To regain her commune with the birds and mammals, she flipped onto her back and slipped along with a proficient, relaxed backstroke, watching the shoreline, water surface, and horizon for amusing activity. Those distractions usually occurred in the form of gathering black clouds, loons diving, bears in a clearing routing out ants and berries, and the occasional canoeist or kayaker paddling unobtrusively by. The few old log and timber cottages on the distant shore were rarely inhabited these days. Their owners, mired in the *in-between* generation, took little time from their high-powered careers to enjoy the pleasures of their youth experienced on the lake.

Kate's best thinking took place when she was swimming. Epiphanies sprang forth; ideas emerged and took form, conundrums were resolved; aches and pains were dispatched, and equilibrium was restored. She preferred to swim in one particular lake, but the activity took her to indoor swimming pools in cities and towns on many continents; into lakes, rivers, seas, and oceans around the world; to oases, estuaries, water-filled quarries, and rooftop residential baths. She swam in fresh water, salt water, chlorinated water, clean water, filthy water, warm water, and frightfully cold water. When she learned that the Asian astrological calendar gave her birth date the revered status of the water dragon, she embraced the descriptive with whole-hearted delight. It was a fit.

A sudden crack, sounding like a whack of lightning, felled a tree, crashing it into the water on the nearby shore. Kate changed direction. Aware of the gathering dusk but wishing to check out the disturbance, she stroked toward the fallen tree. As she approached, a plaid shirt flapping in the water drew her attention toward a snapped and bent tree trunk. A shoulder pushed against a billowing shirt. Kate easily identified the species of the downed tree: a sugar maple. Apart from noting that the body was male, she did not otherwise recognize the occupant of the plaid shirt. The receding ripples of water from the crash and splash of the tree gave the only motion to an otherwise lifeless body. Kate's feet found the rocky bottom. She freed the shirt from its hold on a broken branch of the tree then dragged the heavy, limp, cold body over to the shore and up a slight embankment.

The evening light was fading quickly. It cast the lake in shadow as the sun was setting behind the surrounding hills. Kate mused that she had to stop these late evening swims, taken when the lake was quiet, the parking lot deserted, and the light dim. She could do nothing for the lifeless body whose last breath had long since been taken. She re-entered the water then immediately set off at a fast-paced front crawl. She hated sprinting, but it seemed to be the required response to the situation at hand. Emerging from the lake on the opposite shore twenty minutes later, winded but focused, she grabbed her towel and clothes from the white lifeguards' table at the little beachside day park. As was usual for the late hour, the area was deserted. She ran up to the antiquated pay phone attached to the outside wall of the picnic area change rooms. Frankly, she was surprised that it was even there in 2026. With neither coins nor credit card at hand and her glasses in the car, she quickly discovered that making an emergency call from this phone was impossible. She wasn't sure why she was rushing — the plaid shirt-clad man was dead and may have been for quite some time. She wriggled out of her bathing suit, threw on her clothes, and ran to her car, solitary in the nearby parking lot. She retrieved her glasses and cell phone to place an emergency call. She punched in the number — no ringing, no answer, no signal. Self-counselling — *calm and think* — she pulled out her car keys, returned to the parking lot, got in the car, started the engine, backed out into an open area, turned, and then drove slowly along the road, stopping at the first cottage that had a car parked at it. She knocked on the door to ask to use a phone. The elderly, white-haired woman who answered the knock seemed reluctant to let her in until Kate said, "It's an emergency."

The woman stood back to allow Kate to enter and

motioned to the phone on the kitchen wall, a landline, rare these days but useful in the few wireless dead zones that hid in these hills behind large rock outcroppings. Kate placed the call, reached the emergency service on the second ring, gave a short report with directions, and advised that a boat would be required with strong lighting. Hanging up, she turned to introduce herself and apologize for the abrupt intrusion.

The small, frail-looking woman whose downcast, sad eyes barely connected with Kate's, nodded slightly, allowing back a name: Clare St. Denis.

Kate offered to wait outside for the Sûreté du Québec, the police for the area, and started for the door. Clare St. Denis lurched out of her bewilderment and offered Kate a seat and a cup of tea.

While boiling the water in the kettle, she quietly remarked, "You are the swimmer."

Kate replied, "This lake has many, many swimmers."

"Ah, but you are the first to arrive in May and last to leave in October. Sometimes we don't see you for weeks, for months and a few times — for years." She paused to turn and look at Kate and added, "Then you always return. You used to come with a man when your children were little, but we haven't seen him for a very long time. Once we saw him with another woman and a little girl — neither of them swam, but he did, by himself."

Kate didn't know which was more extraordinary, finding the dead body or listening to this woman relate observations about her personal life at the lake.

Her thoughts were interrupted by another remark from this Clare St. Denis. "Once you did a triple swim of the lake — twelve kilometres. You haven't done that for some years, but we predict you will do it again — maybe quadruple it."

"Who is the other part of *we* you refer to?" said Kate.

A single-word response was all Clare allowed. "Henri."

Kate asked, "Where is Henri now?"

Clare replied silently by placing a hand over her heart. Distant sirens drawing rapidly closer brought them both back to the moment. Kate slipped out the door to wait at the side of the road. Clare hung back in the kitchen doorway.

Kate walked out to the police SUV that had pulled onto the property and introduced herself to the two police officers whose nametags declared they were Officers Archambault and Johnson. They said they would like to take a preliminary statement while waiting for the police motor launch that could put in at nearby Canoe Beach and pick them up from the dock belonging to this cottage. The three strode down to the dock while Clare St. Denis hung back in the shadows of the failing light that were gradually enveloping her white, squared-timber cottage.

Kate gave a brief and factual statement to the officers. "I was swimming along the opposite shore when I heard a loud crack that sounded like lightning hitting a tree. A sugar maple crashed into the water. I swam over to get a closer look and spotted a plaid shirt hung up on a broken branch, flapping in the water. On closer viewing, I discovered that a lifeless body occupied the shirt. I released the shirt from the broken branch and then dragged the body out of the water and up the embankment, where I left it after checking for any sign of life. There was none. Then I swam back to the opposite shore where I had entered the lake at Blanchet Beach. I was unable to make the emergency beach phone work or get a wireless signal to place a call. My search for phone service brought me to the cottage of Madame St. Denis, who lives here." She pointed to the white, squared-timber cottage just behind where they were standing on the dock.

Officer Johnson took a moment to finish writing on his tablet, tapped his fingers against the surface, and remarked, "You were swimming with your clothes on?"

Kate gave him a look of fleeting perplexity then said, "No, I was swimming in my bathing suit. I took a moment to change into these clothes."

"May we see the swimsuit?" Johnson asked. Kate obliged by returning to her car, retrieving her bag from the front seat, and showing him the wet suit.

Officer Johnson said, "This is your car?"

Kate nodded.

"Did you walk here or drive?"

"I drove."

Archambault's hand-held device sounded a communication. A brief exchange in French confirmed the logistics with a follow-up retort from the officer, "*Dans cinq minutes.*" Archambault turned to Kate and Officer Johnson, advising them that the launch would pull around to the dock shortly. He no sooner said it than an engine fired up on the water, and a sweeping beam of light shone well out onto the lake. The three walked down to the dock. Kate glanced back over her shoulder to see Clare St. Denis watching from the windows that looked out over the water.

Officer Johnson said, "Okay, Madame Roarty, show us the way."

Kate pointed in the direction of the distant silhouetted shoreline, advising them to slow down when they got near so as not to disturb the site where she found the body. Johnson quipped, "A bit of *CSI* here, is it?" He missed Kate's eyes rolling in response to his sarcasm.

Johnson's next remark as they slowed on the approach to the darkening shoreline was, "Kathrine Roarty, former diplomat, free agent, divorced mother of two adult children who swims all over the world and periodically gets depressed, show us what you have found."

Kate felt a wave of strong annoyance well up. She bristled, declined to comment, and leapt over the side of the boat, guiding it to a stop as the operator flipped the throttle into neutral.

Officer Archambault quietly said, "We ran a preliminary

check on you on the way here. It's routine."
Kate liked this Officer Archambault. He stood about the same height as Kate's 5'8", with a solid, trim build, dark, thick, slightly curly short hair, and deep brown eyes that expressed emotion consistent with his words and demeanour. His simple attire — blue jeans, a checked shirt, and sturdy leather shoes, reflected a consistency in the way he presented himself to the world.

Kate said, "Gentlemen, you are going to get your feet wet if you want to visit the site where the body is located." The fallen tree prevented the launch from getting any closer. "You may want to take your boots off and wade over. The water is warm. Either way, you are here" — she motioned with her hands to indicate where they were — "and the body is there." She pointed in the direction of a patch of grass on the shore then indicated to the operator where to train the high-beam searchlight. It picked up the plaid shirt in the long grass. Archambault was over the side in full kit. Johnson lingered for a moment, sighed, and followed suit. Kate pointed to where she first saw the body attached to the broken branch of the fallen tree by its plaid shirt. The police launch operator suddenly sprang to life as a photographer, snapping multiple photos where Kate was pointing, surveyed the immediate shoreline then focused in on the body.

Archambault pulled out his notebook, and Johnson waded to shore.

Kate followed, only to receive another sarcastic remark from Johnson. "What else did you do to the body after your herculean heave to get it here?"

This remark sent a series of thoughts through Kate's mind. She could have just gone home and pretended she had not witnessed this scene. Johnson was one in a long line of jerks she had encountered in her professional career as a diplomat. She thought that leaving it had put such exchanges behind her. How naive — these jerks were everywhere. She took a deep breath, allowed the encroaching darkness to mask her annoyance, and said nothing.

Johnson said, "It's Jack."

Kate replied, "Sorry?"

Archambault interjected, "He is Jack, the Franco, I am Guy, the Anglo, and D'Angelo here," motioning to the boat operator, photographer, "we still can't figure out what he is. Are you a typical Frenchy with an Irish name?"

Kate studied them both, paused, then replied, "No, an Iroquois with a tomahawk."

"Christ, sounds like the Meech Lake Accord," said Officer Johnson.

D'Angelo interjected, "Okay, fellas, decide on a perimeter so we can tent it and cordon it off, then we can flip for who is going to stay the night until we can get Forensics out to determine a preliminary cause of death. 'Swim with the wolves' lady here is going to want to head home." The last remark made them all laugh.

"Not before we verify that the cause of death wasn't from a tomahawk," D'Angelo taunted. "Okay, drowning, hit by lightning, then drowned or at the hands of someone who was not happy with the poor bugger?"

Johnson dropped the sarcasm and asked Kate, "Are you familiar with the shoreline and the people who have the cottages along it?"

"If you are asking do I know or even recognize this guy," she pointed to the body that Guy had gently rolled over, "the answer is no. I can't say I really know anyone here, although I've been swimming this lake for thirty years. I have casually observed several generations growing up. I come to the lake to swim, to observe, and to experience, but actually rarely interact with the inhabitants."

D'Angelo, a small, swarthy man, suggesting Mediterranean origins, squatted down and gently riffled through the dead man's pockets. He came up with a billfold that contained some money, a few soggy business cards, a Visa card, and a driver's license. The photo appeared to identify the body as one Vincent Bernard Taylor of Apt. 501, 71 72nd Avenue E., New York, New York.

"Lovely, it's a consular case as well. Natural causes or foul play, it just became much more complex," said Kate.

D'Angelo threw a loonie in the air, and Guy teased, "Is it a three-sided coin?"

D'Angelo replied with resignation, hunching his broad shoulders. "Right, never mind, I'll stay. Huguette is off with the kids visiting her grandparents in Gaspé, so probably I would have done McDonald's and watched bad movies, anyway."

"If you are going to stay, you will have to forego both," said Guy.

D'Angelo patted his tummy with a broad hand and quipped, "It will likely do me some good to go without fries and burgers. As long as we have bug dope, I'll be fine until morning. Just come back with a large triple-triple and two egg McMuffins. You had better pick up Francine and Tracker as well."

Kate learned that Francine was a search-and-rescue dog handler, and Tracker was her charge, a black German Shepherd in his prime. Together they knew the Gatineau region intimately, having tracked down lost backpackers, kidnapped children, victims of marital discord, runaway prisoners who escaped their escorts during transfer, grow-ops hidden deep in the bush, Hells Angels hide-outs ... if there was something more they needed to know about this death, Francine and Tracker would find it and raise the alarm.

Guy tossed D'Angelo a sleeve of insect repellent, a can of Coke, a granola bar, and a space blanket found in the boat locker and then threw the throttle in reverse as Jack and Kate scrambled aboard.

Jack advised Kate, in a slightly more professional manner,

"Stay around town for the next few days in case we have some follow-up questions." He passed her his card, circling the cell number. "In case you think of anything else."

Kate replied, "I have no immediate travel plans. I'll be back out for my evening swim tomorrow." It was Jack's turn to roll his eyes. Before pocketing the card, she turned it over. Under the insignia for Sûreté du Québec, it read *Lieutenant Jack Johnson, Chef d'homocide.*

Guy pulled up to the dock so she could disembark, then he navigated the craft over to the bay at Canoe Beach. As Kate walked up to her car, she saw Clare St. Denis watching from the north-facing windows of the white, squared-timber cottage. The old woman could probably take it all in, despite the darkness.

The drive home gave Kate time to contemplate what had just transpired. Funnily enough, the dead body seemed to occupy the least of her thoughts. She loved driving the narrow, winding mountain road that hugged the edge of the lake then descended to the river. She asked her on-board communications system to find an all-night French classical/jazz station, then she sat back and let the car find the bends in the road.

Who is this Clare St. Denis with the mysterious Henri who's been watching me swim for thirty years? What is the allure of this very annoying Jack Johnson? She had branded him a jerk yet found him attractive. The physical attraction was easy. The tall, fit, well-built man with classical well-defined facial features and a thick flop of dark hair was pleasant to look at — he was attractive. But there was something more. The jerk-like behaviour seemed to mask a deeper, more complex man to whom she was drawn. She had promised herself, *No younger men.* There were too many issues and liabilities, and her children, now adults themselves, found it annoying when she dated younger men. Even five years younger was a liability. Jack was a young late thirty-something to her fifty.

She told herself, *Drop it.*
   Kate contemplated how this Vincent Bernard Taylor had met his demise. Perhaps it was simply a heart attack, or he had drowned — but of that, Kate was doubtful. She was aware that although none of them had said it, all of them harboured unspoken suspicions.
   How did he get there? The only options were by boat across the lake or on foot down the spine trail and up past Nude Beach, following the shoreline beyond First Beach, or he could have swum across the lake, but he was fully clothed. Kate slowed her car and swung it around in a fast U-turn to head back up the parkway road. The Sûreté du Québec's black Ford SUV sped past in the opposite direction, screeched to a stop, also swung around, and put on the flashing roof light, motioning Kate to pull over. Officer Johnson walked up to the driver's window as Kate was rolling it down.
   "Forget something?" he said, trying to mask the sarcasm that seemed to live within him like a constant companion.
   "I thought I would go back and check the O'Brien Beach parking lot," said Kate.
   "For what?"
   "Maybe a car — I was thinking, there was no boat, and it's unlikely that Taylor swam, given that he was fully clothed, so the only other way to reach that area is by foot along the spine trail. Did you check that parking lot? Was there a car there?" asked Kate.
   Johnson sighed, allowing a simple, "No. We'll do it."
   Before he could tell Kate to continue on home, she had sped off back up the road.
   Upon entering the O'Brien Beach parking lot, she saw a lone vehicle at the far end near the start of the hiker's trail. The SQ officers pulled in beside Kate's SUV. Kate was already out of her car, responding to a large, barking Golden Retriever.
   "It's okay, boy. C'mon, we won't hurt you. Take it easy."

The dog responded well to Kate then turned and snarled at the approaching officers.

"Tomahawk lady is also a dog whisperer," quipped Johnson.

"Oh please," Kate said. "The dog is very anxious."

Kate gently patted the dog while speaking with a reassuring, comforting tone as she fumbled with his tags. In the headlights of the police SUV, she could read a name and phone number, the latter of which she recognized as a New York City area code. Kate had done a contract in Manhattan some years earlier. She squatted down and continued to speak gently to the Golden Retriever while ruffling the fur around his neck. "So you are Big Ben from New York. What's up boy, what's happening?"

Officer Archambault shone a flashlight inside the parked vehicle but could see little of consequence. Johnson had already messaged in the New York plates and was awaiting ID. In a few moments, his laptop, perched on a pedestal between the two front seats of the police SUV, lit up and spat back the plate's information. It was a match to a Vincent Bernard Taylor of New York.

Officer Johnson said, "No sleep for these boys tonight. We will have to get some backup, the car entry boys, *and* somebody has to take the dog to the pound."

Kate said, "I can take him home for now, feed him, then figure out a plan tomorrow."

"The regs are to the pound," said Johnson.

Officer Archambault intervened. "Jack, pounds on both sides of the river will be closed up tighter than a clamshell at this time of the night. Why don't you let Mrs. Roarty take him home, and we'll sort it out tomorrow. We have bigger problems to deal with — why is the dog here and not with his owner — even if his owner is dead."

Johnson nodded his reluctant agreement.

2

Kate and Big Ben headed down the winding mountain road, passed through the dark and quiet village of Old Chelsea, and then drove out on to the main highway that led back to the city. She decided to stop at the twenty-four-hour McDonald's to get a double whatever they might have on the menu for Big Ben. She might even get something for herself, since she realized that she hadn't eaten since breakfast, twenty hours ago.

Big Ben unceremoniously wolfed down two deluxe Angus burger meals, lapped up two cartons of milk, then looked longingly at Kate's chicken snack wrap.

"I see your appetite isn't affected by whatever has happened in your life today," she said as she ruffled the fur on his head. Big Ben seemed to know that was it. He executed a deliberate circular dance, lay down in a tight curl on the passenger seat beside Kate, filling it entirely, then instantly dropped into a deep sleep.

Kate rested a hand on the sleeping dog and said, "Poor boy, it's probably been a very long, confusing day or more. We'll get this sorted out, big guy, but if Vincent Bernard

Taylor is your owner, you may need a new home."

Kate drove on, thinking about Golden Retrievers being excellent swimmers. Her little Cairn Terrier had been an incredible swimmer in his prime, but at fourteen, blind and nearly deaf, his swimming days were behind him. She hoped he wouldn't give Big Ben a rough time. Blind or not, the tough little Cairn was still her alpha male *and* her best friend. Her male feline, Boris, would undoubtedly play an advisory role in the acceptability of this particular houseguest.

Kate pulled on to her short, narrow street, a cul de sac in the old section of Ottawa known as Mont Bleu. Her townhouse was a relatively new infill slipped in among gentrified working class rows sought out by the upwardly mobile. Kate liked the place — it was filled with light, everything worked, and it had a small yard where she and the boys could readily slip outside without fear of distraction from an unkempt garden in summer or an onerous amount of snow shovelling in winter. What was there coexisted with a lush weed cover that provided adequate greenery to break up the grey stonework and concrete array masquerading as a patio. For her little fellows it was more than adequate; it might be a challenge for a creature the size of Big Ben.

They entered the house through the garage. A low, guttural growl alerted her to the little Cairn already poised at the door in a tough, macho stance slightly broken by a quick tail-wag for his best friend, then a guarded stance resumed from what his nose told him was an unfamiliar canine scent lurking just beyond Kate. Kate tightened the leash-hold on the eighty-pound retriever, who likewise had assumed a macho stance, albeit with a certain comical countenance. The Cairn was torn between obedience and defense, as his best friend was clearly inviting this aberrant scent into their home, yet it was his role to protect his house. Kate squatted down to make the introductions. Ben, the guest, was exuberant, indulgent, and solicitous; the Cairn was stiff-legged, wary, and considering. An extensive sniffing survey finally permitted them to move to the next accommodation. Kate took two swift steps toward the fridge and quickly retrieved two bones. Ben wolfed down his offering without chewing; Charlie held his tightly in his mouth while resuming the deep, guttural growling. Ben suddenly slipped into play mode.

Kate said, "Guys, it's 3:00 a.m., do you think we could settle this in the morning?"

All three ascended the stairs to Kate's spacious bedroom, where Boris cat was curled up asleep in the centre of the queen-size bed. She dropped Ben's leash long enough to lift the still growling, tough little Cairn onto her bed — Boris stretched up, yawned, passively considered Ben, then curled up between the pillows, totally disinterested in this turn of events, as if to say, "I'll give the big goof some thought in the morning, just keep him off my bed."

Kate obliged then led Ben to the three-seater wicker sofa placed against the wall opposite the bed. She patted the seat cushions when without hesitation Ben lumbered up, stretched out to full length, and dropped off sound asleep. The Cairn terrier's growling ceased as he launched into his bone. Kate slipped between the covers, luxuriating in the feel of a body finally moving to off-duty mode after a twenty-one-hour day. Boris cat meowed in passive annoyance then slipped into a deep, barely audible purr as he snuggled close to Kate's neck.

Kate awoke to full light and more deep, guttural growling. The retriever's head was resting on the bed with bright, playful eyes staring straight into Kate's face. The Cairn was not happy with this proximity of the nighttime intruder. Boris was posing for a Halloween shoot. Kate closed her eyes again while placing a reassuring hand on the Cairn Terrier. This bought her a few moments to contemplate the events of the previous night. She lay there thinking about the SQ officers, the dead man, and the lake while trying to rouse her weary body before a feline-canine melée exploded on her bed. The handset rang with 5:30 a.m. displayed under the ringing number. She sighed and reached for the phone, answering with a hoarse, "Hello."

"Hi, it's Jack, Officer Jack Johnson here," came a staccato retort.

"Don't you people sleep?" Kate said as she instantly picked up the sarcastic tone of their exchange. She was immediately exasperated with herself and determined to proceed more politely.

"Not when a murder is fresh and revealing," said Jack.

"Oh, so you know for sure that it is a murder then."

"Yes, the forensics team came up at first light and quickly made the determination."

Unable to help herself, Kate said, "And I needed to know this at 5:30 a.m. because…"

Jack did not continue the sarcastic banter; instead he replied with a note of sincerity, "Sorry about calling so early — we were wondering if you could come back up to the lake and give us a hand. A launch can pick you up at Canoe Beach when you get there."

Kate replied matter-of-factly, "I am not a suspect then?"

Jack came back with humour in his voice but no trace of sarcasm. "We haven't ruled you out, but it's unlikely."

Kate agreed to go as soon as possible, begging for a bit of time to sort out the scene before her that she quickly described to Jack.

"Oh, can you bring Big Ben back with you, and do you think you can hang on to him for a few days?" asked Jack.

Kate drawled, "Well…"

Jack quickly followed with, "The regulations are temporarily set aside."

"Okay, how about 9:00 a.m. at Canoe Beach?" Kate said in a tone of acquiescence.

After hanging up, she commanded, "Boys, breakfast, let's

go." All three seemed to know the drill and filed downstairs. The canines begged attentively from the floor while the feline strode possessively across the island countertop, using stately arrogance to solicit the first serving.

Kate threw on her jogging togs, grabbed two leashes, poop bags, the tennis ball, and launcher, clipped up both dogs on separate leashes as though this had always been the routine, and then headed off to the nearby field. She dropped the leashes on the porch and ran back to the kitchen to retrieve a handful of bribery treats — uncertain that the retriever would readily return to this very new acquaintance if she let him off-leash. The leash had become the Cairn's white cane — Kate rarely let him off it since blindness had overtaken him. As well, the days of jogging with him were long gone. The retriever, however, needed a good run — the ball launcher would help out there. Kate tossed the ball dozens of times until her left arm and the supply of treats gave out. The Cairn was also ready for home and a long nap.

Uncertain as to how the dogs would behave toward each other if left to their own devices, Kate picked up the little Cairn, sprinted up the stairs into the bathroom, and closed the door, setting the dog on the carpet while almost simultaneously turning on the shower. Big Ben was already outside the door. Kate commanded firmly through the door, "Ben, lay down." The shuffle on the other side of the door implied compliance. Encouraged by the momentary canine acquiescence, Kate quickly stepped into the shower, soaped up her tired body, then surprised herself by lingering on the rinsing as the image of the fit, muscular Jack Johnson floated through her conscience. Another time she might have lingered longer, but not today. The Cairn's growl punctuated by the retriever's whimpers brought her back to the moment.

Kate exited the shower, quickly towelled off, and then once again lingered, this time over her choice of clothing for the trip back up to the lake. She selected a newly acquired pair of spandex shorts that flattened the bulges and accentuated the contours yet was adequately modest for a fifty-year-old woman. She contemplated the bra drawer, where at least a dozen options awaited selection. She hated bras. More often than not, she did not wear one. They were all uncomfortable. Bra discomfort was distracting, and today she did not want to be distracted. She turned to the shirt rack and chose a slightly loose-fitting spandex top that would allow her to eschew wearing a bra, or so she thought. She took a moment to examine the effect in the full-length mirror. Kate was grateful for a distant Haudenosaunee heritage that gave her complexion a darkened hue; a French legacy that defied the outward expression of aging — at least among women; and an Irish connection that blended to give her well-defined facial features. She was pleased that her genetics had given her a tall, adequately lean stature that augered well to support a confident, quietly intelligent manner.

She towelled the moisture out of her thick, straight, long dark hair and brushed it back off her face to allow it to dry naturally in a preferred slightly fluffed look, betraying only the slightest traces of grey in a few tiny waves along her forehead. The rest of the brown-black hair fell to her shoulders. She paused a moment to contemplate make-up to highlight her deep black eyes, but as was usually the case, she didn't bother to apply any, preferring a natural look that required no maintenance. Her thoughts strayed — what would Jack Johnson see and experience in her?

Time was at a premium. She scooped up the Cairn, paused to give him a loving cuddle, then bounded down the stars two at a time with the retriever on her heels and the cat poised to trip the triumvirate at the bottom of the stairs. One acrobatic leap, holding the Cairn tightly, brought the cat and the retriever face-to-face, and feline claws sank into the nose of the yelping Big Ben. Cat out the door rather unceremoniously; Dettol applied to the dog's nose wounds;

blond fur wiped clean of blood drops; Cairn settled onto his favourite blanket on the chesterfield; key in the ignition and retriever breathing down her neck, Kate eased her SUV out of the garage then sped off en route to the Gatineau Hills and Meech Lake.

Kate yearned for a rich, smooth coffee from 3Sisters, a local coffee shop, but the pressing time dictated that the Tim Hortons drive-thru would be the order of the day. Big Ben wolfed down a western breakfast bagel then drooled at Kate's slightly more nutritious breakfast wrap. After the third bite, she relinquished her selection to the retriever. She pushed the speed limit, only slightly venturing over it, as the police of the nation's capital were notorious for nailing the majority of speeders, drunks, and reckless drivers, many of whom numbered among the elected representatives. Once across the Ottawa River and into Quebec, she could punch it — exceeding the speed limit in that province was a socio-cultural, fundamental aspect of daily life.

Her on-board communications system chimed. The voice activation advised her of an incoming call from the Sûreté du Québec.

"Where are you?" a voice demanded. She recognized Jack's voice. "Jesus, Mary, Joseph, what's with you guys? How about hi, hello, just some slight civility?"

"Sorry — it was a long night," replied Officer Jack Johnson. "So, where are you?"

"On the Parkway," said Kate.

"Good," said Jack then hung up.

Kate took her eyes off the road for a moment to look at the screen and then swerved to miss a snapping turtle easing across the road. She hit the brakes then jumped out of the car while Big Ben launched into a barking frenzy. She pulled a canoe stern paddle from the back of her SUV, slipped it under the turtle, then wrestled it over to the grass at the roadside. She always carried this broad-bladed paddle in the car during the swimming season, when she was going to the lake regularly. Many years before, happenstance had given way to habit, following the first time she attempted to get a snapping turtle off the road. After almost relinquishing her fingers and toes to the creature, the trusty paddle saved the day, albeit not without permanent scarring to its varnished finish. More war wounds joined those early etchings as subsequent turtles bit the paddle that saved them.

Kate sped along the bumpy, winding road to Canoe Beach, where a launch was indeed waiting to pick up her and Big Ben. She parked, snapped a leash on the retriever, and sprinted across the lot to give the dog a bit of a run.

Officer Johnson was on the shore waiting for her. An unrestrained remark tumbled out of his mouth as she approached. "Ah, that anxious to see me again, are you?"

Kate replied curtly, "Let's go."

He gestured with the fake grace of a bowing prince. "After you," was all he could muster back from that volley.

As the launch lumbered across the lake, Kate glanced up toward the white, squared-timber cottage occupied by Clare St. Denis. She thought she could make out the silhouette of a solitary figure standing just back of the window that was covered by a partially drawn curtain. She imagined that Clare was intently watching this activity. Kate would have to give some thinking time to the significance of Clare in the turn of events as they were unfolding across the waters of this lake.

Kate's attention turned to the shoreline and Big Ben, who was growing anxious, whimpering as the launch approached the now highly visible crime scene of tent and yellow tape. Several people documenting and cataloguing the site were busily focused on their tasks. Kate hopped off the launch while keeping a firm hand on a short lease that tethered Big Ben to her side. She entered the tent then pulled up short, surprised to see a clearly occupied body bag on a table at the centre of the tent.

"He's still here?" she asked Jack.

"He didn't seem anxious to go anywhere for breakfast," Jack quipped.

"Jesus," Kate said faintly.

Guy Archambault stepped into the tent and provided some much-needed information without the attitude that accompanied Jack's delivery. The forensics team had found a bruising at the base of the vic's skull that seemed to continue up into the hairline. They called for expertise to weigh in on their findings, and the chief coroner had decided to drive up from Montreal. The counterpart on the Ottawa side, who would normally be the go-to in this case, was away in Calgary attending a conference. They were expecting the Montreal coroner within the hour.

"We thought you could give some assistance with the landscape context. As well, when Francine returns with Tracker, we want to see how he reacts to Big Ben."

"If only that dog could speak," mused D'Angelo as he entered the tent munching on an Egg McMuffin.

Kate shivered and withdrew Big Ben back into the open air and away from his dead master — at least that was the presumption about the relationship between the dead man and the very alive dog.

Guy Archambault joined Kate and the dog in the open air. The breeze blowing up the lake gave a refreshing feel to an otherwise oppressive heaviness surrounding the scene.

Guy said, seemingly to anyone who might be near, "He is a good guy and very accomplished at his work. Just give him a chance. He can be awkward around people he likes."

As Kate and Big Ben were the only other souls in immediate proximity, Kate turned to look at Guy and said, "I beg your pardon?"

Guy repeated, "He likes you. This complicates things for him. You should be a suspect, but we all know you are not.

We know that you are telling us the truth. It is a gut reaction and not logical, *and* it is a distraction from the investigation of this crime, but there you have it. We simply have to deal with it. He is behaving like a bit of a jerk around you. Give it time."

Kate reined in the compulsiveness that had earned her the label *undiplomatic diplomat* in her previous career and replied with a simple, "Okay."

Jack bounded back onto the launch, fired up the engine, brought the lumbering craft about, and headed back across the lake. Guy said, "The chief coroner must have arrived at the landing."

Midmorning activity had begun on the lake. Canoeists, kayakers, stand-up flat-boarders, and swimmers dotted the surface of the gently rippling water. Motorized boats rarely disrupted the serenity of the lake. Those that were there transported goods and inhabitants to the far shore not accessible by road. A police launch traversing the lake on this early summer day several times before noon was undoubtedly attracting attention, particularly among the home and cottage owners that ringed the fjord-like shoreline.

Kate's attention drifted to the white, squared-timber cottage directly across the lake, where Clare St. Denis undoubtedly stood just back from the window behind a partially drawn curtain, watching everything that was going on. The attentiveness of this elderly long-term resident of the lake was more than idle curiosity.

Kate was lurched from her reverie to see the launch already plodding back across the lake. Officer Jack Johnson was at the wheel with a very small woman standing beside him. Kate stuffed down her embarrassment. She realized she had made the classic assumption that this chief coroner would be a distinguished-looking gentleman.

Within moments, Archambault was doing the introductions. Kate was shaking hands with Dr. Isabel Bosum, who

Kate guessed to be a northern Quebec Cree. She had bright, sparkling eyes that projected power, confidence, and competence well beyond her small stature. Dr. Bosum shook Kate's hand firmly, warmly remarking, "Ah, the swimmer and corporate forensic investigator." Jack's quick look drilled into Kate's eyes. It appeared Dr. Bosum had access to a more comprehensive dossier on Kate Roarty than the officers could pull up through their routine driver's licence search.

Kate proceeded to introduce Big Ben as though he were one of the boys. Dr. Bosum spoke to him in like manner, barely having to bend down to address him. "Hey boy, you could probably tell us the whole story and save us a lot of work, energy, and plodding couldn't you? Alas, God gave you eyes to see, ears to hear, and a nose to smell, but very limited vocal expression. Stay with us, boy, we'll work with what we have."

Dr. Bosum added, "Guy, Jack, D'Angelo, let's have a look at the victim. Mrs. Roarty, would you mind waiting out here for a bit with Big Ben?"

Kate resumed her contemplation of Clare's cottage across the lake until soft growling disturbed the quiet. Francine had returned with Tracker, the black German Shepherd police search dog. The two dogs had not yet met. They were now spontaneously making their acquaintance. Both were big, powerful, fit, pure-breed canines, the shepherd a working dog, the retriever a pet, or so it seemed. While Kate knew dogs, she knew them as pets. Francine, on the other hand, was experienced with both working dogs and pets.

"What do you know about this fellow?" Francine asked as she ruffled his neck fur.

"Only that he seems to be attached to the dead guy in there," said Kate.

"He is a pretty sophisticated pet," Francine said as she walked around, looking at him.

She tried a few basic commands in English, to which

he responded in a well-trained manner, much as Kate had experienced with him at home that morning.

Just then Dr. Bosum emerged from the tent, walked over to Kate, introduced herself to Francine and Tracker in the same gracious manner she had greeted the others, and then said to Kate, "Let's take a walk. Can you try to recreate the experience you had out here?"

Kate nodded, relinquished Big Ben's leash to Francine, then made her way over to the fallen tree. Dr. Bosum followed closely behind. Kate recounted everything as she remembered it. As she spoke, she watched Dr. Bosum listening very attentively, surveying the water; the site where the body was found; and the fallen tree, which she examined very closely, even though the forensics team had taken samples from a number of points on the tree. Dr. Bosum studied the lake, following the trajectory to the tree and where Kate had dragged the body out of the water and laid it down on the shore. She remarked, "We need to get a couple of kayaks and look at this from the vantage point you would have had while swimming along the shore. I would like to put in and follow the route you swam from the time you entered the water, encountered the body, dragged it out then re-entered and swam back across the lake."

She walked over to the SQ officers, spoke softly, then Kate heard a cryptic utterance, "*Oui, madame*," from Jack Johnson, who re-boarded the launch and headed back across the lake.

Kate followed the line of Dr. Bosom's gaze. Her eyes fell on the squared-timber white cottage on the opposite shore. Kate liked this Dr. Bosum, whose perceptions seemed to run ahead of the pack, sniffing out the realities carried on the wind, recreating a spiritual integrity that may have been fragmented by deluges of deception and human intrigue.

Guy approached them with a questioning look. Before he spoke, Dr. Bosum responded to his body language. "Yes indeed, Officer Archambault, we have to get the deceased out of here. I called the Quebec regional ambulance service that should arrive shortly to transport the victim back to my lab in Montreal. The paramedics can transport over and accompany the body back across the lake when Jack returns with the kayaks."

"Kayaks, ma'am?"

"Yes, Officer Archambault, I want to paddle out on the lake with Mrs. Roarty to get the same vantage point she experienced when this whole scene came down while she was out there swimming. Unfortunately, I don't swim, but I can handle a kayak."

She turned to Kate and said, "Excuse me, I was being presumptuous, assuming that your skill in the water extended to handling a kayak."

Kate replied simply, "Of course."

Each woman picked up a life jacket, donned it, and headed for the kayaks, collecting the paddles at the same time. Dr. Bosum stooped and picked up her kayak with the ease of a seasoned paddler and the strength of a weightlifter. Clearly, her diminutive stature was not to be underestimated.

The gentle ripple of the water against the boats added an auditory dimension to their otherwise silent passage as they paddled out toward the spot in the lake where the drama had begun to unfold. Dr. Bosum surveyed across the lake while Kate followed her trajectory. Her eyes alighted on Clare St. Denis's cottage. As quickly as her gaze rested there, she spun in a panorama survey back to the fallen tree where Kate had found the body of Vincent Bernard Taylor. Their respective silence reflected the thoughts they were each mulling over.

"Had you not been out doing your evening swim, Kate, this could have been a difficult homicide to solve. As it is, the complexity of the context in which our Mr. Taylor lost his life will be a challenge to unravel. I hope his body will tell us more than we have now. I know it is highly unusual to make this request, but can you work with the officers on the investigation? Your expertise in IP forensics may prove invaluable. The SQ remains wanting in such expertise. If you agree, I'll speak with the local SQ chief to do up a contract. Would $500.00 a day plus expenses suffice?" Kate winced, but before she could speak, Dr. Bosum went on, "I doubt they could scrape together anything more than $750.00 a day."

Kate nodded. Her mind raced. What about the commitment she had made to do the Istanbul investigation on the microchip company? Actually, she recalled entertaining a bit of reluctance about that job. Apart from planning it around the Lord Byron open-water swim, the job held little allure. As well, she hated to be away from her little Cairn Terrier, whose advancing years were taking a toll. She wanted to be around him as much as possible, knowing their time together was short, and his abilities were diminishing almost daily now. Thankfully, her neighbour frequently looked in on the little Charlie dog, took him on short walks, and even took him over to his place so he would have company when she was out. Otherwise, she was anxious to be the little dog's eyes, ears, and his devoted companion as much as possible. The latter he had extended to her for more than fourteen years.

She heard her name being called softly but firmly. "Kate, can we follow the course you took from here to the fallen tree, then back across the lake to where you exited the water and made your way to get help?"

"Yes, of course," Kate said.

She took the lead, paddling slowly and deliberately and letting the gentle rippling of the water against their kayaks take over as the only sound disturbing the silence. She spoke sparingly — when there was factual information to communicate. She let Dr. Bosum consider the context in which this crime had taken place. Her thinking was almost palpable above the silence of this watery habitat. A slight upward motion of her head and Kate knew she was ready to traverse the lake, following the route Kate had swum the previous evening.

They pulled into Blanchet Beach. Officer Jack Johnson was already there, ready to retrieve and return the kayaks and hand Big Ben over to Kate. Kate, Dr. Bosum, and a rambunctious Big Ben walked the road to the white, squared-timber cottage. As they approached the door, Big Ben became quite excited. Kate knocked, after a long wait the door opened, and Big Ben lunged through it, greeting Clare St. Denis with the enthusiasm of a long-lost friend. Clare ignored the dog, but the retriever did not ignore her. Kate could barely restrain him. Her planned introduction was suspended by the unexpected behaviour of the dog. Dr. Bosum stood back, watching the dynamic, then stepped into the breach, introducing herself.

"Madame St. Denis, I am the chief coroner with Sûreté du Québec and have been called in to investigate the body found in the lake yesterday. May I ask you a few questions?"

The withdrawn, white-haired old woman nodded silently, motioning them to sit at the faded yellow Arborite kitchen table while she put the kettle on. Dr. Bosum was soft-spoken, unthreatening, albeit direct and unsparing in her words as she spoke to the woman. "Madame St. Denis, a man died across the lake sometime in the past thirty-six hours — it appears that the victim did not die from natural causes. Do you know anything about it?"

The old woman quietly shook her head.

"Do you know this dog, Big Ben?" asked Dr. Bosum. Again, the old woman shook her head. Big Ben's whimpering provided a different reply. Clare St. Denis looked away, then down to pour the water into the teapot. She set her offering on the table, along with a plate of biscuits, milk, sugar, and three cups and saucers. They all sat in silence as Big Ben quietly whimpered — an ominous presence. Kate took a biscuit from the plate and held it up to the old woman with an unspoken request, to which Clare nodded acquiescence.

Big Ben stopped whimpering long enough to devour it. Kate caught a slight softening in the woman's eyes, and then it was gone, replaced by a steely reserve.

Dr. Bosum drank her tea, apologized for the intrusion, and signalled their departure. Kate dragged the reluctant retriever out the door. They regained the road and kept to the edge of the narrow, winding passage until they reached Canoe Beach parking lot, where Dr. Bosum walked to her car, unlocked it, and turned to Kate. She said, "We'll be in touch. I have to spend some time with the deceased to get his story. Therein lies my expertise."

Kate thought otherwise. She believed this woman possessed an extraordinary understanding of the human psyche, alive or cadaver.

Jack strode over to Kate's vehicle as she was lifting the back door for Big Ben to get in. "Can you join us tomorrow at our headquarters in Gatineau?"

"Sure" said Kate.

"Make it after lunch, say 2:00 p.m. That will give us time to set up the operations centre and assemble what we have so far."

As Kate got into her vehicle, she acknowledged him with a nod. A moment lingered between them, which Jack Johnson broke by saying, "I'll text you the address, floor, and room number and make a parking arrangement for your vehicle. Oh, and can you bring the dog? We need to see if he is microchipped." Kate closed the car door, hiding the flush she felt creeping over her face.

Big Ben whimpered, straining in the direction of Clare's cottage. Kate pulled out of the parking lot and headed down the winding lake road back to the parkway and home to her little Cairn Terrier. Their time together was growing very short — each moment they had was precious. She felt her eyes water as she contemplated the days to come when the little fellow would have passed on and their years of companionship would become frozen in memories. She was grateful for her few friends who were dog people and could understand the emotion that accompanied the passage of a canine best bud.

Breathing on her shoulder interrupted her reverie. Big Ben was supposed to be riding caboose in the back of the vehicle. Despite his size, he had slipped over the back seat and moved in as close as he could get to Kate. She patted him. "Okay, boy. Maybe you can help by being the eyes and ears for our little Charlie dog." She had the feeling that the big dog understood her remark.

3

Kate snapped the seatbelt into place on the direct, nonstop British Airways flight from Ottawa to London. The timing of this trip was the perfect antidote to relieve the grief she was feeling over the loss of her best bud, wee Charlie dog. Despite the presence of Big Ben loping about her house, it felt empty and sad without the little guy. Together they had spent more time in one another's company than apart during the nearly fifteen years he had been with her. They enjoyed wilderness adventures during all seasons, world travels, child rearing — the little dog had contributed more to raising her children than the husband she had in her life for a decade or so. He was her comfort and confidante at home and on the thousands of kilometres they walked together in all weather and times of the day and night. Now he was gone. She never missed the former husband; she would always miss the little blond Cairn Terrier.

Kate slipped into a deep sleep, as she frequently did aboard aircraft during take-offs. It was a time she could totally relax, comforted by the fact that there was nothing to do for the duration of the flight. Her book slid off her lap as her mind yielded to a short, deep power nap. She awoke slowly and calmly as the events of the last two weeks seemed to fold through her mind in an ordered, categorized manner. She surprised herself by savouring the time spent with Jack. He had been his usual, brusque, sarcastic self until she called to say she was staying home with her little dog, whose remaining days and hours were rapidly slipping away.

Kate and the little Cairn Terrier had returned from a short and slow walk to find Jack sitting on the porch with a bag of Thai food and a bouquet of flowers. Charlie dog, despite his infirmities, seemed to welcome this stranger to his mistress's life. Jack unfolded his hand filled with tantalizing liver bits under the dog's nose. True to form, the terrier gobbled them up while making another lifelong friend. He was always a good reader of character among the people that came into Kate's life.

The little fellow had experienced a very tough night. Kate knew the time was close. She rang the hospice vet in the morning. The vet said that she could be at Kate's house by 2:00 p.m. The two best friends spent the morning in a tight embrace. They took a couple of short walks, and on the second walk Charlie dog let his mistress know that it was time, that she was making the best decision for him; the right decision for both of them. The kindly young vet who had recently established this hospice business attended to Charlie dog and Kate with compassion and caring, giving them time for the Cairn to slip into a deep sleep and then away. Kate held him for many hours long after the vet departed.

This trip, at the request of the Sûreté du Québec and the recommendation of Dr. Bosum, along with Officers Jack Johnson and Guy Archambault, was superbly timed. Big Ben acquired the protective custody of Jack, with Guy and D'Angelo as backup guardians.

The context of the contract that Kate took on with the Sûreté du Québec was going to meetings in London with the UK security services MI5, MI6, and GCHQ. The cause of death of Dr. Vincent Bernard Taylor might have been a tiny projectile embedded in the medulla oblongata section of the brain that is responsible for breathing, heart, and respiratory functions. While the projectile did not appear to be responsible for shutting down these systems through damage, Dr. Bosum believed the tiny imbedded microchip might have been programmed to send a destruct signal that would have stopped Dr. Taylor from continuing with his life, almost instantly. She was able to determine that these vital functions had shut down, but she was not able to ascertain what had caused them to cease functioning. While Big Ben was healthy, happy, and bounding about like an overgrown pup, he too possessed a chip of similar technology that could have been readily mistaken for a standard pet microchip. However, the scanning did not yield any of the standard information stored on pet microchips such as breed, ownership, address, and phone number. Rather, it yielded what seemed to be an encrypted code.

When Dr. Bosum gave the code to Kate, she immediately reached out to her network of cyber geek contacts, mostly twenty-something guys who slept all day and worked all night. Bryant was the candidate to light up with the challenge. He got back to Kate with an apology for a delay in responding. He explained that when he first broke the code, he didn't believe the connections, so took a number of verification steps to be absolutely certain that the info he passed on to Kate was accurate. When Kate logged onto the site they had set up for such communications — it was highly protected and also encrypted — she could tell by the red-alert colouring of the message sitting in the inbox of this software that there would be a "wow" factor in what Bryant had discovered. His message read,

Kate, what are you up to this time? This chip code originates with MI5, MI6, and GCHQ, the British Intelligence services. It has multiple layers of classifications that lead the decoder on a distracting, winding trail. Be careful with this, Kate, it's more sophisticated that anything I have seen in the netherworld of intelligence encoding. Essentially, the code reveals that the chip was housed in a projectile that was launched remotely, programmed with the DNA of the target and set to activate when it lodged in the medulla oblongata area of the brain. It would almost instantly shut down the respiratory and heart systems, causing all vital functions to disappear in moments, killing the living organism that possessed the DNA signature, where it was implanted. If lodged in any other part of the DNA tissue or a DNA that did not match, it would probably remain benign, doing no damage and would likely go undetected. It seems to have a dormant state where it could inhabit a targeted DNA and only become lethal when moved to the medulla oblongata area of the brain. I suspect that's what the dog is carrying around, since the device shows no signs of being activated. The other chip, however, may have carried out its task and shut down that living being — what or whomever that may have been.

Kate had not given this information about the victim or the dog to Bryant.

While in theory Kate had nothing to do until her flight reached London, she nevertheless reviewed the entire case as she understood it to date and pondered this highly sophisticated technical aspect of the killing of Vincent Bernard Taylor and the implication for Big Ben. The murder was beginning to look like an assassination. What did this man know, or what was he engaged in that would elicit such elaborate measures to get rid of him? Were MI5, MI6, or GCHQ involved, or had their technology been co-opted or … a shiver went through her … both possibilities? Should she treat these British intelligence services as friends or foes, or both? Kate tried to doze off, knowing she would have little time for sleep or rest once she hit London. She opted for a fifteen-year-old, mediocre feel-good in-flight movie, *Midnight in Paris*, to pass the time and encourage her to nap, at least for a bit.

The flight landed at Heathrow on schedule. Travelling only with a carry-on, she made her way through customs and immigration then proceeded quickly to the Tube kiosk, where she topped up her Oyster card to enable movement around the city of London on subways, buses, local ferries, and trains. Kate loved this ease of getting around London. It was also a great walking city. The legendary taxis were actually slow and very expensive, not to mention that using them could be a bit of a compromise to anonymity. London taxi drivers loved to talk and for a few quid would readily hand over all kinds of information about the folks they transported around the city. They ranted about the introduction of driverless vehicles that Kate saw as an inventible evolution in transportation.

She caught an airport train downtown then switched to the Piccadilly tube line to descend at South Kensington, where she had rented a ground-floor studio flat on a quiet residential street close to one of her favourite public swimming pools, with a schedule that could accommodate the crazy hours she knew she would keep during this visit. Kate found the key in the beak of the brass rooster perched among the greens in a tiny sidewalk garden by the private entrance and let herself in. The place was bright, spotless, and sweet-smelling from both the fresh scent of flowers in a vase on the tiny kitchen table and the aroma of coffee grounds already spooned in the paper-lined basket of the five-cup pot that sat on the kitchen counter. Kate flicked the switch on the side of the water-filled percolator and flung herself prostrate onto the double-size comfy bed. It was shortly after 10:00 a.m. Her flight from Ottawa had landed a few minutes before eight. The gurgle of the completion of coffee perking awakened her from her slumber. She downed two large mugs of the delicious brew, grabbed her swim stuff, complete with soap, shampoo, body cream, and a tiny towel, and headed off to the 11:00 a.m. swim at the South Kensington pool.

Kate was in luck; there were few patrons in the pool. She remained in the shower only long enough to scrub away the travel grime and staleness, then she slipped into the water. Awkwardly, she banged out a kilometre before she had to yield her solitary lane to more swimmers. After a second kilometre, navigating more carefully to avoid running into other lap swimmers, she emerged refreshed with the pain gone from her hips, and standing tall in the shower, she felt ready to launch into the rigours of the day.

As she exited the women's change room, she glimpsed a person she thought she had noticed on the way in. She brushed away a feeling of unease by rationalizing that it was quite likely another patron of the pool arriving and departing from the late-morning swim just as her. Kate breezed into a Starbucks to pick up a double latté, single espresso on the way back to the flat. She had indulged her pleasure in the familiar both by going to this pool and stopping into this coffee shop. While waiting for the brew to be prepared, she glanced around and let her eyes settle for a moment on a person that her mind's eye had caught previously when she was letting herself into the flat. She shook her shoulders and allowed that *fatigue-breeds-paranoia* thought to process then pass beyond her mind. She decided that she had best only undertake logistics today, get a good night's sleep, and then begin her rounds of enquiry tomorrow.

Kate walked along the narrow, intriguing residential streets, interspersed with commercial areas, finding her way to the little flat on Rosary Gardens. Before retrieving her key to let herself in, she walked past the address and peered up and down the street, but saw nobody who looked out of place on the street. She returned to the doorway and quickly went in — next time she would look up to see what the windows might reveal. She set her bag and coffee down and slowly moved about the small flat. Everything appeared as she left it, but she had a feeling that the flat had been entered while she was out.

Sighing, Kate lifted the lid off the coffee cup, dumped the contents in a tall, slender, white, porcelain mug with a handle big enough to fit four fingers, and sat down to drink it. She moved over to a tall winged-back chair, pulled her laptop onto her knees and reached to unzip it from its thin, white protective carrying case when she saw her proof that someone had indeed been there. She was always careful to fully close the zipper. It had not been opened at the airport, but now she looked at the zipper that had been drawn up and over the length of the computer, but the last little bit around the bend of the corner had not been closed. She routinely made sure to do that to ensure that any USBs tossed in the case would not fall out. The snooper had not taken the same care. She went through her personal belongings in the little apartment thoroughly but could find nothing else disturbed in any way. The laptop did not appear to have been opened and accessed, but following the level of sophistication she had experienced with this investigation so far, she suspected there was no need to open a laptop to take off whatever the intruder wished to see.

Since Kate had entered the world of commercial espionage, she knew she would be dealing with a level of skill often well beyond her capability. It was her network of cyber geeks who rarely left their man caves, who worked in solitary concentration, who she paid handsomely — always electronically — and whose bank accounts grew, rarely accessed except to buy newer, more sophisticated hardware, software, spyware, and hacking knowledge, usually from one another. Their real names were seldom revealed, and trust was built from the network. An unworthy intruder was caught swiftly and tossed out resoundingly then tied in a bundle of cyberspace restrictions so tight that they were usually left completely locked out of the digital world.

Kate trusted her geeks, and they trusted her. When she was working a contract, they extended a sense of security she rarely derived from contacts that she met in person. She reflected back to her first exposure to this cyber-geek netherworld, when she was still a diplomat assisting in orchestrating an infrastructure contract involving many players and three quarters of a billion dollars. She trusted few of the players; the stakes were high; the egos even higher; the corruption in the form of bribes, manipulation, politics was palpable but always just sufficiently beneath the surface that she couldn't call it. Then she heard from trainonthetrack2030. The message came in during the night with an audible delivery that woke her up. She stirred from a deep sleep, grabbed the BlackBerry from the bedside table, disturbing the Cairn Terrier and the black cat that shared her bed, entered her password, and opened the latest unread message. It read, **Follow your gut, you're right, we got your back.** The sender was trainonthetrack2030. She read it twice, scrolled up and down, and then the message vanished — it was gone. She set the BlackBerry back down while the pets claimed more of the bed they shared, and then they all fell back to sleep.

Her final diplomatic assignment had brought her to West Africa to facilitate commercial engagement in building the region's infrastructure, most of which was woefully inadequate or non-existent. She worked hard and long but with little success. She decided to leave this career to work on her own, liberated from the oversight of bosses usually out of their depth. She experienced the proximity of corruption circling like hungry wolves, stalking the most vulnerable of the prey. She yearned to distance herself and her work from the impenetrable bureaucracies caught in their own stranglehold of ineptitude, like a swirling vortex that never descends nor ascends, continually sucking in but never disgorging.

She took her before-work morning walk with the little Cairn, whose wagging tail signalled that he was readily accepting greetings from his fan club throughout the neighbourhood. She sipped her coffee and thought about the nocturnal message accompanied by audible delivery. Did she imagine it? Did she dream it? If it was real, who sent it? Why? Why her? Who was **trainonthetrack2030**? While the handle was long, it was easy to remember. It introduced her to a cyber-geek world that would eventually surround her with brilliance, protection, expertise, and caring never known in her diplomatic, archaeological, or business consulting careers. It gave her the connections she required yet allowed her to develop the solitary approach to her profession and life that provided comfort and familiarity.

Kate drew herself back to the present and the logistics for the appointments she had planned for the next day. MI5 was first on the agenda. It was relatively easy to get to by catching the tube at Gloucester Road, then taking the Circle line to Westminster, where she could walk or bus it over to number 12 Millbank. Connecting with MI6 was a little more complicated. She was fully expecting to play a bit of cat-and-mouse until she got to the right person or people within the bowels of that organization. She was exhausted but had to stay awake in order to go to bed at a normal time to curtail the impact of the time change and jet lag. It was already midafternoon. If she kept moving, she could push through another five or six hours. She slung her laptop over her shoulder, clipped into place the cross-chest buckle, and then slid her passport and credit cards into an inside pouch secured under her arm. She slipped loose money and her Oyster card into her pocket. This time the exit from her apartment involved a turn around the block to see if her intruder had decided to return.

Kate walked briskly with the determination acquired during her earliest international travels some thirty years before. Despite a forward demeanour to her gait, she examined every single vehicle and passerby on the street. Only a small Vespa aroused suspicion. While the bike was parked and turned off, it appeared that the after-market GPS device remained turned on. She maintained the same gait, feigned a call on her iPhone, and clicked a photo of the screen of the GPS on the Vespa. Within a few moments, she had her answer. The destination was number 12 Rosary Gardens — the row house where her short stay flat was located. Given that there were at least two other flats in the same row house, it did not necessarily mean there was any connection to her would-be intruder, but she would increase her vigilance.

Kate completed the circling of the block and re-entered her flat. She was satisfied that no intruder had returned. She went out again and locked the door behind her then took the underground to Piccadilly Circus and walked over to Soho, an area she always found interesting, imagining what it must have been like when her mother was growing up there. It had evolved into an Asian quarter, first Chinatown and now, in more recent years, although retaining the label, most of the occupants were from Southeast Asia — Vietnam, Cambodia, Malaysia, Laos, the Philippines, and Thailand. Eateries, confectioners, souvenir shops, herbal and massage therapy dispensers, hair stylists, and beauticians pushed against the few remaining play houses and film theatres that dotted the more confined Soho landscape of twenty-first-century urban London.

Kate walked on then slipped into a pho café for a bowl of noodle soup and lemongrass tea. The place was quiet. It was late afternoon, when most would-be patrons were filled from lunch and not yet ready to indulge in dinner. She took a seat affording her a clear view of the entranceway, passage to the washroom, and windows into the street. While she might not readily recognize a possible pursuer, she would at least see everyone who came and went, giving her the opportunity to imprint a face, body carriage, expression, or general demeanour. She settled in with her book, a constant companion to her frequent solitary dining. In fact, not another soul came and went during her hour-long sojourn in the cafe. The waitresses changed shifts; the kitchen yielded bursts of Vietnamese, Khmer, Cantonese … a flurry of wiping down, sweeping and restocking, seeming to ready the restaurant for the evening rush took place, but nothing else of consequence transpired.

Kate paid, left a generous tip, although she was not sure what for, since little extra effort went into serving her, then she departed back out onto the street, still tired but fed, exercised, and stimulated by the dynamics of the street activities. Maintaining an inward hyper vigilance and an outward calm was tiring, especially when she was already battling travel fatigue. She glanced at her watch then up at a billboard for a film theatre. *Man of Steel4* was playing in Imax 3D at 6:45 p.m. Perfect, it was 6:30 p.m. Despite bad reviews, she had wanted to catch this latest *SupermanAI* iteration. The smash, bang, and futuristic high-tech aspects of the film would likely keep her awake and alert. She succumbed to one of her few vices — popcorn, rationalizing that the crunching would also help keep her awake. The theatre was almost empty, which was surprising given the time of the evening — perhaps Soho was more of a live theatre district, or this was a really bad movie.

If it was bad, she did not care; she enjoyed it. The unrelenting action and noise did indeed her awake. By the time she returned to the flat, showered, and donned athletic grey shorts and t-shirt for sleepwear, it was nearly 10:00 p.m. She checked the locking mechanism on the door and adjacent windows then slid between the fresh, cool sheets. Sleep overtook her before she could even turn to face the door and window.

She awakened ten hours later in the same position, confused, disoriented, and filled with a sense of grief. She leapt out of bed and strode over to the small shower cubicle, attempting to shake free of the blows of grief compromising her body, heart, and soul. She turned on only the cold water and stepped in, shocking herself into the present of where she was, who she was, and that wee Charlie dog was only a cherished memory. Kate gradually added warm water, soothing herself into comfort as tears flowed freely down her cheeks, mixing with the shower water and slipping away down the drain. The sobs that exhaled at the same time washed away into deep pants and breathing. Kate exited the shower remaining wet and naked, put the coffee on, extracted her iPod and found suitable meditation music, then settled into a session of mindfulness, despite the late hour. She knew these thirty minutes would give her the concentration and strength she would need for the rest of the day. Her body air-dried as she meditated — her practise was rudimentary but effective. She rose with equilibrium restored, dressed as she downed her morning coffee, a dish of mixed berries with Greek-style yogurt, and she was out the door. She noted that a late-evening swim would be possible on Tuesdays and Thursdays. She entered it in her iPhone scheduler with both visual and audible reminders an hour and a half before the start time.

She departed from her flat quickly and strolled briskly to the Gloucester Road Underground station, then, true to her logistical plan of the previous day, she boarded the Circle line, exited at Westminster, then started to walk in the direction of Millbank. Within moments, she sensed that she was being followed. A bus stopped beside her at the red light at the intersection, and a disembodied voice graciously acknowledged her request to board then quickly pulled off into traffic with the turn of the green light. She tapped the cyber monitor and asked if the bus route went close to Millbank.

"Yes, just a short walk away. You will be advised when the stop approaches."

Kate swiped her Oyster card and sat down. Within a few minutes, the cyber panel called out *Horseferry*, and then it more quietly reinforced the automated broadcast with, "Here you are, passenger." Kate swung off through the front door, since no passengers were embarking. She sensed that she had lost her tail, real or imaginary. At the main gate to MI5, she produced her passport and her Sûreté du Québec temporary ID. She was given an MI5 temporary pass containing an instant photo ID that must have been taken as she approached the security guard window. Her passport was retained to be returned when she surrendered the building pass. She was given directions to accompany a uniformed military type who would take her to a Mr. Braithwaite, the deputy director of Intergovernmental Affairs and International Liaison. It was a start.

She was shown into a small, spartan modern meeting room which moments later Mr. Braithwaite entered and introduced himself, along with Agent Sloane and an intern, Whistlethorpe. Kate looked at Sloane and caught her breath. For just a moment, she felt as though she was standing before a replica of a younger version of herself during the early days of her diplomatic career. Whistlethorpe, in contrast, was petite in stature and Asian in origin. Braithwaite exhibited a stereotypical countenance of an era gone by — aloof, conservatively dressed in a dark suit and white shirt, clean-shaven — a rarity these days. They all exchanged business cards and took a moment to tap their handheld devices to transfer the contact information into their digital address books. Kate glanced at the surveillance monitoor in their small meeting room. Braithwaite followed her sight line and remarked simply, "Regulation."

In a polite, formal, but not dispassionate voice, Mr. Braithwaite said, "Mrs. Roarty, welcome to MI5. What can we do for you? I understand you are familiar with London, and you are not looking for a job." A trace of a twinkle flashed in his eyes. Young intern Whistlethorpe looked a tad uncomfortable at his remarks, while Agent Sloane, seemingly more experienced in general and evidently familiar with her boss's approach, smiled softly, poised to capture the important exchange, if any, that might occur between the visitor and her boss.

Kate provided a thumbnail sketch of what had brought her to London, MI5, and Mr. Braithwaite in particular.

She told Braithwaite that she was by profession a commercial espionage private investigator — she imagined she wasn't telling him anything that he did not already know.

She went on to say that she had come to the case by happenstance and then summarized it as she knew it to date. She told them that the Sûreté du Québec determined the cause of death was related to a projectile containing a micro computer chip lodged in the victim's brain. A top forensic coroner had concluded that the projectile itself would not likely have been responsible for the death of this man in any physical trauma sense; rather, the microchip might have been programmed to shut down the vital functions in the tissue where it was lodged. It might have entered the area of that brain long before the victim actually passed away.

Mr. Braithwaite listened carefully while Whistlethorpe took seemingly very detailed notes. Agent Sloane made a few notes but mostly appeared to study the communications dynamic between Kate Roarty and Jonathon Braithwaite. When Kate paused, not wishing to reveal all, just enough to stimulate a dialogue, Braithwaite's only comment was a predictable remark. "Where does this involve MI5, or the UK in general, for that matter?"

Kate replied, "The microchip implant has a UK-based

digital signature."

Braithwaite exhaled perceptibly and said, "MI5 would like to have a look at it."

Prepared for this question, Kate replied, "It is in safekeeping with the Sûreté du Québec."

"I am surprised that the communiqué requesting this meeting did not originate with CSIS to MI6," said Braithwaite.

"My contract is with Sûreté du Québec. If the communications had gone that route, I would not likely have had this opportunity to meet with you and your unit, Mr. Braithwaite."

"Mrs. Roarty, would you like some tea while we continue this discussion?"

Kate accepted then witnessed a slightly strained dynamic as he turned to Whistlethorpe with a request to retrieve the fixings from his office. She agreed reluctantly, seeming to shudder as she set down her tablet, rose, and left.

Braithwaite returned to Kate, saying, "Mrs. Roarty, I am sure you are aware that we in the UK have similar jurisdictional challenges that you folks in Canada experience among your CSIS, RCMP, provincial police forces in Ontario and Quebec, and the offices of solicitor and attorney general bureaux."

Kate nodded.

"Having said that, MI5 does indeed have a good grasp of the capabilities of high-tech companies in the UK. We could probably find out if we have companies that have developed this type of technology, who they are selling it to, and how it is being used."

Kate nodded again, surmising that Mr. Braithwaite probably already had this information, since Dr. Bosum's preliminary research had already identified a connection between the technology and the UK secret services. He turned to Agent Sloane and in a comfortable, familiar tone asked her to retrieve a list of the companies that might be doing this kind of work. Sloane readily agreed and left, almost colliding in the doorway with the intern.

"Ah, tea, nectar of the gods. Guess that makes me old-school," quipped Braithwaite.

Kate replied, "Then that makes two of us."

Intern Whistlethorpe was not so brash as to roll her eyes, but both fifty-somethings sitting before her sensed she was doing so internally. Kate looked at this young woman and thought with gratitude, *Ah, no bosses and no employees, now that is the nectar of the gods.*

Kate allowed a bit of familiarity to enter her tone and approach as both she and Jonathon Braithwaite were sussing one another out. "I admit that getting the day underway without coffee — several cups of coffee — would be a challenge that I would rather avoid. Tea thereafter, as the day goes on, sits very well indeed."

Braithwaite nodded in acquiescence as he poured their tea, pushed forward a tray of milk, cream, sugar and honey, and then offered some to Whistlethorpe, who graciously declined. He went on to pour a cup for Agent Sloane, adding only a dash of milk. He did this in a habitual manner that suggested some regular occurrence in their daily lives. By the time they had taken their first savouring sips, Sloane had returned with a single piece of paper in hand. She saw the cup of tea and thanked him, picking it up as she sat down.

Setting down her cup, Agent Sloane said, "There appears to be only one company in the UK working on such technology, but they ran into financing challenges a couple of years ago and slipped into a dormant state, laying off most of their employees. The principals, a CEO, head of R&D, and a financial planner, CA type, have been globetrotting looking for venture capital. They burned through their early rounds of angel investments, cobbling together about fifteen million pounds. A UK VC group with participation from a few Japanese members came up with sixty million pounds. The company never did get the last fifteen million pounds after the Japanese earthquake crushed any financing options from that country. We stopped looking in on them about twenty months ago after they failed to attract capital from a Boston syndicate that specializes in this kind of stuff, as well as no play from an Indian VC group and a Brazilian innovator consortium. The UK and the continent have rather dried up on any VC activity not heading toward an Initial Public Offering. There have been few, if any, IPOs on any exchanges since the American meltdown. At any rate, the company is called iBrain Inc."

Kate and Braithwaite pondered the information Sloane had provided while they sipped their tea. Sloane looked at them as she too put her teacup to her mouth. She set the cup down and then casually added, "Maybe we should pay them a call."

Braithwaite nodded then turned to Kate, saying, "Mrs. Roarty, I am sure you are headed over to MI6 when you finish with us here at MI5. If you can give us a couple of days before you do that, we can make a call on iBrain and let you know about our findings. It would at least give us a status report on the activity of the company."

"I can agree to this proposal," Kate said. While she was anxious to move as quickly as possible, this development was heading in the right direction. She did have some IP research to do for a client she kept on the back burner. She doubted she would get paid for her work, because the little company had a great product but was flat broke. She believed in them, so she would likely do it pro bona or for some future shares plan in the company, should they ever get their concept launched into a commercialization process. There were a few angel investors in London she might be able to interest in hearing her pitch about the concept. Doing so could be a short cut to determine if they were backing any other developers working on the same approach. She would let her client know as soon as she returned to the Rosary

Gardens flat then try to set up some appointments for the following morning.

Her cell phone chimed as she strode back toward a nearby underground station. It displayed "private," which suggested she should pick it up. The male caller responded to her greeting in a questioning tone. "Mrs. Kate Roarty from Canada?"

Kate replied, "Yes."

"This is Agent Nigel Rathbone with the International Relations unit of the Government Communications Headquarters, GCHQ."

"Yes."

The very polite, youthful-sounding voice of Agent Nigel Rathbone went on to request a meeting. She agreed and preempted the date and time proposal with her own at 9:30 a.m. Thursday morning.

Mr. Rathbone said they could send a car to collect her. Always wishing to maintain control as much as possible, Kate said she would go to their offices on her own and asked for the details.

Mr. Rathbone cleared his throat. "The late direct train departing Paddington Station at 7:48 p.m. will get you into Cheltenham a bit before 10:00 p.m. It's a trip of two hours and fourteen minutes. All other departures are longer, and many require a change. This would be best."

Kate did not reveal her ignorance of the geography. "Thank you, I'll likely take that route," she said.

"You might wish to set up our meeting for a day later. I would be delighted to book a room for you in Cheltenham."

Kate inwardly sighed but outwardly agreed.

"Right then," came the courteous response, and then Rathbone hung up.

Kate thought, *But how will I know where the reservation is, and where in the GCHQ complex do we meet?*

Before she arrived at 12 Rosary Gardens, a text came in confirming a reservation and the time and place of their meeting Friday morning. Kate read the details for the reservation, which was at a Clematis House, a five-minute walk from the train station, then seven minutes by car to GCHQ for a 9:30 a.m. appointment. The note ended with an instruction to bring her bathing suit, cap, and goggles. Kate sent a one-word reply: **Agreed**, and then pocketed her phone. She felt the script was already written; she was simply carrying out her part. She wondered further — had the written script actually started back on Meech Lake during her evening swim? She shook herself clear of the thought, recalling that she often entertained the same ideas about her engagement in many aspects of her life — the adoption of her son, forest fires, the suicide death of a crew member on an archaeological dig, becoming a diplomat…

Kate checked the time, gathered her swim stuff together, including a titanium digital-coded lock, and headed out with a plan to stop for a bite to eat before, hitting the late swim and some vigorous laps. She loved to people-watch and soon spotted a café terrasse with an attractive medium-priced menu where she could sit in the shade and watch people hurry by and drift in from the street to meet friends who had already arrived, or, like her, they made a spontaneous decision and just stopped in. There were few other solitary diners. For a moment, she breathed deeply to chase away the pang of loneliness that had lurked about like a petulant child since she was very young. A maître d' showed her to a seat facing out into the street with her back to a wall. She happily accepted it and knew the tip amount was already beginning to build. She declined the liquor list but requested a tall mineral water with lime slices. It appeared almost instantly, carried to the table by a young waitress whose image flashed through her mind in the same manner she had experienced when leaving the swimming pool that morning. Kate dismissed the thought, thinking she really needed to eat before she began to hallucinate. She ordered a seafood medley, pasta primavera from the same waitress, then settled back to people-watch and keep an eye on her server. She observed an exchange with the maître d' — not entirely outside the realm of possibility, since they worked together. Kate made a point of taking note of the characteristics of both to remember should she encounter them again.

The meal came, served with a delicious, delicate mixed-green salad. Kate gratefully accepted fresh pepper from a large hand grinder that the waitress generously distributed on both the salad and the pasta. She sampled both and then settled in to enjoy the meal. While savouring the pasta, the feeling that she was being watched came back and continued throughout the meal then on out into the street as she headed toward the community complex where she had swum the previous day. She wondered if perhaps the GCHQ service was watching her, since its agent, Nigel Rathbone, had advised her to bring her swimming gear to the planned meeting several days hence. She didn't really need to ponder why she was being watched; rather, what aspect of this investigation interested the watchers. If the GCHQ organization was involved in the development of this technology, the implications were likely far-reaching and multi-faceted. At this point, Kate just wanted to know where it came from, what its applications were, and most importantly, what its role was in this case.

Kate paid the bill for her meal, left a very generous tip, and exited the restaurant, walking briskly in the direction of the Kensington Chelsea pool. She circled the short block and approached the restaurant from the opposite direction just as her waitress was coming through the door.

She smiled while saying, "Shift over."

Quick on the uptake, the would-be waitress replied, "Oh, I am sorry, Mrs. Roarty, did you forget something?"

Kate responded, "No, just giving you time to catch up; we may as well walk together, since we are headed in the same direction."

The young waitress let her discomfort betray her demeanour long enough for Kate to continue uninterrupted.

Looking straight ahead as they walked on, in a quiet but purposeful and commanding voice, Kate asked, "Who are you, who do you work for, and why are you following me?"

Kate stopped and turned to face the young waitress with such engaging intensity that a reply emerged without hesitation.

"My name is Liz Bruan, Agent Liz Bruan. I am with GCHQ. I am responsible for ensuring that you get to your meeting at GCHQ without incident."

Kate studied her carefully for a moment then decided there was some truth coming from this Agent Liz Bruan. "And do you have identification to support what you have just told me?"

Without prompting, they walked on. Liz Bruan handed over a card while saying, "Nigel Rathbone is my boss."

"And do you swim as well?"

Liz leapt to her reply. "I swam varsity at university and was offered a spot on the UK National Team — breaststroke."

Kate said, "Ah, a good surveillance stroke."

"Actually, it's the first time my swimming has been a useful asset in getting an assignment."

Kate found herself growing to like this confident, albeit inexperienced young agent.

She gestured back to Liz. "So they haven't had you swim the Bosporus."

"Not yet, but you have."

Kate smiled a second time then bantered back, "Oh, that was in celebration of Lord Byron — an annual iconic swim that traverses the Bosporus. My swimming is for fitness and serenity — I don't compete, I swim slowly and steadily."

Liz replied as they arrived at the main entrance to the pool complex, "Yes, I know."

Kate inwardly rolled her eyes and asked, "So now, to be thoroughly convincing, will you join me in a swim? I assume a waitress's outfit isn't the only togs you carry in that bag."

It was Liz's turn to smile, and in that instant, Kate knew they were not alone. With Agent Liz Bruan in the pool, there would be at least one other agent on oversight surveillance. They changed into their gear and quickly slipped into the pool. Kate could see from under the water that on this point, Liz had been completely truthful; her breaststroke was executed with exquisite, precision, speed, and grace. Her economy of energy in motion and quick, smooth turns were a delight to observe and admittedly easy to envy just a little bit. Kate needed a good workout. She swam for nearly an hour and a half, mostly with the front crawl, but the backstroke and breaststroke provided a medley of variation that both her psyche and body enjoyed. She even allowed her guard to relax a bit, figuring the younger agent could both swim and maintain an adequate surveillance with the help of whomever she was teamed up with outside the pool.

As if on cue, Liz exited the pool the moment Kate ended her swim. She was in the change room ahead of Kate, apparently checking it out before Kate got there. In this the agent was deft, staying alert and one step ahead of Kate. She showered quicker than Kate; dried off quicker, applied skin cream, and dressed with a speed and ease that was impressive.

Kate emerged from the women's change room to see Agent Liz Bruan waiting a discreet distance from the entrance but not far enough away for her subject to slip by without being seen. In a humorous tone and with a slight grin, Kate asked, "Where to now?"

Liz replied, "Wherever you wish, this is your gig."

"I am still adjusting to the time difference, so I'll head back to my flat. I assume you know where it is," said Kate.

"Number 12 Rosary Gardens, unless you moved in the last few hours," responded Liz in a matching jesting tone.

They made the walk back toward her flat together, Kate in contemplation of the twists and turns occurring on the fly with this investigation. It was beginning to feel that it was becoming as much about her as it was about Vincent Bernard Taylor, or perhaps more importantly, the microchip that had been lodged in Taylor's brain. Liz, on the other hand, seemed to be actively engaged in observing every minute detail of the landscape and people who occupied it. Kate appreciated that in time this young agent would learn to do both functions while communicating in body language and demeanour a nonchalant indifference. It is maturity that develops that astute ability to observe and analyze simultaneously. For the moment at least, Kate surmised that two of them working at it might be better than one. That sense of being watched accompanied them on their walk. Kate considered then advanced the question.

"Liz, do you have a feeling that we are not alone, that is, that we are being watched?"

Liz gave a one-word, cryptic response. "Yes."

Kate breathed in heavily then continued in silence.

They reached 12 Rosary Gardens when Liz offered, in a slightly authoritarian manner, "Why don't you let me go in first."

Kate turned the key in the lock and stood back to allow Liz to go ahead into the flat. The sense of trepidation was palpable. Liz returned in a few moments, advising Kate that all seemed to be clear. Kate entered — it may have looked clear, but it did not feel clear. A scan of the flat revealed that all was in order, yet that sense of something amiss persisted. Kate decided to let the young agent go and get some sleep while she dealt with this mystery on her own.

Kate smiled at Liz then asked, with a typical slight truth underlying her feigned humour, "Do I have a recognizable escort on the train tomorrow?"

Liz said only, "Third seat back on the left, good night." And she was gone so quickly that Kate's grin still lingered on her face. Young Agent Liz Bruan regained her stature as she exited the flat and strode away up the narrow street.

For a moment Kate felt a role reversal take place, not unlike that which periodically occurred when she pushed her long-suffering therapist into the client position. The therapist was skilled; usually she quickly reclaimed her ground, a position that she communicated well through body language, voice, and a sense of authority. Liz would not require thirty years to achieve the level of professional prowess that Kate Roarty had built up during that period of time. Despite the twenty years that separated these two women, Kate was becoming aware that Agent Liz Bruan would close in on her level of proficiency very quickly.

Kate entered the flat, experiencing a lingering unease like the traces of bad cologne that persist long after the offending user has left. She did a thorough check and did not find anything untoward added, missing, or disturbed. Her mind wandered back to the microchip that was implanted in the brain of Vincent Bernard Taylor, deceased. She knew there was a connection to that situation and this experience. It would be her job to connect the dots.

Her phone vibrated — the call display indicated Sûreté du Québec. The response to her hello was a bark from Jack Johnson. "Hey, you abandon your dog to a stranger and don't even call to see if it is okay?"

Kate allowed herself to get sucked into the banter. She replied, "*My* dog? I don't think that ownership would stand up in a court of law, Officer Johnson." She followed in the same jovial tone, "So, how is he doing?"

"Eats well, farts when he is dreaming, runs like Northern

Dancer, and whines when we get within two kilometres of your house."

"And why would you be within two kilometres of my house?" Kate asked with a little less playfulness.

Jack's tone became serious. "Listen, Kate, we are going to speak with you on a secure line when you go to MI5 tomorrow morning, okay? Dr. Bosum already set it up with that Braithwaite fellow. Your meeting with him is at ten, but go earlier. Braithwaite's unit will call us as soon as you are there and cleared through security, but the call will be private, just with you, okay?"

Kate hit the 'end call' button then plugged in her iPhone to recharge. She headed to the bathroom then stopped and returned to the phone, carefully examining the thin cable and the plug-in. It appeared to be the one she had been using since she got the iPhone more than a year ago, but to the touch the slender cable felt ever so slightly different — perhaps a bit thicker. She was convinced she was simply becoming paranoid. She threw off her clothes and got into bed, but she lay wide awake in the comfort of the bed. She rose and spent a half hour making handwritten notes in a small notebook that she always carried with her. Periodically, she glanced toward the phone, over which she had thrown a pillow.

Still wide awake and preoccupied with the iPhone, she unplugged it, separated the cable from the charger unit, and set it in the bathroom then placed her phone in her carry bag, zipped it up, and put it as far away from the cable and charger as the small flat would permit. Finally, a thirty-minute session of mindful meditation enabled her to clear her head, relax, and slip off into a very deep sleep.

4

Kate awoke as morning light was slipping around the edges of the blinds and curtains in her flat. She lay in bed considering the events of the previous day, her behaviour upon returning to the flat the evening before, and what was to unfold — known and unknown — on this new day in London. Agent Liz Bruan figured in her reflections as well. She was grateful to have a few moments to linger in bed as she sorted through the crowd of thoughts, impressions, concerns, and an elevated sense of anxiety, all pressing like commuters on the underground platform at rush hour. She shoved it all aside in favour of savouring the last thoughts she recalled before falling asleep — Jack Johnson — masculine, handsome, and so goddamned annoying. He was getting in the way of maintaining a clear focus on her aspect of this investigation, inserting himself into her thoughts like the melody of a six-part harmony. Yet what had he done? Nothing — it was Kate who allowed the preoccupation to creep in and take hold.

She slid out of bed, put the coffee on, took a quick shower while it was brewing, made a few routine other client calls, dressed, and headed out. The recurring presence became pervasive as she closed and locked the door. Kate half expected Agent Liz Bruan to fall in step beside her and was pleasantly surprised to walk on alone. She purchased a newspaper chip, picked up a latté, then headed down into the underground to take the tube out to Westminster. Lack of wireless reception in the underground made this means of travel quite pleasant. Folks were quiet, talking softly to one another, reading books and newspaper chips, and dozing off. When she surfaced from the underground, she noticed that she was quite early, so she took a seat at a sidewalk café, ordered a bagel and cream cheese, then continued reading the newspaper. The young waiter with a slight east European accent — Polish, probably — told her, without hesitation, to finish her coffee and enjoy her paper while he went to get her bagel. Another substantial tip was in the offing. When the bagel and cream cheese arrived, the plate was adorned with a finely sliced strawberry fanned out like a tiny ostrich tail. Kate picked away at both as she went through the international news section of *The Independent,* marvelling at how much more worldly it seemed than Canadian news sources.

Just as she was about to pay her bill, she was approached by Jonathon Braithwaite, who politely asked to join her then smoothly picked up the tab from the waiter that had served Kate — he also seemed well acquainted with Braithwaite. Braithwaite smiled and said, "I often stop here for a coffee and a read of the morning news before hitting the turbulence of a busy day at MI5. I was about to go when I noticed you. I didn't see you arrive."

Kate didn't quibble over the bill that he had just paid but said, "Please join me," motioning to the empty chair opposite her at the small round table.

"You have come along earlier than we had arranged," he remarked.

"Yes, I understand I will have a call with my contractors at

Sûreté du Québec before we meet," replied Kate.

"Ah, yes, Agent Sloane rang me to that effect."

Kate did not let on that she had noticed the discrepancy of information between what Braithwaite just communicated and what she heard from Jack Johnson the evening before. She also decided to sit on any reference to her encounters with GCHQ, at least until they formally met, if at all.

Braithwaite digressed to small talk. "Do you enjoy our fair and ancient city?"

Kate was completely forthcoming in her response. "To be frank, I love this city — everything about it. I first came here at the age of nineteen to visit a very old grandmother whom I adored — it was many years before I returned, however. A posting to West Africa during my diplomatic career offered the opportunity to make several return trips when I could roam about as a tourist. It was glorious." She abruptly stopped, surprised by the exuberance of her response.

"Perhaps your first visit while still an infant introduced an attraction that stayed with you throughout your life," remarked Braithwaite.

While not surprised that MI5 was in possession of these details about her life, the remark put her back on her guard. She was aware that Braithwaite might very well have presented it to demonstrate that he had the upper hand.

She stood up, saying, "Shall we?" then gestured to the pavement that led toward Millbank and the MI5 complex. Within ten minutes, they were passing through the main gate with only a very brief stop at Security, where Braithwaite collected the temporary pass for Kate and handed it to her. Before she could throw the thin cord attached to the ID card over her neck, he had swiped them through and into a corridor that was familiar from her previous visit. He showed Kate into a small meeting room and excused himself for a few moments, whereupon Agent Sloane and Whistlethorpe, the intern, joined her almost immediately. Braithwaite returned with a tray of tea and biscuits, poured cups for all, passed them around, then convened the meeting. Whistlethorpe could barely hide her embarrassment — a dynamic that did not elude Kate's watchful eye and was met with a barely perceived grin from Agent Sloane. As Kate added milk to her tea, she mused on the contrasts — a very modern grey steel, glass, and light maple interior architectural surrounding wherein tea was served in traditional Wedgwood china from the turn of the twentieth century. The faint white noise of humming desktop computers, abundant viewing screens, handheld devices, tablets, and scanners of every description contrasted with a cone of sharpened pencils in the centre of an otherwise starkly barren meeting room. Kate wondered who used the pencils then thought perhaps they were part of the décor rather than being there for use. She itched to pick one up, just to get a reaction, but since she did not need a pencil, she did not scratch the itch.

Jonathon Braithwaite was speaking, and his voice lurched her back to the moment. She bought time to refocus her thoughts by sipping on her tea. Then Agent Sloane began talking, and Kate gave her undivided attention. She wanted to win this woman's trust swiftly and decidedly, to make her feel like what she had to say was the most important communication in the universe. Success could carry her a long way in building the relationship.

"It seems iBrain continued its search for money and caught the interest of an accelerator group out of San Francisco with some rather innovative approaches to putting financing deals together. A group of eight or more angel and VC investors from the Bay area and Silicon Valley north" — Kate looked up — "Ottawa/Kanata, that is, stepped up to the plate with another nineteen million pounds, some of which was an infusion of private equity, and they were off to the races. I think we lost track of them when they remained so quiet in the UK. Some of their original researchers were hired through a Canadian brain drain program that complemented a credible base already established in Ottawa. Additional talented researchers were taken on in California. What gets even more interesting, your Vincent Bernard Taylor put the first offshore VC package together, funds raised mostly out of a New Jersey investment group."

Kate took all of this in then responded, "Okay, we have a snapshot of the evolving financing picture — which sounds healthy. What about the work on the technology?"

Agent Sloane responded, "Yes, you are right, but before we get to the technology side of the equation, let's look further at the financing. iBrain attracted a lot of money that of course has not paid out any dividends, since they don't yet have a marketable product. The new investors came on board for the promise of the future — they are not too interested in sharing the spoils with those earlier investors who, by the way, as far as we can determine put upwards of £130 million in the iBrain pot. These guys are still hanging around checking on their technology development. They too are chasing the promise of the future to recoup their initial investments and ultimately to realize a handsome profit. The very nature of these types of investors are motivated by high risk, high returns — get in early, rapid growth, and get out fast.

"As you may know, the regulatory environment varies from country to country and across international boundaries, but the basic principles are more similar than different. The rules of the VC game are that these guys make their profits with the equity they have in the company. They are also hanging on to their prospects usually through an acquisition, when a technology is in prototype phase and ready to go into commercialization."

Kate was fully aware of the process, but she found the summary presented by Agent Sloane served as a good snapshot of what MI5 knew, what they considered important, and what approach this organization might take in a further investigation.

Agent Sloane continued. "We think iBrain has a prototype. In all likelihood, only the inner circle of technology developers and the most recent investors know about it. Your Dr. Vincent Bernard Taylor may have been closing in the prototype when he met his demise. We are presuming that it's related, but we don't know how."

Before they could continue their discussion, a quiet knock came to the door. Intern Whistlethorpe answered then spoke quietly to Braithwaite, who looked up and said to Kate, "Your call has come in from Canada, so let me show you to a private room where you can take it, and we will reconvene here when you are finished."

Kate nodded and followed Braithwaite out and down the corridor into an unoccupied office.

"You won't be disturbed in here," said Braithwaite. He picked up the phone, punched a few buttons, listened for a moment, then handed the device to Kate and left.

Kate took it and said, "Yes."

It was Dr. Bosum who spoke first. "Kate, this is Isabel. I have Jack and Guy conferenced in." Kate warmed to the familiarity of the introduction.

"How are things going in London?" Dr. Bosum asked.

"Interesting," Kate replied, knowing that Isabel's prompt was a politeness that would solicit more detail later.

Jack and Guy chimed in with hellos to Kate, then Guy took over. "Kate, we took Big Ben to the vet to get his chip read. The vet told us that he had not previously encountered this kind of ID chip. It seemed to have a double layer with the standard information connecting the dog to our Vincent Bernard Taylor of New York, as we expected, but that info panel appears to overlay another panel that reveals a distinct likeness to the chip we discovered in Taylor's brain."

Dr. Bosum joined the discussion at that point, saying, "We are reluctant to tamper with it or remove it for fear Big

Ben will suffer the same outcome as Dr. Taylor."

"Don't worry, Kate," said Jack, "we are taking the very best care of this dog that we can. In fact, until we can deal with this chip, Big Ben will be in the company of two officers at any given time — including myself and Guy or both of us. Francine is also on standby to give us a hand if we need it."

Kate exhaled as she continued to listen. She allowed a fleeting thought — *Lucky Big Ben.*

Dr. Bosum asked, "Kate, can you find out as much as possible about the technology?"

Kate gave them a thumbnail sketch about the financing surrounding the development of the iBrain technology, which she believed was related to this chip.

Guy remarked, "Despite all of the high-tech focus, we are still dealing with the rudimentary motivator of many crimes — money."

Kate replied, "I don't think we would be jumping to huge conclusions by saying that it is a contributing factor to this crime or series of crimes concerning this technology.

Jack interjected, "Kate, can we digress for a moment?"

Kate replied, "Yes, of course."

"We think your phone is compromised," Jack said.

Kate responded, "I think you are right."

Jack went on, "We've arranged with MI5 to issue you a new phone that will give you anonymity and security. The Brits are a bit ahead of us in using this technology, but we will catch up quickly. One of Braithwaite's techno geeks will set you up. Your phone will be a new iPhone 10 with cellcrypt technology that will give you both anonymity and secure text messaging. To put it simply, it will give you security for real-time short-lived messages that can neither be stored nor forwarded — like a real-time verbal conversation that isn't recorded. The technology is activated only when both users have cellcrypt and the key to use the encryption; otherwise, it's a normal mobile phone. It will identify all incoming calls for you, regardless of any encryption being employed by the caller. However, it will give you the option to place outgoing calls — voice or text — anonymously. Kate, don't lose it or get it stolen, and do not turn it in to any security collectors during your rounds of meetings and visits in the UK. Figure out how to keep it on you at all times. After MI5's techno geeks set you up, transfer the data you require for the old mobile phone to the new one and ensure no trailers are dragged over to the new device. Your old phone will be disposed of by them."

Kate sucked up her breath at that remark. That cell phone, with an accompanying plan, had cost her a small fortune. She had purchased it only a few months ago.

"Kate," interjected Dr. Bosum, "SQ will pay out your old plan then cancel it. You will not be out of pocket. When you are finished working with SQ, we will get you a new consumer device and compensate you for the new plan you will have to set up."

Kate agreed.

Jack asked without the usual brusque sarcasm that accompanied his speech, "With that bit of techno administration addressed, do you have a few moments to fill us in on what you have found out and your experiences since arriving in London?"

Kate brought them up to date on MI5, MI6, and GCHQ, including agents Rathbone and Bruan. She took a bit of time describing the actions of Liz Bruan. Kate was usually rather brief and to the point, so she surprised herself by going into much more detail than was her custom in the client-contractor relationship. All three listened without interruption until she finished, then Dr. Bosum asked, "Do you trust these people, Kate?"

Kate gave a measured reply. "I imagine they have the same level of guardedness and deception among and between their organizations as we in Canada have among CSIS, RCMP,

CSEC, CBS, DND, Foreign Affairs, and various provincial jurisdictions." She reinforced this observation by saying, "The difference is here in the UK, I really feel the proximity to the rest of the world and hence the opportunity for compromise and infiltration by non-friendlies." She paused then asked, "Are we sure this call is indeed private?"

Guy responded, "We are never a hundred percent sure, but MI5 wants the same privileges with us on some investigations they are engaged in in Montreal. We would be surprised if they jeopardize these favours so early on in this investigation. It's a quid pro quo arrangement."

They said their goodbyes and hung up. Kate was surprised to note that the call had lasted a little over seventeen minutes, during which time they had covered a broad territory. She was glad to have this team that she trusted as her contractors. She pushed away the distraction of lingering on Jack's voice and thoughts of his strong and masculine demeanour. She was pleased at the absence of derision that so often peppered his approach when speaking with her. Perhaps it was the presence of Dr. Bosum on the call that tempered his tendency toward sarcasm.

Kate exited the office into the corridor that led back to the meeting room. In an instant, the intern, Whistlethorpe, was at her side, offering to show her back to their meeting room. Agent Sloane was already seated, totally engaged in activity on her mobile. Before she could reclaim her seat at the table, Agent Braithwaite re-entered, remarking casually but in a rather efficient manner, "Shall we resume then?"

Kate nodded.

Jonathon Braithwaite provided a recap of the discussion they had before Kate's phone call. Kate greatly appreciated it, as she felt a wave of fatigue creep over her. It must be a bit of lingering jet lag. A cup of tea with some extra sugar provided a quick pick-me-up. Agent Sloane was watching her intently when Kate looked over in her direction. The efficient intensity of Braithwaite's voice drew her back to what he was saying.

"We have to get a closer look at the iBrain technology, and more importantly, we need to get a handle on its applications."

Agent Sloane suggested they make a joint visit before Kate went off to GCHQ. Kate agreed and further suggested that they make back-to-back visits to each of the research sites in the UK, Canada, and the US. This approach could thwart any alerts going out from the iBrain research sites that would hinder their intelligence-gathering. Braithwaite nodded his assent and offered his team to coordinate the visits. As well, he offered to use one of the MI5 agents in Ottawa so they would not have to bring in the RCMP, CSIS, or SQ. Kate reminded Braithwaite that she worked for the SQ. She did not reveal her surprise at Braithwaite freely allowing that MI5 had agents in Canada. Dr. Bosum's voice was resounding in her mind: *Do you trust them?* She answered *Yes and no*.

Kate advised Braithwaite that while the plan had merit, using an MI5 agent in Canada would require agreement by her contractor, the SQ, whose only jurisdiction was the province of Quebec; therefore, they would have to liaise with CSIS and/or the RCMP. In the meantime, she would like to proceed with the visit to iBrain in the UK, with or without MI5. She noted an alert but very subtle body language exchange between Braithwaite and Sloane. Whistlethorpe appeared oblivious to the dynamic and continued making notes.

Kate was anxious to get out of MI5 and move on with her own agenda. She rose and asked to be directed to the MI5 techno geeks, where she could pick up the new mobile device. Whistlethorpe leapt up to volunteer to show her the way, leaving Braithwaite and Sloane behind in the meeting room.

Kate met with a stereotypical techno cyber geek who could well fit into her private cyber-geek network. She was comfortable. The guy's name was Anton, information gleaned from a nameplate on his desk rather than by any greeting from the young man. Kate offered her name and a hand, neither of which was acknowledged. Anton went straight into setting her up with the new mobile phone. He showed her the device and carefully explained every detail of its functioning. Kate was overwhelmed with the detail but let him continue without interruption until he finished. He paused and without looking up said he would explain it all again. Kate asked for the 101 version. Anton went through the entire detailed description again in a very focused and methodological manner then stopped talking and paused, handing the device to Kate.

"Thanks, Anton, can you tell me what I need to know to use this device effectively?"

Anton replied precisely, demonstrating each step of his instructions. "Turn it on and off like this; recharge it like this; activate the anonymity function on outgoing calls like this; activate the incoming ID and tracker function like this. It has an integrated GPS, which can be activated like this. Otherwise, it operates like a more advanced iPhone 10. This technology cannot be compromised — yet. The phone is ready for use."

Kate nodded and handed him her old phone, which he took and mounted on a dock beside the new phone.

In a few short moments, still without looking at Kate, he handed the new phone back, saying, "All of the data has been transferred to the new phone, and the old one is stripped."

"Thanks, Anton," said Kate as she left his office.

Intern Whistlethorpe hurried on after Kate. In the corridor, Whistlethorpe remarked, "Wow, you did well with Anton. Most people get really frustrated and yell at him."

Kate replied simply, "Anton knows his stuff thoroughly."

She headed down the corridor to the reception area with Whistlethorpe in tow. Kate removed her visitor's ID, handed it to the agent, and was gone before the young intern could reply. Kate breathed in as she hit the pavement in full stride when she felt her phone vibrating to the tune of "O Canada." She retrieved it and answered, slightly sarcastically, "Very funny." Anton gave her instructions on how to change the vibration and ring tone, then hung up.

The number of players and complexity of this case was growing faster than the various angles Kate could consider. The objective of the SQ was simple: identify the killer(s) and build a case to ensure a conviction. Kate was sensing that the murder of Vincent Bernard Taylor was anything but simple. It was apparent that the web of investors, the number of technology developers, and the institutes supporting them, the application of the technology — credible or criminal — and the intelligence operations involved or becoming involved were making this a quagmire of deception and intrigue. The entire picture might remain elusive to each and every player. Where did a frail, cautious old lady living in a modest squared-timber house on Meech Lake in the Gatineau fit into the web?

Kate self-counselled to see through the complexity by keeping her role focused and simple and then laughed inwardly, wondering how possible that could be. She returned to 12 Rosary Gardens caring not if her flat had been entered again, for what would be observed, learned, or found that had not already been achieved? However, after a ten-minute power nap she did decide she was already becoming too predictable. She grabbed her swimming togs, heading to the Underground, where she could get on to the Circle Line that would take her to Lancaster Gate, the nearest station to Serpentine Lido, a very old and famous outdoor swimming pool big enough to lap out several kilometres without too many turns. The 2012 Olympic long-distance swimming events had been held there; hence, she imagined that the pools and changing facilities would be quite modern and functional — at least to that era — fourteen years ago.

She reached the pool-side in less than a half hour and one and a half hours later emerged from a three-kilometre swim, stress-free, invigorated, confident, and not in the least bothered by the complexity of the case that was unfolding before her eyes. Further, as she looked around, it appeared that she had successfully eluded her surveillance team. There were a few other swimmers seriously plying their way through the warm water — none gave the impression of having any other motive for being there. Kate showered, changed, and headed off in search of pho and green tea with enough time remaining to return to 12 Rosary Gardens, pack her carry-on rolly, and head to Paddington Station, where she would board the train for Cheltenham, Gloucestershire. She made the entire outing without being tracked, thus proving that the new mobile device was not likely compromised.

A sense of lightness and autonomy accompanied her all the way back to 12 Rosary Gardens then on to Paddington Station, where young Agent Liz Bruan resumed her tail function. Kate decided to play the game and walked past her without acknowledgement. Once on board, she slipped into a deep sleep as the train pulled out of Paddington and awoke only enough to reconfirm that she was still headed toward Cheltenham, although she assumed Agent Liz Bruan would have addressed any issues there. She arrived rather refreshed despite the late hour and readily walked the short distance to Clematis House, where she was greeted in name by the proprietor and shown to her room.

5

The young man — probably the son of the proprietor — told Kate that breakfast was served from 6:30 a.m. onward and that Nigel Rathbone had asked him to remind her to bring her swimming togs to GCHQ. Kate nodded, thanked him, and closed the door, wondering if maybe she had to swim across a moat to reach these auspicious offices.

Once again, sleep came quickly and easily beneath a weightless enveloping comforter and soft, almost delicate white sheets. She was surprised to awaken almost seven hours later. She scrambled to shower, dress, and get down for breakfast. Kate was ravenous and devoured everything in front of her, along with several cups of delicious hot, steaming coffee.

As she headed out to the waiting GCHQ car, the young proprietor she had met the night before asked, "Will we see you back this evening, Mrs. Roarty?"

Kate surprised herself when she realized she did not have a clear return plan. She quickly replied, "If I find it is too late to return to London, is a room available this evening?"

The young man responded, "Absolutely, we will keep

your room until you ring us and let us know your plan." He handed her a business card and held the door for her to pass through out to the black Ford Explorer SUV. She mused that it must have been a government contract, as it was the same as the MI5 SUV she saw earlier. Agent Liz Bruan was waiting for her at the main entrance to GCHQ. There was no moat to cross to enter, rather a series of checkpoints requiring a menu of badge-swiping, retina display, and palm display as they entered the inner labyrinth of the organization. A very handsome — in a British sort of way — late thirty-something, Nigel Rathbone, greeted Kate in the atrium where her escort, Agent Bruan, left without a word. Kate revealed surprise.

Nigel quickly said, "Don't worry, she will be fine once she has had a cup of coffee. She is a bit miffed that you eluded her most of yesterday, and she received a slight reprimand for sloppy surveillance. Personally, I doubt that she was sloppy at all, rather, you are very good at what you do."

Kate allowed a very slight smile but said nothing in response. She quietly studied this man whose voice had revealed his appearance and demeanour before she met him. Fit, dark-haired, conservatively attired in expensive suit pants and grey open-necked dress shirt, he was a well-spoken middle manager experienced at the balancing act of keeping everyone happy above and below his station of responsibility.

Nigel continued in a polished yet familiar manner. "Before we get down to the seriousness of our meeting, can I have the pleasure of showing you our new indoor pool completed only a few weeks ago?"

Kate nodded and followed Agent Rathbone across the atrium into a parallel atrium that housed exclusively the largest indoor pool she had ever seen. Nigel beamed like a schoolboy as Kate could not contain the deeply impressed expression lighting her face. "It is 153 metres long and filled with fresh slightly saline water kept at eight-three degrees

Fahrenheit. Everything in the change rooms operates on high-performance sensors. There are three surround Jacuzzis that will therapeutically relieve any stress, tension, or pain from injury. It is free for all employees to use on the twenty-four-hour clock. We all swim, and we know you do, so we thought you might like to complete your exercise regime while you are here."

Kate nodded once again and replied, "Thank you, I accept your offer. It is indeed a beautiful facility. I have never seen a pool this big ... and so pristine."

Nigel replied, "The only bigger pool I am aware of belongs to the Kalifi family in the UAE."

"Yes, I swam in it last year. Although it was built a decade ago, it was only opened to women in 2025."

As they walked through the pool atrium to an office complex, Kate was admittedly distracted by attempting to calculate the number of turns required in a 150-metre pool for a three-kilometre swim. She stated out loud, "Twenty."

Nigel stopped. "Pardon, Mrs. Roarty?"

Kate laughed. "That would be twenty turns for a three-kilometre distance — extraordinary, although I do swim very slowly in comparison to the triathaloners that I witness churning up the water almost everywhere I go to swim."

Nigel suggested, "After their meetings are finished or for a break during the process, we can take a swim. Despite many swimmers, the pool is so big that it is rarely crowded, so timing is not an issue.

Kate heard a voice in her head repeating, *Do not leave that mobile anywhere.*

Kate followed Nigel toward the office tower beyond the pool atrium. She found herself memorizing every detail of the interior landscape of GCHQ as they proceeded toward their meeting location. They entered a small, intimate meeting room not unlike the one she had come to know at MI5. The décor was light and airy — maple on the lower wall panelling, door, and conference table accented by frosted chrome around the door frame, the windows, the lighting fixtures, and the lightly cushioned chairs. She suspected it was all maple veneer over steel structure. It seemed a lot had gone into establishing a sense of physical comfort in the work environment at GCHQ.

Nigel observed Kate taking in her surroundings. "This place had been slated for massive renovations that four successive administrations all put off for budgetary reasons. After the Berlin Wall fell, we decided that in addition to the necessity to completely overhaul the electrical and computer systems, we needed to create an environment that left the Cold War era behind. The minimalist Scandinavian influence took hold, and after four years of excruciating disruption, the contractors produced this working environment. While an aerial view of GCHQ suggests a futuristic structure, it was actually designed and constructed from a renovation growing out of the original historic setting. Our systems are almost paperless. Most of the old guard reached retirement age during this renovation era, so the human transformation was also occurring. Many of the old guys have small retainer contracts that we tap into when we need historical context, but the median age has dropped from sixty to forty-five years. It is interesting that among the small number of women who retired, few were interested in continuing an attachment to GCHQ. They moved onto to rich personal lives, writing, travelling, gardening, golfing, and interacting with their extended families. Even when we reach out to them for help on certain dossiers, they decline — offering only non-paid consultations if we are really stuck. Our personnel profile has changed dramatically since that era. My generation includes more than thirty percent females, and the under twenties, more than fifty percent. We may have to introduce affirmative action for men."

Kate listened attentively then made only two remarks.

"Ah, your Agent Liz Bruan would be the latest generation. Our Canadian CSIS, RCMP, CSEC, and Global Affairs are following the same route, although National Defence clings tenaciously to a male-dominated environment."

Kate thought that Agent Nigel Rathbone was telling her about GCHQ in this manner for more reasons than just to be chatty.

"Kate, we wish to be open and forthcoming with you. We reviewed your career, and your life, for that matter, before inviting you into GCHQ. Few foreigners enter this facility, and even fewer who work in the private sector."

Kate replied, "Except a large number of building contractors."

Nigel responded, "Yes, of course, these workers were from the private sector, but they were all UK citizens and fully vetted before being granted access to GCHQ."

Kate said simply, "Are you sure?"

Nigel bowed his head slightly but declined further comment on the subject.

Kate followed with, "I don't mean to put you on the defensive, but my impression is most of the Western developed economies, such as ours, lack a sufficiently large pool of skilled workers in the building trades. Workers from Eastern Europe who come into Canada on temporary work permits fill many specialized crafts. I imagine the EU offers even more liberal access to the UK building trades."

Nigel continued to decline further verbal comment but once again bowed his head in assent.

Ever the analyst, Kate was considering the exchange. *Is this directly relevant or a distracting tangent?*

She held the thought as an attendant arrived with a tray of tea, coffee, milk, sweeteners, and biscuits.

As she accepted a cup of tea, she smiled and playfully remarked to Agent Rathbone, "I am no longer certain as to who initiated this visit — me, GCHQ … or perhaps both;

regardless, let's have a chat."

Nigel responded, "Right to it then. Shall we begin with Vincent Bernard Taylor?"

While Kate raised her eyebrows slightly; she otherwise contained her surprise and replied, "Go ahead."

"We understand you are involved with the investigation of his death … under mysterious circumstances, which I believe your SQ has classified as a homicide."

Kate nodded and remarked, "Go on."

Nigel continued, "Perhaps we can be of mutual assistance on this case."

Kate skilfully allowed nothing in response as she drew out what GCHQ knew or was at least willing to divulge in the interview. "What can you tell me about Dr. Taylor and his untimely death?"

"Of the latter, nothing as yet. However, we do know a bit about his background. He was a software expert who did some contract work in intelligence surveillance for both the US and the UK. He was rather self-educated in the early years before acquiring a PhD from MIT specializing in cyber detection. His credentials were in high demand when he started out, and many academic institutions courted him. He found that MIT's flexibility in permitting, even encouraging, copyright protection attractive enough to stay on there and lend his services in academia, which came easily to him. MIT was generous in letting him work as a private consultant as long as he fulfilled his academic duties. He rarely taught more than one term per academic year and supervised his graduate students from abroad, where he had contracts in Europe. Most of his students were so delighted to be taken on by him that they readily agreed to the rather hands-off conditions of the academic relationship. It seems many of them went on to attractive research positions through contacts garnered while under the supervision of Dr. Taylor. Some of them joined him on contracts abroad. A few set up their own companies following graduation."

Kate took it all in then asked, "What do you know of his family, his friends, his earlier life?"

Nigel was silent for a moment before responding. "Taylor was an only child born to Henry Vincent Taylor of Keswick, in our Lake District, and Clare St. Denis of Bayeux, Normandy, in France." Kate couldn't help but sit up taller when she heard Clare's name.

"The two met during the Second World War. Clare was a Red Cross nurse working at a hospital in Bayeux, and Henry was a junior officer with the Sixth Airborne Division who landed above Juno Beach on D-Day. Henry was seriously injured on landing but survived and eventually recovered. They fell in love as Clare nursed him back to health. After the war, they immigrated to Canada. Both had relatives in Quebec and Ontario. Clare's father's name was Bernard, and Henry's father was Vincent. They led a hard-working, spartan but rather charmed life eventually enlivened by the arrival of their baby son, Vincent Bernard. They acquired a modest house in Montreal. On a summer vacation, they went to Gatineau in West Quebec during a visit to your nation's capital. Henry found the setting quite reminiscent of Keswick in the Lake District. With Clare's blessing, they purchased a lakeside property on Meech Lake, and together with the help of friends and cousins erected a small cottage.

"They passed many summers there, first living in a tent while building the cottage then living in the cottage as they constructed out buildings, planted a garden, established a small apple orchard, put in a large dock, landscaped the property, and built a boat. The area was a popular weekend getaway in the forties and fifties. Henry became known as Henri — that was the way Clare pronounced his name. It seems Henri experienced periods of melancholy — they would likely be diagnosed as PTSD in today's terms. He also had a weak heart. He collapsed and died of an apparent heart attack while chopping wood at the cottage when the boy was about eleven.

"Clare never returned to Montreal; rather, she stayed through the winter and thereafter permanently at Meech Lake. As time went on, she became reclusive, although independent and quite self-sufficient. With the proceeds from the eventual sale of the house in Montreal, she was able to send the boy off to Brebeuf — a Jesuit boarding school in the same city. Vincent was fully bilingual, having acquired English and French from each parent, as well as going to an English school in Montreal and a French school in Chelsea, Quebec. He was an outstanding student at all of the schools he attended. It seems he was a gifted intellect, quite athletic, with commanding leadership and organizational skills. He also demonstrated effective debating prowess and oratory abilities. As his mother became more reclusive, Vincent eschewed the repressive gloom that surrounded the once delightful lakeside cottage. His visits home became less and less frequent, and the relationship finally became estranged. It seems there were years of little or no contact until shortly before Vincent died."

Kate listened intently. When he paused, she remarked with a gentle softness in her tone and a slight smile. "Mr. Rathbone, should you ever decide upon a career change, may I recommend raconteur, novelist ... biographer."

Nigel smiled and allowed that his own father already occupied that domain.

Kate replied, "In the words of my father, you come by it honestly."

That exchange was a more effective icebreaker than any earlier chitchat the two had engaged in.

"Kate, we have been following the trail of Vincent Bernard Taylor off and on for a number of years. That surveillance intensified several years ago and continued until his death. Although he was a Canadian citizen by passport, he was something of a citizen of the world, or at least the US, the UK, and France — all of the places he had called home at different times."

The seemingly taciturn Kate replied, "Did GCHQ kill him?"

Nigel replied, "No, Kate, we did not, he was more important to us alive."

Kate replied singularly, "Why?"

Nigel continued in a surprisingly forthcoming manner, skilfully reeling Kate into his confidence. The dance of the analytical intellects was readily apparent to each of them and even more so to the silent observer in the room, Liz Bruan, who had quietly slipped in and sat down to a nod from Nigel.

"We know Dr. Taylor was involved in an extraordinary amount of technology development for clandestine surveillance and espionage. He was a partner to most of the technology in R&D with his students and the principal investigator of many research projects. His work, and that of his close-knit network, had the interest of all Western superpowers, namely the G8 and beyond to the G20. We never sensed that he was politically motivated, although he was not without political savvy. Rather, he was inspired by brilliance in innovation and to a lesser extent monetary gain. Although he lived comfortably and did not seem to want for anything, the monetary motivation seemed largely to do with fuelling the insatiable R&D burn rates characteristic in this field of technology development. He made generous venture capital loans, advanced angel investments to new promising starts-ups, and paid abundant salaries to newly minted PhDs at the top of their game. He purchased the latest technologies to facilitate the R&D.

"Vincent's mother lived on a modest pension and never asked for anything of Vincent. In recent years, the prodigal son seemed to figure out that she could no longer manage the taxes on the Meech Lake property, so he paid them up ten years in advance — I suspect to remove any acrimonious debate about the issue — and bought her a four-wheel-drive SUV that would better handle the winter road conditions. We think he also took out a snow removal and landscaping contract with one of the locals. Then there was the matter of the dog."

Kate leaned in. "Dog?"

"Yes, he acquired a dog a couple of years ago, from which he became inseparable. The dog went everywhere with him, including to the UK. He maintained a EU canine health passport for the dog akin to exemptions coverage given to guide dogs. The dog became well trained and well travelled, but not by Dr. Taylor. Then suddenly Taylor paid his mother a visit and left the dog with her.

"While generous, even GCHQ resources could not be justified in the surveillance of the dog, so we reluctantly had to drop it. During the brief few weeks that we kept an eye on it, the dog never left Clare St. Denis's side."

Kate said nothing, expecting Agent Rathbone to reveal that GCHQ knew the dog was in her care, or more accurately the care of the SQ and herself. This piece of information seemed to be unknown to the agent. Kate decided not to enlighten him.

Nigel abruptly stood up, inviting Kate to take a swim break. Kate agreed enthusiastically and followed Nigel to the door of the women's change room. Upon entering, she found a salon with floor-to-ceiling change cubicles and keypad lock doors. Each cubicle contained a generous-sized bench, clothes racks with hangars, a keypad storage locker, a floor-to-ceiling mirror — back to front — on two walls and a shelf with hair dryer, lotions, soaps, shampoos, three voluminous towels, and an enveloping robe. A partially frosted door led to a spacious private shower. Kate wondered what the masses enjoyed then remembered that she was well acquainted with public swimming pools in London. She slipped into her bathing suit and cap while allowing the "wow" factor to settle. She followed the instructions to key in her own personal code and placed all of her valuables, including the phone, in the locker. She noted that the inside of the locker was steel-lined and fully sealed. Kate closed that door feeling the contents were quite secure. She then followed the same procedure for the door to the room. A pictorial sign indicated the direction to follow to the pool, where she found Nigel waiting wrapped in an equally voluminous bathrobe. His was monogrammed with 'NR' on the pocket and right cuff. Kate looked at the monogram then noticed 'Guest' was similarly embroidered on her robe.

Nigel smiled. "Right then, shall we?" He gestured toward the pool.

Kate reminded him that she was neither a fast swimmer nor a competitive one. Nigel allowed that he was both fast and competitive but tired rather too quickly for his own liking.

Kate decided to measure this vast pool by counting the number of turns. She climbed out one hour and twenty minutes and twenty turns later, having completed three kilometres in an hour and twenty minutes — a good time for her. Nigel was dressed and sitting at a round table on the edge of the pool, where lunch for two was already laid out.

Kate apologized for her tardiness, but Nigel raised his hand in protest. "I swam half your distance in half your time. This gives me a chance to catch up on routine work. Please join me here after you have showered and dressed." Kate nodded and headed off to the change room. She went directly into the shower, relishing the soft, delicate soap and shampoo products. When she opened the locker, all appeared as she had left it. She felt confident that her personal items including the mobile had not been compromised. Further, she felt none of the apprehension that she had experienced at the seemingly undisturbed 12 Rosary Gardens.

When she emerged onto the pool deck, Nigel appeared engrossed in reading his tablet, much as he had been when she left.

He looked up, smiled, stood, and gestured to the other seat for her to sit down. Kate accepted willingly, realizing that despite the large English breakfast, she was famished. The fruit display, cucumber sandwiches, and the cold gazpacho soup looked enticing. She dug in with less genteel manners than her host. Nigel smiled and joined her in enjoying the soup. Before moving on to fruit and sandwiches, Nigel wiped his mouth with a cloth napkin and said, "Kate, will you work for GCHQ on this case?"

Despite having rather perceptive inclinations, this was last thing she had expected Nigel to say. It was her turn to wipe her mouth with a napkin in order to buy time to restore her inner composure.

She looked at Nigel for a moment before saying, "Agent Rathbone, I am hired on contract with the Sûreté du Québec on this case. I cannot and will not work for GCHQ as well or instead of SQ."

Nigel responded, "Fair enough, let's carry on then. Do you have some questions of GCHQ?"

Kate felt the case wrapping on more layers of complexity as she struggled to communicate an outward calm and control. She would play his game but on her terms.

She asked, "Is GCHQ involved in developing a biosurveillance technology?"

Nigel answered, "No."

"Is MI5 and or MI6 involved in developing a biosurveillance technology?"

"We don't think so."

"Is or are there UK-based companies involved in developing a biosurveillance technology?"

"We believe so."

"Are these companies collaborating with Canadian

counterparts?"

"Yes."

"Who are they?"

Nigel answered, "Now there is the rub."

Kate sensed the exchange might descend into a non-productive debate, so she opted to call it off. "Agent Nigel Rathbone, what do you say we take a break and resume tomorrow morning? I hadn't planned to stay over a second night, but I can — the kindly folks at Clematis House told me that I can keep my room there for a second night if I wish. We can take time to digest what we've learned … exchanged about this case … and perhaps come up with a strategy for collaborating on our investigation."

Rathbone readily agreed and proposed they resume at 9:30 a.m. the next morning. He escorted Kate back through the various security checks, advised her to hang on to her personalized security badge for re-entry the next morning, then left her at the last exit. Kate moved forward then stopped as she heard her name being called.

"Mrs. Roarty," said Rathbone.

"Yes?"

"Bring your swimming togs again," Nigel called back with a faint grin.

Kate nodded and gave a slight wave then continued out into the town of Cheltenham.

She returned to Clematis House long enough to confirm to the proprietors that she would indeed stay a second night. Kate switched her footwear to trainers and headed out to see this high-tech town. The walking gave GCHQ a context within the community of Cheltenham and Kate time to think about what she had learned before she rang the SQ crew.

"GCHQ is the largest local employer, engaging nearly 5,500 of the mostly highly educated, upwardly mobile employees, numbering among Britain's best and brightest. These people work, work out, eat, and sleep. They are purpose-driven minimalists who rarely frequented theatres, galleries, sports facilities, libraries — their needs and obligations are met within the confines of the high-tech 'donut' where they go to work. They prefer to live in newish homes filled with modest furnishings and austere artwork." Kate learned all of this from a forthcoming and eloquent waiter at a pleasant café terrasse where she stopped for a late afternoon latté and a gander through an online guide tool to Cheltenham. The waiter, Daniel, added that he thought Kate would fit in. She smiled then asked about dogs.

"No dogs," replied Daniel.

Kate threw back, "Then I wouldn't fit in."

Daniel smiled and returned to his duties.

Kate walked on, taking in the details of the town of Cheltenham, the information she had obtained from Nigel Rathbone, and the phone call she had to place to her SQ team. She spotted a tranquil park, empty of visitors, and decided this was a good place and time to make her call. Dr. Bosum picked up on the third ring and greeted Kate warmly.

"Kate, let me bring in Guy and Jack on the call so everybody hears the same discussion first-hand."

Kate agreed, slipped in her earbud, and waited on hold for a few minutes until she heard Dr. Bosum's soft voice again.

"Kate, are you still there?"

Kate smiled and replied, "Indeed I am, Dr. Bosum."

"Oh please, make it Isabel."

"Agreed."

Then she heard a French accent, "*Bonjour*, Kate," from the voice of Jack Johnson.

Her heart raced. Jocular Guy Archambault came on with, "How is my favourite spy today?"

Kate said, "Oh, please," aware that she had said nothing to Jack. "How is Big Ben?"

Jack replied, "Johnson is chopped liver, but the dog is a prince."

Isabel jumped in to joke in her gentle voice. "Thank you for that illuminating report, Jack. Kate, what do you have to tell us?"

Kate related the entire contents of her meeting with Agent Nigel Rathbone. The other three listened without interruption until she finished.

Then Guy said, "Sounds like they do not know that we have Big Ben. We had better keep it that way."

Jack chimed in, "So are you going to become a double agent?"

Dr. Bosum added, "She just blew her cover by telling us. Kate, I have to tell you, after our last call, I was feeling that we were getting a bit out of our depth. There is one senior contact I have in CSIS who I would trust with my soul. We met this morning, and I brought him up to speed. He is content to let us continue as we are while I keep him informed. We speak the same northern Cree dialect, so we can have very detailed discussions without any compromise to cyber eavesdropping."

"Good."

Jack interjected, "We have been keeping an eye on Clare St. Denis, but I think we will increase that vigilance if for no other reason than to determine complicity, or if she is in danger."

"I learned from GCHQ that she is Dr. Taylor's mother, so complicity or danger may well figure into the investigation," said Kate.

"Christ god," replied Guy.

Dr. Bosum advised that Kate should go ahead with her plan to meet again with GCHQ, further develop the relationship with Rathbone, and continue to communicate her loyalty to SQ. Best not to advise him that CSIS had entered the picture.

Guy added, "We will let D'Angelo know that swim with wolves is now off swimming with spies." His levity brought a laugh from everyone on the call. They hung up, and Kate restored the mobile to her pocket then took in the beauty of the Zen-like garden before strolling off toward the restaurant district. She was pleased with the call, not only from a professional perspective, but she enjoyed the personal sense of connection. Just hearing Jack's voice was enough to draw her more toward further consideration of him. Also, while Kate had determined never to work for anyone again after she left the diplomatic service, she was admittedly enjoying working with this little SQ team. It gave her the combination of independence and autonomy, along with backup and support to carry out the job.

The light was beginning to fail as she walked on in search of a cozy restaurant. She decided to place calls to each of her children before settling in to dinner. That way, with the time change it wouldn't be too late to reach them. The calls with her son were rarely more than a few minutes in length, while those to her daughter often exceeded an hour. She made the short call first.

Dominic, her twenty-two-year old, picked up with a grunt on the first ring. The usually brief call was surprisingly long, meandering, and interesting. This sometimes occurred with Dominic. Kate had learned just to keep listening, because it might be months before he was as forthcoming again. Dominic talked about his love life, his new apartment, the people he loved and hated at work, cycling to work, partying in the village, drinking, drugs, clothes, and shoes. By the time the call was over, Kate was thrilled with having made such a good connection with him. Sometimes her son simply hung up after a minute or two. Kate had never gotten used to his unpredictable behaviour. This time, it was nice not to have to recover from the call. She was now famished and ready to savour a quiet dinner in the aftermath of a successful chat with her son. She would call her daughter the following day or early evening.

She came across a restaurant called Vanilla that she had read about in the Michelin guide. The roasted butternut squash soup, listed among the appetizers on the menu, was enough to lure her in for the evening meal. After the soup, she ordered a sea bass fillet with wilted spinach and colcannon potatoes. She settled for a glass of house white wine, a Sauvignon Blanc of recent vintage, both adequate to the palate and complimentary to the cuisine.

Kate walked back to the Clematis House Bed and Breakfast. As she strode through the chilly, slightly damp evening air, she was surprised to realize that she had not reflected upon the day's meeting with Agent Nigel Rathbone; rather, her mind was preoccupied with the pleasure of the swim, the joy of the phone call with her son, and hearing Jack Johnson's voice during the call with the SQ team. She was also charmed to see many canines out strolling with their human companions. Contrary to the waiter's assessment, Cheltenham was indeed a dog town.

She paid the bill, bade farewell to the proprietors of Clematis House, and descended into the street with her small rolly luggage in tow. The same car from GCHQ that had been waiting for her the previous day was there again. She got in, momentarily reflecting that this could be an easy way to get kidnapped, then settled back for the short journey. It was during these moments that she gained clarity in the delicate chess game she was about to play with GCHQ in general and Agent Nigel Rathbone in particular. She was confident that she had the complete trust of the SQ team to make the best judgment calls she could entertain at any given moment. She sensed that even if she unwittingly strayed from the best course of action, the SQ would be there to back her up. She did not trust Agent Rathbone or the view he offered on the GCHQ organization. The jury was still out on MI5, and she was not yet in a position to adequately assess MI6.

Kate had to remind herself that she had only been in the country four days — barely long enough to get over jet lag. She hoped that, at the very least, the twelve years of living she had over Agent Rathbone would give her the adequate edge to stay ahead of the game. Maybe, just maybe, her diverse personal and professional experience would serve her sufficiently well in the number and complexity of quick and precise decisions she would have to make over the coming days. Although she enjoyed visiting the UK, she also yearned to be back in her own home and swimming at Meech Lake.

The car pulled up to the main entrance of the GCHQ. She exited the vehicle and breezed through the security checks, following the procedures she had experienced the previous day using the ID card she had been given. Kate fully expected the rolly and her shoulder bag to be inspected, but no such request was made of her. Of course, the cyber surveillance technological capability was probably already carrying out a myriad of non-invasive scanning and probing of everything she had with her, including her person. As Kate passed through the third checkpoint, Nigel strolled up to meet and greet her. He escorted her to the meeting room they had occupied the previous day. A fresh tray of tea, coffee, milk, sweeteners, and scones with jam had been laid out as though awaiting her arrival. Liz Bruan was already seated, this time with a small notebook in front of her and a sleek gold pen poised in the thumb and forefingers of both hands. Another person, a man Kate had not previously encountered, occupied the titular head of the table. Nigel introduced Kate to Director Claude Mason. He offered Kate a business card that confirmed his title, organization, and contact coordinates, but nothing more.

Mason readily responded to the body language that Kate

thought she had carefully concealed. He addressed Kate perfunctorily. "Indeed, I could be anyone. However, I am who the card indicates I am. If you require more information, please ask, and I will be happy to oblige."

Kate quickly recovered — not missing a beat. She asked, "Director of what?"

Claude Mason answered, "Technology IP forensics. Your line of work, I believe."

Kate nodded and moved to her next question. "What is your role in the death of Dr. Vincent Bernard Taylor?"

Mason answered, "None."

Undeterred by the cryptic authority in his voice and manner, Kate went on. "Then to what do I owe the pleasure of your company?"

Mason replied, "Like you, the microchip that was lodged in the brain of Dr. Vincent Bernard Taylor when he died interests GCHQ."

Kate liked his candour and decided to yield ever so slightly. She would move a pawn forward but keep it well protected. She replied, "Yes, SQ is interested in learning what role that microchip played, if any, in the death of Dr. Taylor. The autopsy revealed a general systems shutdown, but we do not know what caused that shutdown."

Mason responded, "You suspect it is related to the microchip."

"Possibly."

With a slight impertinence in his tone, Director Mason asked, "Then how can we work together to uncover this mystery?"

Kate studied the two men without response. Director Claude Mason poured the tea and added a precise amount of milk, then, much to Kate's surprise, he tipped a dash of maple syrup into the brew before passing it to her. She allowed a smile, and he returned the same. Clearly, this man was a pro. He appeared to be in his mid-forties, very fit, eloquently turned out in tailored trousers, monogrammed shirt, no tie, no rings, and a very plain but expensive watch. His hair was matte black, speckled with brown where normally a man of this age would exhibit some greying or white. She thought it was dyed and then recalled that her father, at twenty years older than this man, had the same hair colouring, albeit thinning by his mid-seventies. Since she had not yet seen him standing, she could not determine his height.

Mason suddenly softened and shifted to the personal. "Mrs. Roarty, may I call you Kate?"

Kate nodded.

"I understand that one of your many passions in life is swimming."

Again, Kate nodded.

Mason continued, "It has been my lifelong passion since swimming in the sea on summer holidays as a child, then swimming Varsity at Cambridge and MIT. My first assignment was to Perth, Australia. Admittedly, I embraced the opportunity with enthusiasm because of the swimming reputation of the population there. Monitoring gold theft, slipping out of the country as plating in a variety of technologies, was not the high point of my life. However, the swimming was superb."

Kate responded, "I am merely a recreational swimmer with no interest or inclination toward competition."

Claude responded, "Ah, but what you lack in speed, you make up in endurance."

Kate replied, "Perhaps."

"Rather like the course of your life, I imagine."

Kate half nodded but said nothing.

"Kate, that is the very reason we want you to work for GCHQ on this case. Not only for this admirable attribute, but you are also fully bilingual, in the Canadian context, and you understand Americans, having lived and worked in the US. You have been successful in their very aggressive business approaches. As well, you have carved out an IP forensics niche few others have ventured towards. There are lawyers, but they are too mired in the legalities to actually fully appreciate the depth and breadth of applications we are developing in these leading technologies."

Kate's mind latched on to the most important word in his discourse — *we*.

She backed off from the intensity of the conversation by inquiring after Claude Mason's name. Mason smiled. "My father was a French Canadian from the Saguenay region. He met my mother during the war but went home without establishing a union. My mother married another man who was a Crail fisherman and drowned at sea in the late forties. My father never forgot my mother, and in 1950, he finally wrote her a letter that miraculously reached her half a year later. She responded, which took another half year to reach him, but she sent the village phone number. He called and asked her to come to Canada. She declined, still unable to leave the seaside where her husband had perished. My father, Gilles Maisonneuve, showed up in Crail eight months later. They married immediately, but as his accent and limited English speaking skills were difficult for the locals to understand, his name was even more so. He told the minister to put his name as George Mason on their marriage certificate. Thereafter, he became George Mason to all in the village and beyond. He never returned to Quebec. I was the fourth-born and youngest son of George and Marion Mason. Although my father took on an Anglicized name, I learned early on in life to accept whatever pronunciation of my name was uttered — surprisingly, I'd get 'Claude' more often than 'clawed,' especially after I moved on from the village of Crail."

"Thank you for that background, Claude Mason. How long did you spend in the Saguenay? St. Jean, I believe?"

It was Mason's turn to fail to cover his surprise.

He replied, "Very perceptive, Madame Roarty. My father's

family invited me for a visit shortly after we wrote to them about his sudden death. While he never returned to Quebec, he maintained contact by writing a short note to every member of his family for each of their birthdays, enclosing a recent photograph of some or all members of our family. He had little money, but he always sent a small parcel by sea in September to arrive there in time for Christmas."

Kate remained silent, inviting him to continue.

"The letter of condolence from the Maisonneuve family arrived by special post. It was written in French. We deciphered the basic text, but I wanted to know exactly what was written in that letter. While my parents never attended the Catholic church in our village, I knew my father had been raised Catholic. I went to see the priest there, and he told me to take the letter to the deacon, a Parisian who readily translated the content of the letter for me. As he handed it back, he said, 'You should go — experience that wild land your father comes from.'

"I did and stayed for three years, attending CEGEP, a type of trades high school. As well, I worked in the bush with my uncles in winter and helped on their farms in the summer. Their own sons had all gone off to work in the mines and the cities, where abundant wages were readily available for those willing to work. They came home for major holidays and extended family festivities. The Maisonneuve families always had lots of food, a fire in the stove, much singing and telling of tales, and many, many laughs as I struggled to learn the language. It was total, absolute, and utter immersion. Along with learning the language, I acquired the French Canadian dimension to my heritage. I got to know a father that in many ways I really never knew. While he was gone, I felt his presence in his brothers, his mother, and his dear sisters. Most of my cousins were a half decade or more older than me — rather like my own brothers — they were my self appointed guides. The Catholic church became a big part of my life there because it was a major part of the life of the Maisonneuve family. I never really embraced it in the same way, but it served its purposes. After graduating from CEGEP, a priest asked me what I was going to do next. I had no idea — I hadn't thought about it. He told me I should consider university.

He added that I had a good mind that would flourish with more development. He also went on to say that my citizenship in the UK gave me access to some very fine academic institutions. I stayed on in the Saguenay — St. Jean throughout another winter to help my uncles; however, I increasingly passed my time buried in books. The priest helped me apply to several universities, but when the acceptance came from St. Andrews, my path was charted. I went home to Scotland to study at that institution located within a short distance of where my mother and brothers lived in and around Crail."

Kate found Claude Mason's tale illuminating. She expected that he was recounting it for very different reasons than the interpretations she was applying to it. Her considerations of the details about his Canadian connections were reaching out to latch on to what was retained of those relationships after he left Quebec and whom he encountered at St. Andrews, Cambridge, and MIT to further deepen them. She sensed these seemingly random dots would link up into a picture that outlined the development of a programmable micro biochip implant that was found in the brain of Dr. Vincent Bernard Taylor and perhaps was sitting in the brain of Big Ben. The former had been activated; the latter was dormant but likely vulnerable to activation. She had to see if the SQ was able to get more background on Vincent Bernard Taylor. She suspected Taylor and Mason were close in age, education, technology interests, and maybe even familiar relationships. Maybe Dr. Bosum could hit up her CSIS contact to see if they had a file on him. She would ask, imagining that whatever they turned up would confirm what she already suspected. In the meantime, she would operate on the assumption that her hunches were probably correct. Kate felt certain there was a connection between Taylor and Mason and that Mason knew Taylor was dead before Kate found him attached to a fallen tree on the shore of Meech Lake.

6

The evening train pulled out of Cheltenham Station as Kate settled into a good book. She read little more than a chapter before dozing off into a deep sleep aroused only with the announcement of Euston Station. The London underground had stopped running for the night, so she took a night bus, transferring several times. It was a pleasant, rather quick bus ride from Euston Station via a change at University College Hospital, then on to South Kensington tube station, where she descended at the bus stop and walked briskly up Old Brompton Road, enjoying the cool night air and calmness of the street. The sense of being watched that she had experienced previously did not return.

She placed the key in the door at 12 Rosary Gardens without apprehension, switching on the light as she entered. Although the air was slightly musty, the flat was as she had left it almost three days before. She collapsed onto the bed, and despite the long, deep sleep on the train, slumber overcame her immediately, giving her another four hours before first light cascaded through the one large window. She leapt out of bed, grabbed her swimming bag, and headed straight out to catch the 6:00 a.m. lap swim at South Kensington pool. She backtracked to Old Brompton Road, where a Starbucks was just opening and ready to serve her as the first customer of the day. She went to pay when the waitress put her hand up and said, "First customer always gets the order free along, with a warm croissant."

Kate was indeed getting a good start to the day. She dropped a one-pound note in the tip jar and headed out, covering the nearly two kilometres to the pool in record time, even as she enjoyed her latté and croissant. Kate half expected Liz Bruan to plunge in beside her, but the young GCHQ agent did not make an appearance. The pool was busy with fast and serious swimmers churning up the lanes.

Kate stayed in the next to slowest lane and struggled to keep up the pace. After an hour and ten minutes she emerged to shower, shampoo, and dress, arriving back at her little flat on Rosary Gardens shortly after 8:00 a.m. She was feeling rather smug at having accomplished so much before the workday was underway. She supplemented the earlier croissant with yogurt, blueberries, and almonds, another cup of fresh coffee, and orange juice. She checked her email, reconfirmed the appointment by phone with MI6, an Agent Nadeem Hazan, then settled into some serious note updating before making the early call to the SQ team. Unexpectedly, her phone rang. A simple hello was responded to with a very masculine, "Woof, this is Big Ben calling for Kate Roarty."

Kate laughed. Big Ben continued, "I am in desperate need of a swimming buddy, can you come home soon?" It was Jack Johnson impersonating the retriever. Returning to his normal but beautifully and lightly Quebecois-accented voice, Jack said, "I hope we didn't wake you."

"No, not at all. I have already done a 2.5-kilometre swim, had breakfast, and was working on updating my notes from the visit to Cheltenham," replied Kate.

Jack returned to a jovial voice. "Did you hear that, big boy, she's already swimming the Thames."

Kate laughed again. "No, just the Kensington pool."

"Kate, can you reschedule your visit to MI6 for a bit later and go up to Cambridge and have a chat with a Professor Michael Pepper?"

Kate replied, "Certainly, and who is this Professor Michael Pepper?"

Jack told her what he knew. "It seems he was an advisor and some sort of mentor for our Vincent Bernard Taylor when he attended Cambridge in the eighties. He is retired now and pretty old but seemingly still has a sound mind. I got you a phone number. It goes back a while, but there is no indication that he's moved since he retired more than a decade ago." Kate took down the number and the last known address for Professor Michael Pepper.

Jack continued, "Dr. Bosum is off dealing with a train explosion in the Eastern Townships, but she did take a moment to follow up with her CSIS contact in response to your text request. Guy has gone with her, and D'Angelo is having some family time before the kids go off to summer camp. His wife is a bit worn out, and she lost her last week of holidays due to some crisis or another in the office."

Kate was enjoying this rather normal everyday chat from Jack.

Then Jack said, "Let's talk again soon, Kate. I'm holding the fort and praying for no more murders until we are back up to full staff again, but the wicked are rarely so considerate. Oh, my only sleeping partner has four legs, bad breath, and snores. Dr. Bosum told me that I couldn't let Big Ben out of my sight. My career depends on it."

Kate replied softly, "Thanks for the call, Jack. It was so nice to hear from you. I will keep you posted."

Kate looked at the phone number for Michael Pepper and decided to call it straight away. An older gentlemen's voice responded on the first ring.

"Professor Michael Pepper?" enquired Kate.

The older voice responded, "This is he."

Kate briefly filled him in on the reason for her call. They confirmed a meeting for noon at his home in Cambridge the following day.

Kate was pleased to be on a train once again. This time it was a short trip, barely more than an hour from King's Cross Station to Cambridge, where she was going to meet with Michael Pepper, Professor Emeritus from King's College. Dr. Bosum's CSIS contact had dug up this name as an advisor assigned to Claude Mason when he attended Cambridge. Kate walked the slightly less than two-kilometre distance from the train station to a row house off Mill Street. The walk gave her a chance to acquaint herself with the Cambridge neighbourhood and collect her thoughts for the interview with Professor Pepper.

As per instructions from Professor Pepper, Kate rang the doorbell beside the singular bright red door on the narrow laneway signed Orchard Street. After some minutes the door swung open and a voice asked, "Mrs. Roarty?"

Kate stepped into the threshold, allowing a moment for her eyes to adjust to the dimmer light, where she saw an old man in a wheelchair beaming up at her with an exuberant smile.

She answered, "I am Kate Roarty."

"And I am Michael Pepper. Please come in," he replied.

Kate closed the door and stepped forward with her hand outstretched to greet her host. He took it firmly then warmly said, "Please follow me."

Kate did as requested, walking down a corridor into a brightly lit kitchen, where a tray sat on the counter made up with tea, sandwiches, a bowl filled with grapes and biscuits.

Michael Pepper said, "It is such a glorious day I thought we could go up to the terrasse and have tea. I am able to make up a tray but have my challenges navigating the lift with it. Can I ask you to carry it?"

Kate replied, "Of course."

"I will go ahead, and you can follow with the tray." He laughed and said, "I hope you don't mind it won't be a NASCAR race to the roof. These lifts are liberating but very slow. My great-grandson keeps telling me that it needs booster juice."

Kate laughed as she fell in behind Professor Pepper on the slow ascent. They reached a landing that he navigated along then positioned himself on the second lift. Kate carefully stepped around the platform of the lift on the first level, leaving it in position for his descent later on. They reached another landing, where Professor Pepper pushed a button and the door swung out onto a rooftop garden. Kate emerged behind him in instant awe of the beauty she took in.

Michael Pepper said, "Welcome to my Secret Garden."

Kate gazed about, replying, "You have done Frances Hodgson Burnett proud, although I doubt this garden was ever abandoned."

Professor Pepper smiled back. "There you are absolutely right — this was a project I started after the accident that left me in this wheelchair. With the help of my middle son, Andrew, who built the trellises and installed the many gadgets that help me to reach up and down, this garden gives me many hours of pleasure. Much to the dismay of my family and housekeeper, I often fall asleep up here. Andrew's latest project is to install an all-weather on-screen sensor system complete with an alarm, since I often forget to bring the mobile phone up with me. Although I don't get enough exercise," the very slender Professor Pepper said, "the fresh air always makes me feel hungry. Shall we have our tea while we chat? I am delighted to have the pleasure of your company, Mrs. Roarty."

"The pleasure is also mine, Professor Pepper," said Kate.

He replied, "Please call me Michael. Despite my British

heritage, I have never been much on formalities. Can you first fill me in on the circumstances of Vincent's death?"

"Of course." Kate proceeded to paint the picture of what she knew so far, including her connection with the case, giving enough to draw him in without disclosing too much that could inadvertently implicate him.

While he listened, he poured the tea for them both, munched away on his sandwiches, and devoured most of the grapes.

Finally, he said, "Kate, please eat, or you will be left with having to scurry downstairs to make up another tray for yourself."

Kate found that she was ravenous as she scoffed down the sandwiches and drank the tea.

He laughed and said, "I think the fragrance of my secret garden arouses hunger cravings. My daughter-in-law, Andrew's wife, sends the grandchildren over when they fall off on their eating — especially healthy foods."

Kate paused for a moment to ask, "Michael, can you tell me what you know about Vincent Bernard Taylor?"

Michael replied, "Of course, what I can tell you is history. I have had little contact with him in recent years. Kate, to talk about Vincent Taylor properly means to speak about a group of scholars I had under my wing in the late eighties, early nineties. If you are up for a bit of a story, can I ask you to go down to the kitchen, fill the teapot, and grab anything else down there you may wish to eat or drink? I will use the handy loo that Andrew installed for me over in the corner there. There is also a powder room just off the kitchen if you need to avail yourself."

Kate obliged with, "Back shortly."

She descended to the kitchen, put the kettle on, and used the loo. The loud whistle brought her back from the *Sunday Times*. She found a bowl of mixed blueberries and raspberries that she added to the tray, along with a few more biscuits and the remainder of the grapes. Michael was waiting comfortably for her when she returned.

Michael said, "Shall we begin?"

Kate settled herself and nodded.

"Vincent came to me after reading the classics at St. Andrews. He was on a full scholarship. He possessed a bright, enquiring mind that had already been refined by the rigours of St Andrews. He was one of six graduate students assigned to me — a heavy load, as these lads, while quite self-sufficient, were all very bright, demanding, and intellectually ambitious. From the onset, they had one dimension in common. While they all had an excellent grounding in the classics, they wished to move into the sciences. I became the facilitator for them to reach that objective. It was a tough go, as they all had to reach back into preparatory classes at the undergraduate level. I was at the pinnacle of my career, publishing a lot, giving advanced lectures in quantum physics, and supervising this core of the best and the brightest. Frankly,, their intellectual capacities and zeal for work far exceeded my own. During the early weeks, I spoke long into the night with my wife, Anne, about my dilemmas with these lads. She always had such clarity on these human conundrums."

"'Put them together,' she said. It was such an obvious and simple solution. She cooked many an evening meal for these lads as they revised in preparation for various exams in the sciences. The whole of their first year with me was devoted to these make-up requirements. It was all very unusual at Cambridge. I often ran interference for them with the administration authorities. To be truthful, my wife and I were thrilled with having them around. They added an energy and excitement to our rather routine lives. I was their academic mentor, and she was their counsel on life. You know they all came to her funeral — from the four corners of this planet — when she was killed in the car accident that left me in this wheelchair." He paused a moment, and

Kate did not intrude upon his silent reverie. He lifted his tear-filled eyes, allowed a smile to creep back across his face, and then continued.

"After some many months of my tutoring and my wife's joyful counselling, one night as we lay in bed happily worn out from an intense exam preparation week, Anne said, 'Michael, I believe all of the boys are homosexual.' I was stunned — it had not entered my mind. She went on to say, 'Times are changing and will continue to change, but they will nevertheless have a tough go of it.' I lay silent for some moments then said, 'Anne, it can't be. What about Peter Pocklington? He is engaged to be married ... to a woman we have met.'

"Anne replied, 'Yes, Peter is a bit of an exception. I think he may swing both ways.'

"In the end, Peter was tragically killed in a car accident on the way to spend a weekend with his fiancée. The boys were devastated by the loss of Peter, and so were we. The five lads formed an even tighter circle and for a time shut out the rest of the world, save their studies and our home. Anne often made up the beds in the spare rooms and on the divan in the parlour for whoever was staying over. I worried that it was becoming quite a burden for her, but she loved it and would have it no other way. The boys kept the dining room and parlour filled with flowers, and every once in a while when we went away they scoured the house from top to bottom and left the most delicious meals waiting for us upon our return. Our own young adult offspring were off making their mark on the world, so we were delighted to have this interlude."

"There was Vincent and Peter?" Kate prompted.

"Ah, yes, the other four," replied Michael. "There was Matti Toivenen from Finland, a fine, exacting, yet infinitely curious mind. He went off to do doctoral work in biotechnology at Johns Hopkins in Baltimore and then returned to take up a position at the Karolinska Institute in Stockholm. He eventually specialized in neurology — brain tumours, Alzheimer's, Parkinson's, non-specific dementia, etc. He drops around occasionally when he is passing through London giving a paper. I can still see him when he first walked through our door — a muscular young man of medium height with thick white-blond hair and ice blue eyes that despite their opaqueness radiated warmth unusual for the reserved Scandinavian manner. There was nothing pretentious or formal about him. His mind was clear and focused. He was easy to like. His only allowed distraction was to return home for cross-country skiing competitions several times a year. He would come back victorious, none of us ever understanding how he managed these victories without training.

"Then there was Kiran Patel from Bangalore, India, the opposite of Matti. He came from a well-educated family; his father was an internist. He was the only son, with five sisters. He loved to cook, having eschewed every effort of his mother and sisters to chase him from the kitchen. He learned well and every so often produced an Indian meal that delighted the palates of our entire household. There was much jest about his cooking, usually dealt with by a threat to heat up the next batch of curry to burn the sphincters of all those who teased. Kiran was a very dark Indian, despite light-complexioned parents. The boys teased him that he was a weekend fling when his father was in surgery. That could very well be the case, as he was the youngest after the five sisters. Nevertheless, he was handsome beyond words. As pale as Matti's eyes were, Kiran's were deep, penetrating, and magnetic — and if a heterosexual man can say it of another man — intensely sensuous. The lads kept their sexuality very private. Anne perceived much more than I ever did — we suspected that a relationship developed between Matti and Kiran, although there was never any evidence of it here. Kiran's other passion and outstanding ability was in cricket.

He always put the cricket schedule first, declaring that if he died tomorrow, as long as he was playing a match, he would die happy. We all believed him. He tried to enlist the others in the game, but the only concession they ever made was to watch on the telly any televised matches he played in. He presented a striking athletic figure on the field — lean, muscular, and compact, exacting and economic in his play. We had several jovial celebrations of his victories. After the lads moved on, sometimes we received postcards from Matti and Kiran vacationing together somewhere or other, and from time to time they gave papers at the same conferences. Kiran eventually returned to India and set up a very successful biotech business. He was also on staff at Christ College in Bangalore, although it was likely a loose connection as he does an active lecture tour to the best research institutes in the world. He has consulted in South Africa for many years. He seems to have evaded all efforts by his mother to marry him off."

Michael paused. "Kate, I'm forgetting. Please go down into the parlour and bring the photo of the boys. It is sitting front and centre on the high table against the wall opposite the window."

Kate was happy for the opportunity to stretch. She bounded downstairs, sought out the parlour, and easily found the photograph of the five boys, registering that it must have been taken after Peter died. From Michael's description, she could readily pick out Matti and Kiran. She glanced around and saw other framed photographs of the lads but thought it best to bring only the one Michael requested. When she returned to the rooftop, Michael was asleep. He roused as he heard the door close. Kate asked if he would like to take a break and offered to return later or the following day.

Michael replied that he would like to get through introducing the lads. They had two or three to go.

"There was Giorgio Beretta from Milan, Italy. We loved Giorgio — he was like a teddy bear, stocky, almost cuddly, not at all like the northern Italians, who were typically quite Austrian in their appearance and outlook. He would put his arms around Anne and declare, 'Madam Anne, you feed my soul.' They laughed, and he spun her around."

Again, Michael's eyes teared up, and he paused. He looked up at Kate and said, "You know, I lost Anne tragically and much too early in life, but oh the joy we had together. Ah, Giorgio, while he had some early classics training with the priests, he studied structural engineering and was already on his way to becoming an earthquake design specialist when he came to Cambridge. He was very strong on math, physics, and chemistry and had the ability to transfer that knowledge to quantum physics. We had many intense discussions well into the night. Anne sent him to bed in a spare room more frequently than she sent the others. Giorgio believed the brain was the next great frontier. He wanted to apply his many theories to understanding not only how it worked but also how it failed, and when it did, so catastrophically. He did not want to become a surgeon and grappled long and hard in search of the most effective portal into developing solutions for the dilemmas of the brain. He eventually went the pure science route and followed Matti to Johns Hopkins. Giorgio was always anxious to return to Italy, and finally an opportunity attracted him to the San Raffaele Institute in Milan. Like the others, he had a startup, a well-launched company, deeply engaged in brain structures research. His financial backers reluctantly let him transfer the business to Milan. Italy provided a generous repatriation grant that was too attractive to turn down. It included a percentage payback to the venture capital investors, an approach that was unique to the startup investment world at that time.

"Giorgio was so devastated by Anne's death that he finds it too emotional to visit here. Every so often, he calls and sends a disability car to pick me up, and I meet him at some fine restaurant in London. It is a nice outing for me. I am always fascinated by whatever he is pursuing. Even though I am a very old man, out of touch with the advanced research these boys are doing, he always asked my advice, input, and assessment, and he always carefully measures what I have to offer. While he writes scholarly papers in the neurosciences, he has produced several textbooks as well. They have all been dedicated to Anne and me. I feel so honoured and only wish that Anne could be here to enjoy the honour as well."

Kate said, "Michael, I rather suspect that Anne is fully aware of the accomplishments of all of her boys and tips many a glass to their success."

"Ah, but we must not forget Claude, the Scottish French Canadian. Claude was a swimmer. While we adapted to Kiran's cricket and Matti's cross-country skiing, we also had to accommodate the varsity competitive swimming schedule for Claude, not to mention his swimming escapes. Swimming varsity was part of his scholarship; although never presented as such, it was tacitly understood. Claude seemed to take each part of the handsome spectrum that the boys brought to humanity and fold it into a Nordic Greek god. His features, like his brain, were fine, exacting, and performance-bound. Claude had to swim. He not only swam competition but also swam in cold, open water, and very long distances. He swam the English Channel in an annual competition between Cambridge and Oxford. His times were very respectable. I believe he medalled."

He paused. "Claude swam the Thames when it was filthy, before it got cleaned up and became fashionable to swim in. After a serious bought of gastroenteritis, Anne did some research and gave him a list of much cleaner waters nearby he could easily get to when he had to satisfy his need for long, contemplative swims, which she believed he actually preferred to competitive swimming."

Not only could Kate relate to this part of the description of Claude Mason, but she could also fully appreciate it, as it reinforced her experience of him.

Michael continued, "I have had less contact with Claude than the others — perhaps because of his clandestine career pursuits. He works for GCHQ. When I read about a very expensive pool installation at the Government Communications Headquarters in Cheltenham, I suspected Claude had something to do with it."

Kate had very much warmed to Michael and felt she could trust him. She replied, "You are right, Michael. I believe it was his initiative. I just met with Claude Mason in Cheltenham a few days ago and swam in the enormous pool at GCHQ. I would say that Claude is evangelical about swimming."

Michael laughed. "You are correct there, and his evangelism succeeded with me. He got me involved in the Masters Swim Club at Parkside Pool. Swimming was a big part of my rehabilitation after the accident. I was given a lifetime membership to the pool there, which I suspect Claude had something to do with making possible. I still go three times a week."

Kate smiled and said, "Swimming may be the glue that binds us together. It's a lifelong passion of mine. There are few items I always carry with me — a swim suit, hat, and goggles are among those items."

Michael beamed and remarked, "Kate Roarty, private investigator, would you like to accompany me on a swim to Parkside Pool? It is a five-minute walk from here. I was going to forego it today in order to meet with you, but now I realize that may not be necessary. There is an afternoon lap swim from three thirty until five that I enjoy when I don't make it to the morning swim. I could get you in on a guest pass."

Before he could prod further, Kate readily agreed then said, "I hope you don't mind if I swim for the entire one and a half hour session."

"Fine by me," replied Michael. "You can find me afterward in the reading room. Which brings us back to Claude. He was desperate to get on with his formal education. He thought he was headed into medicine, but he developed an interest in robotics. Giorgio and Vincent shared this interest. Giorgio brought a good deal of consideration to the table with his engineering background, while Claude and Vincent read widely on the subject and were the first to acquire personal computers. Within months our home was rewired, and a 'command centre' took over the parlour. Vincent had a real bent for design, and Claude became almost obsessed with American military applications that were developing in robotics. The Canadians were doing some interesting work in medical applications for prosthetics and microsurgery and for the space program, foremost of which was the Canadarm. Vincent came in one day announcing that he thought MIT was the place to go to pursue a doctorate in robotics. Giorgio was intrigued, but it captured Claude's imagination more intensely. Artificial intelligence wasn't yet an avenue of study, but it was on the horizon. Claude had a lot of make-up work to do. He was possessed: reorienting his thesis, taking physics courses, and corresponding with professors at MIT. Vincent took a more measured, gradual approach. Claude was the first to head off to MIT. Vincent followed a year later.

"I suspect that during the year Claude was on his own, the British Secret Service came knocking. Claude had already set up a robotics company of some sort — MIT was pretty liberal in encouraging its students to commercialize their technology developments.

"Vincent flew over to Boston on an exploratory visit while he was awaiting acceptance and word of a scholarship from MIT. He shared little with me beyond the academic approach, but he talked to Anne about the personal side and about Claude's activity there. Even with me, Anne did not share a great deal, but she allowed enough that it seemed

Claude was venturing into high-tech commercial espionage.

"Not long after the visit to MIT, Vincent received word about a very handsome scholarship — the full Monty, so to speak — and after picking up his MSc here, he was soon gone."

Michael broke off and said, "This is a good point to break and head off for our respective swims."

Kate agreed, gathered up their plates, cups, and bowls, then she headed back downstairs. Michael followed down on his two lifts, arriving only a few minutes after Kate. It gave her time to load the dishwasher, put the milk away, and set a cover over the butter.

The walk was refreshing but barely long enough to work out the kinks before plunging into the pool. Michael seemed to be well known. He was warmly greeted by attendants in the lobby and then by the duty lifeguard. An assistant helped Michael into the pool. The pool was almost empty, giving him a lane to himself. Kate could easily see him under the water as she swam. While his legs exhibited little movement, his upper body ploughed through the water with power and precision. His two limbs accomplished more than many swimmers managed with all four. She suspected that it was the age difference that gave her superior stamina, because it certainly wasn't her skill.

She watched Michael for a few laps then let her mind focus on 'the lads.' They were all involved in neuroscience in one manner or another. Was it possible that they were all working together on some clandestine project? They were simply too connected personally, professionally, and scientifically for it not to be so.

These men were all brilliant; leaders in their field, all well credentialled with PhDs, stature, status, *and* they were all gay. It seemed there was an intimate relationship between Matti and Kiran, and possibly between Claude and Vincent. It appeared they all stayed connected with one another and with Michael Pepper.

Why was Vincent killed, and who killed him? Was there dissension within the ranks? Had they got ahead of themselves so far in the technology development that it scared one or more members of the group or scared someone else? She needed a whiteboard to assemble everything she had learned, to exhume the critical elements to help her connect the dots.

After her swim, she showered, changed, and found Michael waiting in the reading room.

He beamed questioningly at her. "Good swim?"

Kate replied with a huge, breast-filled inhale, "Great swim!"

"Kate, while all of the sleep studies advise against caffeine after lunch, there is a delectable sidewalk café around the corner that serves passable decaf and wonderful real latté. We could order a large with a single shot in slight compromise," said Michael.

"Lead the way," replied Kate.

A young waitress brought the lattés and greeted Michael. "It's nice to see you, Professor Pepper."

Michael said, "Superb. And did the thesis get submitted last week, Miss Beth?"

"Indeed, sir, it did. And Canberra has indicated a willingness to take me once I send proof of my thesis completion and acceptance."

"Scholarship?" he asked.

"Of course, Professor, and plane fare, along with settling-in expenses."

"Congratulations, Beth, well done and in record time, I might add," he added.

Beth replied, "The dead are waiting, sir."

Michael answered Kate's enquiring look with, "Forensic anthropology. Which brings me to you, my dear. Was anthropology an antecedent to the technology forensics that now occupies your professional pursuits?"

Kate replied, "Well, yes, yielding forth from a twenty-five-year circuitous route."

Michael smiled then allowed, "I thought so," then added, "I think there is enough privacy here that we can continue on about the boys, if you like."

Kate provided a brief summary of what Michael Pepper had recounted so far, to prod the resumption of his story. "Vincent goes off to join Claude at MIT, but in a different, albeit related field. Did they become flat mates?"

"Not at the outset, as Claude's place was very small and chosen for its proximity to both a pool and open-water swimming when the season permitted. His preoccupation was robotics and artificial intelligence, while Vincent focused on neuroscience and nanoscience. Their faculties were different, but I think in time their professional interests merged, and their personal lives blended. By this time, Anne was no longer with me, so my social information became very limited. Like the other lads, they also launched start-ups; separate at first, then they went through an M&A that resulted in the creation of iBrain."

Kate sat up taller.

"While both of the antecedent companies were registered in Massachusetts with something called a Delaware exemption, the new company was registered in the UK. Kate, I am an academic; these corporate machinations elude me," said Michael. "All of the lads were involved in small companies that were opening, closing, merging, morphing, going public, staying private … being acquired, going broke. It defied my comprehension. I think I was born a quarter century too early."

Kate nodded. "In the course of my technology forensics research on behalf of my clients, I encounter high-tech corporate evolution and devolution on a regular basis. While these lads, as you call them, are highly intelligent and often highly strung, I don't encounter murder, although I am sure that many murderous thoughts are entertained among the various players in the business. Further, I came to this case while swimming — an evening swim in a very pretty lake — happenstance, although," she laughed then added, "it is beginning to look like another common thread linking the various players." They both sat in quiet contemplation, finishing off their respective lattés.

"Can I walk you back to your house? I will try to catch the 6:00 p.m. train to London."

Michael replied, "Perfect, my son and his wife are coming around this evening for dinner and a bit of whist."

Kate left Michael Pepper in the hallway of his house and headed off in the direction of the train station. If she walked briskly enough, she thought that she could just make it in time to slip directly onto the train. Luckily, she had purchased a return ticket. She hoped to make it back to Euston Station in time to check a cyber supply shop that she had spotted in the shopping concourse at the station. She was in desperate need of a holographic rendering to help her get a visual on all the elements and characters of this case. She needed to purchase the software and the projection aperture to make it all possible.

As is so often the case in the UK, the train arrived precisely on time. Luckily, the shop was still open, and she found everything she needed. The projection device was hardware, while the highly specialized software was a download purchase that she completed with a cyber tech right there in the shop.

7

Back at 12 Rosary Gardens, Kate liberated one wall of a few pieces of artwork so there wouldn't be any distracting background to the holographic whiteboard imaging. After her swim at the Kensington Pool the following morning, she would stop at the library and do a search for photos and bios of all of the lads and of Michael Pepper. Libraries were continuing to get their entire holdings uploaded to cyberspace, but the archives still held a lot of data not yet uploaded. In the meantime, virtual nametags would suffice. After a couple of hours she stood back to appraise her work. Once complete, she could send the holographic rendering to SQ via her encrypted phone. Kate developed a legend along the left-hand side of the rendering so as not to mix up any of her plan. She placed the names of people on it in brown outline, places in blue, the relationships captured by black lines, and so on. She began with the traditional crime elements, including means, motive, and opportunity, but she was fully aware that the advanced technology characterizing this case would blur the lines of this analysis. The holographic rendering offered the opportunity for each member of the investigative team to consider the elements of the case from every vantage point.

She was sufficiently aware of the rapidly evolving capabilities of unmanned systems. While applications were not intended for clandestine or criminal activity, they certainly could be and were already integrated into the toolkits of both espionage and criminal activity. For the moment, Kate colour-coded a category she called IP, for intellectual property (*hic sunt dracones*) in a rich grey. In modern technology/science, IP was a controversial entity, pointing to the pot of gold that indeed the most heinous of crimes could and were being committed in the pursuit of possessing these latest capabilities. Working in this niche had yielded a nice living for Kate, tracking down the migration of IP for leading-edge technologies and restoring the intellectual property rights to their rightful innovators. Success paid out handsomely, failure resulted in maxed-out credit cards and unpaid bills. She preferred the reward and comfort of the former, so she took on a very small number of cases as she built her portfolio of successes. She couldn't help but wish that this case had come to her before it resulted in murder. She hoped she could lasso it before more death and destruction resulted from the conflict among the many players.

Kate stood back to survey her work and thought that just to be on the safe side, given the previous invasion of the flat, she better have a back-up for her holographic rendering. She retrieved her mobile and sent it out to several different encrypted email addresses that she used only for her IP cases. She also saved it to the hard drive on her laptop and on an encrypted USB and finally sent it to **trainonthetrack2030**.

Before collapsing into bed, Kate reopened the holographic rendering and threw up a number of questions marks querying the direction the investigation needed to take. Top of the list was the role of MI6, where she was headed the next day. Her mind was on overdrive; she decided to bring herself down with a session of mindful meditation. Her level of fatigue readily succumbed to the soft, introspective strums of the classical guitar repertoire saved on her iPod. Surprisingly, this session took on a life of its own and lasted over an hour. She felt restored to a gentle calm and slipped into a deep sleep without any other preparations.

Kate awoke to the image of Jack Johnson smiling and holding a Cairn Terrier pup on his arm. The image was so vivid that she thought it was real before her conscious brain engaged and she realized where she was and that she had to have been dreaming. Still, it was a nice dream, and she lay in bed a little longer, trying to hold on to the warm feeling that the image had brought to her. Her mind gently marinated on his name — *Jack Johnson*. Kate realized that "Jack" might simply be an Anglicization of his given name, Jacques. She made a mental note to ask him. If it was indeed Jacques, it made it easier for the flow with a French pronunciation, including his surname. She leapt out of bed, put the coffee on, and pulled out berries, yogurt, almonds, and juice from the fridge. She glanced at the clock in hopes she could make it to the early swim. The phone rang. She hit the talk button.

"*Bonjour*," said Jack Johnson.

"That's a fast turnaround to my request for information."

Jack replied, "This is not a work call, it's a personal call." Kate remained silent. Jack said, "Kate, are you still there?"

Kate managed a guarded, "Yes."

Jack replied awkwardly, "*C'est bon. Ça va?*"

Kate replied, "*Très bien, et toi?*"

"*Formidable, merdre*," said Jack.

"*Excusez-moi*," replied Kate.

"Ah, Kate sorry, I slip into French when I get nervous speaking with *les anglaises*."

"That is fine," said Kate. "We can speak in French or English, whichever you prefer, especially on a personal call."

Jack said, "Ah, you're probably up early to head off for

your swim, and I've interrupted your morning routine."
"That's okay, Jack, but isn't it 2:00 a.m. where you are?" replied Kate.
"Yes, but I couldn't sleep. I was thinking about you."
Kate surprised herself by saying, "I fell asleep last night thinking about you, and I woke this morning with an image of you in my mind."
With almost schoolboyish enthusiasm, Jack exclaimed, "Really, tell me."
So Kate told him about how she was wondering about his name and the image of him with a Cairn Terrier pup on his arm. He replied, "It is Jack."
Kate said, "What is Jack?"
"My name is Jack. My mother thought that since I had an Anglo surname, I should have an Anglo given name. My father and grandmère wanted to call me Jacques. Since the name Johnson has a four-hundred-year history in La Belle Province, she considered that it was more of a French name than an English name. My mother was a very decisive person, advising them that the name was Jack, and that was that. She insisted on writing my name on the baptismal certificate herself so the unilingual priest didn't screw it up. She conceded on the middle name, Antoine."
Kate replied, "Jack Antoine Johnson, I rather like the naming your mother decided for you. Is she still alive?"
"Sadly, no. I still miss her very much. I think her passing had a lot to do with the end of my marriage. When my mother was alive, I was happy with everything about my wife Micheline, but afterward, I think I wanted my wife to become my mother. It destroyed us, and she found somebody better. I should have done some counselling, but it was too late, she moved on and made a good life for herself."
"And you?"
Jack said, "Oh, I buried myself in my work and triathlons. Both didn't leave much time for anything else. Fortunately,

the triathlons nearly destroyed my knees, so after successfully doing an Iron Man, I quit. It's everything in moderation now, with enough room for martial arts."

"Jack, how long ago did your mother die?"

"Six years."

Kate felt relieved — six years was long enough to work through the loss of a mother and the collapse of a marriage.

"Kate, enough about me, what about you?" asked Jack.

Kate laughed. "I thought the SQ already knew all about me."

"Kate, we only know what the official record tells us, and that's often not much. We rarely learn anything about feelings, emotions, hopes, and dreams," replied Jack.

"What were your words the first time we met?" said Kate. "*So, Kathrine Roarty, former diplomat, free agent, divorced mother of two now adult children who swims all over the world and periodically gets depressed, show us what you have found.*"

"Wow, you have a good memory. Sorry about that — to be honest, I was so shaken by my reaction to you the first moment I saw you that my mind became as unhinged as a high-school kid contemplating a first date."

Kate teased, "Oh you were thinking about dating me then." She imagined Jack blushing in a search for a smart response.

"Not then, but I am now." It was Kate's turn to blush, feeling like a teenager. *Jesus, no — not another younger man.*

"Kate, you still there?"

"Yes, of course," said Kate.

"Can we try dating when you get back? Or do you want me to come there?" Jack said in a very earnest tone.

Kate laughed. "Jack, I don't think it would be appropriate for us to date."

Jack replied, "Why not? Neither of us work for the other; we are both unattached, and we are both interested — aren't we?"

Kate replied, "And there is the other thing."

"What other thing?" said Jack. "You are interested in another guy?"

"No, our ages," said Kate.

"Kate, we are old enough to date."

"Our age difference," she said in exasperation.

"Am I too old for you, Kate? Oh, I get it, I am not old enough. You want some guy you can make hot cocoa for and tuck in for an afternoon nap."

Kate laughed. "Okay, enough, enough."

"Kate, I'm closer to your age than to your daughter's age, and even if I wasn't, what would it matter? A grampa is never going to keep up with you. You need a guy like me."

Kate said, "Okay, when I get back, let's try a date or two. Now, I have to go. Bye." And she hung up before her heart exploded.

Her phone beeped with a text message: *Bye.*

She grabbed her swim bag, switched off the coffee pot, and headed out the door, pausing only a moment to lock it, then set out at a brisk pace in the direction of the Kensington Pool. She arrived a bit late to do the one-and-half-hour swim she had intended to put in but was pleasantly surprised that she covered her distance in record time — for her, that is.

As she exited the shower, she heard a voice say, "I had a hard time keeping up with you." It was Agent Liz Bruan.

Kate, caught a little by surprise but not showing it, said, "Oh, back on duty, are you?"

"No, actually, I'm taking a few days off. I am staying with my great-grandmother, who lives just around the corner, and I rushed over to get in the early swim before she wakes up."

Kate looked at her. "I know it sounds far-fetched, but it's true. My great-grandmother swam here herself until a few years ago, when navigating the wet floors in the change room and getting in and out of the pool became too challenging. She's ninety-eight years old and says, 'Elizabeth,' she has always called me Elizabeth, 'if I fall and break a hip, shoot me on the spot.'"

Kate replied, "I share that sentiment with your great-grandmother."

Liz said, "Would you like to come over for tea and scones — you can meet her yourself?"

Kate thought this was a very clever ruse, or Agent Liz Bruan was actually telling the truth. She replied, "Another time, perhaps — my day is rather full."

Liz slung her bag over her shoulder. "I have to pick up the scones at the bakery before they run out. Bye."

Kate thought she detected a trace of affection in the farewell. It sounded a bit like her daughter. She made a mental note to ring Danielle today. She gave a little wave as Liz headed west, and she headed east. Liz did indeed step into a little bakeshop before the traffic light turned green. It gave Kate a chance to proceed across the street and out of sight.

She returned to 12 Rosary Gardens, where she took the time to further contemplate the holographic rendering then remembered she had intended to stop in at the Kensington library to transfer up photos of any of the lads and others she could locate in the digital archives. She was a bit frustrated at her forgetfulness, realizing seeing Liz Bruan must have distracted her from her morning plan. She would have to pay attention to that — in her line of work, focus was of paramount importance. At fifty, she was too young to claim age as a culprit.

She would have to get to the library later today — for the moment, MI6 must occupy her fullest attention. Kate was painfully aware that she was still lacking a key contact there. One did not pay cold calls to this organization. She considered her options; get back to Jonathon Braithwaite at MI5, ring Claude Mason at GCHQ, or the team at SQ. At any rate, she thought she needed to speak with Braithwaite by way of follow-up to the GCHQ visit and to identify a suitable contact over at MI6. Further, she wondered if Jonathon Braithwaite and Nigel Rathbone were acquainted, i.e., shared alma maters, friendships, or rivalries. They were about the same age and could have crossed paths before they embarked on their respective professional careers. There could be some easy research, followed by a little more in-depth investigation if superficial linkages suggested that their connection might have greater depth.

Kate faced the situation, picked up her phone, and keyed in Braithwaite's number. She allowed her phone to display the caller number. Jonathon picked it up on the first ring and in a quiet voice said, "Kate, can I ring you back later this morning?"

Kate replied, "Sure, or can I meet you at your office at 2:00 p.m."

Jonathon said, "Good, see you here then, bye."

This gave Kate time to return to the South Kensington Centre to spend time in the library.

Kate's time in the library was productive, assisted by a very competent library technician. Her research time was cut in half. She found bios with accompanying photos for all of the lads and for Michael Pepper as well. The technician directed her to *Who's Who* among doctoral holders in the world. She found Vincent Bernard Taylor, Matti Toivenen, Kiran Patel, and Giorgio Beretta. Peter Pocklington had not received his PhD before his untimely death; nevertheless, the library technician came up with a photo from his year at Cambridge. Claude Mason was not listed in the *Who's Who*, but the technician found a bio for him on the government employees' database. His biography did not mention a PhD. She was doing so well with the assistance of this library technician that she pressed on for bios and photos of Braithwaite, Rathbone, and even Liz Bruan. The library technician advised Kate that because some of the individuals worked in sensitive government jobs, she would have to take a digital scan of her passport and have her sign a declaration indicating that this information would not be used in any illegal and clandestine manner. Kate agreed.

Rathbone and Braithwaite were the most interesting connections she uncovered. The lads had taken that honour the day before. Rathbone and Braithwaite studied at Bournemouth University, where they obtained undergraduate degrees in Forensic Archaeology and Anthropology. As well, it appeared that they both played varsity tennis on scholarships. Kate had thus identified their connection and their possible rivalry.

Kate thought both MI5 and GCHQ would require graduate degrees or at least favour them. The library technician readily found the trail for both. While Braithwaite had gone on to graduate studies at the University of Dundee, specializing in intellectual property, Rathbone had gone to the US to attend MIT. It seems he wandered around the Applied Cyber Security Program for a year, taking a variety of courses in Ethics in Cyber Security & Cyber Law, along with Forensics, then was admitted to a graduate program and completed a Masters in History, Anthropology, and Science, Technology, and Society (HASTS).

While the trail the technician followed did not reveal it, Kate suspected that both Rathbone and Braithwaite were recruited on campus by the UK secret services.

Kate was beginning to see that a trip to Boston to explore around MIT where Messrs. Mason, Taylor, and Rathbone all spent time, studied, acquired credentials, and undoubtedly interacted would be helpful. She also wanted to find out what happened to Mason's graduate studies.

Kate returned to 12 Rosary Gardens and added all of this information to her holographic rendering then sent the update to the same encrypted repositories as before. She added SQ — Dr. Bosum, to the new recipients list. She also sent it to her trusted cyber geek, Bryant, with a simple note: *safekeeping trusted friend.*

8

Kate glanced at her watch. She had enough time to grab a bit of lunch then head to MI5 to meet with Jonathon Braithwaite.

She stopped into a little Vietnamese café near the Gloucester Road tube station and enjoyed rice-wrapped vegetable rolls, a seafood noodle soup, and green tea.

Once again, she passed smoothly through all the security checkpoints with the temporary ID that had been set up for her at MI5. Jonathon greeted her as she got off the elevator. "Welcome back, P.I. Kate Roarty." Kate smiled at the Americanism he used to address her. Braithwaite continued, "We will soon have to start issuing you a paycheque."

Kate replied, "No need, I'm already getting one — contract payments, that is — from SQ. GCHQ offered me a job there as well, but I declined."

"Ah, so it was a productive visit then?" asked Braithwaite.

Kate replied, "Oh, that is all in how you define productive. The swimming was good; the train connection easy and smooth and the accommodation pleasant."

"I gather the personnel you encountered were not entirely forthcoming?"

"Mr. Claude Mason was abundantly forthcoming in an oblique sort of way. Agent Braithwaite, are you acquainted with Nigel Rathbone, I mean beyond your current professional association?"

"Yes, indeed, Mrs. Roarty, we are more than well acquainted," replied Jonathon. "We did our undergraduate studies together at Bournemouth, and we both played varsity tennis. We moved in the same circle of friends and girlfriends, I might add. I went off to Dundee for a year to read for my Masters, and he went to the States — MIT, and stayed there a while. We lost track for a few years until he turned up on a case I was looking into. I had been working at MI5 for several years, and he had just started with GCHQ. We reconnected and have maintained a loose contact ever since." Braithwaite further allowed, "Rathbone is a very clever chap who doesn't take kindly to being trivialized — real or imagined. I think he hopes to run GCHQ one day."

Kate was mentally making the checks in her mind that confirmed assumptions she had already made about these two. She was pleased at how forthcoming Agent Jonathon Braithwaite was on the subject of Mr. Rathbone. His frankness gave her a sense of being able to trust MI5 more than she trusted GCHQ, although that was easy, since she did not trust GCHQ at all.

"Kate, was GCHQ able to tell you anything about Dr. Taylor and the technology associated with his demise?"

"Not directly," said Kate. She needed to give Braithwaite some useful information in this quid pro quo exchange. "However, I did learn that Mason and Braithwaite studied together, both here in the UK and at MIT. I had an interview with one of their old professors."

Nigel sat forward and said, "Kate, that is interesting."

"Yes, I plan to pursue that further — perhaps get in the face of it in Boston."

"You will keep us in the loop as well?" Jonathon asked.

They both knew Kate's reply was insincere yet necessary. "Of course, Agent Braithwaite."

"Kate, I have a contact for you at MI6 — another school chum, although less well known to me than Nigel Rathbone. His name is Anthony Blythe. Terribly handsome, I might add, but I am not sure how clever he is. I recall him as a womanizer and crammer who relied heavily on charm and was always ready to avoid hard work, but he has done well for himself, considering. He, Rathbone, and me are all at about the same level in our respective organizations within the intelligence service of Great Britain. I understand he has acquired a female boss that he has neither been able to bed nor best, so his clipped wings may present a smoother demeanour than has been his less mature persona. I can only wish you luck with this interview."

Kate thanked Braithwaite as he walked her to the lobby. "No sidekicks today, Mr. Braithwaite?" she added as she shook his hand.

He smiled and replied, "Agent Sloane is on leave for a few days, and young Whistlethorpe is back on a course rotation, which is part of the three-year intern program she is following, so it is just me. I hope you were not disappointed." He bade her farewell. Kate sensed he wanted to say something else but held back.

As she walked toward the tube station, she received a text from Braithwaite that said, **Meeting with Agent Anthony Blythe today at 4:00 p.m. — see directions, keep safe.** Kate was surprised by the last two words.

Kate descended into the Westminster tube station, where she boarded the train on the District Line. She noted that she had to change at Victoria for the Victoria Line to Vauxhall, the underground station closest to MI6. The journey wouldn't take much more than twenty minutes with sufficient time to walk to MI6.

Kate navigated the London underground system with

ease. She contemplated the fact that neither MI5 nor GCHQ acknowledged anything to do with the microchip implanted in the brain of Dr. Vincent Bernard Taylor, yet her cyber-geek contact, Bryant, was quite certain of the code signature connecting it to MI5, MI6, and GCHQ. Kate pondered the disconnect between what Bryant had discovered and what these organizations were willing to acknowledge. Were they just playing her, stringing her along to gather what she knew and what she was learning? Were there multiple levels of clandestine activity within these organizations that would limit such information about the microchip technology to a very few? Were they using Kate to track what they couldn't explore themselves? The questions flooding through her mind abounded; suppositions were many as well, and the concrete answers remained few.

The three organizations of the British Intelligence Service claimed to work closely together, particularly since the threat to National Security within the era of the al-Qaeda and ISIS threats. However, Kate was well acquainted with the culture of these organizations through the mirror of her own country and her exposure to others. In fact, the intelligence services competed more than they collaborated — for resources, intelligence, stature, access, recruitment, and for the glory of success. Failures they retreated from, rarely assuming responsibility and often seeking to blame others, both individuals and organizations.

Kate was about to experience yet another extraordinary display of architecture. The new MI6 building was completed in 1994, but more than thirty years later, it still projected a futuristic aura. Kate had the impression that the British were anxious to celebrate, even broadcast the elegance of their secret service. The British Secret Intelligence Service edifice, also known as MI6 and frequently referred to as 'LEGOLAND' or 'Babylon-on-the-Thames,' was located at 85 Vauxhall Cross in the southwestern part of central London, on the bank of the River Thames beside the Vauxhall Bridge. She recalled seeing the building in the Bond film, *Skyfall*. Kate loved films.

She exited the Vauxhall underground station, oriented herself, then headed north onto Bridgefoot and picked up the busy Wandsworth Road that took her to the bridge crossing. She was grateful for the time to walk and to admire the view from Vauxhall Bridge. The breeze blowing across the bridge cleared her mind and enabled her to focus. Kate was glad of having left the meeting with MI6 for last — having wet her feet, so to speak, with MI5 and GCHQ. She suspected MI6 might hold the controlling hand in this activity. Anthony Blythe may have been portrayed to her as a lightweight in order to throw her off. She counselled herself to keep all options open but determined to gain an audience with his boss.

Sooner than she wished, Kate was standing before a monstrous, elegant structure that communicated Babylonian and Mayan architecture in the design, the stonework, and the way the light struck the sand-coloured exterior walls. She wanted to walk around it and admire the beauty of lines and creativity conveyed by the architecture of the building. Her artistic side was grateful to have the opportunity to enter 'Babylon-on-the-Thames.' She became quickly aware that she must not allow her investigation to be distracted by the perception of power projected by the building. She allowed Nigel Rathbone to get away with that behaviour on the first day of the meeting at the GCHQ, although she retrieved the focus on her investigation as she moved up the chain of command to Claude Mason.

Kate located the entrance on the Albert Street Embankment and passed through the now very predictable security procedures — personalized visitor's pass — that held her retina and palm ID, as well as biographical details.

She walked unescorted across the cavernous foyer to a

bank of elevators, where she took a lift to the sixth floor. Agent Anthony Blythe, a less fit, less well meticulously dressed man with rumpled hair and an annoying demeanour, met her there as she exited the lift. "Welcome to Babylon," said Blythe as he thrust his hand in her direction. She took it to complete the obligatory handshake. Then he asked the predictable question: "First time to MI6?"

Kate replied simply, "Yes."

"Impressive structure," he followed.

"Yes."

Agent Blythe showed her into a small, sparsely furnished meeting room, the interior of which was totally eclipsed by the view. She held back any outward expression of awe but took it all in. The highly professional and very competent IP forensic investigator stuffed the schoolgirl exuberance of the experience into its rightful compartment. She would give vent to the expression in an appropriate time and setting.

A tray of tea, coffee, milk, sugar, and maple syrup, along with orange and apple wedges was already laid out. The presence of the maple syrup did not go unnoticed. Kate readily accepted the offer of coffee and helped herself to several orange wedges; the strings had been removed. This guy was smooth — now was time to explore the substance.

Kate went straight to the point, providing a thumbnail sketch of the death of Dr. Vincent Bernard Taylor and the microchip implant believed to be the cause of his demise. Agent Blythe listened and took a few notes on an Android device then asked why this investigation had brought her to the UK specifically, and the British Secret Intelligence Service in general. It was time for Kate to play the bait card.

She said, "The microchip implant bore the encrypted signatures of MI5, MI6, and GCHQ."

Blythe did a poor job of feigning his surprise at her reply. He studied her for a moment and then said only, "I see. Of course, we would have to have a look at it to verify such a claim."

Kate said, "It is in the possession of the Sûreté du Québec — as you know, I am a private investigator on contract for the SQ to assist with this investigation. The SQ concluded that Dr. Taylor was murdered. Put simply, SQ needs to know who killed Dr. Taylor and why, then lay the charges for that crime."

"Mrs. Roarty, there are very serious implications to what you have just related to me. I needn't tell you that we checked you out rather thoroughly and accepted the recommendations of our colleagues in GCHQ and MI5, with whom you have already met. Given the lateness of the day, would you be overly troubled by a request to return tomorrow morning to meet with our director, Karen Palmer? I would gladly arrange a meeting now, but she is tied up in another part of the city and not expected back until very late."

Kate said, "That would be fine."

"We know you like your morning swim, and alas, unlike the facilities at GCHQ in Cheltenham, Babylon does not have a pool, although we do boast a very comprehensive fitness facility for employees. Could 10:30 a.m. tomorrow morning work for you?"

Kate nodded, showing no reaction to the confirmation that she was probably being watched very closely. Perhaps on this point the three entities of the British Secret Intelligence Service were indeed collaborating.

Unlike the initial greeting upon arrival, Agent Anthony Blythe escorted Kate back to the main lobby. She thanked him, offered her hand, and said, "Tomorrow at ten thirty then."

Blythe took her hand, lingered just a moment too long before letting go, then said, "Mrs. Roarty, can I show you a bit of our fair city by night this evening?"

Kate thought, *Ah, Anthony Blythe's standard modus operandi emerges.* She replied, "Thank you, Mr. Blythe, I know the city well, and I have plans this evening. Shall I see you here in the morning, then?"

"Of course, Mrs. Roarty," replied the slightly chastened Mr. Blythe.

She turned and walked out the entrance, saying to herself, "Thank you, Mr. Braithwaite."

She was exiting the building as the flood of a couple thousand employees were ending the workday. Kate thought the underground would be packed, so she walked in the opposite direction until she found a deserted little park with a bench. She sat down and pressed the button with her daughter's name. She was delighted when Danielle picked it up on the third ring. She loved her daughter's staccato response: "Mom."

They enjoyed a long, newsy chat. Her daughter, the inveterate poet, traveller, lover, and inquisitor, was continuing to have the time of her life. She wanted to join Kate in London so she could check out a young man — a composer she had met while attending a fine arts workshop at Banff in the Canadian Rockies. Nothing would please Kate more than to explore London with her daughter, but she delicately explained that she was working, and the covert dimension to her work could put Danielle in danger.

"What about you, Mom?" Danielle replied.

Kate said, "Danielle, I always come home."

"Okay, okay, but someday, someday soon we have to do Europe together."

"We will, Danielle, someday soon." Then she rang off with their hallmark exchanges entrenched in Danielle's childhood from a delightful book titled *Anna Banana*. "Bye!"

The throngs of commuters had cleared as she returned back across the Vauxhall Bridge. Kate paused to Google Danielle's composer-conductor's name to find that he had a performance in the young artists series at Sadler's Wells. She knew both the theatre and the area, so she decided to continue straight up to the theatre, pick up a ticket, and have dinner in one of the trendy organic restaurants nearby. She would not meet the man, but a chance to hear his music might tell her something about him. When she reached the theatre, she was delighted on two counts: one that a good and rather inexpensive ticket was available, and two, that the young composer's work was to be performed by an equally celebrated young choreographer. She loved dance, having been submerged in it for years in support of her son's career, so she was very interested to read the description of the performance to be presented in a series of vignettes embracing ballet, modern, and lyrical dance adapted to the compositions of the adventurous and risk-taking young composer. Ah, and now she wished that both of her children, grown and proud, were at her side.

At intermission, she made her way to the small lobby in search of a washroom and some juice. While she found both, she also saw Agent Liz Bruan laughing with a couple of people who appeared to be about the same age as her, although presenting a somewhat more artsy appearance.

She approached the small group and said hello to Liz, remarking that it seemed they had the arts in common as well. Liz replied in a gay, light manner that Kate had not previously observed in her. "Oh, Mrs. Roarty, it's nice to see you. Are you enjoying the performance?"

"Yes, indeed," said Kate.

Liz said, "Oh, these are my friends, Caleb and Isabel — we all know the composer and his style of music, but I am afraid we are less well versed in the dance, although we are really enjoying the vignettes."

Kate greeted Liz's friends then replied that she too was thoroughly enjoying the vignettes. "Dance is my strength; my son is a very fine dancer. He has taught me a great deal about it," she added.

The lights dimmed to signal the beginning of the next set. Kate returned to her seat convinced that Agent Liz Bruan was attending this performance as a private person, or these folks were very good at stepping up their game.

Professionally, Kate would prefer to slip out before the end of the performance. Privately, she was there to learn what she could about the composer, so she would stay until the end and even linger longer in case the post-performance offered up an opportunity to get a better sense of this young man who had mesmerized her daughter.

Admittedly, despite her best efforts to focus on the music, Kate was captivated by the dance performances. The company was well-trained, versatile, adventuresome, and experimental, wilfully pushing the boundaries of traditional choreographic interpretation. One vignette almost totally alienated its audience in a brutally athletic display of disdain, then seduced it back into endearment with tender caresses of lyrical mysticism. Was the dance interpreting the music or music interpreting the dance? Each artistic expression seemed to emerge in conflict and in complement. The overall effect revealed a synergy in the working relationship between choreographer and composer that achieved a formidable artistic expression. Kate was pleased she had come to the performance; perhaps in so doing she learned a bit about the composer that she could share with her daughter.

Kate walked back up along John Street toward the Angel underground station. The cool and fresh evening air invited most theatregoers to stroll along in animated exchange about the performance. As Kate neared the intersection that yielded to the entrance to the tube station, she saw Liz Bruan being seated with her friends in a fusion Japanese restaurant. Kate registered the same thought that she had entertained earlier about the agent. Either she had attended this performance as a private person, or she was very good at stepping up her game.

Number 12 Rosary Gardens was becoming her sanctuary, especially since she no longer felt an outside presence when returning to the little flat. Sleep came quickly and easily, requiring no relaxing measures to encourage slumber to overtake.

The following morning, Kate returned to MI6 with ample time to meet with Director Karen Palmer. She had restored her focus to the task at hand. The performance at Sadler's Wells had provided an artistic and intellectual interlude to the preoccupations of investigating the Vincent Bernard Taylor case.

Agent Anthony Blythe met Kate at the security check, greeted her warmly, then engaged in mundane chitchat as they made their way to the reception area outside the office of Director Palmer. They were not kept waiting, and the secretary showed them in straight away. Kate was surprised to find herself in the office of the director rather than in a spartan meeting room devoid of any personal expression. Karen Palmer thanked Agent Blythe, who unexpectedly realized he was being dismissed. Kate watched this woman's eyes follow her employee across the room and out the door. Once the soft click of the closing door was heard, Director Karen Palmer exited from behind her desk, offered her hand in greeting, and motioned for Kate to have a seat in the lounge area of her spacious office. A morning refreshment tray was laid out already, bearing very fine china and displaying the predictable array of tea, coffee, milk, maple syrup, biscuits, and sliced fruit.

Palmer poured a coffee for both of them, remarking that they probably still needed an additional caffeine fix for the day. Kate smiled and nodded, taking one of the cups.

Kate observed a woman professionally attired but in a very personal way, exhibiting nothing stereotypical. The office displayed paintings, photos, and colours, all quite tasteful and very personal, none of which Kate expected to find. There were photos of a slightly younger Karen Palmer with two young adult women, the same young women with a man and another of Karen and that man. All three photos communicated a joy and warmth that Kate did not expect to see in the office of a director at MI6. In all cases, the photos included a large, red blond Golden Retriever dog not unlike Big Ben waiting for Kate at home in the care of her SQ team. A life-size stone, very authentic-looking inuksuk occupied one corner of Karen Palmer's office, and two colourful, masterfully woven textiles were draped long and languid on two of the four walls. Kate observed in Palmer a small but not petite woman of about her own age. Her carriage was confident, warm, and not at all officious. When Palmer spoke, her grey eyes reinforced the strength and controlled emotion that lay behind her words. Kate liked this woman. She could work with her.

Palmer said, "It's a pleasure to meet you, Mrs. Kate Roarty. It is not often we work with Canadians on our activities, but whenever we have, we have found them to be companionable colleagues."

Kate nodded but did not speak, allowing Palmer to continue.

"It's rare that we engage with a private investigator, regardless of country of origin. However, we have been impressed by the way you operate. In some ways, from the British perspective that is, it is typically Canadian — low-key and understated, not to mention your adept use of our public transportation system." Palmer smiled in an almost endearing manner as she said this last remark. "You do not harass, intimidate, or alienate; rather, you ingratiate yourself to those who can help you do your job. Our agents could take a page from your modus operandi. Coming to this work as a third major career change undoubtedly helps to bring out this effective approach you employ. We in the UK tend to be lifers in the intelligence business."

Once again, Kate was hearing a British agent reveal the she had done her homework on the contact she was about to meet. Director Palmer divulged enough to indicate that Kate would preserve few secrets when it came to this woman and the MI6 organization. Sometimes all Kate needed to do her job was to retain just a few secrets. So far, none of the British Intelligence folks appeared to be aware of either Big Ben or the microchip he was carrying. As well, Kate didn't think that her discussion with Michael Pepper about the lads had been listened in on or revealed to British Intelligence agents.

"Mrs. Roarty, while we are very interested in you and your investigation, what brings you to MI6?"

Kate went straight to the point. "Mrs. Palmer, as you know, my expertise lies in intellectual property investigations. I work for scientists and high-tech companies that are trying to regain the ownership of intellectual property that has been copied, stolen, modified, introduced into new technology developments, co-opted — the full gamut. Emotions can and do run high at times in this business, but it does not usually involve dead bodies. While swimming in a lake in Canada, I came across a body of one Vincent Bernard Taylor. He had been murdered. He had a microchip implanted in his brain. Our forensic investigation revealed that the microchip bore the signatures of MI5, MI6, and GCHQ. I was hired on contract by the Sûreté du Québec to help them find out who killed Vincent Bernard Taylor by investigating the link between this microchip and the cause of his death. I have met with MI5 and GCHQ — they seem to want to know what I know and go to great lengths to try to find that out. I am looking for answers from MI6 — to tell me about this microchip and its link to the death of Dr. Vincent Bernard Taylor."

Karen Palmer studied Kate Roarty for a moment or two after Kate stopped speaking.

"Mrs. Roarty, a bio microchip was under development in the private sector here in the UK. It had medical applications that addressed functioning of the brain — Alzheimer's, stroke, seizures, cerebral palsy, and the like. The company developing the bio microchip morphed through numerous different corporate structures as it sought out financing to fuel a voracious burn rate to support the research and development on the bio microchip. The UK wing of the company seemed to go dormant as international partners came on board with global financing capabilities. When the UK operation virtually shut down, we, the British Intelligence Service, that is, stopped keeping an eye on it."

"Mrs. Palmer, then how do you account for the IP signatures connecting the bio microchip to all three of the UK's intelligence services?"

"Kate, may I call you Kate?"

Kate nodded affirmatively and held Karen Palmer in a soft yet direct gaze.

"MI6 has a unit that follows these high-tech developments focusing on the biology technology interface that has neurological applications. While the research usually starts out to address purely medical conditions, it can be adapted for other less altruistic agendas. We want to know about it before it happens and if necessary shut it down. The complexity of the neuroscience, the technology, and the financing machinations of this kind of R&D keep us scrambling to stay ahead of the curve. We do not have adequate expertise among our rank and file, so we have to enter into limited contractual relationships with those who do have such expertise. Occasionally we luck out, and one of those contractors gets drawn into our ranks."

Kate said, "Claude Mason."

Palmer nodded. "Claude Mason." She paused then continued. "If you can see your way clear to work for MI6, for a short while at least, we could bring you into our confidence; however, we are not prepared to divulge this information to you, given your current status."

Kate replied, "Mrs. Palmer, I am a private investigator

working on contract for the Sûreté du Québec on this particular investigation. GCHQ made a similar offer to me. I cannot and will not betray my client. To be frank, from a professional point of view, my greatest interest in this case is the identity of the rightful IP ownership. What I know so far points to a multi-layered, highly complex title migration so contentious that it appears to have resulted in the loss of at least one life. Clearly, the rights to the intellectual property for this bio microchip have gone beyond commercial clandestine dimensions, involving the intelligence services of several or more countries. Can you tell me how this resulted in the death of Dr. Vincent Bernard Taylor and who, or perhaps I should say what killed him?"

Director Palmer appeared to be weighing her options then said, "Kate, in part you know as much, if not more, than we know about this bio microchip. I believe exposing the applications of the technology will indeed bring to a halt the path of crime that appears to be following in its wake." Kate noted that she had switched from 'we' to 'I.'

"How long do you plan to remain in the UK?" Palmer asked.

"Until I have gathered sufficient information for my client or until my investigations draw me elsewhere."

Director Palmer stood up, obviously bringing the meeting to a close, and walked Kate to the door. "Let's keep in contact, Kate. I have written my personal cell line number on my card. Please feel free to use at any time."

The two women shook hands and parted.

Kate returned to 12 Rosary Gardens in order to do some work using her laptop. Soon after, she headed over to the South Kensington Pool for the noon swim slot before the early afternoon planned call with the SQ team.

While churning through her laps at the pool, Kate half expected to see Agent Liz Bruan, but the woman did not appear, nor did Kate spot any other swimmers who could be carrying out this surveillance function.

When she got back to her flat and opened the door, she found an envelope from MI6 had been slid through the door mailbox. It was an offer of a contract for three months, renewable with fees at ten times what she was getting from Sûreté du Québec. She was disappointed in Palmer for making this move. It suggested that she thought the highest bidder could buy Kate's services. However, it also gave an indication of the level of desperation within the MI6 organization concerning this investigation.

The SQ team was all on the line for the call: Dr. Isabel Bosum, Guy Archambault, D'Angelo, and Jack Johnson. Dr. Bosum chaired the meeting on speakerphone.

"Kate, sorry we have not been available for a bit. There was a tragic accident in the Eastern Townships that required not only my attention but all of my colleagues in forensics with help from Ontario and the Maritimes."

Kate replied, "I presume you are referring to the train explosion; it has received extensive media coverage here in the UK."

Dr. Bosum said, "Can you bring us up to date on your findings?"

Kate did so with precision and detail, leaving nothing out.

Dr. Bosum said, "I can see we are going to have to increase your remittance to cover at least two-star accommodation and throw in some peanuts to boot." They all chuckled. "Kate, we really appreciate the work you are doing for us there. You bring an expertise, insight, and ability to work internationally that we simply do not possess in SQ. We may have to bring in CSIS more formally than the arrangement we currently have through my contact." Dr. Bosum solicited input from the others.

Guy said, "Kate, I wonder if we might want to take the heat off a bit. You have successfully made contact with all levels of the British Intelligence Service; you have gleaned a lot of information from Professor Pepper, and you are exposed with no back up there. The Boston-MIT angle needs to be flushed out, *and* Big Ben misses you." Another gentle chuckle came from the team.

Dr. Bosum agreed with Guy. "Yes, Kate, why don't you come home for a bit; work with us to put together everything you have sent us and told us then prepare to go off to Boston. I rather think that while you will be leaving the UK for the moment, the British Secret Intelligence Service will keep you in their sights wherever you go — you have both impressed them and made them uncomfortable. Now, I must return to my dead bodies, whose method of communication I better understand, and leave you three to the exploration of the behaviours of the living. I only implore you to try to keep everyone alive. My morgue and others about the province are full in the wake of this train explosion. The bikers have been on a bit of a rampage lately, and a run of nasty domestic disputes among the rich and famous is leaving far too many corpses in the villas of La Belle Province."

With that, they all hung up, and Kate logged into the Air Canada website to find the next flight to Ottawa. She booked the only direct flight for the next day — that would give her time to follow-up for her backburner client, tie up a few loose ends, and have an early swim before catching the train out to Heathrow Airport.

A text message beeped on her cell phone.

Send flight info. Ben and I will pick you up at the airport. Champagne complimentary. Jack

Kate smiled then texted back the flight details.

She let her mind switch quickly to the little company she had done a bit of IP research for when she had some down time shortly after she first arrived in London. She had really wanted to cobble together a bit of financing for this client as well. She called an angel investor she had a private lead on, a fellow named Graham Burke. Surprisingly, he picked up. Kate introduced herself and explained the reason for her call in as few words as possible.

Graham Burke replied, "Mrs. Roarty, where are you now?" Kate gave him her address. "I'm only ten minutes away. I just dropped off my son for his music lesson. I have to pick him up after it's over. I know a nice little café not far from your street that makes delicious lattés. I could pick you up if that can work for you?"

Kate readily agreed, saying she would be out on the pavement in ten minutes. She threw off her clothes, leapt into the shower, then realized that she had showered at the pool only a short time before — regardless, the pink grapefruit body wash she loved freshened her up. She slipped on clean blue jeans, a white, snug-fitting, tailored blouse, and a delicate gold necklace. The outfit was completed with a fine tweed jacket, red lightweight trainers and a soft red scarf that went with both the trainers and the tweed jacket. She loaded the USB containing the company presentation, quickly scrolled through it to refresh her memory, then slid the laptop into its skin and slung a small leather bag over her shoulder. Kate stepped through the door and turned to lock it as a late-model Audi SUV pulled up alongside the curb.

The window rolled down, and a small man sitting in the back seat said, "Mrs. Kate Roarty? I'm Graham Burke. Please hop in, and we'll be off to the café Blanchenoir. It's just a few blocks from here."

Kate did as she was told and greeted the thirty-something man as she got in the vehicle. They barely had a cordial exchange of pleasantries before the Audi pulled up in front of a café painted white with black trim around the doors and windows, complimented by a black-and-white-striped awning reaching out over black wrought-iron chairs adorned with black cushions and scattered around small round tables painted white — a charming effect. Kate was smiling at the scene before her when she heard Graham ask, "Inside or terrasse?" Considering the task at hand, Kate reluctantly opted for inside, where it would be quieter and with fewer distractions.

They were seated in a corner but with a full view of the street. The menu was comical, listing two full pages of various types of coffees presented in cartoon format. Both she and Graham selected the medium-sized, no frills lattés. While they waited for their orders, Graham told her about the café and his connection to it. While he spoke, Kate studied this small, handsome man with a very dark complexion, Asian facial features, and a perfect upper school British accent spoken with a hint of California American English laced across his vowels. Graham broke her gaze and said, "Kate, like you, I'm a mongrel. I just display it outwardly, while you hold it inside."

Kate flushed in embarrassment. "I am sorry." Then she thought, *This man is almost as beautiful as my son.*

The lattés arrived, and Kate opened her laptop to launch into her spiel for her little company. Graham placed his hand on the top of the laptop and said, "Kate, just tell me about your client. What are they developing? Who are they? How much do they want?"

Kate relaxed, took a sip of her latté, and responded. "The company is called JED, and the product name is Hearit. The company has three employees, a principle investigator and two technicians — one technician is medical and one is a sound geek who knows everything there is to know about sound. The latter is self-taught. He has Asperger's, and his lifelong obsession — if a quarter century can be referred to as lifelong — is sound. The other technician is highly skilled in lab procedures and scientific documentation preparation.

"The principle investigator, a young PhD, is passionate about his work but has no money to move it ahead. He has sold everything he owns; sleeps in his lab; gets food from the food bank and hitch-hikes to meet prospective financiers. The only financial commitment he maintains is his athletic membership, where he works out, swims, and showers and tries not to steal juice bottles, fresh fruit, and sandwiches from other patrons. I met him in the lobby of the club as he was chowing down on my cranberry chicken sandwich. His product is brilliant in its simplicity and applicability. It is designed to refine the distinction of sound, particularly for musicians who fried their hearing capacity early on in their careers. It can also enable children with profound hearing impairments to become skilled musicians — children who may have been bypassed for musical activity because of their limited hearing abilities."

This point caught Graham's attention, but he simply nodded, prodding Kate to continue. "While you would have to go straight to the principle investigator for the minute detail, my understanding is that the sound processing capability of this technology development improves sound distinction one hundred fold for the profoundly deaf and improves mildly hearing impaired profiles to exceed the limits of the average hearing capability found in our populations. The company needs to produce prototypes, test them, and develop a marketing plan. They estimate another twelve to eighteen months for research and development and would try to undertake it for about 250,000 US dollars."

Graham said, "No."

Kate felt the typical swing from optimism to letdown in the search for R&D money for these small, brilliant companies. She replied, "Okay, it was worth a try," and took a sip of her latté.

Graham turned to look at her and said, "I mean no, they cannot possibly do it for that amount of money. They need money for salaries, facility rentals, materials, super highspeed connectivity, travel to conferences, assemblage of test populations, and time without the worry of running out before they bring the product to market. I will provide 750,000 US dollars through an angel investment facility

— probably your Canadian NACO. The National Angel Capital Organization is holding its AGM in the Rockies in the fall. I am planning to attend, not so much because of the conference but because of the beauty of the setting that I want to introduce to my son, along with exploring the Banff School of Fine Arts. I would like to meet your little triumvirate then and there, when they can dazzle me with the developments. In the meantime, I'll cut you a banker's cheque for 0.4 million US dollars that you can carry back. I will plan to give them the balance at Banff, when we can sign some sort of equity sharing agreement. Don't worry, Kate, as long as those three are with the company, it's theirs. I just want a little equity in the action to realize a return on my investment."

Kate sat back as delight washed over her. Graham made a call to convey instructions on cutting the cheque.

"How long are you here, Kate?" he asked while holding his hand over the phone.

He processed Kate's reply with an offer to have his driver bring the cheque to her then run her out to Heathrow. Kate agreed.

"Now I should get back to collect my son. Can I drop you back at your flat?"

Kate declined, explaining her wish to walk.

Graham said, "I am delighted to have the opportunity to meet you. I followed the McLaughlin case you did — brilliant work on the IP trail. Ultimately, that work decided the case in their favour, returning the IP ownership to the McLaughlins, thus enabling them to continue with the R&D on the stem cell-generated bio stents. Many stem cell-grown bio stents had been implanted this past year. So far, the success rate is phenomenal, moving this form of heart repair into a new heart treatment landscape. The bio stents had the capability to adapt to the flow requirements of the arteries, maintaining a consistency in the circulation of the blood through the heart. While the previous metal or mesh stents represented significant technological advancements in the treatment of heart disease, the stem cell-generated bio stents were far superior.

"I hope it will be the first of many encounters. I made my fortune young, as a consequence of being able to take advantage of an educational system that fostered my obsessions, as well as a rather indulgent mother. While I am very cautious about whom I elect to finance, I am blessed with pretty good judgment, although it is not infallible. I was intrigued with you and your very different background while I followed the McLaughlin case, so this opportunity is serendipitous as far as I am concerned. The level of investment I have proposed is on the high end for angels. It's your integrity that is making it possible for JED. Let me know when the young scientist is eating properly again."

Graham dropped a ten-pound note on the table as they headed for the door. He handed Kate four business cards without having to explain that one was one for her and three for the JED investigators.

Kate walked back to 12 Rosary Gardens feeling lightheaded — she resisted the impulse to tell JED right away but decided to wait until the cheque was in hand.

The visit to London had been so intense that she decided to spend the remainder of the day completing the holographic rendering on the Taylor investigation. She could then send it off to SQ. Since flights were always hard on her, she would do the early-morning swim as planned and have some leisurely time before leaving for the airport, now that she would have the luxury of the pick-up compliments of Dr. Burke.

Graham Burke's driver arrived as planned and handed an envelope to her that contained the bank draft and a note from Graham. The driver loaded her bag into the boot of the SUV and headed out into traffic, clearly knowing every back road and shortcut to get them to Heathrow. As she settled back into the seat, her cell rang. It was Graham Burke. "Kate, are you in some kind of trouble?"

"Not that I know of. Why?" she answered.

"When I arrived at my office this morning, a group of British Intelligence agents were already here waiting for me. Their cards indicate they represented all three levels of our beloved secret service — the Government Communications Headquarters in Cheltenham, MI6, and MI5 here in London. Is there something about JED you haven't told me?"

Kate sighed, "Oh, Graham, I am so sorry. It's another case I am working on that brought me to London in the first place. It is totally unrelated to JED, although there is an IP dimension to it."

"You mean you didn't come here just to see me?" Graham laughed. "Listen, Kate, I don't need to know what this is about. I already told you, it is your integrity that attracted me to working with you. Having said that, if you ever need my assistance, particularly in navigating this UK environment, please don't hesitate to ask. I can deal with these folks. I have already have — have a good flight."

"Graham, can you tell me the names on the business cards these three gave you."

"Sure, they are Agent Beth Sloane, Deputy Director Nigel Rathbone, and Agent Liz Bruan."

Kate ended the call and sat back in the full realization that the British Intelligence Service would be watching her very closely as long as she was working on the Taylor case. It felt good to have a friend — always wary, but she believed that she could trust this Graham Burke.

Kate arrived at Heathrow in good time. She tried to check in electronically but received a *see an airline agent* message. The ticket agent advised her that her ticket had been upgraded to business class. She was handed a new ticket and boarding pass then directed to the business travel lounge.

She was delighted by this development but still wanted to browse the airport bookstores and purchase some Butlers chocolate and South African wine, duty-free, for gifts. When she finally eased into a comfortable seat in the business class lounge and selected several of the complimentary newspapers, she took a moment to send a thank-you text to Graham for the upgrade. Her iPhone beeped a few moments later with a text message from Graham that read, **Good idea, but it wasn't me. Must be one of your other many admirers?**

Her relaxed feeling was short-lived as she approached the lounge airline agent to find out who had called in the upgrade. The agent obliged immediately then frowned. "It says here, 'Classified.'" He swung the monitor around so she could see what he was reading. Kate immediately knew who it was: MI6 — Director, Karen Palmer. She surveyed the lounge but did not see anyone she recognized. Was this just a luxurious upgrade, or would she be accompanied under close surveillance, or both? It was too late to do anything about it. She decided to sit back and enjoy the ride.

9

When the aircraft levelled off after takeoff and the personal monitors were restored to full use, Kate decided to catch up on various blockbuster movies she had missed over recent weeks. They were effective bedtime stories — the next thing she heard was the captain announcing the descent into Ottawa International Airport. Her heart skipped a beat in anticipation of seeing Jack Johnson waiting for her by the wall fountain as she descended down the escalator. There he was, clutching a large bouquet of flowers in one hand and the leash holding Big Ben tightly to his leg in the other hand. Big Ben saw her first and began to wiggle and whine. In a moment, all three were wrapped in a spontaneous embrace.

"Kate, it's so good to have you safely home," Jack breathed into her hair.

"It is good to be home," Kate said as she pulled from their embrace to retrieve her bag from the carousel.

"Wow, the first one out, that's a good sign. Let's go," said Jack.

As they exited the arrivals hall, that feeling of being watched crept back over Kate. Jack had an unmarked cruiser that he had left sitting at the curb. They piled into it and sped off back to her house. When she opened the door, a sense of warmth and security wafted over her. Then she spied the dining room table set for two with champagne on ice and the aromas of roast chicken and butternut squash wafting out from the oven. Jack said, "Kate, the moon is full, the sky is full of stars, and you have been on a plane for hours. If you are up to it, let's take Big Ben for a romp in the field, and you can work out the kinks."

Kate reached for her fall coat. She didn't mention that having flown business class, she did not have any kinks.

Jack threw Big Ben's ball for him a number of times, then, while the dog was searching for the ball, he pulled Kate into his arms and kissed her with a warmth that washed over her, wiping away all else that was on her mind or crowding her heart. She wanted to be with this man, kissing him, being held by him, being cared for by him. If time stopped right now, that would be fine. A whine interrupted their embrace. Kate and Jack laughed, ruffled the dog's ears, then turned to walk home.

Kate and Jack enjoyed a long, leisurely dinner, slowly draining the champagne and chasing it down with a few glasses of the South African Sauvignon Blanc Kate had brought back from the duty-free shop at Heathrow. Jack confessed to assistance from Guy Archambault in getting the meal into the oven while he and Big Ben headed to the airport to meet Kate. After the meal, Jack declared himself too drunk to go home, and Kate jovially concurred with his assessment. They made their way to Kate's bedroom and onto the bed, where they fell into a deep sleep, tight in one another's embrace with Big Ben at their feet.

They awoke in the early hours of the morning, when love-making came easily, gently and naturally. Slumber overtook again until the late summer sun was high in the sky. Jack and Kate spoke few words as they caressed in bed, in the shower, and while they dressed — only when the coffee was perked and poured did they begin to speak. Their conversation flowed warmly and freely, wandering through the preoccupations of their lives, their pleasure at being together and finally the developments of the Taylor case. Big Ben was bundled into the car, and they headed off to nearby Red Pine Grove, where they could stroll deep into the woods in the cool breezes of a late summer day. They were both forced to acknowledge, as they discussed the Taylor case, that Kate and Big Ben were flirting with danger as they came closer and closer to the vortex of this biotechnology maelstrom.

Finally, Kate confessed that she had to fulfill her obsession and head up to Meech Lake for a long swim. While she had maintained her fitness adequately while in the UK, not a single pool anywhere in the world was a substitute for the pleasure of open-water swimming. It not only addressed her physical needs — plying through the fresh waters with only the trees on the shoreline, the approaching autumn breezes, the loons, and the occasional wild animal sightings — but the activity also restored her spiritually, quieting her soul and enlivening her psyche. She received no argument from Jack; rather, he said he had to put in some hours at work preparing for the Taylor case meeting the following day.

He proposed they meet at L'Agaric, a café terrasse in the village of Old Chelsea across the Ottawa River in West Quebec and en route to Meech Lake. There they could sit outside, with Big Ben under the table, and enjoy a leisurely evening meal. The food was nothing short of delicious. The reputation of the place with many patrons was long and endearing. The establishment didn't take reservations, so they agreed that whoever arrived first would secure a table and confirm the acceptable presence of Big Ben.

They returned to the house — immediately upon entering, Kate felt the ominous presence that had dogged her in the early days of her visit to the UK. She told Jack, whose shoulders slumped with the news.

"Kate, I didn't want to spoil your return home," he said. "We swept your place yesterday afternoon with the help of Dr. Bosum's CSIS contact and found a number of bugs. We were quite certain that we got them all, but to be certain that the house didn't become compromised again, Guy stayed until moments before we arrived from the airport. He was also handy at getting the dinner in the oven."

Kate took this in without surprise. She related the details of her surveillance in London, Cheltenham, and the upgrade of her plane ticket for the trip home, then said, "I think I have to accept that this will be my life until we get through the Taylor case."

Jack put his arms around her from behind, burying his face in her long hair falling silkily to her shoulders. "Kate, you are one tough broad — we'll get the debuggers back here again and install some security of our own. We can go through your vehicle and computer as well. In the meantime, we will have to be careful about what we say around here. I can stay here tonight and we can head over to SQ-Gatineau together in the morning."

Kate smiled. "You are welcome to stay over as my lover. I don't need a guardian."

He replied with a playful grin, "Think of it as a side benefit."

When Jack left, Kate immediately sent a text to her JED client. **News, meet me at Stella Luna 11 a.m. today.** She hoped the young scientist had paid his smartphone bill so that he got the message and could respond. A reply came back immediately. **Okay you buy?** Kate smiled and responded, **With pleasure.** She was anxiously anticipating the look on the young scientist's face when he unfolded the bank draft from Graham Burke that Kate was bringing to him.

She glanced at her watch — ah, not quite enough time to walk, but she could easily make it on the bike. She changed to more suitable biking attire, clipped on her helmet, and headed out. The route there was almost all downhill and across the Rideau River, where she could see the resident swans on a good day. Kate took particular delight in spotting the gay pair — swans mate for life. When Patch swan died, Buddy swan rejected all dames he was presented with — on a hunch, the swan keeper brought in a very handsome young black male swan, and it was a match made in heaven. Buddy swam on happily with his new mate. As Kate peddled across the Bank Street Bridge, there they were, the old gent Buddy with his young Casanova.

She parked the bike in front of the café and double-locked it — stealing bikes was a long-standing Ottawa pastime. Kate ordered one large latté with single espresso and double milk for herself, a large cappuccino for her young scientist, as well as a mouth-watering panini piled high with grilled chicken, cranberries, avocado, and many crunchy greens. She complemented that order with fruit-laden waffles and maple syrup. She asked the waitress to keep an eye on the young man she would be sitting with, and when his plates were emptied to bring him a dish of their homemade three-flavour gelato. The waitress agreed with a smile and a nod — her agreeable response was awarded with a large tip.

Kate grabbed a newspaper sitting by the window and selected a large, round table to give them room for his triple-course snack and their specialty coffees. Just as she took her first sip of the steaming, frothy latté, the young, gaunt scientist came through the door. He greeted her warmly with a tired, boyish grin and grabbed the cappuccino practically before he sat down. The delightful young waitress placed the panini and waffles in front to him. "Kate, I can't afford this," he said, recoiling in alarm.

"It is on me, but yes, you can afford this feast. We will tack it on to my fee." The poor man's shoulders sunk further. Kate had to put him out of his misery.

"Take a few bites of your food, then we'll talk about what you can afford." Kate wanted his blood sugar restored before she gave him the bank draft. He did as instructed, and she watched a glint brighten his foggy eyes. She handed him the bank draft.

He stared in stunned silence. Finally, when his voice found expression, all he could say was, "What is this?"

She replied calmly, "It is a bank draft for four hundred thousand dollars. It's like cash — rarely used these days in favour of cyber transfer. There's a second portion for three hundred and fifty thousand that Graham Burke will give to you when he meets you and your team at the NACO conference in Banff in a few months."

She handed the young scientist three of Graham Burke's business cards then fully explained the details of the meeting and the terms and conditions of the investment Burke was providing. The young scientist took them and studied the information on the card as he carefully listened to everything Kate was explaining to him. When she finished, he placed both hands on his head and dragged his fingers through his hair as though massaging the news into every pore of his cranium. He looked up. "I have to call the guys."

He pulled out his phone to read a no-service message. Kate handed him her phone, and he made the two calls, telling both of his technicians the same thing: "Quit your job." They were both working minimum-wage service jobs to pay the rent and eat. "Meet me at the lab. We have money — enough to bring this baby to market. To prove it, I'll bring pizza and champagne." He leaned back in his chair. "Kate, I don't know what to say."

She replied, "You don't have to say anything — just make it work. I will take care of the IP issue and make sure you have the best intellectual property lawyer in the city."

He finished his waffles and panini and was about to get up when a bowl of Stella Luna's homemade gelato was place in front of him. Kate derived a great amount of vicarious pleasure from simply watching him lay into it. After he finished, she walked up to the Scotiabank with him, where he deposited the bank draft to his JED company account. They said their goodbyes and each peeled off in a different direction on their respective bikes. That was the last bank draft Kate would carry. Cyber technology had superseded the need for guaranteed paper drafts, as vulnerable as cash currency. Playing the role of courier was nerve-wracking — especially when under surveillance by all levels of the British Secret Service. Kate pedalled home and jumped into her SUV to drive up to Meech Lake for a swim — a very long swim, provided it was not shortened by electrical storms or bodies on the lake.

Within forty minutes, Kate reached the winding road that took her along the shoreline of Meech Lake to the farthest end. Despite the recent distractions, she loved this setting. She was already beginning to feel the solace it brought to her psyche. The SUV climbed the hill, passing Clare St. Denis's white, squared-timber cottage. The old woman's SUV was parked in front. Kate wondered if Clare would be watching her as soon as soon as she hit the water to traverse the lake. Kate had to let it go — she was determined to preserve the comforting embrace the lake offered her as she plunged into the cool near-autumn waters.

She swam long and hard, allowing leisure to overtake her strokes only when she finally felt her body loosening and stretching out. She observed the shoreline from the vantage point of a backstroke and some breaststroke. Mostly she luxuriated in the strength of her front crawl, oblivious to the watching eyes from behind laced curtains in the cottage or from invisible satellite surveillance. After more than an hour plying along the north shore of the lake, Kate reluctantly took a broad turn to head back along the opposite shore. The water was cool. She knew once she exited the lake, the cold would come out of her body like a polar bear on the hunt. With her ears just below the surface of the water, she could hear the ping of an outboard motor drawing close. While there were few boats on the lake, and most cottage owners used them only to ferry people and goods to and from the properties on the north shore, occasionally — very occasionally, a visiting boater unfamiliar with the protocol on the lake would come close to swimmers, kayakers, and canoeists. There was nobody else on the lake except Kate and this lone craft bearing down on her.

In order to deceive what she rapidly became aware of as an attacker, she prepared to dive at the last possible moment so she could stay deep and swim hard. Kate drew strength into her body, readying for the dive of her life. An image of her daughter synchro-swimming came into her mind. She recalled the fast, efficient feet-first dives she saw her execute many times during her years on the synchronized swimming team. Kate had never done it; never even tried it herself, but now her powers of observation were to be put to the test. The boat was almost upon her when she dove fast and deep by elevating her arms in two swift motions, giving her a rapid descent of a metre or so each time. She then turned to a horizontal breaststroke when she was certain the boat had cleared the spot where she had been. Hoping that she had maintained her orientation in the murky waters, she swam hard, while trying to stay as deep as possible, toward shore. She could hear the ping of the engine but focused all of her energy and concentration on reaching the shore. Finally, completely breathless, Kate surfaced to find that she had swum farther out into the middle of the lake. The motorboat was trolling along the shore, anticipating that she would surface there, so the lone occupant did not see her come up for air then dive again. While Kate had envisioned many scenarios over the years while swimming in Meech Lake, this was not one of them.

On her second feet-first synchro-like dive, she reoriented herself and swam toward a small island that was closer than the shore and could offer her some shelter from sight. She did not waste energy or time to search out the location of the boat when she surfaced; rather, she took in air and dove again, hoping the attacker might believe she had drowned. The pinging of the outboard motor stopped abruptly. Once behind the small island, she surfaced alongside a dock, where she could see across the lake through the space between the underside of the dock and the surface of the water. While she could not see much detail, the boat appeared to be disabled — the motor was not running, and the occupant seemed to be paddling as the boat slowly sank. The boat was close to the southern shore, and the occupant appeared to make it into shallow water.

Kate decided to make the half-kilometre swim back to the beach area, where she had started out from, as quickly as possible. As she neared the beach, she could see families of picnickers arriving and several more cars pulling into the parking lot. She should have a bit of safety among the numbers of people there. She left the water and changed, quickly grateful for the folks who were coming for dinner and an evening swim in the soft light of the setting sun.

Kate expected to find her car disabled. When it appeared to be intact, she waited until the parking lot was cleared of people before she hit the unlock fob from as far away as she could stand and still make it work. All was okay, but she waited a couple of minutes before approaching the vehicle. She even checked underneath before tentatively opening the passenger door to retrieve her cell phone from the locked glove compartment. She walked away from the car, called Jack, who picked up on the first ring, and told him what had happened. He told her to stay there; he would have the SQ on the road as quickly as possible. They would shut down the dead-end road, thoroughly check her car before she turned it on, try to locate the boat and motor, and hopefully find the occupant.

Jack didn't take the time to tell Kate, but protocol also required the SQ to notify the RCMP, since the prime minister's summer house was at the end of that cul de sac. He mobilized Guy, and within fifteen minutes they were at the top of Meech Lake road, having shut down all exits from the area. As they exchanged information, an SQ SUV towing a Zodiac arrived. Jack quickly gave them the instructions and information they needed before sending it on to the boat launch. A explosives disposal van was already there, awaiting instructions. Guy escorted them the four kilometres along the road to where Kate's vehicle was parked. SQ officers were on the beach, ordering picnickers to remain there until they could be given the all-clear to return to the their vehicles.

It took only a few minutes for the bomb squad to confirm that her vehicle was safe to turn on and drive. Jack called to tell her that the disabled boat had been located. He wanted her to meet him on the road just above where it had been found. It was about halfway between Clare St. Denis's house and the swimmers' beach. Kate drove slowly along the narrow road and pulled into a half-moon driveway big enough to hold two vehicles. Jack pulled up in his SQ SUV a few moments later. Despite his professional responsibilities, he took Kate in his arms and held her tight, whispering into her ear, "Thank God you are all right."

They pulled away, and Kate sighed, "Let's have a look at the boat that the officers have found." They bush-crashed down to the shore then doubled back along the narrow strip of pebble beach navigable on foot. The officers were examining the back end of the boat, where the motor was affixed. Kate confirmed that it certainly looked like the boat that tried to run her down — then she saw the motor. It was fused and melted to the aluminum hull. Kate could not contain herself — the pent-up stress exploded out of her.

"Jesus, Mary, Joseph — Christ, what the hell."

A recognizable voice behind her said, "Are you declaring this mess an act of God's whole family, Kate?" Kate turned to see Guy with Big Ben held tightly by his leash. Seeing the retriever, her stress dissipated as she threw her arms around the big, loveable dog that whimpered in delight.

"What am I, chopped liver?" remarked Jack, observing this effusive display of affection.

Guy replied, "Nah, you are just a man upstaged by a dog — that's our lot in life."

Kate took a playful swing at Guy and smiled sheepishly at Jack. She asked, "Any sign of the boat operator?"

"None so far. We are going door-to-door and combing the nearby hiking trails. There is no sign that he was hurt — we are looking for a man, aren't we?" asked the officer in the abandoned, destroyed aluminum watercraft.

They all turned to look at Kate, who replied, "I think so, but I'm not sure. The boat was a long way off, and I was in the water with goggles on. The goggles have a tendency to reduce the depth of field, making it more difficult to discern detail at a distance."

"Kate, did you see anything else — anything that could have caused the damage to the motor?" asked Guy.

"No, nothing, but then I swam underwater, surfacing only to take in air. I could have easily missed whatever happened." Having said that, Kate had a pretty good idea what caused this damage, but she would hold that thought until she was in more restricted company.

She added, "Let's go have a chat with Clare St. Denis." Both Jack and Guy nodded in agreement, and they set off back up through the bush to the road. It was a short walk to the old woman's house. Jack drove the SQ SUV over, and Guy and Kate walked. Kate felt certain the old woman had something to do with what had happened. It is always hard to imagine seniors engaging in criminal activity, but sometimes they do and in very vicious ways.

Jack had already knocked on the door as Guy and Kate approached. There was no answer, so he knocked again and nodded to Guy, who circled around the back of the house — the side facing the water where there were more windows. There was movement in the house, but he could not discern any detail. He drew his sidearm and nodded to Guy, who did likewise. Kate backed up and took refuge behind a large old oak tree. The inside door opened slowly, and Clare St. Denis asked through the screen door if she could be of assistance. Jack asked her to step out into the garden, where they could have a short chat. The old woman hesitated and looked back — in an instant, with one smooth movement, Jack moved ahead, opened the screen door, encircled the woman's waist with one arm and lifted her over the threshold of the door and down into the garden, where Kate pulled her to safe cover behind the tree.

Jack asked, "How many in the house, Madame St. Denis?"

In a soft monotone she replied, "One."

"Does he have any weapons?" Jack asked without looking at her but keeping his eyes on the house.

"Yes," she replied. Jack called for back up and signalled to Guy that the person in the house was armed. Within moments, a number of SQ officers descended on the location. Kate peeked out from behind the tree and saw D'Angelo making his way up the slope, keeping low with his sidearm drawn.

Jack asked, "Madame, who is this person in your house? Do you know him?"

Clare St. Denis replied, "I don't know who he is — he came here shortly after the murder across the lake and said I was to call him if she — pointing at Kate — ever returned to the lake alone to swim. He said he would kill me if I didn't call. So when I saw her go into the lake, I made the call. I had no idea what he was going to do."

Jack asked, "Did you see what he did with the boat on the lake?"

She hung her head and mumbled, "Yes, I thought he had killed her. When I saw the SQ speed by, I became hopeful that she had survived. The next thing I knew, he burst through my door. I am sorry, I didn't know what to do." She hung her head.

The brief interlude gave the SQ officers time to surround the little house and train a gun on every opening. The door opened, and a man appeared. He threw a gun out and walked down the steps. He was surrounded, cuffed, and led off to a waiting cruiser. Guy and D'Angelo went in and soon emerged, giving the all clear. The old woman slid down the tree, coming to a rest in a clump at the base. Guy called for the paramedics already on site to come over to attend to her. She had fainted.

Kate remarked, "My corner of paradise is becoming rather sullied. I think I have lost my swimming hole until this entire affair is resolved — a shame, it was part of my coming-home fantasy. Whenever we can free ourselves from this mess, can we grab a bite to eat and chat? I am starving."

"It's a date, probably a bit on the late side. Guy can take care of the fellow in the cruiser, but I want to have a chat with our Madame St. Denis."

Kate said, "Let me take Big Ben for a walk."

Jack replied, "Kate, it can only be within sight of the officers we have on the road — this guy had to have a buddy who clearly got away, but he may not be very far." Kate agreed and headed off with the retriever. Jack went into the house to speak with Madame St. Denis.

It looked like half of the West Quebec police force was spread out along the Meech Lake road looking for additional clues as to the identities of whoever tried to kill Kate. They were aware it was connected to the earlier murder of Vincent Bernard Taylor, so they were taking their work very seriously, checking every cottage, house, boathouse, and garage along the lake within ready access of the road. Francine, the search dog handler, came out from the edge of the lake with her big black shepherd, Tracker, on a tightly held leash. She had taken Tracker to have a thorough sniff around the boat in hopes that he would pick up some useful identifying scent. She greeted Kate and ruffled Big Ben on the head. Suddenly Big Ben began a low, guttural growl and Tracker went into high alert. They seemed to have been drawn by the same stimulus. Francine unleashed the shepherd, gave him a command, and he was off, with her not far behind. Big Ben strained to give chase as well, but Kate held him tightly, allowing the retriever to go in the same direction but completely under her control.

Tracker moved quickly, halting frequently at Francine's command, while Big Ben strained to follow in the same direction. Tracker stopped at an abandoned-looking boathouse that had already been checked by the SQ officers. Nose to the ground, he was intensely sniffing back and forth across the double-door entrance. Francine called for backup and motioned to Kate to stay back while Big Ben strained to continue. Within moments, the SQ backup arrived and surrounded the boathouse while Francine opened the door and entered, followed by well-armed SQ officers. They emerged moments later with a man nursing what looked like badly burned hands and scorched clothing. Big Ben went nuts. It was all Kate could do to control him. Tracker was already leashed and fully controlled.

Jack caught up with Kate and stopped to observe the scene, remarking, "And a nice quiet walk with the dog."

Kate smiled and replied, "Two dogs. There is always safety in numbers. Maybe I don't have to give up my swims in the lake after all."

Jack replied, "I don't think we can question this guy until he's treated for his burns. I have finished with Madame St.

Denis for the moment, so let's regroup at SQ headquarters. Would you mind driving in convoy with us back to Gatineau, Kate?"

She wanted to protest but thought better of it and reluctantly agreed.

The beautiful autumn evening offered them the opportunity to carry out their original plan of a café terrasse dinner at L'Agaric in Old Chelsea with Big Ben curled up under the table, snoring lightly. It was hard for them not to refer to the day's events. However, as they could not risk being overheard, they were forced to talk about everything but the current situation. It was a good stress reliever for both. Guy joined them for coffee and dessert then a stroll in the bright moonlight along the paths in the mature wood across from the restaurant as Guy brought them up to speed on everything and advised them of the plans for the meeting on the case in the morning. Dr. Bosum was coming up from Montreal, and the superintendent would sit in as well. They would start at 10:30 a.m. to give Dr. Bosum time to get there. In the meantime, both Kate and Big Ben required ongoing protection. Kate sighed.

Jack smiled and said, "I am volunteering — to provide the protection, that is. I can use the overtime, and we won't have to work with the Ottawa police, yet."

Guy laughed, and Kate threw her hands in the air. "Let's give Officer Johnson a run for his overtime money," and they were off running across the field.

Guy said to Jack, who was still standing still, "Well boss, you volunteered — I'm going home. See you in the morning."

Kate arrived at the Gatineau SQ headquarters early with Big Ben in tow. The dog was well exercised from a long walk along the nearby Ottawa River. Kate was well fuelled by a large coffee. The walk limbered her up both physically and mentally before the "all hands on deck" meeting on the Taylor case.

She was pleasantly surprised to find her holographic rendering already launched in the investigations room obviously dedicated to this case. There were additions to what she had provided, most notably images of the two culprits arrested at Meech Lake the previous day. The notes under one photo read, **Marc Brault, age 26, PhD candidate MIT, advisor, Dr. Vincent Bernard Taylor, dropped out, employed at iBrain, hands and clothing burned in boat on Meech Lake.** The notes under the second image read, **Simon Waterman, age 25, PhD candidate MIT, advisor, Claude Mason, dropped out after one year, returned to the UK — followed Claude Mason — believed to be an agent in training at GCHQ, specializing in bioterrorism detection.**

Kate was pleased to see Dr. Bosum. The two women greeted each other warmly in the Quebecois double-cheek kiss fashion. The room quickly filled as the Gatineau area superintendent came in, followed by Jack, Guy, D'Angelo, Francine, and a few other uniformed officers Kate had seen previously but not formerly met. Guy and Jack reviewed the case, with a few interjections from Dr. Bosum and an invitation to Kate to cover the London/UK activity that had greatly added to the overall picture that was unfolding. While they were closing in on the motive, which would ultimately reveal the reasons for the crime and hence who committed the acts that led to the death of Vincent Bernard Taylor, they were still a long way from being able to lay charges against anyone.

10

It was agreed that Kate would travel to Boston and nose around MIT to see what connections she could make to thread together the many clues emerging as they moved forward in this investigation. MIT seemed to be a launch pad for many relationships that were emerging in the case. As well, she would try to reach Matti Toivenen from Finland, Giorgio Beretta in Milan, and Kiran Patel in Bangalore, the remaining lads who were part of the original group studying at Cambridge, UK, under the mentorship of Michael Pepper. Kate's safety was a concern to all. Some discussion suggesting that she should have a partner accompany her to Boston was reluctantly set aside at Kate's insistence, advising them that she was a private investigator on contract to SQ. It was not lost on anyone in the room that in fact she seemed to have an unidentified guardian angel watching out for her. Marc Brault had revealed that he thought it was a projectile launched from an unmanned drone that disabled the outboard motor on his boat and in so doing burned his hands. Simon Waterman disclosed nothing about the drone or his reasons for being at Meech Lake. GCHQ through MI6 had already been in touch with SQ headquarters in Quebec City, demanding the immediate repatriation of Waterman. The SQ agreed — he was to be driven to the Montreal airport then shipped out the next day. The two men did not give any indication that they knew each other. Soon after the meeting wrapped up, a junior SQ officer approached Kate to tell her that he had sent her the contact coordinates for Matti Toivenen, Giorgio Beretta, and Kiran Patel.

Kate easily reached Giorgio Beretta, who told her that he would be travelling to Boston in a couple of days to collaborate face-to-face with some business and academic partners there. Kate arranged with him to meet there during their respective visits to Boston. Matti Toivenen was in Lapland and out of mobile phone reach, but he was expected back in a couple of days. She left her contact information on a voice message for him to call her, making a note to herself to follow up in case he didn't call back. She would call Kiran Patel at a time when it would be more likely and convenient to reach him. The time difference between Gatineau and Bangalore was nine and a half hours.

She left Big Ben with Guy while she went to a community swimming pool to get in a couple of kilometres before heading home to make her travel arrangements to Boston.

Kate found that she had returned to hyper-alert mode again, carefully but very subtly watching every woman in the change room then orienting herself to all exits when she stepped out onto the pool deck.

Fifty laps passed quickly and effortlessly as she ploughed through the water alone in the fast lane. She cut short partway through the remaining twenty laps when a young woman entered the fast lane, swimming very aggressively. The same woman came into the change room moments after Kate entered the shower. Kate appeared relaxed and casual, but in fact she was moving quickly in hopes of exiting the change room before the woman was dressed. When she walked out of the community building, Jack was sitting out front in an unmarked black SQ SUV. Big Ben was in the back seat. Despite having brought her own vehicle, she got into the SQ SUV and motioned to Jack to wait. The woman emerged, crossed in front of them, and disappeared among the many vehicles. Jack swung the SUV into the parking lot. The woman had vanished, yet no car had left the lot.

It was late afternoon by this time. Kate simply wanted to head home and make her travel arrangements for Boston. She wished to have some alone time, but there was no shaking her "escort," so she and Jack drove the two vehicles in convoy back to Kate's home. Jack did a sweep of the house then agreed to leave Kate for a few hours, since she was planning to work from home. Big Ben was with her.

"I'll be back later this evening and pick up Thai food for dinner, if that works for you."

"Perfect," said Kate. "I'll supplement it with an Asian salad, cobbled together from whatever fresh greens and other veggies I can scavenge from the fridge." She reached up to kiss him and said "Thanks" as he slipped out the door.

Kate flew out on an early-morning direct flight to Boston. It arrived there by 9:30 a.m., giving her the rest of the day to get oriented, find her way to MIT, and settle in to her accommodation at the Charles Hotel. The inner core of Boston was small, and campuses such as Harvard and the Massachusetts Institute of Technology (MIT) were only about a mile and a half apart across the Charles River in Cambridge. Many of the commercial labs and startup companies that spun out of the MIT Laboratories and Research work were located in various science parks, biotech parks, high-tech parks, industrial parks, and warehouses in the greater metropolitan area.

SQ was covering all of the travel costs associated with the trip. They did not want any security risks taken by Kate, so they advised her to go quality in all of her logistical arrangements. The nearby Wellbridge Athletic Club (WAC) offered daily lap swimming in its private pool. The Charles Hotel provided passes to its guests to freely use the WAC facilities. Kate hoped to find an equivalent to Michael Pepper associated with MIT but doubted she would be so fortunate.

She relaxed a bit once she had made the logistical arrangements to get to Boston. She spent some time browsing around the MIT website, which was both extensive and comprehensive, familiarizing herself with the various relevant departments, biological engineering in particular biological engineering. There she could begin to piece together the story of the microchip implanted in Vincent Bernard Taylor's brain and the connection among the players who more than likely crossed paths at MIT.

Kate was digging as deeply as web research permitted when her cell beeped with a text message from Giorgio Beretta, indicating he would be arriving in Boston the day after Kate and would also be staying at the Charles Hotel. He proposed meeting over lunch in the Rialto, a restaurant at the hotel. Kate texted back agreement and confirmed noon at the Rialto. It was Giorgio who had told Kate to take the train from the airport to the Charles Hotel, saying that it was fast and easy. Kate was rapidly revising her perception of Boston and Cambridge, Massachusetts.

Kate took a bit of time to review the rudimentary logistics of getting around the MIT campus. Then she devoted herself to an intensive study of bioengineering applications in neuroscience. She required a fundamental overview so she could engage in meaningful discussions with key researchers who might be willing to speak to her. She learned that the major breakthrough came with the development of cochlear implants. These were considered a first-generation on-brain microchip. The next generation research had moved into controlling neural circuits. She found the emerging possibilities fascinating. Kate suspected that the implant in Vincent Taylor's brain was a bioengineering generation beyond what had been accomplished to date. It was not yet available or even known in the public domain. It probably began its development at MIT then moved off campus and became clandestine as it plunged deeper into the realm of human control.

Kate was surprised to discover that she had passed hours reading about bioengineering in the neurosciences. She was tired, hungry, and needed some exercise. She grabbed her swimming stuff and the pass for the Wellbridge Athletic Club and headed over for a swim. She had noted a nice little organic food café just up the street from the club where she could grab a bite afterward, so she threw a book in her bag as well.

As she was tired and hungry, she kept the swim short and fast. The shower after the swim combined to refresh her, but her slight hunger had progressed to ravenousness.

The Herb Garden café was still open. She was thrilled to find that it had a self-serve buffet filled with vegetarian items galore. She heaped her plate with tofu, greens, spicy eggplant, and couscous, complimented with a side bowl of lentil soup. The dessert counter displayed a carrot cake with cream cheese icing that she could not resist. The *Boston Herald* was available free of charge for patrons. She paid for the food, put the chip for the newspaper into her tablet, and headed to a quiet corner table facing toward the door and windows that gave a view out onto the street. At this point Kate was feeling that Boston was almost as good as London. As she ate, she quietly reflected on the fact that she had made the trip and navigated thus far without incident or intrusion. The café was emptying out as closing time approached. Satiated by the delectable meal and sumptuous carrot cake, Kate strolled back through the cool evening air. She wished at these times that she was still a runner so she could run along the Charles River while the rowers were out on the water for their morning exercises. She decided then and there to rise before dawn to power-walk along the river to see the shells sculling over the glassy calm water and hear the coxswains barking the commands to the crews to execute their skills with grace, precision, and strength. Kate had never rowed, but she loved to watch it as a masterful example of human focus, speed, and cooperation, particularly in the men's and women's eight-person boats.

The next morning Kate was up, out, and back before seven thirty. She ate in the breakfast room of the Charles Hotel then readied to begin seeking out contacts on campus to whom she could speak about former students and faculty involved in advanced bioengineering applications in neuroscience. On her second cup of coffee, a brainwave hit her. She called her young scientist in Ottawa to see if he had a contact at MIT where she could at least get started. Indeed, he did — he texted the contact info a few minutes later, including a note that Professor Lech Bogdan would be expecting her within the hour. Google Maps indicated that it was a twenty-minute walk from the Charles Hotel to reach MIT and his lab. She enjoyed the brisk walk up Massachusetts Avenue, allowing her time to wander around until she found the building, floor, and lab where she was to meet Professor Bogdan. She had to present photo identification several times as she made her way to the MIT Centre for Neurobiological Engineering. Security took a scan of her and sent it to Professor Bogdan, who called immediately to confirm he was expecting her. She followed the directions and found herself at the threshold of an ultra-modern laboratory that was bright, busy, technologically futuristic, and humming with activity.

She approached the first person she saw, but before Kate could ask for Professor Bogdan, a smiling young man was introducing himself. Kate blushed at her misconception. Professor Lech Bogdan was medium height, taller than Kate, athletic-looking, with spiked blond hair sporting blue, yellow, and green tips. He looked eighteen but had to be over thirty. His smile was infectious, and his eyes danced through a deep, rich blue that must have been enhanced by tinted contact lenses.

He said, "My buddy in Ottawa tells me you need some help navigating our labyrinth of Neurobiological Engineering research and the dudes that do the work."

Kate stammered a "Yes."

"I know I look like I was born yesterday, but I assure you that it was the day before yesterday, so I may be able to help you. Would you like quick a tour, or do you want to get straight to business?"

Kate said, "A tour would really help give some context. My own specialization is IP forensics, but I am not a scientist. Having said that, most of my clients are scientists."

All of Kate's clients for whom she did IP investigations were passionate about their research. Lech Bogdan was no different. He clearly loved the place, the work, his niche in it, and the unlimited possibilities for the future. He guided her around the facility with the nimbleness of a skateboarder, spoke eloquently, and captured Kate's imagination with everything he showed her and described to her. He stopped abruptly and said, "Wow, you must be starving. I am. Let's go eat lunch, and you can pepper me with your questions."

As they made their way to the atrium café, Lech said, "Chad told me what you did for him. The guy is brilliant, you know. You won't regret it. I admire his sense of adventure to go out on his own the way he did — this device he is working on will be the first of many he develops."

They picked up their respective choices of healthy food from the cafeteria-style kitchen, had their plates weighed at the cash — typical for vegetarian fare — and paid. Kate picked up the tab for both, despite Lech's protestations. They sat off in a quiet area under a flowering tropical plant that was clearly celebrating the sunshine channelled to it by the design of the atrium.

Kate decided to speak directly to the reason for her visit. "Dr. Bogdan, I am a private investigator currently on contract with the Sûreté du Québec, also known as the SQ, the main police force for the province of Quebec. As well, I am a long-distance swimmer and do most of my swimming, when I am at home in Ottawa, at Meech Lake in the Gatineau Hills of West Quebec. When I was swimming there a few weeks ago, I came across a body in the water along the shore."

Dr. Bogdan looked up and set his fork down. "This was the body of Dr. Vincent Bernard Taylor."

Kate watched a cloud descend over the bright and fair complexion of Dr. Lech Bogdan. "The autopsy revealed that Dr. Taylor had a bioengineered microchip embedded in the medulla oblongata section of his brain. It first appeared to be a projectile that may have caused his death, but upon further examination, we determined that it was a bioengineered microchip. Regardless, it may still have been responsible for his death. This death is considered a homicide. The SQ believes that solving the riddle of the bioengineered microchip will sort out the motive behind the murder and lead them to the perpetrators. While happenstance exposed me to the case, my background in IP forensics drew me into it. This technology does not exist in the public domain. We believe it had its origins here at MIT, but what it started out as in the labs here and what it evolved into — probably in a privately funded lab — is far more advanced, with seemingly quite sinister applications." Kate watched this vibrant, ebullient young man age before her. His eyes and facial muscles took on a look of despair tending toward misery. Kate decided to give what she had told Dr. Bogdan time to fully settle. She spoke no further and quietly munched on her spinach and mango salad.

Finally, a tell-tale sigh came from the young man, signalling a willingness to speak.

"Mrs. Roarty, you can imagine that this news has caught me by surprise. I heard about the death of Dr. Taylor but that it was a drowning accident. I didn't know him personally — only his lingering reputation. The possible role of the bioengineered microchip you're talking about, on the other hand, is really disturbing. The work we do is consistently motivated by improving the quality of life — for humanity. We're also painfully aware that in the wrong hands these biotechnology developments can have — to use your word — sinister applications — that's not new to research. Sinister applications of medical developments go back more than a century. It was well documented during the Second World War. This is the very reason for the security you experienced today in coming here. To be frank, it is almost impossible for us to protect against what people take out of here by way of personal intelligence or possibly in the form of bioengineered implants. We have some detection devices for the latter, but cybernetics is continually adapting. It is likely impossible to stay ahead of the game. Many of us try to secure the intellectual property of our research as soon as it is practicable to do so — as you well know in your line of work — the outflow of IP can be as fast-moving as spilled milk. We're bound by rigorous ethical standards, but subscribing to them is virtually voluntary. The rigour prevails in a lab such as this one, but when it moves out of here, particularly into a private and clandestine domain, it's almost impossible to track transgressions of the ethical regime. It is conceivable to imagine the scenario you have presented. As well, while we would have to have a look at the chip to be certain, it is indeed possible that it began its development here in these labs. It's not my area of expertise — I can readily identify who is working in the field for you and make introductions, but these scientists are contemporaries of Dr. Taylor. I'm not sure what minefield you would been walking into." Kate suddenly realized that at this very moment she was to be lunching with Dr. Giorgio Beretta at the Charles Hotel.

She had turned off her iPhone so as not to be disturbed while she was with Dr. Bogdan. "Oh my, do you mind if I take a moment?" She turned the phone on to reach Dr. Beretta but was relieved to see a text from him that read:

Flight delayed, reschedule for dinner 7:00 pm same place

She replied: **Agree**

She turned back to Dr. Bogdan, having turned the phone off again. "All set — mercifully, the gods intervened. Let's continue. Dr. Bogdan, I don't want to put you at any risk. It goes without saying that this exchange we are having is highly confidential. Rather than having you make introductions, can you identify one or two key people who may have worked with Dr. Taylor when he was still here and of course who may still be working in the same field? I will take it from there and not implicate you."

Dr. Lech Bogdan lightened up a bit and replied, "Of course, I'm happy to do that — give me a little time to consider the best possible contacts and do some nosing around. I will get back to you as quickly as possible, Mrs. Roarty."

"Kate, please call me Kate."

"Regardless of what comes of this, please don't hesitate to contact me for anything." He smiled with a bit of youthful vigour returning to his expression. He walked Kate through the atrium and back to the main lobby, where he bid her goodbye.

As Kate was about to leave, she posed one more question. "May I ask you if you were acquainted with a graduate student named Marc Brault?"

Dr. Bogdan's face clouded over again. "Yeah, I knew him, very bright and talented, a bit of a renegade and a real loner.

I think he picked up his Masters but dropped out of the doctoral program. He's Canadian, I think — I lost track of him after he left MIT."

Kate thanked Lech, and they parted by shaking hands and committing to keeping in touch. She strolled up Massachusetts Avenue reflecting on the fact that she had quite unintentionally drawn around her a cadre of thirty-something scientists who appeared to be strong-willed, ethical, and willing to help her out. She hoped that she was not putting them in harm's way.

She reached into her pocket and turned her phone back on — to find another text message, this time from Jack.

Call me. Visit you in Boston?

Kate called Jack's number.

Jack answered, "Hey, miss you. How is it going?"

Kate replied, "Good, but this is not a great place to talk. Later?"

"If you agree, later in person," said Jack. "Francine has agreed to take Big Ben. He and Tracker get along really well, and I could drive down, getting there in time for a late dinner tomorrow night … to spend a strictly personal weekend with Kate Roarty."

Kate laughed. "I will certainly have to stay beyond the weekend, and I guess tracking down folks over said weekend might be difficult. I'll have the hotel add you to the room, and you can pick up a key when you register."

Kate checked her watch and saw there would be time for a quick swim and return to her hotel room to make notes from the meeting with Dr. Bogdan before she met Giorgio Beretta for dinner. She liked the Wellbridge Athletic Club. It was secure, with soft lighting and a well designed, spacious change room and shower facilities stocked with high-quality natural cleansing and aftercare products. She needed to bring only her bathing suit, swim hat, and goggles — and even those things could have been supplied had she arrived without them. Thick, soft housecoats were also available in three abundant sizes. While the gym facilities were popular and crowded, the pool was hardly used — at least when she had been there. Alone in the pool, she settled into an easy rhythm that offered an opportunity to meditate as well as to exercise. After an hour, she exited for a steaming Finnish-style sauna then a shower. Kate felt on top of the world as she walked back to the hotel.

A voicemail message was awaiting her from Dr. Beretta. "Mrs. Roarty, I have finally arrived, and I am exhausted from the rather long journey. Can we dine a little later? If later is okay with you, could you ring my room about thirty minutes before we meet for dinner, oh, and change the reservation that is in my name. My room number is 946."

Kate thought this was great. It would give her time to complete her notes, relax a bit, and make a quick call to her son. The latter was preempted by the young man himself as she looked at the display on the incoming call that just started vibrating.

She picked up to hear, "Hey, Mommy, guess what?" It had been years since Dominic called her Mommy.

"Dom — what?"

"I got in — the acceptance came today." Dominic proceeded to read the entire contents of the acceptance package. Kate was thrilled for him — simply proud and delighted. He had done it all himself. The last phone call she had enjoyed with him was long; this one was an hour and a half — a record in their telephone communication history. She said goodbye after listening to all of the many details of the program of studies he was to follow in the coming year. A world order was aligning, Kate mused to herself.

Kate threw herself on the bed when she entered the hotel room. She lay there reflecting upon her children through the years of growing up. Parenting had not come easily to her. She delighted in the young years. She found the teen years difficult. She had been on her own with them since they were young. She came to learn that she simply tried too hard, seeking perfection all too often and not knowing how to parlay the pushback of defiant mid-teens. Somehow, miraculously, they got through it, survived, and were now even beginning to prosper, both in their relationships and in their accomplishments. For all three of them, when at times despair was a prevailing force, dreams were now invading their lives. Most importantly, communications were open to reinforcing how they felt about one another. Although they had a high level of independence, all three of them were drawing closer. Kate fell into a deep power sleep, waking in time to complete her notes then call Giorgio Beretta for dinner.

11

She went down to the Rialto restaurant ahead of Dr. Berretta and sat at the reserved table. The description of the man that Michael Pepper had provided in the context of discussing the lads made it easy to recognize the middle-aged man threading his way through the tables to reach her. She saw the stocky, almost cuddly, teddy bear-like man that Michael and in particular his wife Anne had experienced. Despite his jet lag from the long trip, made even longer by flight delays due to bad weather, Giorgio exhibited a spirit in the way his body moved — Kate could imagine him putting his arms around Anne and saying, "Madame Anne, you feed my soul." She sincerely hoped that this lad worked on the ethical side of brain structures research; that he had not been pulled in the sinister direction taken by some of his colleagues in the discipline.

While Kate was still considering Giorgio as he approached, the disarming man was making the introductions without prompt or ceremony. "Madame Kate Roarty, it is indeed a pleasure. I am Giorgio Beretta."

Kate stood to extend a hand, but Giorgio quickly leaned

in with the French-style double-cheek greeting. Kate was pleased with his warmth and instant sincerity. He pulled out the chair opposite her while simultaneously asking if he could take the seat. Kate smiled, and he sat down.

"I am so delighted to meet you," he said. "Professor Pepper rang me and spoke with intense endearment about the afternoon you spent together, including going for a swim. If Michael likes someone, that is good enough for me."

Kate smiled and replied, "Indeed, it was a very enjoyable and informative afternoon for me as well. He was forthcoming and detailed with the time he spent with his lads."

Giorgio replied, "I hope he spoke about his wonderful wife, Anne, as well."

"Oh yes, I gather you and Anne forged a special bond that continues."

She watched his eyes sadden and the sparkle cloud over for a brief moment. "I do not think I can ever think of her as gone. It is emotionally too difficult to visit Professor Pepper at his home; thankfully, he readily agrees to come to London for our visits when I travel to the UK. May I call you Kate?"

"Of course."

"While I never drink alcohol when I fly, after that journey a glass of wine washes through in delightful acquiescence."

Kate said, "I will join you and defer to what I imagine is an expertise well surpassing my own."

Giorgio flashed a boyish grin then turned to search for a waiter, who caught his eye and came quickly with a drinks menu in hand. Giorgio reviewed the wine then surprised Kate by ordering a South African Chenin Blanc. Kate had expected him to select a full-bodied red wine from Italy.

Giorgio turned to Kate and said, "I hope you will be okay with this South African wine. I enjoyed a lot of it during a stint in Cape Town. We vacationed a few times in the nearby Franschhoek region, where I came to develop a taste for it. This wine was the first to make inroads into Europe at the end of the apartheid era. It underwent many changes under European and American influence until the wineries around Franschhoek perfected a tasty, exciting experience that eschews its cheap, rather dry origins. Ken Forrester added a slight oak taste while leaving it sufficiently crisp to transition from a pre-dinner to a dinner accompaniment." The waiter poured it, Giorgio tasted it, and he nodded then raised his glass to Kate.

Kate sipped from her glass, paused a moment then said, "Lovely."

Kate detected a sensuousness in this man that, had she not known his sexual preferences, would have found him appealing beyond a simple attraction. She was grateful to be able to enjoy both the man and his choice of wine without threat of impropriety. In her years as a diplomat, many of her male colleagues and counterparts were gay — she enjoyed working with them immensely, as their intellects and abilities could be readily appreciated without crossing any lines she might later regret. Working long late-night hours on projects and issues with these men was not accompanied by sexual attraction or partner jealousies that Kate had to tread carefully around with her heterosexual male colleagues. While she never developed an interest in any of them, their female partners and lovers sometimes thought the contrary. It resulted in tensions that she stickhandled poorly, and friendships were lost due to unfounded perceptions. She settled comfortably into her dinnertime discussion with this man. Kate posed a few questions that Giorgio answered at length with seeming integrity and genuineness.

"Dr. Beretta."

"Please, it is Giorgio."

"Can you tell me about the relationship between Vincent Taylor and Claude Mason?"

Giorgio inhaled then replied, "We had better order some hors d'oeuvres and our entrées before we launch into that one." They did so, each selecting a delicately spiced pumpkin/nutmeg soup followed by a light mixed salad with vinaigrette dressing. For entrées, Kate went with a freshly caught brook trout while Giorgio selected a heavier, gamier Arctic char.

Kate began. "Giorgio, Dr. Vincent Bernard Taylor was murdered at Meech Lake in Gatineau, Quebec. I found him when I was swimming there. While intellectual property forensics is my expertise, it was by happenstance that I came across Dr. Taylor. The autopsy revealed a bio microchip implant believed associated with his death. Whether it was the actual cause of his death, we do not yet know, as we have yet to deduce its role and function. Nevertheless, it is technology that is not yet on the market or in the public domain. My expertise appeared useful to the Sûreté du Québec. The SQ hired me on contract to assist with the investigation. I met with Claude Mason at GCHQ in the UK. I have a sense that understanding the relationships among the individuals connected to the case will lead me through the mystery surrounding this bio-engineered microchip and ultimately to who murdered Dr. Taylor and why. Whatever you can tell me that might illuminate some aspects of the case would be greatly appreciated."

Kate felt relaxed but inwardly cautioned herself to remain vigilant as this scientist sitting opposite her was directly linked, through history and relationships, with all of the key players in the investigation.

Giorgio took a sip of his wine, contemplated the rim of the glass, then set it down and began to speak. "I believe Professor Pepper filled you in on how we all came to know one another."

Kate nodded.

"I will try to pick it up from there then, focusing on Vincent and Claude. When we were all at Cambridge and practically lived with Anne and Michael Pepper, we were intense about our studies and our future respective trajectories. Apart from

Peter, who was engaged to be married, the rest of us had little in the way of personal lives. We were intensely focused on our studies; some of us pursued a dedicated sport at a high-performance level, otherwise our lives revolved around science and technology. Michael and Anne's home became our refuge. We were all attracted to men, but we didn't act upon it. It was an earlier, so much more restrictive time. The death of Peter troubled us deeply, even more deeply than our private considerations of his choice to marry a woman. Times changed so very much over the intervening decades. We all loved Anne very much, and I believe most of us confided in her. We were devastated when she was killed in the car accident. With her death went our liberation — we were driven back within ourselves. We had the intellectual and tutorial connection with Michael Pepper, but it was Anne we adored.

"In a short time, we had lost our comrade, Peter, and then our confidante, Anne. We had all moved on by the time Anne died, but Claude had so much more make-up work to do that he remained at Cambridge for another year before he headed off to MIT, where Vincent was already well ensconced. As far as I know, after Claude arrived here, while their disciplines were initially at variance, they began a professional relationship that merged the nature of the research they were doing; their friendship deepened, and they eventually became lovers. They took an apartment together and came to demonstrate an openness about their mutual affections and commitment. I visited MIT in a professional context and made time to get together with them. I was pleased for them, at least in my experience of their relationship. Professionally, they were soaring — in fact, all of us were soaring, and Michael Pepper was beaming with pride. While his accident, the loss of Anne, and long convalescence ended his active academic career, he was, in a way, carried forward by his enthusiasm for our accomplishments.

"In rather quick succession, over the next couple of years or so, we completed our doctoral work and obtained our PhDs. All, that is, except for Claude. We all attended our respective convocations and took advantage of the opportunity to get together. Regrettably, Michael Pepper did not feel up to making the journeys, so we rang him and sent photos of the ceremonies. Vincent was first, then Kiran and Matti, and a year later myself. Claude was there in full form for the first three convocations, but at mine, he attended in body only — his spirit was someplace else. Vincent did not say anything about what was up with Claude, but his concern was palpable. Within a year, Claude had both left Vincent and academic life. He joined the British Intelligence Service, moved back to the UK, and remains where you have encountered him at GCHQ. His advancement up through the ranks has been meteoric. I believe he has already reached a director level.

"Claude was involved in iBrain, a company that had been founded by Vincent, himself, and a collection of other scientists. In their search for financing, I think we all contributed a bit of money to keep their research afloat. MIT was generous in encouraging startups to launch from the security of their labs and business tutelage. iBrain took full advantage of that facility until some sort of falling out occurred that saw Claude ousted from the university, severed from his research at the MIT labs, and from what I understand, his thesis advisor withdrew his supervisory role. Claude did not obtain his PhD. Despite their estrangement, I think Vincent knew the whole story. As far as I know, once he went with GCHQ full-time, he dropped his academic pursuits. He does, however, retain some link to iBrain."

"Giorgio," said Kate, "do you happen to know when the British Intelligence Service began its recruitment of Claude Mason?"

"I am not entirely certain, but I suspect it was during the

year he was on his own at Cambridge, UK, after we had all dispersed — I think he arrived at MIT fully recruited. These are all hunches on my part, Kate, piecing together what I have been able to deduce from Vincent, iBrain activity, and my distant observations of Claude myself."

They both sat in silence for a few moments, playing with the food on their respective plates. Kate took the plunge.

"Giorgio, do you think it is possible that Claude killed Vincent or was at least responsible for his death?"

"I would be lying if I said no. As much as I wish to think otherwise, the thought has indeed crossed my mind," said Giorgio.

While Kate wished to pursue this line of enquiry further, she decided to leave it there for the moment to try to explore the bioengineered neuro-microchip dimension of the investigation further.

"Giorgio, as I mentioned, when the SQ coroner did the autopsy on Dr. Taylor, she found what appeared to be a bioengineered microchip embedded in the medulla oblongata section of his brain. It was simply there. Its role and function, if any, has yet to be determined—"

Giorgio interrupted, "It was lodged in the portion of the brain that controls the basic autonomic functions: breathing, digestion, heart and blood vessel function. It is also something of a transitway for messages travelling between the forebrain and midbrain and the spinal cord." His face clouded over as he mused out loud.

Kate asked, "To the best of your knowledge, was Vincent suffering from any maladies — I am thinking early-onset Parkinson's, Alzheimer's, etc.?"

Giorgio replied, "Not that I know of, but given that the microchip was bioengineered and where it was embedded in Vincent's brain, it represents a collaboration of the expertise that they each possessed. I know Vincent was very interested in addressing diseases of the brain such as Parkinson's and

Alzheimer's, as well exploring the occurrence of Asperger's, autism, ADHD, and the like. Claude's interests, at least while he remained at MIT, were in the effective bioengineered applications of the remedies."

Kate prodded further. "Giorgio, is it possible one or the other or both took their R&D down a sinister avenue, perhaps provoked by sources of financing to support an insatiable burn rate?"

"It is possible — all of our work is susceptible to sinister applications. That is why we race to launch it into the public domain as quickly as possible. Then we get caught in the maelstrom of IP rights — protections and dissemination. We create employment opportunities for people like you."

Kate nodded then went on to postulate, "I am not a scientist, but I am wondering if this bioengineered microchip, when implanted as it was in Dr. Taylor, could have a software control that when activated simply shuts down the host's basic living functions — in a word, kills the host?"

Giorgio replied, "I have not heard of such a device. However, as highly developed biotechnologies are converging, it is entirely plausible."

Kate held back the information about the identical bio microchip implanted in Big Ben's brain. She had not shared that detail with anyone she encountered during the investigation. It appeared nobody outside of her and the SQ knew about it — for Big Ben's safety, it was best to keep it that way.

She glanced at her watch — it was late. Kate was anxious to pick Giorgio's brains as much as possible but appreciated they were both tired. He would be here another few days, so there would be a chance to connect again. She expected Jack would be arriving soon — he might have already checked in. She felt her heartbeat speed up just thinking about finding him in her hotel room.

Giorgio picked up on her cue and turned to summon the waiter for the bill. He would not think of letting Kate share it or pick it up.

"Kate, it has been a pleasure. While the reason to meet is not a pleasant one, I hope that I can be helpful in solving the mystery of Vincent's death. Please contact me any time — I am available to you. My vantage point may be useful. If your IP investigations ever take you to Milan, I will expect you to call on me."

The waiter handed him the device to process his credit card, and they got up, embraced in the French style again, and walked together to the elevators. Kate tapped the sixth floor, and he tapped the tenth floor, the connoisseur club level.

She bid Giorgio goodnight, got off at the sixth floor, walked down the hallway to her room, passed the card by the door sensor, and let herself in. The lights were on, and sprawled across the bed was a very fine sight indeed — a flop of black, curly hair on the pillow, boots kicked off on the floor, shirt open revealing just enough of a hairy, muscular chest and blue jeans loosened, exposing the top of white/black boxers. Jack was in a very deep sleep. She decided to catch a shower, wishing to be fresh and clean for whatever might follow when Jack woke up.

Kate had slowly lathered up under a hot shower when, just as she began to rinse, the door opened and Jack stepped in to join her. Neither spoke as their warm embrace aroused them into gentle caressing under the scents of lightly fragranced soaps. Jack slipped easily into Kate then held her strongly, as he moved her up and down, bringing her to a climax as quickly as would have happened in her teen years. She was surprised, slightly embarrassed, until his caresses returned her arousal. Slowly and smoothly, their bodies led them into a deep tremble together. Jack turned the shower to a light spray and soaped down both Kate and himself, leaving the lather to massage their skin as they kissed along every curve and crevice of their bodies. He entered her again and brought her to a climax then held it for her until she was spent in sexual delight. It had been years since Kate had taken such pleasure in a man's body, so close, so intimate, and so delicious. Jack rinsed their bodies, reached for towels and the robes, and wrapped Kate in hers, wrapped his over his shoulders, then scooped up Kate and laid her gently on the bed, reaching over to kiss her one more time before picking up the phone and ordering a bottle of champagne.

They had not spoken a single word to each other until Kate kissed Jack back hard and long, then smiled and said, "What are we going to do tomorrow night?"

"We will let tonight continue right on through until tomorrow night doing what we love best."

In fact, they were both quite exhausted and fell into a deep sleep before the champagne arrived — they did not hear the tap on the door from the room service attendant who slipped a note under the door that read, *Champagne on ice, call when you wish to have it delivered. –Room service (Dan)*.

Kate awoke early and made coffee, grateful for the milk she had purchased the previous day and put in the fridge. The coffee aroma awakened Jack. He simply smiled as Kate placed the freshly brewed cup in his hand.

"Hmmm, better than toothpaste."

Kate slipped easily down on his morning erection and slid him into shudders before he could set the cup down. She bounced off, threw the drapes open, and said, "Let's walk along the river to watch the rowers on their morning exercises.

Jack replied, "You give a fellow a hard time."

Kate threw a pillow at him. He caught it, leapt out of bed, had a pee, brushed his teeth, and said, "You are on, woman — let's go."

They pulled on jeans, warm sweaters, and jackets, and headed out. They were frolicking like schoolchildren as they made their way out to the walkway along the Charles

River. Kate enjoyed having a strong arm to hold on to as they walked along. A half-hour into the walk, a different male voice said, "Morning, Kate." Lech Bogdan ran past, throwing a wave back as Kate haltingly replied.

Before they reached the Head of the Charles, another male greeting rang out. It was Giorgio Beretta. Jack said, "Well, you have only been here two days, and you already have three guys — that I know of — do I have to take a number tonight?"

Kate feigned a punch then told Jack who they were.

12

The rising sun gradually burned off the mist blanketing the Charles River. The rowing sculls slipped silently into view like phantoms taking possession of the watery domain. The only sounds to break through the dawn were the periodic barks from the coxswain as the craft slipped along the water. Kate and Jack walked briskly, intimately entwined in the warmth of simply being together. Jack stopped and said, "Kate, while you were dining with the other man last evening, I waited tired and dinnerless and was greeted only by a gymnastics workout. I'm starving — can we go for breakfast?"

Kate laughed and broke into a run, turning back slightly to say, "Let's go." Their sprint returned them quickly to the hotel. The breakfast room, while open, was still empty as Kate and Jack selected a window seat where they continued to enjoy the view of the river.

Jack downed another coffee and said, "Kate, will you want to swim this morning?"

"If we can work it in."

Jack said, "I would like to take a long run along the river then do a workout in the gym. Can we do our respective exercise activities at the same time?"

Kate replied, "You are on — it's easy to swim here. The club that the hotel uses is just up the street, and the hours are 24/7."

"I made a dinner reservation for us this evening at a restaurant recommended by a colleague who spent some time here on a training exchange. It's called Salts, just over on Main — we can walk there from here."

Kate was pleased to learn that Jack had made the arrangement. As a bit of a solitary soul, all too often such arrangements fell to her. She could feel this was going to be a memorable weekend. It got off to a great start and just kept getting better.

Jack ate a huge traditional American breakfast with lots of coffee and orange juice while Kate kept it healthy with yogurt, fruit, granola, and nearly matched Jack in coffee consumption. Over breakfast, she brought him up to date on what she had learned from the meeting with Dr. Giorgio Beretta, then they headed back up to the room to collect their respective workout gear. Kate tapped the card on the room's sensor and went in, pleased to find the room already made up. An eerie feeling crept over her, reminiscent of the first days at 12 Rosary Gardens in London. She said, "Jack, did you put the *please clean* sign on the door when we went out?"

"No. Why do you ask?"

Kate said, "That same uneasy feeling I had during the early days in London crept over me again just as we entered the room. It is Saturday. We didn't put the *please clean* card on the door, and yet by 8:20 a.m. the room is already cleaned and tidied. Even in a five-star hotel that would be exceptional service. Perhaps they were watching us and slipped in as soon as we went out, giving them lots of time to go through our belongings."

"Kate, who slipped into the room and what are they looking for?"

"I suspect the room was checked out by the British

Intelligence Service — which branch, I'm not certain — and I imagine they are trying to determine who I have talked to and how much I know. I had my phone and notebook with me, so neither Dr. Bogdan nor Dr. Beretta would be vulnerable. However, now I am worried about them. We got a sense of how far they would go during that last melée at Meech Lake."

Jack mused, "While I can offer protection for you personally, I don't have any jurisdiction in either the US or the State of Massachusetts. Kate, I trust your feeling, but let's look around carefully to see if there is any concrete proof of an intrusion outside a regular room clean by hotel staff."

Surprisingly, Jack was the first to find the proof. His small pouch containing a few important personal documents, including his passport, was in his soft-sided briefcase just as he had left it; however, the passport was in the outside sleeve with the pages facing out. Jack always placed it there, but with the spine facing out. He was one hundred percent certain of that. "Kate, let's carry on as though we don't know that they've been in the room. How do you feel about going for your swim?"

Kate laughed. "It can't be any worse than finding a body at Meech Lake, being shadowed by MI6 at the South Kensington pool in London, then escaping a run-over back at Meech Lake. The Wellbridge Athletic Club is a relatively secure facility, but anyone with a room key from the Charles Hotel can get in. I can't run scared, Jack. I don't operate that way. Discovering your identity might suggest to them that you are here in an official capacity and hence with the SQ organization behind you — that could buy us a little clout."

Kate went off for her swim, her vigilance heightened, but she remained determined to carry on. Jack headed to the gym for a strenuous workout on weights and machines before heading off on a five-mile run along a route he saw included in the room directory of services. Kate slipped into the water at WAC quickly and churned up the first half kilometre before she settled into an easier steady pace through the next two and a half kilometres. She felt the same presence she had felt at the London Chelsea pool when Liz Bruan et al. turned up. Whoever they were, they could watch all they wanted — she could only hope that was the extent of their action. She completed her swim, did a flexibility and strengthening round in the adjacent exercise room, then showered, dressed, and headed back to the hotel. Uneasiness accompanied her on the short walk.

Jack was nearing the end of his run when a searing pain wrenched his shoulder.

He went down, dazed and reaching for his shoulder — he looked at the hand that had reached to the pain in his shoulder. It was covered in blood, and he realized he had been shot. He rolled to seek some cover at the base of a large tree when another runner came to his assistance. He regained clarity in an ambulance racing to hospital.

Kate reached into her pocket to retrieve her phone and turn it back on. There were two text messages. Both said, **Call me**. One was from Jack, and the other was from Lech Bogdan. She called Jack. No answer — he was probably still out on his run. She crossed the lobby. When she was about to call Lech, a middle-aged man approached her with a name badge on his suit indicating he was an assistant of guest services at the Charles Hotel. "Mrs. Roarty?"

Kate stopped, uncertain as to whether to disclose her identity when she saw just beyond him two uniformed police officers. She nodded and accompanied the assistant manager over to the police officers. They went into the privacy of the assistant manger's office. The officers identified themselves and asked Kate for identification. She handed them her Ontario driver's license.

Officer Daigle spoke with the distinct dropped-'r' low-vowel accent of a native Bostonian. "Mrs. Roarty, there has been an incident involving your friend, Jack Johnson. I think he has tried to call you."

Kate said, "There was a text message from him to call, and I did but there was no reply. What's happened?"

Officer Daigle said, "Mr. Johnson was shot while out jogging."

Kate reeled back into a seat.

"He has been taken to the Massachusetts General Hospital, which is not far from here. Can we ask you a few questions?"

Kate replied, "Yes, of course, but I need to go to the hospital as quickly as possible."

Officer Daigle said, "We will drive you, and we can ask our questions en route. As Mr. Johnson was in his jogging clothing, you may want to bring some street clothes for him."

That remark gave Kate a bit of relief. It suggested his injury wasn't too great. Kate regained her composure and said she would go straight up to the room and get some clothes for him. Daigle asked if they could accompany her — she readily agreed then realized that perhaps they suspected she was the shooter. She let them in the room, dropped her gym bag, and went to Jack's bag, where she found pants, shirt, and socks, then decided to bring the whole bag as it was only packed for the weekend. She picked up his shoes off the floor and pulled his jacket off a hanger in the closet. She started toward the door then realized she was dressed in a jogging suit. "Gentlemen, I would like to take a moment to change my clothes." She grabbed black jeans, a white shirt, socks, and shoes, and headed into the bathroom, emerging a few moments later ready to go.

"Mr. Johnson was only carrying a driver's license and a room key when he was shot. Does he have other identification here, including his medical insurance, that you can bring to him?"

Kate said, "Yes, of course," and reached for his soft-sided briefcase.

"May I check his bags and your bag as well, Mrs. Roarty?" He did so quickly then stopped at Jack's SQ ID. He turned to Kate. "Mr. Johnson is a police officer in Quebec?" He read out loud and with perfect French pronunciation, "Lieutenant Jack Johnson, Chef d'homocide, Sûreté du Québec."

Kate replied, "Yes, he is here privately, visiting me for the weekend. I am working in Boston for a week or so."

Daigle pulled out his phone and relayed this information to his superior. His tone softened. "Shall we go?"

Officer Daigle and his sidekick accompanied Kate to Jack's hospital room. The sidekick remained outside while Daigle entered with Kate. Jack was sitting up, bare-chested and with a bandaged shoulder. The first thing he said to Kate was, "We are still going out for dinner tonight. I can leave in another half hour or so." Kate leaned in to kiss him, uncertain how to hug him without hurting him.

Jack asked Officer Daigle if they could have a moment. Daigle reluctantly agreed and stepped out into the hallway.

Jack said, "It's not as bad as it looks. The bullet passed right through the soft tissue. I will have small souvenir scars front and back. The police are looking for the bullet. If they find it, it might help give us an idea as to who is responsible for this."

"A bit of a distraction to an otherwise lovely weekend," remarked Kate, trying to add a bit of levity to the situation. "What are we going to tell them? The Boston police may not be too happy to learn that I am in their jurisdiction investigating a murder of an American citizen. This could become very complicated."

Jack replied, "The murder happened in Quebec, so the investigation is the jurisdiction of the SQ. I think we focus on the IP angle, which is really why you are here in the first place. Besides, I think Taylor was a dual citizen."

"Indeed, that reminds me; I received a text message from Professor Bogdan to call him. I had better do that as soon as we finish with the Boston police," said Kate as she walked toward the door and asked the two officers back into the room. Daigle asked the questions, and his younger sidekick took notes. The Q&A passed quickly and easily with all four of them focused on finding the bullet — it could help identify a path to the shooter. Jack and Kate allowed as much as required but did not postulate a connection to the murder of Dr. Vincent Bernard Taylor.

Daigle offered Jack and Kate a lift back to the hotel in one of the official Boston police SUVs. "I had no idea that the back seats of our regular cruisers are so uncomfortable — bringing Mrs. Roarty to the hospital was the first time I had ever ridden in the back seat. Officer Johnson, do you have a sidearm?"

"I do, an SQ issue, but since I was crossing the border to come to Boston, I left it in the safe at my office in Gatineau."

When Daigle turned to Kate, she quickly responded that she had never owned a sidearm of any kind but had taken several memberships at a shooting range and used the guns provided there. Jack looked at Kate, showing a bit of surprise. "It was a just-in-case measure when I started out as a private investigator. Until now my work has truly been about tracing intellectual property and finding investment for high-tech startups."

Daigle told them that he was actually asking out of concern for their own protection. "You will have to watch your back until we get to the bottom of this."

Jack replied, in slight jest, "I think the shooter took aim

from the front, given the path the bullet followed." Daigle smiled and left it at that.

When they got back to the hotel and into the room, they collapsed on the bed — releasing the build-up of tension they had both been carrying. The room communications monitor chimed. It was Mr. Mendoza, the assistant manager Kate had encountered earlier. He was asking after Mr. Johnson and whether the hotel could do anything to make him comfortable.

Kate thanked him and declined any assistance then quickly asked, "Mr. Mendoza, what time does your cleaning staff come on duty to do the rooms?" He said that they kept at least one cleaner on around the clock, but the routine shift to clean the rooms for the day started at 9:00 a.m. Kate asked if it was possible to find out what time their room was cleaned that this morning. He said he would call her back shortly.

She hit "end call" on the monitor then turned and reached over to Jack to find him sound asleep and snoring lightly. Kate thought this was the best thing he could be doing to help the healing process and dissipate the tension surrounding the drama. As well, the attending physician at the hospital had probably given him some painkillers that had effectively kicked in and knocked him out.

She crossed the room and retrieved the hotel kettle, filled it in the vanity sink, and put it on to boil. She had brought a restorative herbal tea mix she had been drinking in recent weeks and quite enjoyed — her daughter, Danielle, who was well attuned to the efficacy of such remedies, had sent it to her from the west coast. Slipping into a meditation session was not really an option at the moment, but the tea might help restore her equilibrium. While Jack slept and the kettle boiled, Kate called Professor Bogdan, who picked up on the first ring.

"Mrs. Roarty, I am so pleased you called back."

Kate apologized for not returning his call sooner, telling him a friend who came to visit suffered an injury requiring him to go the hospital for treatment. Professor Bogdan was silent until Kate asked if he was still there.

He apologized and said, "Yes, of course."

He asked after her well-being, and she confirmed that she was fine. Then he said, "Mrs. Roarty, my lab was trashed last night. The intruders broke everything, destroyed our experiments, and made off with all of our laptops and some samples crucial to our ongoing research."

Kate's heart sank. "Oh, Professor Bogdan, I am so sorry this happened to you. Are you and your students and staff all okay?"

"Yes, nobody was here when it happened — Mrs. Roarty, do you think this could have anything to do with your investigation?"

"Professor Bogdan, I fear this may be the case." Under the circumstances, Kate decided to be more forthcoming. "Let's not talk any more over the phone. Could you meet me at the Charles Hotel for breakfast tomorrow morning?"

Professor Bogdan agreed to a 9:30 a.m. Sunday breakfast. He mentioned that he was in a masters swim club that trained Sunday mornings. Kate said she was the last person to ever stand in the way of someone taking a swim. He told her that a colleague from Italy was staying at the hotel as well — Dr. Giorgio Beretta. Kate told him that she'd had dinner the night before with Dr. Beretta. When she ended the call with Lech, she wondered if Dr. Beretta might also be in danger. She called his room and left a message for him to call her back.

"You are a busy woman," said a groggy voice from the bed. She leaned over and kissed him gently then said she would be back in a second with a cup of her daughter's recommended restorative tea. It had steeped for a good long time, so it was ready. Jack took the cup she handed him and sipped, expressing pleasure at the taste, then remarked on the soothing feeling it gave him.

The room phone rang. It was Mr. Mendoza, who told Kate that he had spoken to the cleaning lady assigned to her room. The cleaning lady said that when she went to the room, it was already made up and in order. She thought that perhaps the guests had not stayed there the night before.

She checked all around, including the bathroom — everything was the way a guest would find it when just checking in. She said there were clothes and personal items around the suite, so she knew there were guests checked in there.

Kate thanked Mr. Mendoza for the information then returned to Jack, who was now sitting up and looking a bit better. She related what Mr. Mendoza had told her.

"Kate," Jack said, "we had better have a call with the team as soon as possible. I'll get Guy to arrange it." He picked up his phone and tapped the speed-dial number for Guy, who answered straight away.

"Jack, you okay?"

Jack filled Guy in on what had happened and asked him to link up the team for a quick conference call. He winced as he set his phone down. He told Kate that Guy would get back to them shortly. As well, he told her that Guy had said the Boston chief of police called their superintendent — police protocol when a member was injured or worse, killed, in another force's jurisdiction. Then he said, "No matter what, we are going out to Salts for dinner tonight." Kate nodded, although she wondered what this obsession about dinner was all about, but she let it ride. It was clearly important to him.

She climbed up on the bed beside him, just to get close but careful not to bump his injured shoulder. "Can we forego the walk and take a taxi?" He laughed in agreement then winced again as pain shot through his shoulder.

There had a few moments to relax, sip, on their tea and

catch their breath. Jack started to doze off again when both of their phones rang. It was Guy with the team.

Dr. Bosum spoke almost immediately. "Jack, how is the shoulder?"

"I won't be tossing a touchdown for a week or two but otherwise I am okay," said Jack.

"And Kate, how are you?"

"Nobody has tried to run me over in the last few days," Kate replied in a jovial but tired tone. She went on to fill them in on what had happened to Professor Bogdan's lab.

The SQ superintendent advised them that while he hated to see the numbers of investigators increase, it was likely the Canadian Border Security Agency would have to come in, thus bringing in the FBI, the CIA, and CSIS. "We will be tripping over one another."

He asked Kate to try to get as much information as possible on that bioengineered microchip before a law enforcement Keystone Cops was let loose on MIT. Kate agreed. He then said to Jack, "If you can manage to keep from getting yourself shot again, you might as well stay there for a bit. In your condition, you can't come back to work here anyway until you get a medical clearance to do so. You need a bit of time to heal. Mrs. Roarty, Officer Archambault will keep you apprised of all developments on our side. I am sure you appreciate that it was never our intention to have a contract investigator take on such a heavy and risky load. Please understand that you will indeed be compensated to our fullest ability. I hope the bird with the wounded wing there can offer you some protection. Jack, if we can get approval from the Boston Police, we will try to have you equipped with a sidearm. Mrs. Roarty, is Dr. Giorgio Beretta friend or foe?"

Kate replied, "I think friend, but I have had only one long meeting with him — it's too soon to give an absolute certain nod to his reliability."

Both Guy Archambault and Dr. Bosum wished them an enjoyable dinner this evening. D'Angelo, who had been otherwise quiet, chimed in as well and told them that Big Ben was doing well but missing his mistress. They all hung up, and Kate turned to Jack. "They all know about our dinner this evening?" Jack gave her a one-shoulder shrug and a sheepish smile.

Kate glanced at her watch and said, "Why don't we turn our phones off; you have a rest. I would like to do a meditation session, if that won't bother you."

Jack replied with the touch of humour he used often when speaking to her, "I'll doze off to your enchanting hypnosis." She grabbed a pillow, and he put up a playful hand. "Ah, you can't hit an injured bird." Kate laughed and moved over to position the pillow to give support to his arm on the injured side.

Kate turned off both of their cell phones, but before they could relax, the hotel communications panel chimed. It was Mr. Mendoza, who told Kate they would like to move them into a suite on the concierge floor at the same rate as their current room. He explained the suite was more secure, since there was a concierge on duty at all times, and it had the layout of a one-bedroom apartment, which would better allow Mr. Johnson to rest as he recovered.

Kate agreed, advising him that Mr. Johnson would indeed be staying on longer than originally expected, and they would be going out for dinner this evening. Mr. Mendoza offered to supervise the move personally while they were out so they could return from dinner to the new suite. Kate agreed and said they would leave their bags packed and in one place. She turned to tell Jack — but he had already dozed off.

Kate smiled, found her meditation music on her phone, changed into a roomy t-shirt and loose pants, then sat yoga-style on the comfortably carpeted floor for a wind-down of mindful meditation. Jack continued to sleep, so she had a full hour session, longer than usual. She emerged from it centred, calm, focused, and relaxed, with her all of her senses more attuned to the moment. She reminded herself that she must make the time to meditate daily — particularly during this stressful period. It was almost as important as her swimming.

She woke Jack in time to take a bath and dress for the evening. A shower with his shoulder bandages was not an option. She helped him ease into the tub after he protested that it had been years since he took a bath.

Kate helped him on with the new white double-chest-pocket shirt he had brought for the evening. The high-quality silky material slipped easily over his bandaged shoulder. The style accentuated his fine physique. He managed his pants and belt but struggled with his socks and shoes. Kate remarked, "A new wardrobe for the evening. I must say you are indeed looking quite debonair." She dressed to complement his style in black pants, a black silk blouse accented with a brilliantly coloured white-background flowing silk scarf and her Ron White Sabrina Onyx boots that her son had selected for her some months ago when she was visiting him — a rare and luxurious extravagance she kept for very special occasions.

They were surprised to find that they had both brought along leather jackets, which seemed appropriate for the evening. They studied each other in the mirror and playfully remarked on the handsome couple standing before them.

The taxi ride to the Salts restaurant was short and pleasant. When they arrived, they were shown straight away to the table with their reservation. Jack ordered a bottle of fine Marcassin Chardonnay from the Napa Valley. The full-bodied, buttery-smooth oak taste relaxed on their palates as it slipped down from delicate sips.

Jack exhaled in relief, remarking, "We are finally here, so I can tell you." Kate looked at him quizzically but was gracious enough to let him continue without interruption. "It's my birthday. I am forty — no longer a thirty-something, too young for you."

Kate was surprised, embarrassed, and wanted to burst into laughter all at the same time. She set her glass down, leaned over, and kissed him long and hard, then gently broke away. "Happy birthday, forty-something Jack Johnson."

He put his finger over her lips before she could say anything to apologize for not knowing it was his birthday. "Despite everything that has happened today — and you certainly do live life on the edge, Kate Roarty — I can't think of anyone else I would rather be with right here, right now."

The waiter arrived, distracting Kate from her search for words. They each ordered a French onion soup and a pear-and-mâche salad with vinaigrette that they planned to share as a palate-cleanser after the soup and before their entrées. Jack ordered roasted halibut while Kate selected wild bass. Both main courses came with delicate French sauces and exotic garnishes of organically grown American vegetables prepared crisp and light. They settled into an intimate, fresh, and fanciful discussion over dinner, savouring their food and the presence of one another, transported into their own private delight, well beyond the events of the day.

Kate was surprised by the ease of their companionable relationship. They could enjoy periods of silence as well as intense conversation. They expressed and demonstrated a caring for each other that was not smothering — although she suspected Jack would like to move in closer but respected her need for autonomy, independence, and self-sufficiency. Their energy levels were well matched, despite the near decade difference in their age. It seemed both were willing to encourage the experience to move forward — that is, if they managed to keep out of the path of speeding boats and bullets.

After the sumptuous meal, they ordered a single slice of

Salts' house carrot cake with two forks for dessert and one candle to celebrate Jack's birthday. Jack was not partial to cake and was happy to let Kate choose her favourite and then share it. He changed his mind when he tasted a cake made succulent with pineapple, raisins, and buttermilk.

13

They were anxious to walk back, however, grateful to have gotten through the dinner without incident. They walked out the front door to hail a taxi. A white-and-blue Boston police SUV pulled up to the curb, and Officer Daigle jumped out. "Just heading over to the Charles Hotel. Can I give you two a lift?"

Jack said, "Right, just happened to be in the neighbourhood at 11:00 p.m. on a Saturday evening."

Officer Daigle smiled. "*Bon anniversaire*, Officer Jack Johnson of the Sûreté du Québec."

It was Jack's turn to smile. "Good pronunciation there, Officer Daigle." Kate was amused by the camaraderie between these two police officers from very different cultural backgrounds.

As Officer Daigle drove, he told them that the bullet that passed through Jack was found embedded in the ground about thirty feet beyond where he had been hit while running on the river trail. "It's a bullet common to the preferred sidearm used by intelligence and police services in Europe, the UK, Canada, and the US. That's not to say that criminal elements and private individuals wouldn't also be in possession of such a weapon — in this country, anything goes when it comes to guns."

Officer Daigle pulled up in front of the Charles Hotel and then turned to bid Kate and Jack good evening. He paused then said to Jack, "So, you're going to be with us a little longer. You should be more comfortable and a little safer on the concierge floor of the Charles. We will be in touch."

Kate and Jack got out and walked into the lobby of the hotel, where the doorman greeted them by name then reached into his coat to extract an envelope with the new room sensor cards for Mrs. Roarty and Mr. Johnson. In the privacy of the elevator on the way up, Kate said, "Do you have a feeling that you are cast in a play and simply carrying out the script that has already been written and staged?"

Jack replied, "Something like that, except onstage the men usually shoot blanks."

Kate laughed, locked her arm in his, and said, "I am delighted to play opposite this leading man." She passed her room key across the door sensor and remarked, "Let's see what our next adventure beholds at the Charles Hotel in Cambridge, Massachusetts."

They entered a rather luxurious suite with bouquets of flowers in all of the rooms and a bottle of champagne chilling on ice. Jack laughed. "The champagne I ordered last night. Seems like a lifetime ago." He went into the bedroom, sat on the bed, and leaned back with fatigue creasing his face. "I don't know if I should mix painkillers and champagne, Kate. I can try foregoing the painkillers so we can indulge a little at least. It would be a nice way to end my birthday."

Kate poured, they clicked glasses, and toasted before drinking. "To being forty-something, Jack Johnson."

Despite Jack's injury, they made slow, gentle, and quietly sensual love before slipping into a deep sleep, held warmly in one another's embrace.

Kate awoke very early with her mind racing, reviewing all of the details of the Taylor case. She felt frustrated; she had to move it forward. Last night she had been completely at ease with the way the relationship with Jack was unfolding, but now she was restless, ill at ease, needing space and time to think. This morning, the confident, self-assured fifty-year-old felt like a wobbly twenty-something, drawn in by the perception of love, uncertain about its reality. Her adult children were lovers, they had lovers, and they were in love. Surely, Kate Roarty, former diplomat, archaeologist, long-distance swimmer, world traveller, and intellectual property investigator had moved into a more sophisticated consideration of romance. Perhaps the only difference was the accumulation of personal history — the decade of experience was irrelevant. Disease, death, divorce, and abandoned lovers had all intruded upon her consideration of romance. The innocence of youth was long gone, yet here she was, slipping into the embrace of an intimate relationship once again.

She got up, made coffee, drank a cup, then decided to head over to the club for a swim. Apart from the duty attendant, the WAC was empty when she arrived. She loved to swim in empty pools; it gave her so much more freedom to get into the rhythm of the swim rather than concentrating on not running into other swimmers, the buoy lines, or the ends of the lanes on her turns. She quickly changed into her swimsuit and did a race-diving plunge, an entry she hadn't done in years. She churned through three kilometres in an hour and fifteen minutes — fast for her. She felt so good that she continued for another kilometre. She did another strengthening and flexibility routine on the machines in the adjacent gym before showering, slipping on her tracksuit, and heading back to the hotel. The lobby was quiet as she noticed the clock that read, *Boston, Sunday, 7:30 a.m.* Admittedly, she felt a bit smug at having already done a good workout while the rest of the world slept. More importantly, she was calm, centred, and focused. She decided to do a visual call with Guy Archambault. She wanted to add items to the holographic whiteboard projection and look at in the context of the entire case. She couldn't project it here, but Guy could do it there, and they could collaborate on the additions she wished to make.

She entered their suite to find Jack up, dressed, having coffee, and working on his laptop. "Hey, go for a swim?"

"Yes, a fabulous swim — for a pool, that is. Had a machines workout as well. I was banking on our stalkers not getting up this early on a Sunday morning. I think I called it right. How are you feeling?" said Kate.

"Good, much better than yesterday — as long as the wound doesn't infect, I think it'll heal quickly. Even though I was off duty when this incident occurred, I needed to file a written report, given the connection to a case that is part of an ongoing investigation. Thanks for the pot of freshly brewed coffee — it gave me the jumpstart I needed."

Kate felt a change in the air. It seemed they had become Kate, the P.I., and Jack, the police officer. Kate looked at this forty-something man who was undoubtedly experiencing the intrusion of his own personal history — perhaps a decade shorter than her own and not involving children, but nevertheless involving a painful divorce, a long, emotional recovery, and undoubtedly much that she did not know in this very new and tentative relationship.

"Jack, we have been through a very intense thirty-six hours. We both have a lot on our minds, personally and professionally. Let's take this an hour at a time today. Before continuing in a somewhat officious manner — I really enjoyed last evening, in every way. It was very special. I was thrilled to be a part of this moment in your life … and I wish to continue letting this all unfold."

Jack got up, walked over to her, and put his arms around her, wincing from pain in his shoulder. He kissed her lightly before stepping back. "My feelings are the same, Kate. And we have to solve this case. I think I'll spend some time with the Boston police on the bullet issue and see if I can get a sidearm. I will try to stickhandle any intrusion by other police or secret service forces. You have your breakfast with Dr. Bogdan shortly, and I believe you are hoping to follow up with Dr. Beretta."

Kate added, "I have to connect with Matti Toivenen and Kiran Patel as well. While the jurisdictional issues among the various security and intelligence services elude me, I can press on in uncovering the development and applications of the bioengineered microchip. Successfully piecing that quilt together will be key to leading us down the path to solving this crime."

Kate picked up the hotel phone and called Dr. Beretta again — no reply. She left a message. She was concerned but decided to let it ride until after her breakfast with Dr. Bogdan. She had forty-five minutes to relieve her newspaper passion with a browse through the Saturday *New York Times*. She salivated over the arts and books sections, wishing to see and read everything featured there, and then quickly switched to the *Boston Herald*. A small article caught her eye in the "Mergers and Acquisitions" column.

iBrain Gets Cash Infusion

iBrain has successfully attracted another cash infusion to propel forward its uniquely innovative R&D in bioengineered neurological implant microchips that address maladies of the brain and facilitate the redirection of brain functions that have been damaged in accidents, sports, and strokes. A consortium of American, Canadian, British, and Italian venture capital investors banded together to provide $22.5 million. It is a complex financing package that blends the previous three rounds of fund raising iBrain attracted through small- to medium-sized angel investors followed by small venture capital investors. The new consortium has restructured the company with heavy emphasis on financial management, laboratory procedures, and the protection of intellectual property. The untimely death of Dr. Vincent Bernard Taylor, iBrain's Director of Research and Development, has resulted in further restructuring whereby a new CEO has been appointed to oversee all aspects of the R&D but report to the board of directors in parallel with the COO. The new CEO is Dr. Giorgio Beretta of the San Raffaele Institute in Milan. The yet unnamed COO has been recruited from Forbes Global based in London. It is expected that iBrain will move forward into an IPO within the next twelve to eighteen months.

Kate digested this news in the context of everything that had happened. She read the article out loud to Jack. He said, "Kate, we are so fortunate to have you on board on this case. It becomes more complex at every twist and turn. Are you still sure about Dr. Beretta in light of these developments?"

Kate replied, "Dr. Beretta would not have been at liberty to tell me that this was unfolding at iBrain until it was a done deal. I will have to give some thought as to whether this in fact changes my perception of him. However, at least I do understand why I haven't been able to reach him."

Kate got up to head out for her breakfast with Dr. Lech Bogdan. She paused, kissed Jack, then hugged him, still carefully, although he did not seem to wince quite so much today. "Catch you later?"

"My place or yours?" he teased.

Kate made her way into the half-full breakfast room, where she was greeted by a fit-looking, bubbly waitress who addressed her by name and told her she had saved a table over near the window, where she could see the river and have a view of the dining room with adequate privacy. Kate smiled; once again, a server had earned a handsome tip before the orders were even placed. She asked for coffee with a small pitcher of milk then said she would hold her breakfast order until her guest joined her. It gave her time to reread the iBrain article once again, hoping to glean something more from it.

"Hello, Mrs. Roarty." She looked up to see Dr. Bogdan standing at her table. She leapt up to greet him and extend a hug — a bit embarrassed that she had not noticed him arriving. Behind him, the waitress slipped onto the table a large pot of coffee, with pitchers of milk, honey, and maple syrup.

"Ah, I see you are engrossed in the iBrain article," said Dr. Bogdan.

Kate said, "Yes, but more importantly, how are you and your team?"

She noticed his wet hair. He put his hand up to pat it.

"I swim Sunday mornings with a masters team — I think I mentioned that. I showered, changed, and ran over here to meet you on time."

Kate smiled. "I did likewise, but it was a solitary swim at the Wellbridge Athletic Club." She motioned to Dr. Bogdan to sit down and poured coffee for him that he gratefully accepted. Then she said, "Can we go to a more familiar Kate and Lech?"

"Of course, and how is your friend who was shot?"

"He'll be okay; the bullet passed through the soft tissue of his shoulder. Tell me, will you be able to recover your research?"

"Once we absorbed the initial shock at the physical destruction of our lab and began to move into recovery mode, we've become more optimistic than we originally thought. The intrusion of the police, the MIT research lab insurance folks and all was a distraction from actually getting down to seriously assessing what can realistically be salvaged. We worked through yesterday then decided we all needed a break to stand back and catch our breath. We'll go back at it tomorrow. The lab, and the whole building for that matter, has become a security fortress."

The waitress placed menus in front of them, telling them there was no rush — whenever they were ready. Lech said he was starving, since he had forgotten to eat dinner last night, then the early morning swim drew on any remaining reserves he had stored. He ordered a hearty array of healthy foods and carbs — fruit, yogurt, eggs, crepes, bacon, and pulpy orange juice. Kate stuck with granola, yogurt, fruit, and a single medium-boiled egg.

They both spoke at the same time then Kate went on, "Lech, you first."

Lech smiled half-heartedly. "I can't imagine who would do such a thing and why. I guess I have been pretty naïve about the environment I'm working in. Until now, corruption, IP thefts, sinister applications of the developments we have achieved have all been out there — happening elsewhere, not in our backyard so to speak. If the destruction of my lab is linked to the death of Dr. Taylor and untoward usage of our technology, it makes me feel sick. My — our — objectives have always consistently been to contribute to improving quality of life. I'm dismayed, upset, and very angry."

Kate listened carefully without interrupting. She let him get it all out. Then when their food came she invited him to dig in and let him eat most of his meal before she spoke.

"Lech, there are indeed criminal elements involved in this field. I am hoping that if we can gain an understanding of the role and capability of the bioengineered microchip found in Dr. Taylor's brain —" and she thought but did not say *implanted in Big Ben's brain as well* "— then we may learn why Dr. Taylor was killed and who killed him. In light of what has happened to your research, I would understand perfectly if you do not wish to continue an association with me. It is very possible that whoever did this followed me to your lab when I visited you a few days ago."

Lech replied, "The reality is there is no going back. The Boston police are involved. I'd bet the FBI and CIA will join the fray, so if you offer a chance at getting to the bottom of this before a posse of investigators go for it, I'm game. Besides, I like you; you have been honest and forthcoming with me. At times over the past couple of days I felt my researchers and me were being investigated, as much as the break-in and destruction of the lab. I doubt that the Boston police or the university security and insurance services will succeed in identifying and apprehending the culprits responsible."

"I am relieved," said Kate. "I was concerned you might have thought I was behind the incident."

"It passed through my mind, but I quickly rejected the notion. It's true I am a scientist first. Scientists often have an unfounded reputation for being weak on people skills, but in order to undertake successful research that engages a large effective team, a principal investigator has to be a good judge of character, that is, the human strengths and weaknesses that contribute to the overall richness of the dynamic. The individual researchers don't all have to be team players — I don't really like the term and what it implies — in fact, our research attracts a large number of brilliant people who also have certain conditions, like Asperger's. The ability to hyper-focus possessed by some of these researchers can be an invaluable asset. You, Kate, are highly skilled, low-key, trustworthy, gracious, and a loner." He paused, and they laughed. "Of course, you don't have Asperger's."

Kate smiled a bit sheepishly. "The loner tendency is that obvious, is it?"

"Yes, but it works for you and what you do, and it works for me to work with you." Lech continued, "One of my researchers, a tireless worker and kind of a loner, had actually backed up all of our research on his home computer system. Had I known he was doing this, I might have fired him. Now it will go a long way to assisting us in reconstructing our ongoing and current experiments. It gives us the historical data we require for developmental analysis and presentation."

Kate said, "I strongly suggest that he keep this very quiet. It may be best to let the perpetrators think they had destroyed everything."

"I considered that approach — even to the extent of keeping it to a few restricted individuals on the team who I am certain could not possibly be implicated in the destruction of the lab. I'm even thinking of setting up a shadow lab."

Kate thoroughly appreciated this scientist — bright, quick-thinking, adaptable. He represented so much about why she enjoyed in working with this cadre of young scientists — passionate about their work, resourceful, undeterred by adversity, energized by the arrival of each new day. That was not to say that this passion could not be corrupted, disfigured, taken from a thing of beauty to become a vile and detestable aberration unrecognizable from the intentions of its origins.

Kate suddenly looked up in response to hearing her name called. It was Dr. Giorgio Beretta, who was making his way toward their table. He appeared delighted to see Kate and grinned at Lech, who rose to greet him. The men embraced as colleagues then Giorgio moved around the table to do likewise with Kate. She asked him if he would like to join them for a late breakfast. He graciously accepted and sat down.

Kate decided to cut to the quick before engaging in small talk. "Congratulations on your appointment to iBrain as its new CEO of R&D."

Giorgio grinned. "Thanks." He betrayed no discomfort. "Kate, I am sorry that I couldn't tell you that the appointment was in the works when we met. I was one of three short-listed candidates. It was under complete lockdown until the announcement was made."

She said, "I surmised as much. Are you aware of the misfortune that befell Dr. Bogdan?"

Giorgio was either a superb actor — his body language did not betray a single suggestion that he was aware — or he truly did not know about the attack on Lech's lab. He turned to Lech questioningly. Lech gave him an abbreviated version of what had happened, leaving the description of the lab at totally destroyed.

Giorgio's face went ashen. "How can I help to begin the rebuilding process?"

Kate interjected, "I believe it is connected to Dr. Taylor's murder and the bioengineered microchip implanted in Dr. Taylor's brain. It doesn't stop there; my companion and member of the Sûreté du Québec who was here on a visit for the weekend was shot while out running along the Charles River. I think that incident is also connected to the Dr. Taylor murder."

Giorgio's colour did not improve — in fact, his previously sparkling eyes darkened. Kate poured him coffee, and he ordered two croissants, cheese, and cranberry jam with a boiled egg and a dish of blueberries on the side. He said, "Let me have a few bites of breakfast before I engage on this — I have been running on fumes since their dinner two nights before." He ate a croissant with cheese, the dish of blueberries, and then looked up first at Lech then over to Kate.

"These incidents must be connected to iBrain. I am the new CEO of R&D, and I don't have a clue what is going on within the company that could lead to this criminal behaviour, but I will get to the bottom of it, expose it, clean it up, and ensure those involved are held accountable in a court of law and within the neurological research and development community. Lech, I cannot imagine losing your lab in that manner — not only a compromise to the existing research but also the loss of the data accumulated over a number of years."

Kate sensed that perhaps the wagons were beginning to circle. She looked up to see Jack making his way toward their table but not seeing her. She excused herself and went to him.

"Jack, come and join us for some breakfast," said Kate.

Kate made the round of introductions as Jack pulled over a chair from the adjacent empty table. He gingerly struggled out of his jacket, slipped it over the back of the chair, and eased himself into the seat. The two scientists sized up Jack, and he did likewise. Giorgio spoke first. "What we all have in common is knowing Kate, and perhaps a connection to iBrain."

Jack said, "You folks have the biotechnology expertise. The Sûreté du Québec wants to solve the murder of Dr. Taylor and get to the bottom of what role, if any, the bioengineered microchip implanted in Dr. Taylor's brain played in contributing to his death. I would rather not meet the same fate while we are investigating it. In fact, I came to Boston-Cambridge to visit Kate, not to investigate the case, although admittedly it was this case that brought us together in the first place and brought Kate here."

Giorgio grinned. "Ah, the things men will do to get their women. You are a lucky man — the Kate Roartys of the world are few and far between. Dr. Pepper's summation of Kate when he rang to tell me about her visit was, 'She is as good as they get.'"

Jack flushed a little, looked at Kate, nodded, then dug into the breakfast that the waiter had just placed in front of him.

Kate mused about the three very different men sitting with her. What they had in common, she hoped, was that they were all good and decent. She wanted to trust her judgment on that assessment but warned herself to let the jury continue to deliberate and move slowly in bringing in the final verdict. It was not lost on her that all three of these men had already trusted their judgment in assessing her strength of character, and she came up not wanting in the least. She would hold this thought for now and revisit it when a long solo swim gave her the opportunity to think and reflect.

While Jack ate, Kate took a few moments to fill him in on Giorgio's considerations in his new role as CEO of iBrain.

Jack listened, finished eating, put his utensils down across the edge of the plate, took a gulp of coffee and said, "We all have to remain out of harm's way as well. Each of us sitting here has experienced direct or indirect violence as a consequence of our association with this case." Giorgio looked slightly perplexed but said nothing. Jack picked up on his confusion. "Dr. Beretta, you have become CEO of a company doing brilliant neurological research. I think there is also a dark element at work within the company, and while you may have been on the periphery of it, you are now stuck in the muck. If you want to save the company, continue the research, and ferret out what ails it, you are going to have to get your hands very dirty before you can wash them clean and move forward."

Giorgio nodded. "Indeed," he said quietly.

Kate felt herself fill with pride, surprised at how clearly Jack had grasped the situation and articulated it. She made a mental note never to underestimate him.

Jack continued, "I am not here in an official capacity — although I am hopeful that might change. Police forces worldwide cling tenaciously to their jurisdictional territories. Intelligence and security services, on the other hand, step across these lines all the time. Kate's role is to try to gain an understanding about the bioengineered microchip, and despite recent developments, she can continue in that role."

Giorgio said, "I'll stay on a little longer in Boston, but given several international locations of iBrain's labs, I want to visit them all as soon as possible. I can keep in touch easily wherever I go."

Lech added, "I have a lab to rebuild."

Jack laughed and said, "I have a shoulder to heal."

Giorgio glanced at his watch. "I'll be on my way." He signed the bill that the waiter placed in front of him, shook hands around the table, and walked over to embrace Kate Italian-style then hurried off. Lech summoned the server and asked for the rest of the bill. The server said portions of the bill were covered in some of the room rates, and Mr. Beretta had covered the rest. They all looked surprised, but there was nothing they could do — Dr. Beretta was gone.

Kate asked Lech back up to their suite for a bit to strategize on how to proceed. He agreed but said he would have to get back to the lab soon for the next round of cleaning up and sorting out. Several of the lab technicians were already there.

After they were in the privacy of the room and Kate had poured mineral water with lime for all of them, she said, "Lech, do you trust the researcher who backed up the work without letting you know that he was doing it?"

"This guy has my back. That's probably the reason he did it. We go back a very long way."

Kate pushed further. "If a payoff, extortion, threat of violence, or even death were involved, would he remain solid?"

Lech said, without a moment's hesitation, "Yes."

Kate exhaled, then said, "Okay, maybe there's a chance to rebuild your work and ensnare the culprits at the same time. Can you focus your technicians on the cleanup, appearing as though you are going to start all over again? Drop a few comments here and there about taking years to get to where you had been. Act a bit down but not defeated."

Lech nodded, slipped into his jacket, and left.

14

Jack said, "Jesus, am I glad you're comfortable with all of this IP forensics activity. I'm much more accustomed to sex, betrayal, drugs, and money."

Kate smiled. "And you don't think this isn't about the same thing, Lieutenant Jack Johnson, head of Gatineau Homicide? Don't let the academic credentials, research, and biotechnology deceive you. These guys are smart, but they are careless. They're vacillating between sophistication and thuggery. I am not a homicide investigator, Jack, but in my limited dealings in IP forensics, and life in general for that matter, such behaviour suggests there's dissention within the ranks. There are too many players on the field, and nobody knows where the ball went."

Jack smiled at her analogy then nodded. "Guy is going to call in a few minutes so we can make additions to the holographic white board projection and get a more visual sense of where we are going."

Kate's cell phone rang. She picked up, assuming it was Guy, but it was her daughter Danielle, with her signature staccato. "Hi, Momma, call me back?"

Kate said, "Okay," and hung up. "That was my daughter, Danielle. I'll call her back — can you call Guy and tell him to hold the call for a bit, if that can work for him?"

Jack nodded, but Kate saw a cloud creep over his face. As she dialled Danielle's number, she wondered why. She made a mental note to follow up after the phone calls.

Danielle bubbled over with excitement about her new place, new job, a weekend canoe trip, an online herbal studies course she was taking, and the beloved shepherd dog that had become the focus of much affection, attention, and many anecdotes, not to mention a long list of misdemeanours. The rescue dog had a propensity to consume everything eatable within a two-metre reach of her cavernous jaws. The most recent reports included seven pounds of Polish sausage sprung from her brother's fridge, two hundred west coast salmon canapés awaiting the conclusion of a wedding ceremony, a bucket of homemade fresh ice cream en route to the neighbour's chest freezer, a half dozen steaks marinating before an evening barbeque with new roommates, and an iron pot of fermenting beer waiting to be bottled. Danielle loved the dog. No matter the number of misdeeds, the shepherd had a forever home with her daughter. Short of importing Cesar Millan, it was unlikely the shepherd's behaviour would improve in the short term.

The chats with her daughter were all too infrequent. She hated to cut any of them short, but after telling her that she was in Boston on a contract, she promised to call back later that night then hung up. Jack had connected with Guy and arranged for their call as soon as Kate was off the phone from Danielle. His mood continued to be distant and a bit gloomy. Kate worried that she had inadvertently said something untoward, or perhaps some after trauma from being shot was setting in. She felt a brotherly closeness to Guy and wished he was nearby to ask, but that would not have been diplomatic. Jack was, in fact, Guy's boss, although it rarely seemed to be the nature of their relationship. They seemed to be good buddies.

By the time they were finished catching up with Guy, Kate was surprised to notice the sun setting. She turned to Jack and said, "Hey, despite all, we can't stay cooped up in here like caged animals. If you are up to it, let's go out and get some air while the sun is setting over the Charles."

Jack still rather sombre, said only, "Good idea, let's go." As they were about to open the door to go out, a knock sounded. Kate looked through the peephole and stepped back to let in Officer Daigle.

"This is a surprise on a Sunday evening — in Boston, er, Cambridge."

"Same thing. May I come in?"

"Of course," said both Jack and Kate simultaneously.

"Our respective bosses have talked, and they reached an agreement to give you a sidearm from our arsenal. We wanted you to have a weapon type that you had already been checked out on in Quebec. You can go around to our firing range any time if you want to brush up on using it." He handed Jack a handgun and two magazines. "Seems the Glock 17 is a standard issue with the SQ, and it's one of our standard issue as well. I brought along a left dress, right dress, and back holster." Daigle got Jack to sign for the handgun, reviewed its operation, and gave him a card showing the location of the firing range.

"I gather you Canadian folks rarely if ever use your guns. We're a little different here, however, the procedure is the same if you fire the gun. A full report must be submitted as soon as possible after the incident. Unlike your police forces, it is not necessary to file a report if you just draw your sidearm but don't fire it. Lieutenant Johnson—"

"Please, it's Jack."

"We treat homicides quite differently here. Our annual rate is ten to twelve times your rate in West Quebec. I believe you investigated six murders last year — we had sixty-two for the same period. Believe me, we wish it were a lot less. Regardless, we don't want a police officer, especially the head of Homicide of a foreign force, shot and killed on our watch, so we are counting on you to make a significant contribution to keeping yourself alive while you are here."

Jack saluted him.

"We will still watch out for you whenever we can until we apprehend whoever shot you." Daigle turned to Kate. "Mrs. Roarty, I wish I could outfit you as well, but given your P.I. status, it is impossible. Be careful. Shall we walk out together?"

Jack and Kate both thanked Officer Daigle profusely as they headed to the elevator. On the street, Daigle bid them farewell, jumped into his blue-and-white Boston police SUV, and sped off. Kate and Jack walked over to and along Mount Auburn Street to Story Street, then on past the Monroe C. Gutman Library to Radcliffe. Walking past Radcliffe was impressive for Kate. She hadn't realized it was so close by but should have, since it was the women's back door to Harvard when Harvard was an all-male institution. Kate had dreamed of going to a place like Radcliffe when pursing a liberal arts degree was an honourable direction for a woman. As it turned out, her undergraduate anthropology degree and graduate science degree obtained from Canadian universities had proven to be quite useful.

Kate and Jack chatted about their post-secondary education as they walked along — they still had so much to learn about one another. While Jack was still in a sombre mood, it seemed to be safe territory to discuss. Kate learned from Jack that he had received all of his education in French in Quebec. He took law enforcement at CEGEP then went on to the Université de Montréal, where he studied the classics, psychology, and business. He did his Masters in public administration at U. de Québec. He loved the years he spent first in Montreal and then in Quebec City. Both cities were interesting and fun places to live, and both universities were excellent institutions. They had been walking for an hour when Jack spotted a pub and suggested they grab a drink. He had a tall local beer and Kate ordered a glass of white wine.

"Kate, I didn't tell you the whole story about my wife … and daughter."

Kate was surprised to hear of a daughter. She allowed an indulgent silence to encourage him to continue.

"After Micheline left and we divorced, she moved to Sherbrooke with our daughter, Elizabeth. When they still lived in Gatineau, Elizabeth spent a lot of time with me. Then Micheline and her new man, Jacques — spelled the French way — both got jobs at the Université de Sherbrooke and moved there. We had a plan that Elizabeth would alternate years between us, back and forth — crazy idea, really. Micheline was very happy with her new man. Elizabeth seemed to like him, and she was still very young to be away from her mother, so she went to Sherbrooke. I drove down every three-day stretch I had off and even took a small apartment in Sherbrooke so we would have a place that was familiar to Elizabeth when we were together there.

Micheline was going to attend a conference in Calgary and suggested they drive up to Ottawa. She could leave Elizabeth with me then take the direct flight out to Calgary. I was thrilled, and so was Elizabeth — she hadn't been back to see her friends since leaving, and she would be here for my birthday and her birthday, which were just two days apart. They never made it. Their car was hit head-on by a drunk driver passing on a double line. Micheline, Elizabeth, and the drunk driver were all killed instantly. That's it. That is all — it was four years ago. Elizabeth was about to turn eight."

They sat quietly and said nothing, Kate digesting what Jack had just told her and Jack flushed with relief that he could tell Kate about it. Finally, Jack started to speak again.

"I got through my birthday okay — having you with me made me feel alive, then getting shot and surviving was like proving I was alive. When I heard you speaking to your daughter this afternoon, the grief just washed over me. I will never experience the obnoxious teenager, the lovely young woman, or hear a message on my voicemail that says 'Bonjour, Papa, c'est Elizabeth ici. Appele-moi. Je t'aime. Beth'."

Jack's eyes filled with tears. He looked over at Kate, who struggled and searched for the right thing to say, but there never is a right thing to say at such times. She reached over, took his hand, and held it. "Thank you for telling me."

Jack stood up. "Kate, let's get out of here." He left a twenty-dollar bill on the table and they were out the door and into the street. Kate locked her arm in his as they walked along. She just wanted to hold him and make the pain go away. But she knew … she knew he had to experience the pain to feel alive. She knew a parent never gets over the loss of a child. The best they can hope for is in time to learn to live with it. Some never do. Her parents never did.

The streets were quiet, almost deserted when a scooter came up the road driving on the wrong side. Jack pulled Kate behind a parked car as it sped on by. They huddled low for a moment. Kate thought that perhaps Jack was overreacting, but she let him carry through on his reaction. They rose and quickly crossed to the other side of the street then crouched behind another car. The scooter returned, moving slowly this time — a gun was visible in one hand of the rider as he proceeded up the middle of the narrow street, checking either side around and between cars. Suddenly, police vehicles converged, sealing off both ends of the block. The scooter sped up, drove over the end cruiser, then the rider lost control of the small machine and skidded to the pavement. Three officers were on top of him almost instantly, and it was over. Officer Daigle emerged from his SUV at the other end of the block. Other officers checked along the street in case the scooter rider was not acting alone as Daigle, Kate, and Jack met, and Jack said thanks.

Daigle said, "For a guy who only investigates half a dozen homicides a year, you sure attract a lot of threats."

"Are you sure it's me this guy is after? It could have been Kate."

"Or both of you," said Daigle. "I'll find out who he is and what he is up to then give you a call."

Kate bent down and picked up a small black cylinder-like device while the officers were talking. She put it in her pocket.

"There's a nice little Italian restaurant over on Huron Street called Pulcinella's. I know the owners. You'll be safe there, and the food is great. It's only a mile from the Charles Hotel. Do me a favour and get a cab back to the Charles afterwards — I'll drop you off on the way back to headquarters with scooter boy here."

Jack and Kate saluted and once again hopped into Officer Daigle's SUV. Scooter boy was loaded into a paddy wagon. Jack said, "Are we going to have to start paying for taxi service from the Boston police?"

It was a short drive over to the restaurant. Officer Daigle went in with them.

They heard a welcoming voice. "Daggy, where's Maria?"

"Hey Vincento, I'm still on duty. Can you give my friends a quiet, secluded table, and make sure they take a taxi back to the Charles Hotel when they are ready to go?"

"Of course. A glass of wine for the road?"

"Sorry, Vincento, no can do. How is *your* Maria?"

"As hot as the day I married her."

A pleasant-looking middle-aged woman approached from behind and snapped a towel at Vincento's behind and then said, "You behave yourself, old man. Daggy, it is so nice to see you." She reached forward and greeted Kate and Jack. "Welcome."

"Sorry, Maria Rosa, gotta run. We'll come over with the

girls after the game on Thursday. Call Maria Christina in the morning — ciao."

"Ah, that man, always saving the city." She stood back, sized up Kate, and Jack, "You are in love — let me show you to the lovers' table."

"Eh, Maria, you just met them. She says that to almost every couple that comes in." Vincento headed back to the kitchen, shaking his head.

The restaurant appeared to be a little hidden gem. If the food was as good as the atmosphere was charming, they were in for a superb meal. Kate thought it would be a perfect antidote to Jack's mood, memories, and the would-be assassin.

Maria Rosa seated them and then asked for their wine preference. Kate said, "Could we put ourselves in your hands for the wine and food?"

Maria flashed a full, engaging grin and replied, "*Absolutemento*. You will not be disappointed."

She brought them a large carafe of the Pulcinella house red. "A Pinot Noir — for my lovers. The Pinot Noir is made from the grapes the wine makers love to hate. It is the prettiest, sexiest, and most demanding yet least predictable. Enjoy!" And they did.

Despite the trauma of memory and action that had occurred during the day, they settled into a relaxing, romantic mood made more so by the ensemble of delectable dishes Maria placed before them. Each arrival was a delightful surprise. They started with baked sardines stuffed with escarole, black olives, and pine-nuts complemented with a Toscana mixed-green salad, followed by tortellini with celery, onions, carrots, ground beef, and tomato sauce, as well as potato dumplings served with shrimp in arugula pesto sauce. They tried to skip dessert, but Maria would have none of it. She insisted that they at least try her very own tiramisu. When Vincento came out to tell them the taxi was waiting, they rose completely satiated with a warm, comfortable glow, having thoroughly enjoyed a fine dining evening. They would have loved to walk back to the hotel, but they had promised Officer Daigle they would take a taxi. They were grateful to be without any more distress for the evening.

"Kate, do you realize that I arrived in Boston only two days ago?"

"I was just thinking about that myself. It wasn't exactly the weekend we had envisioned, was it?"

"Some parts of it were beyond my wildest dreams — actually, most parts of it were beyond my wildest dreams. You know how to keep a man dreaming, Kate Roarty."

Kate slipped her free hand into her pocket and touched the cylinder she had picked up from the street. She pulled it out and held it up to the light.

"What's that?" Jack asked.

"I'm not sure, but I think it may have something to do with a bioengineered microchip," said Kate.

The new week and Jack's continued stay with Kate in Boston brought on more personal and professional developments. A visit to the hospital confirmed that Jack's wound was healing well with no cause for concern. His discomfort, while annoying and limiting in terms of regular exercise, seemed to be gradually diminishing. He had to visit a psychiatrist to assess the presence of post-traumatic stress following the shooting before SQ would agree on his official return to active duty. The psychiatrist recommended that he take at least a full week off. A week would provide time for the wound to heal as well as keep him in a reduced-stress lifestyle while he was processing being shot. He wanted Jack to consider any triggers it might have tripped as a consequence of the shooting. The fact that the shooting occurred on his birthday, which was the fourth anniversary of the death of his daughter and ex-wife, led the psychiatrist to suggest but not require some ongoing counselling. Kate thought the counselling might be a good idea, but Jack just blew it off. However, he did agree to see this psychiatrist again at the end of the week. He doubted he could find someone of his calibre in the Gatineau-Ottawa area when he returned there.

Officer Daigle called to say that they had enough on the scooter boy to detain him with charges for at least a few days. Damaging police property would do it while they considered attempted murder. He had some IDs on him gleaned from a number of passports and drivers' licences he was carrying. Several of the officers thought he was carrying a revolver, but it didn't turn up. He asked if Jack or Kate had seen a revolver. Kate said they would come in to look at the IDs and go over the incident. After they ended the call, she photographed every angle of the device she had picked up on the street during the attack from scooter boy, in case she had to hand it over to Officer Daigle. Kate drove Jack's SUV. Officer Daigle said they could park in the precinct lot.

15

Officer Daigle greeted them warmly and showed Kate and Jack into his office. He pulled out the three passports and three drivers' licenses. Each was paired with the other for a continuity of identity if required. Kate paired up the drivers' licenses and passport for Marc Brault, a Canadian. Jack said, "That's him. We arrested him in Gatineau when he tried to run Kate over with a motorboat while she was swimming in Meech Lake. I guess we must have released him on bail."

Officer Daigle ran his ID through the Interpol port that brought up his arrest. "He doesn't seem to have had any other run-ins with the law. He studied at MIT on a student visa for two years then got a temporary work permit to work for a company called iBrain. Until now, that's it."

"Two attempted murders — that's a big it," said Jack.

Kate looked at Jack, who nodded. "Officer Daigle, this is what we know so far."

Kate laid out the entire story captured in her memory, with some prompting from Jack. He interjected periodically to clarify the policing angle of the story. Daigle listened quietly and carefully, having asked if he could record it. Jack and Kate agreed. When they finished, Daigle said, "So this Marc Brault could be responsible for at least one murder and three attempts?"

Jack nodded. "Or some variation thereof — clearly he is not working alone — we suspect under instructions and somehow linked to iBrain."

Kate said to Officer Daigle, "While undoubtedly protocol requires me to hand this device over to you, I would prefer to hang on to it to see if we can determine how it functions and if it is linked to the bioengineered microchip embedded in the brain of Dr. Vincent Bernard Taylor."

Officer Daigle picked up his desk phone and hit a speed dial button to advise a respondent he would be there in a moment. "Let's go down to the photo lab and get it thoroughly documented before it goes on a walkabout with you."

As they walked along, Officer Daigle asked Jack how his shoulder was coming along. Jack told him that he had been to the day clinic for a follow-up, and it seemed to be healing well, with no risk of infection so far.

"Then you might want to take a run over to the firing range and do a few rounds with the Glock."

Jack nodded.

"I think a couple of our new recruits are heading over there shortly — I can see if you can get a lift with them. Theoretically, you shouldn't be driving yet."

Jack jokingly responded, "The Mrs. drove us over to the precinct."

Officer Daigle introduced Jack to a couple of young officers, who invited him to join them. Daigle and Kate walked back to his office. "Kate, there's a method to my madness with Jack. A couple of hours at the firing range will help release stress, desensitize him to the sound of gunshots, increase his confidence to actually fire the gun in defense if he has to, and give him something to do. It's hard when someone of his calibre and rank is sidelined."

"Officer Daigle, you have been very thoughtful and kind to us since this whole business started."

"I am sure the SQ would do the same for ours, should there be a need in Canada."

"I hope so," said Kate.

"It will be over soon, and then you can go home, although scooter boy may require us to get to know one another even better over the coming months."

Kate nodded.

She made her way down Massachusetts Avenue in Jack's SUV. She hit his saved MP3 buttons and enjoyed La Chicane, a popular French Canadian band that Jack must like. She imagined Jack and his daughter singing together on road trips like she and her daughter used to do.

She hit the steering wheel in frustration, swearing aloud in her solitude. "Jesus, life is not fair. Not fair for Jack, and not fair for Dr. Taylor." She surprised herself at her outburst. She was normally cool, calm, and collected — too much so — in her personal life, but it worked in her professional life. Perhaps she too was feeling the stress of this case. It certainly was far more volatile than her previous cases. Then again, none of them had started with a dead body. She was usually on a paper hunt that involved the people who produced those bits of paper. She had developed an effective research technique that was getting good results. This case, however, seemed to do a better job of putting her and others in harm's way.

Kate had missed her morning swim and needed a meditation session to get centred again. She made a mental note to be sure to address that deficiency before the day was out.

Now, she had to find a parking spot — a large Annex P sign leapt out in front of her. There was one space left. She wheeled in. Lech had told her he would meet her at reception, since security continued to be over the top in the lab building. An iris and fingerprint detector had been installed, although it was not yet fully operational, since the security staff required training. Three pieces of photo ID were required to get into the building. This was giving his American students grief because they rarely had more than two pieces of photo ID. The international students had passports, which helped. Kate could easily fulfill the ID requirement, but she needed to get the device in as well.

When Lech greeted her at reception, she suggested they go for coffee before heading up to the lab. Kate retrieved the device, placed it on the table between them, then studied Lech very carefully as he examined it. She trusted her assessment of his reaction. He had not seen it before. He did not know what it was. He was curious and ready to assist in analyzing it.

Kate asked how neural implants were usually installed.

"Surgically."

"Could such an implant be implanted remotely?"

"It usually involves a neurological team, even for the most routine procedures."

"What if a bioengineered microchip held the DNA signature of the target? Is it conceivable that this device could be a remote launcher?"

Lech said, "Okay, let's take this thing up to my lab and try to figure it out. If you let me, I will carry it so we can get it past security."

Kate walked into a lab transformed from what she had seen the previous week and prior to the break-in and trashing.

Lech said, "It might be best to try to lift as many DNA markers off the device as possible." He slipped it into a DNA scanner. "Some of the fingerprints may have left enough oil to make it possible to lift DNA signatures. However, they are only as good as the DNA inputs into various databanks. It's a bit like trying to match fingerprints. It's only possible if fingerprint DNA markers have been taken and entered into the databases. The scanner I have in the lab is more robust than most portable hand-held scanners that are not much bigger than your cylinder here."

Kate was drawn into the focus and attention he was applying to this task. He had experienced the destruction of nearly five years of his life's work just days before — probably at the hands of some sinister and very dangerous element that had its origins at MIT. Nevertheless, he was willing to assist her in following the trail back to where the research took a dark turn that may have ultimately led to a murder, several attempted murders, the destruction of his lab, the restructuring of a company, and who knew what else. It was not his specific research, but it was related to the nature of the biology-brain technology interface capability under development to enhance brain function.

While Lech worked, Kate reflected on the series of bright young men who had assisted her in this investigation. The high-stakes game of validating the property of the mind or intellect including knowledge, discoveries, and inventions took her through a forest of know-how, patents, trademarks, copyrights, trade secrets, industrial designs, reports, and publications. It was essential to locate then navigate the correct path to determine the rightful ownership of the intellectual property, thereby enabling her clients to attract financing, enter into partnerships, and commercialize their technology developments. Only then could her clients receive recognition for the contribution of a body of often quite valuable work. In a David and Goliath scenario, her clients were Davids. They were passionate, committed, and driven. Their IP rights had often been bled away by the Goliaths of the scientific community. Kate was successful at restoring the IP to the rightful owners. As she watched Lech work, she realized she had no David in this investigation, and the Goliath out there lacked definition. She had to step back and open her mind. The SQ was paying her, therefore, the SQ was her client — hardly a David. The client simply wanted to know who killed Dr. Vincent Bernard Taylor so the perpetrator could be arrested, charged, convicted, sentenced, and jailed. The why of the crime was only important insofar as it would give her client a motive and therefore a greater opportunity to obtain a conviction. Kate needed the holographic whiteboard projection, a swim, a meditation session, and a David, if only to focus her approach to making her way through the quagmire and over to a grassy knoll on the other side.

"Lech, is there a pool nearby where you swim?"

Lech looked up from his DNA scanner and smiled. "For sure, it's a short walk over to the campus pool, and there's a lap swim starting in a half an hour. Do you want to go?"

"Yes, very much so. I have my swim gear in the car."

"Okay, let's head over, Kate. There's a terrific soup and sandwich place near where you parked where we can grab some lunch afterward." Lech locked the device in a newly installed safe — only he knew the entry method and codes. He grabbed his swim bag, and they headed off, stopping to collect Kate's swim stuff from her car then carrying on to the pool.

The walk to the car was longer than the walk to the pool. Lech led Kate into a massive modern structure, the Zesiger Center, that housed two varsity swimming pools. The sights and sounds from outside were filtered out from this indoor atrium-like swimming environment. They headed off to their respective change rooms and met up a few minutes later to enter lanes side by side and settle into long, invigorating lap swims. Kate could see from under the water that Lech was a skilled and efficient swimmer, well trained in technique.

He slid through the water with very little disturbance on the surface. Observing Lech's ease in the lane beside her was inspiring. Her technique was much more rudimentary and her speed slower, but she was thrilled to work out the stresses of the day. She settled into an aggressive front crawl for one and half kilometres, followed by a one-kilometre smooth, efficient backstroke that pulled out and lengthened her muscles, bones, and joints. The natural light streaming in through massive windows added an aesthetic experience to the physicality of the swimming activity. She wound down a final half kilometre with a medley of strokes before exiting to see Lech also finishing up.

They met in the foyer and headed back to Kate's car to drop off her swim stuff then go for lunch. As they approached the lot, they saw a cordon of yellow police tape, police cruisers, and specialized vehicles surrounding the site. They quickened their pace to get closer but were stopped by the cordon and the scene beyond. In the melée of what looked like a bomb disposal unit, ambulances, and police with automatic rifles at the ready, Kate spotted two familiar faces: Officer Daigle and Lieutenant Jack Johnson. She approached a nearby officer and asked him to let the officer in charge know that she was there.

While waiting, Lech said, "This looks like it has something to do with your car." Kate kept her eyes on the policeman who made his way toward Officer Daigle and spoke briefly. Daigle's gaze surveyed the gathering, landing on Kate. He touched Jack's arm, and he turned to see Kate.

In one smooth motion, Jack strode to her side, seeming to barely touch the road as he moved. He enveloped her in a tight embrace, breathing into her hair. "Thank god you are alright. We thought you were in my car when it blew up."

Kate and Lech looked at each other then simultaneously exclaimed, "Blew up?"

Jack said that the alarm on his car fob had started flashing.

He tried to reach her and left voicemail messages, but no response. "At first I thought maybe you had set it off accidently. I called Dr. Bogdan's number as well but only got his voicemail. Then I got worried, so I called Officer Daigle in case he had been in touch. He said no, but he was on his way to a vehicle explosion on the MIT campus near the neurosciences labs. He picked me up on the way."

Kate said, "We were swimming at the campus pool."

"The only thing left of the vehicle was a license plate that blew off in the explosion and was lying on the ground some distance way. It was my Quebec plate. The first responders had already called it in and ID'ed it. We were in Officer Daigle's car when the ID came in — my ID. Daigle already knew that I had loaned you the car this morning. There isn't much left of it."

"I'm so sorry, Jack."

"Now that I know you are okay, the only thing I really cared about in the car was an old CD that Elizabeth and I made together when she was seven. It was a bunch of our favourite songs. It was always a comfort to listen to it."

Kate's heart sank further. What else could she do to this poor man? In three short days since coming to visit her in Boston, he had been shot and had his car blown up — on his fortieth birthday and the anniversary of the death of his daughter and ex-wife. She was dumbfounded, and her face must have yielded that sentiment.

Jack was at her side to give comfort. "Kate, don't worry about the car. The combination of the SQ and my insurance will take care of it."

Kate was not consoled. "Jack, we don't know if the target was you or me."

"Or both of us," said Jack.

Officer Daigle joined them. "Kate, I am so relieved that you were nowhere near Jack's car exploded. Once again, I will have to get a statement from you. Dr. Bogdan, could you stay around for a bit, as well?"

"Of course," replied Lech.

Kate's heart sank further for Lech Bogdan. She unwittingly kept dragging him into the deceit, corruption, and destructive underside of the otherwise altruistic nature of bioengineering neural research that engaged him.

Officer Daigle started back to the crime scene then turned and walked back to Dr. Bogdan. "I know you have extensive security personnel and measures at your lab, but I want to increase it by placing a couple of our officers there until this situation gets resolved. We will work with your campus security folks." Lech nodded then made a call to his head lab technician to let her know this would be happening.

Once it was established that nobody had perished in the explosion, the investigation proceeded quickly and was wound up by late afternoon. Officer Daigle suggested they go for coffee to discuss next steps.

"I am hoping that you two will agree to our forensics people sweeping your person and belongings. It seems your movements are known practically before you make them. I would love to just lock you up so we can keep you safe. I'm not sure that even sending you back to Canada would give you any greater degree of safety." With a short laugh, he added, "The Boston police might send the SQ a bill after all of this is over — particularly if the perpetrators are Canadian citizens, like the one we have in custody — Marc Brault."

Lech said, "Kate, would you and Jack like to join me at the Soup and Sandwich Kitchen? I think there is still time to get a bite before it closes for the day. It's up the street, so if the police need any of us, we will be nearby."

Kate agreed and asked Jack, who said he was famished. He spoke briefly with Officer Daigle, who nodded. Jack caught up to Kate and Lech, who were headed in the direction of the shop. "I'm hoping they'll be willing to do a large order that I can bring back for all of the officers at the site of the explosion," Jack said.

Lech said. "I often bring back a few orders to the lab, so they should be able to do something."

The owners of The River Run Soup and Sandwich Kitchen were more than accommodating. Mary Lou said her brother was just coming back with a canteen wagon they had to service construction sites. She would restock it and send it over. She took their orders and got to work preparing a fresh batch of sandwiches, perking more coffee, and adding soup, fruit, cakes, and confectionaries. Just as they sat down to eat, Mary Lou's brother came in and loaded up the truck. Jack called Daigle to let him know that the canteen truck was on its way with food. He gave Mary Lou his credit card info so she could bill him for the total amount.

They were all thinking more clearly after food and beverages. Lech suggested to Kate that they go back to the lab to continue the DNA work. Jack would head back to the crime scene.

"The bomb squad guys said there is a bit of debris that may give them something to work with. Did you lose anything of value?" said Daigle.

Jack told Daigle about his daughter's CD and said that otherwise he had cleaned the SUV out rather thoroughly before leaving Gatineau. Luckily, he had brought his briefcase and luggage — only a weekend bag — up to the hotel room.

Jack added that the SUV was getting old, but Elizabeth had liked it. "We spent a lot of time together in it."

Daigle was aware of the loss of Jack's ex-wife and daughter. It had come up on the ID search, including the date. He thought he couldn't imagine losing his own daughters — this guy had had a rough go of it. Now he was finally beginning to move on with his life when he was sent running through a minefield. He had a good feeling about the match with Kate Roarty, despite the age difference, but he wondered if they would both survive this case to enjoy the relationship. His head of bomb squad forensics came over to say they had finished and were ready to go. Daigle told Jack that was all they could do, but he did need to get official statements from both him and Kate. Since Jack was once again without wheels, he could get a lift back with him, and Kate could make her way over with Dr. Bogdan when they were both finished in the lab. He had to get a statement from Bogdan as well.

16

The scanner yielded up a large number of DNA markers on the exterior of the device and a heavy concentration of one DNA signature from the interior. Lech said, "Let's see if we get any matches when we run it through the DNA databases."

In passing, he asked if Kate had ever submitted to a DNA scan. Kate replied, "It's becoming a way of life with all of the intelligence agencies I have visited on this case. I have also submitted several times when researching IP trails."

The exterior revealed two distinct matches: a Marc Brault and a Simon Waterman. "The interior match, that's what the device was programmed to target, was to—" Lech paused, took a deep breath, turned to Kate, and said, "I suppose Kate Roarty is not an uncommon name?"

Kate felt both elevated and deflated; elevated, in that this was another bit of evidence circling around the bioengineered neuro-microchip and deflated that it was another indication that a group of people seemed to want her dead. It also brought her closer to believing that the microchip implant was directly connected to the death of Dr. Taylor.

Lech said, "Let's take this data output with us over to the

Boston police. We can explain it to them, along with giving our statements concerning the explosion. They will find this information useful."

Kate thought it would indeed them more grounds to hold on to Marc Brault and set up an airport security watch for Simon Waterman, although she suspected he was skilled at getting past any kind of security.

As they left the lab, Kate checked her cell phone to find a message from Dr. Bosum asking Kate to call her. Kate's return call got her voice mail, so she left a message suggesting they do a full team call at 6:00 p.m. She would call Guy to see if he could coordinate it. It probably should include the superintendent, since there had been more developments of concern.

Dr. Bogdan and Kate took a cab over to the police precinct and met Jack and Officer Daigle. Lech gave his statement to Officer Daigle while Kate and Jack went off to be scanned for bugs on their person and belongings. The scans turned up nothing; however, the police scans could only detect bugs with metal and plastic. If the trackers were bioengineered, they would remain undetected. They regrouped with Officer Daigle, and Dr. Bogdan and Kate explained the results of the DNA scan on the biocylinder — renamed as such for its content.

For the first time, the cool, affable, easy-going Officer Daigle lost it. "How the hell do we solve a crime where the technology involved in the crime is beyond us?"

Kate said, "Let's not get distracted by the technology. On the one hand, we are dealing with a highly educated cadre of people specialized in bioengineering research targeted at manipulating brain function. On the other hand, we have witnessed genuine thuggery in the approach being used to steer us off track. Officer Daigle, can you let me demonstrate the anatomy of this crime, plugging the car explosion and the shooting of Jack into the larger picture that begins with finding the body of Dr. Vincent Bernard Taylor? I have the software for a holographic rendering projection, but not the hardware on hand."

"Absolutely, be my guest, Kate Roarty, PI. We have both the software and hardware. Officer Manley can show you to the room where we can run it. Lieutenant Johnson and I will be along to join you shortly. If you like, we can conference in your SQ Officer Archambault while we put it together. I just want to get to the bottom of this before our respective intelligence services take it over, leaving us in the position of having to mop up but never knowing what the hell is going on. I think we are only ahead of their entry into the fray by a few hours, if they aren't already there." Kate and Jack nodded in agreement.

"CSEC, CSIS, CBSA, the RCMP, our own Canadian Intelligence Services may have insinuated their organizations into the landscape as well. We already know that the Brits are fully engaged, if not actually the instigators," said Kate.

Jack sent a text to Guy. **Setting up the holographic rendering projection at BP. Need your assist. JJ**

Kate and Jack headed back to their suite at the Charles Hotel for their call with the SQ team. Both were feeling a bit frazzled, wanting to push the case forward while being stymied by distracting elements.

Kate said, "I know using the holographic rendering can be a bit theatrical. Nevertheless, it really helps to see the whole picture. I think we have to be very careful not to lose sight of the fact that a man was murdered. The bioengineered neural microchip implant in Dr. Taylor's brain is an important dimension of the whole picture, but it is not the endgame — at least I don't think it is."

The SQ team call was helpful in bringing everyone up to speed and reintegrating Kate and Jack into the fold. The dynamics that occurred during Jack's brief visit to Boston had frayed their SQ team connection a bit and pulled them in the direction of the Boston police. Jack's superintendent and Dr. Bosum were not at odds with this development — the working relationship appeared to be mutually beneficial. They shared the same concern that the entry of the intelligence services of Canada and the US might prevent them from getting the crime solved before it descended further into a quagmire of international espionage. Dr. Bosum assured the team that she could keep her contact at CSIS reined in, but if other parties within that organization were drawn in, there would be little she could do.

The superintendent was concerned about the battering his Gatineau head of homicide seemed to be receiving at the hands of thugs associated with the case, but he was the first to point out that it was unclear whether Jack was even the target. They were all aware that both he and his SUV might have been unfortunate stand-ins for their contract P.I., Kate Roarty. Kate advised him that the analysis of the interior of the device at the scooter boy crime scene indicated she was DNA target.

Dr. Isabel Bosum told the team that she had been in contact with the University of Ottawa Brain and Mind Research Institute. She contacted a scientist who would be taking a look at the bioengineered microchip implanted in Dr. Taylor's brain. "Dr. Pierre Alarie is aware of research and development in this area. He is quite certain that it hasn't yet moved into the public domain, nor has it even gone to human trials. However, the network is finite, working in no more than a handful of countries including Canada, the US, and the UK. He was rendered silent for a moment when I told him where we found the chip. Dr. Alarie was acquainted with Dr. Taylor, particularly when Dr. Taylor was working at MIT. According to Dr. Alarie, Harvard recruited Dr. Taylor to join their Neuro Discovery Centre that was working primarily on degenerative diseases of the brain — Alzheimer's, Parkinson's, ALS, and Huntington's. The Harvard focus was drug challenges, which frustrated Dr. Taylor. He tried to forge a collaborative relationship between Harvard and MIT, largely to retain the biotechnology interface approach that he was pursuing through bioengineering channels. He seemed to have engendered conflict and confrontation where it hadn't previously existed and finally left to build up an R&D company he was involved in called iBrain. After that, Dr. Alarie lost track of him until he read of his death."

Kate thought, and Dr. Bosum said, "Once again the trail leads back to iBrain."

Guy chimed in, "While our boss man has been dodging bombs and bullets in Boston and the rest of you are bringing science fiction to life, I have been having tea with Clare St. Denis. I check in on her when I am in the area."

Jack interjected, "Guy, you have no reason to be in the area."

"Precisely," Guy continued. "She is a tough one to wear down. I am just trying to build a bit of trust with her at this point. I am certain she knows a lot she isn't telling us. She could very well be implicated in the whole scenario. I want to try her with Big Ben again soon. That dog knows her and knows that cabin."

Kate said, "Be careful you don't put Big Ben in harm's way."

"That is why I haven't taken him there again. By the way, Kate, he knows your name. He wiggles all over when we say your name and give him your sweatshirt."

"My sweatshirt? Oh, let's not even go there."

The superintendent said, "Since you seem to pack a lifetime into each twenty-four hours you are in Boston, can we do a call at nine in the morning, day after tomorrow? That will be about thirty-seven hours from now — should be enough time to experience the next incident, investigate it, and write it up."

"*C'est dr*ôle, mon patron, à la *prochâine, salut.*" The call ended.

Kate sank back onto the sofa while Jack flung himself back on the bed, forgetting about his injured shoulder. He moaned in distress as Kate came to the rescue, helping him to ease the shoulder free. He looked strained and tired as he closed his eyes to rest for a few minutes.

Kate said, "If you want to rest for a bit, I could use the time for a little meditation session. I doubt the music will bother you as it is quite peaceful and soothing."

"*Allez-y*," was all Jack could mumble before falling into a very deep sleep.

The thirty-minute meditation session lengthened to nearly an hour. Kate emerged restored, centred, calmed, relaxed, and very, very hungry. She showered and put on a set of fresh, clean clothing, thinking that she would leave a note for Jack to join her, if he wished, when he awakened. She came out of the bathroom to find him lying calmly with his eyes open and smiling. "Never underestimate the power of a power nap," he said.

"…and a power sleep," Kate said. "You were in a deep sleep for almost an hour and a half — hungry?"

"Starving — let's go grab something in the dining room."

Jack leapt off the bed and said, "Give me five minutes."

He was in the shower before she could reply, emerging exactly five minutes later, fresh, clean, in a change of clothes, and raring to go. He stopped before going out the door, turned back, picked up the holstered revolver, slipped it gently over his bad shoulder, and Kate helped him draw his sports jacket on over it. As they walked to the elevator, she wished they were going out to walk along the river then head up some side streets to find a little, quiet, romantic bistro. She knew better than to even propose it. They had enjoyed eight safe hours. Best not to push the envelope.

17

The dining room was moderately full. The maître d' found them a quiet table in an alcove by the window, where they could see the lights glistening across the water of the nighttime river and also easily survey most of the dining room. They ordered a bottle of white wine before even deciding what they would eat.

"I probably shouldn't, since it might render the antibiotics ineffective against fighting infection, but I think my brain needs the gentle wash of alcohol." They clicked glasses before taking their first sip, and Kate almost choked and set hers down. Jack followed her gaze to two men about his age, deeply engaged in conversation.

"Do we know them?" he asked.

"I do. They are Dr. Giorgio Beretta and Claude Mason."

"These two men together, here — one on a meteoric career advancement who now heads up iBrain, and the other whose brain is mired in British intelligence."

"Remind me never to underestimate you in any way, Jack Johnson."

He smiled and said, "Your wine is getting warm, Kate

Roarty. We can probably get through our dinner without them noticing you. I really do think we need to eat before taking on any more excitement."

The waiter returned, and they both ordered farm greens and squash soup to address their immediate hunger but not assault it. Kate ordered stuffed, braised cabbage that included farro, porcini, chestnuts, tomato sauce, and stracciatella. Jack went with a more robust paprika-marinated swordfish garnished with smoked squid, red curry squash, Brussels sprouts, and ginger. Kate told him that Giorgio had said Rialto's was a very fine Italian restaurant.

While Jack thoroughly enjoyed his meal, Kate ate her dinner because she was hungry. Jack motioned for the waiter and gave him a note directing him to Dr. Beretta's table. Kate gave him a puzzled look. "I invited them over for coffee and dessert."

Dr. Beretta read the note handed to him by the waiter. He looked over in Kate's direction and smiled broadly when he caught her attention. He spoke to Claude Mason then nodded to the waiter, who returned to Jack and Kate and said, "If you will give me a moment, I will set up a larger table where you will be more comfortable with four people." Kate and Jack nodded. They moved over to the new table. It added to the feeling of neutral territory.

Kate introduced everyone. Jack and Giorgio acknowledged having previously met. Giorgio said, "And the woman who knows us all, Kate Roarty, P.I."

"Gentlemen shall we have coffee, dessert, and a digestif?"

Giorgio smiled abundantly, while Claude nodded in acquiescence. Jack caught everyone by surprise, including Kate, when he said, "That depends. I'm not keen on taking any part of a meal with someone who tried to kill me or Kate by shooting at me and blowing up my car."

Giorgio sputtered in alarm, "You don't think we would do that, do you?"

"I don't know. You tell me, Dr. Beretta, or perhaps your friend here can enlighten us."

Claude spoke in French to Jack. "*Desolé*, Jack Johnson. *Peut être je peut t'assister. C'est mon travail, comme toi, mon ami.*" Jack looked furious. "I can agree on the work but not on any friendship. There is a murder and three attempted murders on two people. We are going to lay charges against those responsible."

"I am sorry you think I may be part of that circle. My job will be even greater to get you to trust me. I am willing to take on that challenge. Are you willing to at least consider that I may be trustworthy?"

Jack did not reply; rather, he just stared at Claude Mason with simmering furry.

To break the tension Kate interjected, "Gentlemen, shall we order?"

A bit deflated, the group decided to give over to Giorgio's expertise in Italian cuisine. He ordered coffees, bitter digestifs, and a small platter of cheeses and bite-sized fruits — berries, grapes, and almonds, that seemed to please all four of them.

Claude spoke again. Kate had forgotten the charming tenor tone to his voice.

"Lieutenant Johnson, this entire situation is a mess. In part, that is why I am here. I, like all of the other lads who were under Michael Pepper's tutelage during graduate school at Cambridge, contributed to iBrain in the early stages. It was Vincent's brainchild, so to speak. We are hoping that under Giorgio's leadership, the firm will get back on track, the sinister elements will be exposed and expunged, and the research can move ahead. The investigative work that Kate has done is already helping Giorgio to plan a navigational path through the various iterations of the firm. We think that by following the IP trail, we will be able to identify where the sinister developments of the R&D broke off, where those applications are being worked on, and who is doing the work. It's very dangerous — we don't want to lose him too. We have been in touch with our colleagues, Matti Toivenen and Kiran Patel. Kate, I think you are at least acquainted with them and have been in contact. They too made small investments in iBrain during the early stages, and although like me they have pretty much written off getting any financial return, their expertise may prove invaluable."

Kate nodded and at the same time noted that Jack was relaxing. She was relieved. Cool heads needed to prevail if they were going to make headway quickly before anyone else got hurt and an army of secret service agents came crawling all over the investigation.

"Mr. Mason, how many agents does the British Secret Service have in Canada and the US on this case, or two cases, however you wish to look at it?"

Claude paused, looked directly at Jack and answered, "Three besides me. There is one in Gatineau/Ottawa and two here in the Boston area."

Giorgio blurted out in very restrained manner, "Jesus, Claude you didn't tell me that."

Kate spoke very quietly. "Claude, can you tell us the story?" All remained silent, patiently waiting. The brandy digestif was taking effect, relaxing and calming all four of them.

"I don't know the whole story. I don't think anybody does. The British Intelligence Service recruited me for my expertise in neuro bioengineering. I wanted to finish my doctoral studies before going to work for them. MI6 was reluctant, but GCHQ was willing to wait if I agreed to perform a few minor tasks while at MIT. In fact, I was on the GCHQ payroll for most of a year without having any requirements placed on me. Vincent and I were growing closer, personally and professionally. I had not told him about my involvement with the British Intelligence Service. He believed I would join him in building the R&D at iBrain.

"Vincent became heavily engaged in raising funds to feed the voracious burn rate of the growing company. His focus was the R&D and the money needed to keep it going. He made the classic mistake of small science companies that grow rapidly without any return on their investments. He was trying to be the CEO, CFO, and chief of R&D. An international fundraising round reached deep into financing capabilities beyond Vincent's scope of analysis. Some very sinister elements stepped up to the plate, seducing the young firm with abundant and readily available cash. GCHQ picked up on it through their ongoing money laundering surveillance. They came to me with a plan to infiltrate iBrain as an investor so they could more readily navigate the interior landscape of the company. I wanted to tell Vincent and directly involve him — GCHQ would not agree to the disclosure of its involvement. I was caught between a rock and a hard place. It was leaked to the senior echelons of MIT that I was an MI6 agent. Karen Palmer was connected in high places in American academia and facilitated the leak, thus keeping the spotlight off GCHQ and limiting the knowledge of my role to a very few. For a short time, MIT let it unfold. I was just months away from completing my doctoral work. Then the dean of bioengineering called me in and told me I had to leave immediately. There was no discussion about the details, but when I tried to buy time just to complete the application trials for my research, he said if I wanted Vincent's status to remain as it was with MIT, where iBrain was enjoying a high level of credibility, it would be in everybody's best interest if I quietly left as soon as possible.

"When I returned to our apartment, a package was waiting for me with a first-class ticket to London and two sets of keys for a car and a flat in Cheltenham. Clearly, the immediate future was out of my control. The flight left in twenty-two hours. I put a bottle of wine to chill and prepared a special dinner. When Vincent came home, we enjoyed the dinner, made love, and I told him everything. He was furious and devastated. He left with Big Ben and didn't return before it was time for me to leave for the airport."

Giorgio interjected, "Big Ben?"

With near comic relief Claude, Jack, and Kate responded simultaneously, "The dog."

"I took the flight to London and continued on the train to Cheltenham. We were out of touch for some time. At GCHQ I began to learn how deeply iBrain had been infiltrated and compromised. However, the good side of the work, so to speak, continued seemingly unaffected by the growing sinister element. In the UK, iBrain appeared to be a dormant firm with a few researchers and little of consequence going on. The bone fide company was thriving with labs in the US, Canada, Italy, Denmark, and India — yes, all of the locations to where the lads had dispersed. As well, there were several more laboratories operating under the umbrella of iBrain but beyond the administrative reach of the structure that Vincent had established. The stem cell work, the neuro bioengineering platforms and robotics micro surgery techniques, were converging into a very exciting suite of treatment for Alzheimer's, Parkinson's, stroke recovery, and a whole host of maladies of the brain, where altering targeted brain functions from within would dramatically improve quality of life. A very tiny microchip containing programming as complex as anything required to launch a space ship into orbit was designed to hold a stem cell biomass grown from healthy DNA of the target patients. There would be no need for accompanying medications; the stem cell biomass of the host would mitigate rejection. The performance of the bio microchip could be tweaked remotely from a master external hard drive control centre. It could even be radically changed as bodily performances controlled by the brain were repaired, adapted, bypassed, or stimulated from different healthy areas of the brain. The work was exciting and moving very fast. The brilliance and mastery was beautiful in its simplicity. The scope for refinement and new development seemed almost infinite." He paused to sip some water.

"Claude, please continue," urged Kate in a gentle, firm, encouraging tone.

"A couple of the investors with lucrative Saudi and Qatari backing brought two small companies into the consortium. One was a nanotechnology company that integrated well with our bioengineering research team, the other was a southwest US R&D firm specializing in miniaturized unmanned drone technology; military applications had been its bread and butter. These guys were a band of cowboys — all highly intelligent, newly minted PhDs and decorated ex-military types having done tours in Iraq and Afghanistan. The company's stated objective was to miniaturize and power up all unmanned drone technology. Its slogan was *The final frontier: the human brain*. Culturally, these guys were from another planet, but they knew their stuff. Their imaginations appeared boundless, and they added a certain buzz to the consortium. As they learned about the development of the bioengineered microchip that was being designed to control and stimulate brain functions, they saw a role within the suite of converging technologies folded into iBrain. These guys were interested in three applications: to physically launch and control the direction of the chip, implant it remotely without any surgical intervention, and then to stimulate the thought processes of the host brain. Despite their brilliance, these cowboys equated brain function with thought process. Ayman al-Sawahari, successor to Osama bin Laden, was still alive when they first joined iBrain. They actually did a presentation that demonstrated the remote launch, control, and implant of the bioengineered microchip. It connected with its target host by DNA attraction, then, once successfully implanted, brain images were sent to the chip that influenced the host's action to flee, surrender, or suicide. Quite glibly, they believed that the untowards of the world, as they define them, could be dispatched quickly and permanently, thus eliminating the necessity to create vast armies to battle it out."

Kate said, "Claude, this company is CCTech — Cerebral Control Technology Inc. — and they got their startup funds from the US Defense Advanced Research Projects Agency, or DARPA."

"Yes."

She added, "CCTech has consistently skirted the edge of intellectual property integrity. Please continue, we are beginning to get the picture."

"GCHQ promoted me to director as compensation for pulling me out of MIT before I finished my doctoral work. I was immediately put in charge of the iBrain file and conducting surveillance on the CCTech activity. I took a wide berth around Vincent to give him time and distance to work through his personal and professional approach to me and what I had become. He never contacted me. I understood he had gone up to his mother's place in the Gatineau for a while then returned to Boston and resumed his work. Admittedly, I used my position to keep an eye on him — to protect him from the CCTech guys, if necessary."

"Did the CCTech reach spread rapidly throughout the various lab sites of iBrain?" asked Kate.

"Yes, you could say they went viral, but their success rate in gathering a committed following to their cause was slow and small in numbers. Most of the Canadian and European researchers were ethics-bound and unmovable. CCTech threw a lot of money out there, and some of it did stick. They fanned out through their networks in International Defense R&D, Science, and Technology. There was uptake in Canada, the UK, India, and Finland, as well as the US. Kiran and Matti kept an eye on developments in India and Finland, and I watched the UK and Canada. A lot of money that passed through CCTech was thrown at fuelling the R&D, tilting it in the direction of the CCTech objectives. After the initial euphoria wore off, many of the principal investigators in most of the labs became wary of the CCTech cowboys and pulled back. However, the collaboration between bio-engineering, nanotechnology, and unmanned drone technology was already well integrated, and was, shall we say, running amuck."

Jack interrupted, "Claude, are you familiar with a young ex-student by the name of Marc Brault?"

Claude nodded. "A CCTech recruit from the MIT/iBrain lab. He was a very bright, promising mind out of Quebec who had lots of good lab experience through several private sector members of BioQuebec. He was from a working class family with few resources to support his studies in the US. CCTech dazzled him with a handsome paycheque, and he bit. I understand SQ has him in custody — probably saved his life. I think the cowboys were prepared to sacrifice him in order to put a halt to Kate's investigation."

Kate said, "Ah, so my hunch that an unmanned drone knocked out the boat trying to ram me at Meech Lake was accurate."

"Yes, Kate, my man, Simon Waterman, was trying to intercept Marc Brault when all of that business came down. Thank God, you are a skilled swimmer. We think Brault's assignment was to take you out. They probably figured he could navigate the cultural landscape of West Quebec more easily, being native-born and raised, but Marc is a scientist gone astray, not a killer. It's too bad he has got himself in so much trouble."

Jack said, "It will be a very long time before he sees the inside of a science lab again. The SQ released him on bail. He crossed the border and tried to finish off his assignment, this time on a scooter." A slight look of surprise crossed Claude's face, suggesting he was unaware of this development. "He drove the scooter into a police cruiser — it earned him a free pass to jail."

Giorgio said incredulously, "This sounds like the Wild West."

"Well, you are in America," said Jack.

Giorgio continued, "It gives us a greater understanding of what has been happening. It brings us closer to who may have killed Vincent and why and the role the chip implanted in his brain may have played in his death."

Kate said, "We need to stop CCTech, and the best way to do it is to bring into play the weight of intellectual property protection in many jurisdictions, within the US and Canada as well as internationally. These cowboys have transgressed legislation governing copyright, trademarks, patents, and trade secrets, as well as committed assault, attempted murder, and possibly murder. Going the IP route isn't sexy, but it carries weight."

Claude said, "It is this approach that led the British Intelligence Service into trying to recruit you on this investigation. We thought that, given your proven track record in restoring intellectual property rights to their rightful developers, you stood a better chance of taking CCTech out than any of us did. SQ already demonstrated the smarts to hire you. CSEC had nothing but glowing reports on your successes."

Kate swallowed the reference that confirmed she was also under CSEC surveillance and pressed on. "We could probably stop CCTech in its tracks with an arm's length list of charges. If we could have each individual principal investigator within CCTech charged, we may be able to make arrests with huge bails set for release, embargo their labs, and have passports seized. That could tie up their cash and mobility for a very long time — perhaps ultimately bankrupt the company. The Saudis and Qataris would likely run for cover when the media gets a hold of the story, thus drying up CCTech's financing gravy train."

Jack dialled a phone number, reaching Officer Daigle. "Hey, Daggy, Marc Brault is still in custody, right?" He listened to the reply then hung up and told the others what Daigle had said. "A couple of heavyweights with a big-time lawyer tried to spring him this afternoon, but it will take at least a week to even schedule a bail hearing."

Kate refocused the group back to the account from Claude Mason. "Gentlemen, it is very late. We all have a lot to digest. Claude, thank you for being so forthcoming — it is not typical of an employee of any intelligence service to provide such a helpful account. Shall we reconvene for breakfast, when Claude will tell us the real reasons British Intelligence became so interested in iBrain?"

Giorgio looked up in surprise, first at Kate and then to Claude, and he knew Kate had seized the upper hand and would not relinquish it until this investigation was concluded.

Kate and Jack walked silently to the elevator, ascended, and continued their quiet contemplation. As the door clicked behind them in the privacy of their suite, they embraced then quickly yielded to aggressive, passionate sex. The only restraint they exercised was caution not to aggravate or further injure Jack's shoulder. Their sex was self-assured and vigorous. The tentativeness they had experienced in their earlier lovemaking had given way to a confident, consuming eagerness in the exploration of their bodies. Their attraction to one another sprang into an intense, all-consuming gratification that left them spent, enveloped in one another's arms and slipping off into a calm and welcome sleep.

18

The chiming of his cell awakened Jack early from a deep sleep. He picked it up on the second ring in hopes that Kate could continue sleeping. It was Officer Daigle. "Hey, did I wake you?"

"Yeah."

"I have the day off since you guys made me work through the weekend. I can pick you up to go car-hunting, if you like."

Jack sat up, surprised and pleased with the offer. "Okay, what time?"

"Meet me out front in a half hour — I'll bring you a coffee. What do you take?"

"Just cream, oh, and a very large cup."

"Right, ciao."

Jack kissed a sleeping Kate very gently then headed to the shower.

He left a note propped on his pillow for Kate then quietly slipped out into the hallway, shrugging on his coat as he waited for the elevator. He forgot his gun and started back, then reconsidered and left it, since he would be with Officer Daigle.

Despite Jack being a few minutes early at the entrance to the Charles Hotel, Daggy was already there. Jack eased into the front seat beside him, gratefully accepted the coffee, took a sip and said, "Great."

"Good, I thought since you would probably be screwing your brains out all night, you would need some coarse stuff to launch you into the day."

Jack smiled and laughed. He was comfortable with the police fraternity banter. The gals could dish it up just as well. They even embarrassed him at times.

"New or used?"

"What?"

"Do you want a new or used car, truck SUV, ATV, Harley, bicycle…"

Jack laughed again. "I haven't thought about it. Big. Yeah, maybe new. I've never bought a new vehicle. Usually fixed up something promising — made it like new."

"Okay, so you'll let the factory do it this time."

Jack liked that concept.

"Big. SUV or truck, self-drive or driverless?"

"SUV."

"One of my cousins has a Land Cruiser dealership. He sells other Toyota SUVs as well. Want to take a look?"

"Okay."

Daggy pulled a U-turn, rounded the corner, and sped out into traffic.

"She's great."

"Yeah, drives well."

"I mean Kate, you ass. Drink your coffee."

"She got any kids?"

"Yeah, two, a boy and a girl, both in their twenties."

"Good relationship?"

"I think so. I haven't met them. The girl is in her mid-twenties, lives out in BC. The boy is younger — lives in Toronto. They talk on the phone — especially the girl. The boy, not so much. There might be a bit of defiance there, but Kate never complains. She always speaks of them with great pride. Seems the dad left when the kids were very young. They divorced, and Kate raised them, pretty much on her own."

"They'll be good for you."

"Hey, man. We haven't got that far not anywhere near."

"You will."

"Let's keep focused on the new vehicle."

"Why?"

"It's easier."

"Okay."

"New wheels it is then."

They drove onto the lot. Within two hours, Jack had signed the purchase contract for a matte gold exterior/black interior Land Cruiser. The standard feature package seemed to include every bell and whistle he could imagine. He wanted larger mud flaps and running boards that could be installed for pick-up the following day. As they drove off, Jack remarked on the amazing sound system. "I feel like a twenty-year-old. Can I buy you one of those humungous American breakfasts somewhere?"

"It's a deal."

Within fifteen minutes, they were walking into Mike's Diner on Washington Street, a couple of blocks from Massachusetts Avenue.

The staff, as well as a few patrons, greeted Daggy warmly. They took a booth with a view of the street outside and most of the interior of the restaurant. The owner came over. "Hey, Daggy — you looking for somebody?"

"No, Ricky, I'm off duty, just bringing my friend here to the best breakfast diner in Boston."

"Absolutely. So what can I get you, or will you just trust me?"

"We'll trust you, Ricky, and the big guy needs coffee

right away."

Jack smiled, said thanks and leaned back, relaxed, with a twinkle restored to his eyes. "Reminds me of the kind of places we had in the small towns around where I grew up."

Daggy said, "Jack, I've been looking at your Gatineau on Google Earth. It seems to be all hills, trees, lakes, and rivers, and probably a lot of snow in winter. No wonder you don't have many murders. There's hardly anybody to kill."

"Oh, there are people, a half a million permanent residents and a couple million tourists. They manage to get themselves into enough trouble. The offspring — my generation — are dispersed across the country, but they love to come home. When they do, old family tensions arise, skeletons rattle in closets, drugs are sought to mollify nerves, lots of drinking happens, and some scores get settled. Hunting season and boating season offer up some 'accidents,' and the rest are clearly identified murders — about a half dozen a year. It stays relatively constant." He sipped his coffee then said, "You should come up, bring your family to ski or swim whichever season you prefer. We would make you feel welcome."

Daggy smiled and said, "You know, there are those police exchange programs. I could swap with someone in the SQ and go for a school year. That could be a real experience for the whole family."

Jack nodded. "Daggy, I would be happy to help you put it together if you decide you really want to come up to Quebec. We do speak French as a first language in Quebec."

"*Bien sûr, mon ami. J'aimerais travailler en français toujours pendant un an,*" said Daggy.

Jack threw his head back in laughter. "Officer Daigle of the Boston police, you never cease to amaze me."

Ricky put two massive breakfast plates down in front of the two men. "I see you enjoy Daggy as much as we do. Men like him don't stand on every street corner. My boy slipped off the rails in his early teens. Daggy cared and made a difference in his life, and now my boy is making a difference in the lives of many others."

"Hey, Daggy, we could use that kind of expertise with our youth in Gatineau. These young guys are the ones being lured into the cross-border drug scene."

The two men wolfed down a breakfast filled with nutrition, taste, and the sense of comfort food but no grease. While they ate, Daggy told Jack about the food in this restaurant. "The eggs are whipped whites served in benedict style, the meat is natural ham and sausages that Ricky's father makes exclusively for the restaurant. The berry medley is what his cousins on Martha's Vineyard grow and ship twice a week to the restaurant. The fruits change with the season and are frozen for the winter months. The fruits and vegetables are grown with tender, loving care — no pesticides and no rapid, forced production. Ricky's wife installed a summer kitchen at home, where she bakes all of the whole-grain breads made from natural grains they ship in from cottage farmers in the region. That way she can work for the restaurant and be home for the kids. Ricky wanted to make good food available to common folk. These prices are affordable, and if a customer eats only one meal a day, it will have been a healthy one. He opens at six in the morning and closes at four. While he misses breakfast with the family, he's always home in time to make dinner and sit down with his wife, children, and whomever else happens to be there. Bring Kate for lunch one day."

"She will like it — I'm sure. This place is inspiring."

Jack's thoughts drifted to Kate. Daggy studied him. "She is right for you, Jack. I didn't know either of you a week ago. This business makes us a good study of character. Unlike many of my colleagues, I haven't become cynical about humanity. The goodness shines out even more against the underbelly of what we see people do to one another. You are both good people who are falling in love. In the midst of getting shot, the car explosion, deceit, and deception, you are navigating your way. I'm enjoying watching it. As my Marny would say, 'Oh Daggy, another trek of vicarious pleasure for you. Your girls are going to grow up to be hopeless romantics.'"

"Speaking of Kate—"

"Were we?"

"Yes, we were, my man."

"Daggy, switching to our jobs — even though it's your day off — we need to meet with some guys key to the developments in the case."

"Okay, but first, we need a session at the shooting range. Are you game?"

"Yes, but I didn't bring my revolver. It's locked up in the safe back at the hotel."

Daggy flipped down his credit card to pay the bill, and before Jack could protest, he said, "You get the next one. We can swing round to the hotel to pick up your gun — it's only a few minutes out of the way." Daggy waited in his SUV at the entrance to the Charles Hotel while Jack ran up to the room.

The door was ajar. He stood for a moment and listened but heard nothing. He entered, checked all of the rooms, then strode into the bedroom, where the closet housing the safe was located — the safe was open, the gun was gone, and so was Kate. He hit Daggy's number on speed dial and told him what he had found.

"I'm calling for backup," replied Daigle.

Nothing else appeared disturbed in the room. A few other items they had put in the safe were still there. Kate's swim bag was on the floor. He checked inside it; the bathing suit was wet. As he looked around, he could see that the room had been cleaned and the note that he had left for her on the pillow was folded and sitting on the kitchen counter. As he looked around, he surmised that she had returned from her swim, happened in on someone, perhaps initially thought that he had returned and then ... only she could fill in the rest.

He heard his name being called by a familiar voice. It was Officer Daigle.

"What've we got, Jack?"

Jack related what he had found and didn't find.

"Did you try Kate on her cell?'"

"No, I figure she would have alerted me if she could, and I don't want her cell to ring in case she can't retrieve it to silence it."

"Send her a text message."

Jack did so immediately. In hotel suite, safe open, you ok?

They waited — no reply.

"Let's use the GPS to track her location." Jack reached D'Angelo on their respective cell phones. He was in the station in Gatineau.

"D'Angelo, we need to trace Kate's cell."

"Oh, she didn't lose it, did she?"

"No," said Jack.

"You guys had a fight?"

"D'Angelo!"

"*Desolé, patron.* I am on it. Give me a few minutes."

Guy came on the line, and Jack filled him in.

D'Angelo came back with, "One Bennett Street, Cambridge. That's the Charles Hotel."

"Can you try to isolate the signal so we know where in the hotel she is, or at least where her cell is?"

At that moment, Mr. Mendoza, the hotel assistant, manager tapped on the door.

Officer Daigle greeted him. "Oh good, you are here. Mrs. Roarty is missing. Can we check the hotel cameras? We want the entrances locked down until we find her or determine she isn't in the building." He gave the same instructions via digicom radio to the police officers already on site.

Jack said, "Get someone to check on Dr. Giorgio Beretta. No, wait — he's on the same floor as this suite." Mr. Mendoza picked up the hotel phone and had his room number in an instant: 946.

At that moment, two more officers arrived outside the room. Officer Daigle requested the service sidearm from one of them, with a brief explanation. He handed it to Jack. Both officers were also carrying rapid-fire rifles. Jack and Officer Daigle proceeded down the hall to room 946. Jack pressed his ear to the door — nothing. Neither Officer Daigle nor Jack was wearing a flak jacket. They stood on either side of the door and knocked — nothing. Mr. Mendoza came down the hall with his master sensor card and handed it to Daigle. Jack and Daigle looked at each other. Daigle passed the card across the door entry mechanism. It clicked open. Jack's cell vibrated. He looked at it in hopes that it was Kate. He waved Daigle on. They entered and found Dr. Beretta apparently asleep or unconscious in the sofa chair. Jack checked his pulse. It was strong. Daigle called for an ambulance, while Jack laid him on his back on the sofa and checked his mouth and airway. Breathing, although a bit weak, was present. There did not appear to be any obstructions. He loosened Giorgio's clothing and elevated his legs. By the time the paramedics arrived, Jack had completed all of the standard first aid procedures. He reported all to the paramedics, who carefully examined all around his head, neck, and chest for injuries. There were none.

The paramedics slipped him onto the stretcher, strapped him in, and headed out. Officer Daigle digicomradioed his team to update him and instructed a cruiser to lead the ambulance to the hospital then provide a guard for Dr. Beretta until they got to the bottom of what had happened to him. He concluded his instructions with, "This is a possible attempted homicide. The perpetrators may be very dangerous."

Officer Daigle and Jack checked over Dr. Beretta's suite very carefully. It was identical to the one Jack and Kate occupied. Nothing appeared out of order. His laptop was open on the desk, and two cell phones sat beside it. All were password-locked.

One cell was an iPhone and the other a BlackBerry, and they found a little Nokia in his suit jacket pocket that was not locked. He seemed to keep it for communication with four contacts: Mama, Luca, Mario, and Renata. Jack smiled — probably all family in Italy. While Jack was looking at it, it started to ring, displaying the name Mario. Jack answered, and a voice speaking Italian said something that Jack could not understand. Jack tried responding in French, but the voice answered in English. "Who are you?"

"Uh, my name is Lieutenant Jack Johnson. I am a police officer. Who are you?"

"Has something happened to my brother? I am Mario Beretta."

"Mr. Beretta, I must be cautious. Can you describe your brother to me?"

Mario did so quite exactingly.

"Did he call you recently?"

"Yes, last night."

"Where was he calling you from?"

Mario sounded exasperated, "I don't know — he had gone to Boston on business — I thought he was still there."

Jack searched his mind for yet another identifier to confirm the connection before he allowed any information. "Mr. Beretta, where did your brother obtain his PhD?"

"Johns Hopkins. Please tell me is my brother okay?" Jack then told him everything he knew about Giorgio's condition and the hospital he had been taken to. He passed on both his and Officer Daigle's cell phone numbers, explaining that he was a police officer from Canada, while Daigle was with the Boston police force. He would call as soon as they knew more about Giorgio's condition. Then, just before hanging up, on a hunch he asked Mario if Giorgio had mentioned the names of anyone he was going to see in Boston. "He mentioned some woman named Kate, Irish last name, that was going to help him with some IP issues with one of his research companies."

"Kate Roarty?"

"Yes that's it — that is the name."

"And the name of the company?" asked Jack.

"iBrain — his problem child that he has a share in — it belonged to a buddy of his who died recently. Some American company had been giving iBrain a lot of grief. Giorgio was hoping to get it sorted out on this trip."

"Thank you very much, Mr. Beretta, you have been very helpful. We will call you as soon as there is any change in your brother's condition."

19

Officer Daigle and Jack started for the door when Kate walked through it holding the Glock out front, police entry style. As soon as she saw it was Jack and Daggy, she dropped her hand to her side. "Jesus, guys, what are you doing in Dr. Beretta's room?"

"What are you doing holding a drawn gun in Dr. Beretta's room?" said Officer Daigle.

"Looking for the intruder," said Kate.

Officer Daigle raised a hand then spoke into his digi-comradio. "Kate Roarty has been located but the lockdown continues. We may still be looking for armed and dangerous suspects. Nobody is to be let in or out of the building until I give the word." Kate and Jack listened to a series of barked acknowledgements delivered back over the digi-comradio service and Daigle following up with a couple of his team members to make certain everyone heard his updated instructions.

Kate told them, "When I returned from swimming, the door to the suite was unlocked and slightly ajar. I entered to find a uniformed cleaning lady in the bedroom who said hello and continued her work. I felt uneasy. Mr. Mendoza had described the cleaning practice when they moved our room to this concierge floor. I recall him saying that the cleaning staff had been instructed never to leave doors to the hallway ajar, because it's too easy for someone to slip in, steal something, and leave quickly undetected. I told her I needed to change her clothes. The woman said she could leave and come back or go and clean the kitchen. I told her the kitchen would be fine. I closed the door, unlocked the safe, and retrieved the gun then exited the room. I saw the woman disappearing out the fire exit door at the end of the hall, and I gave chase. I followed down four or five flights when the woman exited the stairwell onto the floor. By the time I got there, the floor was empty. I checked the stairwell all the way down to the ground but didn't want to exit into the lobby carrying the Glock. I heard sirens, but I wasn't sure if they were from Boston Street activity or involving the hotel."

Jack interjected, "Was your cell on, Kate?"

"I turned it off while I was tracking the intruder."

"We thought that an intruder might have kidnapped you. Kate, may I have my gun now?"

"Of course." She handed Jack the Glock. She sensed his stress, annoyance, and relief. "Jack, Officer Daigle, I am sorry that I didn't find a way to communicate with you. It all happened so fast. I am so accustomed to operating alone."

"That is why SQ hired you, Kate, and for your expertise in IP forensics. You found Dr. Dr. Taylor because you were out on the lake swimming alone in an electrical storm."

Officer Daigle defused the tension. "Kate, the important thing is you are safe — Dr. Beretta did not fare so well."

They filled Kate in on how they had found Dr. Beretta. Kate said, "You know, your description is similar to the way we found Dr. Taylor — except, of course, Dr. Taylor was dead."

"And whatever happened to Dr. Beretta could have been your fate as well, Kate."

Kate nodded. "How is he?"

"No change as far as we know."

"I have a thought I would like to run by Dr. Bosum," said Kate.

Jack explained who Dr. Bosum was to Officer Daigle while Kate made the call. Dr. Bosum picked up on the second ring.

"Kate, how are you?"

"Looking forward to seeing you soon. In the meantime, are you in your lab, or more importantly, do you have Dr. Taylor's autopsy report at hand?"

"Yes to both questions," said Dr. Bosum.

"Was there any kind of analgesic or sedative in Dr. Taylor's toxicology report?" asked Kate.

"Yes, there were both, but only traces."

"Can you give me the details, or more importantly, can we put you in touch with the medical team that is treating Dr. Beretta here in Boston?" Kate looked at Jack and Daigle. Daigle took the phone.

"Dr. Bosum, this is Officer Daigle of the Boston police. I will get in touch with the hospital and advise the attending physician that you will be calling. In case there is a miss, is this the best number to reach you at?"

Dr. Bosum said, "Yes, very good then, and it's a pleasure to speak to you. Jack and Kate have spoken very highly of you and your team."

Dr. Bosum gave Officer Daigle a bit of time to reach the attending physician, then she was on the phone to Massachusetts General Hospital. — she noted that is was the same hospital Jack had gone to —She asked for a Dr. Sanchez in Trauma, who was expecting her call. When they connected, Dr. Bosum gave him a brief introduction concerning Dr. Vincent Bernard Taylor and the findings captured in the toxicology report from his autopsy. She said, "For now, all you need to know is that these two cases may be related, and the first victim is dead."

They compared notes on their respective toxicology reports and found two substances in common: an analgesic and a sedative. Dr. Sanchez said, "Dr. Beretta's condition was so perplexing that we did a brain scan. We found a tiny microchip implanted in the medulla oblongata section of his brain."

Dr. Bosum said, "The same as our Dr. Taylor," and she thought but did not say *Big Ben*. "We think this microchip is bioengineered and was implanted without Dr. Beretta's knowledge or permission. It may have an external activation mechanism that we are still investigating — in fact, your unconscious man there may know as much as anyone about what we are dealing with — he is a research scientist, so saving him could save him."

Dr. Sanchez thanked her and hung up with an invitation to call back with any further questions.

Dr. Bosum closed the loop with Officer Daigle and Kate then spoke briefly with Jack, who had just gotten off the phone with D'Angelo, advising him that the GPS placed both phones — Kate's and Jack's — side by side at the Charles Hotel.

"Daggy, may I call you Daggy when you are on duty?" asked Kate.

"We had better do Officer Daigle when other officers are around."

"I am so sorry to once again ruin your day off."

"We had a good morning. You are okay, and if Dr. Beretta pulls through, it will all have been worth it."

"Did Jack mention the meeting we wanted to have with you?"

"He tried to, but I kept putting him off."

"One of the people who would have been there is Dr. Beretta. The other is Claude Mason, a director at British Intelligence — the GCHQ people."

"Oh Jesus, he's here in Boston?"

"Yes, with more of his merry band of spies."

"Christ, we'll be crawling with CIA and FBI in no time," said Daigle

"Not to mention our guys — RCMP, CSIS, CSEC, CBSA," added Jack.

"Look, fellows," said Kate. "This isn't my thing, running around with a gun, people getting shot at, run down, car blown up. I have to refocus on what I do well. The intellectual property theft can bring them down. I can do the IP work, and you guys — all of the forces that want to get in on it — can do the round-up. I need my cyber-geek network and my own command centre — a reliable, super-high-speed encrypted system — to move on this as quickly as possible. I have that at home. With seventy-two hours of solid focus and concentration, I can track the route the IP has taken. I have a hunch that if CCTech tumbles, the rest of it will fall into place. I have to go home — now."

"Would tomorrow morning be soon enough?" asked Jack.

"Early morning before dawn, before rush hour, before these insanities are at it again," said Kate.

Officer Daigle looked at Jack. "I'll get my cousin on it."

"On what?"

Jack replied, "I bought a new SUV this morning. It will be ready to go tomorrow, but maybe we can get it sooner and drive home."

"I'll have it here at 5:00 a.m. tomorrow morning, ready to go. Now, since you have the gun in your hand, let's go pick up the holster and head to the firing range. I want you to see the shrink again before you go. We'll see if we can get your Friday appointment bumped up to late today. Kate, can we leave a uniformed outside your door until you leave?"

Exasperated, Kate said, "Oh, whatever. I need to get on to the IP trail now. I can get started with my cell and laptop if you can keep out intruders, the bomb squad, and any would-be assassins."

Jack and Daggy, feeling like little boys being chastised, both said, "Right."

They all headed out of Dr. Beretta's room, secured it, and returned to Jack and Kate's room. Jack retrieved the holster, they headed for a quick pee, then the two police officers were on their way.

Officer Daigle said, "Keep the safety lock on, Kate."

As soon as the boys were gone, Kate threw off the clothes she was wearing and put on comfortable, loose-fitting clothing suitable for meditating. She selected some clarinet concertos on her tablet and settled into a meditation session. The session started as a mental battle with invading distracting and disturbing thoughts traipsing in from every corner of her mind. She started by chasing them out. That just increased her anxious ridden clutter. Gradually, as she felt her breathing beginning to harmonize with the clarinet resonance, she climbed down, slipping in a calm rhythm. As each frenetic distraction stepped up to the door, she simply dismissed them with *not now*. She envisioned herself swimming, slowly, strongly, and effortlessly traversing Meech Lake. Her strokes and breathing synchronized; her centre and equilibrium were restored, and her direction and focus emerged. Nearly an hour had passed when she rose feeling calmed, centred, and sharp. She poured a glass of water, sliced a whole lime into it, walked about the suite thinking,

then she went to her laptop and signed into the protected, encrypted site she had set up with her brilliant cyber-geek contact, Bryant. Daylight hours were not his delight, but she hoped on an off chance he might be available. She sent a message:
Same case, intensifying, need your help. IP chase to the finish. Dangerous.

Bryant's handle lit up. I'm in — call me.

Kate reached Bryant on the phone.

"Have you run into a company called CCTech?"

"Yup, brilliant, very, very bad boys. No ethics. Ex-military types. Dangerous. Shoot to kill. Into some shady drone stuff."

Kate said, "We — I want to take them out on IP transgressions."

"These guys don't care. They are in it for the money, the power, and the glory — such a waste of good brains. They came home from Iraq and Afghanistan with their brains intact but their morals bankrupt."

Kate gave Bryant a thumbnail sketch of what she thought happened with the technology convergences after CCTech moved into the iBrain fold.

"Whatever you think they did, it will be a hundred times worse," said Bryant. "Jesus, Kate, you really live on the edge. What happened to those nice, easy IP chases we did when you started out? This is really dangerous stuff."

Kate told Bryant she suspected CCTech had compromised several technology platforms in redesigning the bioengineered neuro-microchip so it could be remotely launched and activated. She went on to tell him that rather than doing clinical trials, they were putting it out there to test on target individuals — people that pissed them off. "The latest victim is the new CEO of iBrain, Dr. Giorgio Beretta."

"Wasn't he a buddy of your dead guy, Taylor?" said Bryant.

"Yes, that's correct," said Kate.

"And you've got British Intelligence all over this — every

branch of their service. I haven't been able to figure out if they are competing or collaborating with CCTech. Any other dynamos leaping into the fray?" asked Bryant.

Kate said, "The Canadian and American intelligence service counterparts are probably biting at their heels. I would not be surprised if the defense R&D institutes aren't all excited by the prospects of the CCTech technology applications. They are probably at least dabbling in it without the knowledge of their governments. My plan to bring them down is not sexy. There are no moon launches in this approach. It will be to simply track, document, expose, and charge. I think we can get them on the entire suite of IP transgressions — patents, trademarks, copyrights, trade secrets — that can put them away long enough and deep enough. The original iteration of this technology will have the chance to become part of neuro medical treatment for the masses."

"Kate, these guys won't go down without a fight. It will be a technologically sophisticated fight to the death. You can't do this on your own or even just with the help of my network. You need an army."

"I think I am amassing it. What will be crucial is when to call them in. Okay, back to the IP chase." Kate told Bryant about three technologies key to the bioengineered neuro-microchip that she was fairly certain CCTech had totally compromised. "We should be able to hit them with everything once we've got it adequately documented. You will have to reinvent yourself after this comes down. There might be a time delay in getting compensation to you, but it will come."

"Kate, I only ever spend money on software, hardware, and pizza. You are good to go with me. As usual, let's keep our contact to a minimum. I've got my marching orders, and you need to march."

"Okay, I'll send you everything I have on these technologies via our encrypted link. If Dr. Beretta revives, and I can safely bring him in, I will. We could then have a lot more to work with on the IP front. Oh, and one final digression — can you get me a reading on Karen Palmer, MI6?"

"It's done. I did it when you went to meet with her a couple of weeks back. I just hit the send button on it."

Kate went into the folders she had already assembled on the various IP trails she had amassed on iBrain technologies and lifted the micro-drone technology interfaces with the bioengineering platforms and the stem cell manipulation. There were dozens of newly developed technologies moving through the pipeline and modifying faster than the speed of light as they went. Kate examined the IP trail that had come on board within three months of CCTech joining the consortium up to the present. There were twenty-two in that period. She selected three cold, clear cases and forwarded all of the documentation to Bryant.

20

Jack and Daggy arrived at the firing range, picked up ear protectors, and headed out. Daggy went first, firing several rounds, taking out the target, then he stepped aside for Jack to take a turn. Jack's hands felt clammy as he stepped up for his round. He pointed the Glock then started to shake. He couldn't squeeze the trigger. Daggy stood behind him, wrapped his arms around Jack's hand, and pulled the trigger six times. Jack was spent and let his arm hang down.

"Now you do it. Six rounds."

Jack's hands steadied, and he fired six rounds.

Daggy said, "Good, that's probably six more rounds than you will fire during the rest of your career. You are going to be fine. Since we are here, empty the magazine with a little better shooting." Jack did.

"Regardless of what the shrink says — that's where I am taking you next — you will be fine. Just watch your moods — anger — withdrawal. Stay on top of it."

Jack got a clean bill of health from the shrink, although once again, the psychiatrist recommended that he get some counselling about the loss of his ex-wife and daughter. "If you don't, these things have a nasty way of biting you at the most inopportune times. Unprocessed grief can play havoc with relationships," said the psychiatrist as he shook Jack's hand on his departure.

Before leaving the hospital, an intern checked Jack's wound. It was healing nicely. The intern removed the existing bandage and replaced it with a waterproof patch bandage that covered the area with no added bulk. Jack picked up a box of the same bandages at the pharmacy before leaving.

Daggy met him at the hospital entrance and proposed that he and Marny come over for dinner in the hotel suite. Marny was happy to package up her standard Italian cuisine and bring it over. Jack called Kate with the plan, and she readily agreed. He said they would likely be there in about an hour.

Kate said, "Perfect. I got a lot of IP work done and will just continue working on it until you get here." Then she asked, "Any word on Dr. Beretta?"

"We'll check on him before we leave the hospital."

Daggy and Jack went to the secure area where Giorgio was being treated. His attending physician was at the desk when they approached, and two uniformed policemen were outside the door, with hospital security at the elevator and the exit doors from the floor. Daggy and Jack showed their service IDs and were allowed to proceed. Dr. Sanchez recognized Officer Daigle and greeted him.

"I was just going to call you. The information the Canadian pathologist gave us was really helpful. We cleared his system of the sedative and analgesic then revived him. He seems fine, although we are continuing to monitor him closely. He has spoken to his brother, Mario Beretta, but we didn't allow any other calls through."

"Have there been other calls?" Jack asked.

"Yes, four calls that we declined and two visitors that were turned away in the lobby — all male, both calls and visitors."

"Can we talk to him?" asked Jack.

"Yes, of course, he's quite alert and able to speak. In fact, he appears to be almost normal, apart from that microchip in his brain. Under normal circumstances, we would be ready to discharge him."

Dr. Sanchez showed the two officers into the room. "Dr. Beretta, these are the two police officers who found you."

"Jack Johnson?"

"And this is Officer Daigle of the Boston Police," said Jack. "Are you up to talking to us?"

"Yes, of course. Do you know what happened to me?"

"Not conclusively, but Kate has a theory. I believe she discussed it in with you in relation to Vincent Bernard Taylor." Giorgio nodded. Jack said, "You have the same kind of bioengineered neuro-microchip implanted in your brain as the one chief coroner Bosum found in the brain of Dr. Taylor. We think it is connected to iBrain research and more specifically to the CCTech branch of iBrain's technology development."

"Jesus, like we previously discussed, my own company running amuck right under me. Has anyone been in touch with Claude Mason?"

"No, it's possible that he was trying to reach you, but until we are certain he isn't part of the conspiracy trying to harm you, we are guarding access to you here in the hospital, both in person and by phone," said Officer Daigle.

"What makes you think Claude has anything to do with this?"

"The part that Kate didn't tell you, but I will tell you now, is that the microchip in Dr. Taylor's brain had several British Intelligence IP signatures on it."

Giorgio leaned his head back on the pillow. "I think I am getting a headache."

Daigle said, "We'll leave you to rest. I would like to speak with you again as soon as possible. Here is my cell number.

Call me at any time." He wrote the cell number on the back then handed Giorgio his card. "The uniform will remain on guard at least until tomorrow."

Daigle was formulating a plan to try to keep Dr. Beretta, Jack, and Kate safe.

They stopped by Daggy's house to pick up Marny and make sure homework was going to happen with the girls. A young cousin who was a university student was going to spend the evening with them and provide some guidance on the essays that each of them had due shortly. Jack found Marny to be exactly the kind of woman he was expecting — warm, caring, loving, and very, very funny. Her smiles, plays on words, gentle teasing of Daggy, and self-deprecating manner had him smiling and laughing within moments of meeting her.

Back at the hotel suite, Marny had the same impact on Kate. It was like Marny swept in, and tension swept out before the door even closed behind her. Daggy poured the wine, and Marny laid out an antipasti platter of salami, mortadella, and prosciutto, along with cheese, greens, and bruschetta. They grazed away, talking and laughing. Both Daggy and Marny were very interested in the Gatineau, a subject near and dear to the hearts of Jack and Kate. They laughed over anecdotes about the French-English cultural differences in their everyday lives as Marny's delicious pesto tortigliano slipped down with yet another fine red wine from her grandfather's wine cellar — all homemade, of course. She added a contorni of green and yellow vegetables steamed and lightly oiled. They wound up their picnic meal with homemade gelato from Marny's sister's restaurant and coffee. Marny and Daggy bade their farewells, and Daggy said he would be back at five in the morning with Jack's new SUV.

21

As they closed the door behind them, having collected the plate they had given the officer on duty, Kate said, "I feel like an old couple bidding the in-laws farewell after a wonderful visit."

Jack slipped his arm around her and said, "Kate Roarty, I would be very happy to become that old couple with you."

Kate smiled, they kissed warmly — rather like an old couple — then Kate instantly pulled away. "We have to pack. We're leaving in six hours."

Jack said, "My packing will take me about ten minutes. I think this is your issue, my dear. Can I help?"

Kate declined, saying she was too accustomed to doing her own packing, but if he wouldn't mind putting the dishes in the dishwasher and tidying the kitchen while she got to it.

Kate awakened a moment before the alarm was to go off at 4:00 a.m. and quickly turned it off before it wakened Jack. She leapt out of bed, put on the coffee, and turned on the shower. She was enjoying a refreshing reverie when Jack joined her in the shower and both quickly soaped down and rinsed off.

They quickly towelled off, downed their coffees as they dressed, and readied to leave. Following Daggy's instructions, they did not check out. The uniform accompanied them down to the lobby, where Jack's new Land Cruiser was waiting for them at the entrance. Daggy was in the driver's seat — but there was another person in the back seat.

Daggy greeted them and said, "I want you to leave right away. The guest accompanying you will be with you for a bit. It's maybe the best way to keep you all as safe as possible and get this case solved. You will remain registered at the hotel, and he will remain registered at the hospital. Jack, we have notified both American and Canadian border security that you will be carrying a handgun, and the plates are temporary from my cousin's lot just to get you up to Canada. You can send both back in the fullness of time. All of the vehicle documentation is in a white pouch in the glove compartment. Oh, and here's a little something for you to listen to on that fancy sound system you have in this pick-up. There are two copies — keep them separately."

Jack looked perplexed but took the CD case and the keys, put their bags in the back where there were two bags already, and got in. Kate got in beside him, remarking, "Pretty deluxe, I'd say there, Lieutenant Johnson." Then she looked into the back seat as Jack picked up what she was looking at while adjusting the rear-view mirrors.

"Dr. Beretta!" exclaimed Kate.

"Officer Daigle thought it was a good idea, and so do I. I hope you do not mind."

"Yes," said Kate, and Jack agreed, albeit a bit haltingly.

"Let's get out of the city, then we can talk." Jack took a moment to program the GPS then enter the coordinates for the trip. The melodious female voice guided him over to the M-28 N then onto the I-93 N, and they were headed for New Hampshire. He turned off the GPS voice and looked down to see two Starbucks coffees on the cup console between the front seats and another one in the back. Dr. Beretta — Giorgio said, "I have cakes, grapes, and apples, as well as sandwiches that Officer Daigle handed to me for a late-morning stop — he said his wife had put the care package together for us."

Kate said, "As my mother would say, bless that guy."

"And as a buddy of his, who owns a diner in Boston, said yesterday, 'You don't find one like him on every street corner.'"

They had cleared the metropolitan area before sunrise and were speeding across the lowland estuary of urban Massachusetts. Settling into the ease and comfort of the new vehicle, they soon climbed through hilly countryside, crossed the Merrimack River, and followed the most direct route north to Vermont and home to Quebec.

Kate said, "Giorgio, we are going to Montreal first to meet Dr. Isabel Bosum, our chief coroner who did the autopsy on Dr. Taylor. She has been in touch with the Ottawa Mind and Brain Institute to give us a hand on understanding the bioengineered neuro-microchip. Of course, you may be able to tell us as much, if not more than they can figure out."

"Or work with them to fill in what CCTech has done to our original biotechnology platform."

Jack looked at him from the rear-view mirror and said, "So you really aren't in bed with the cowboys at CCTech."

Giorgio looked stunned and shocked. Kate was studying his face very carefully and once again thought he was either a brilliant actor or the genuine article. She was leaning on the side of the genuine article.

Jack's cell rang. He dug it out and handed it to Kate. It was Guy. "Hi, Guy, This is Kate. Jack's driving, and we haven't dug out the earphones or figured out the onboard communications system in this new vehicle."

"I can see both of your GPSs are on the move, coming this way." Kate switched the phone to speaker and put it on the jack.

"Guy, we have a guest travelling with us, Dr. Giorgio Beretta, the CEO of iBrain. He is coming for his own safety and to work with us to move as quickly as possible on the IP trail. He has the same chip in his brain as the one Dr. Bosum found in Dr. Taylor's brain. We think he acquired it yesterday."

"*Tabarnac*, another bomb on the loose. Can we ... er ... talk ... *peut -être en français?*"

"Dr. Beretta *parle en français très bien, mais*. It's okay, Guy, go ahead."

"I think we are all on the same side." Jack looked in his rear-view mirror at Giorgio. "If we discover otherwise, I have a loaded Glock under my arm. Kate is pretty adept with it too." He
looked at Kate.

"*Calisse,* less than a week in the US, and you've both gone cowboy. I hope in more ways than one. *Bonjour*, Monsieur Beretta. *Ecoutez*, all hell is breaking loose here with the intelligence services moving in. Dr. Bosum is trying to keep a lid on it, working with her guy in CSIS, but the lid blew away in the west wind — the garbage is about to tumble out."

Kate said, "We are about three hours south of Montreal, just coming down out of the White Mountains. If the border crossing is swift and smooth, we should be pulling into the chief coroner's office in three hours."

"Okay, we can hold the cavalry at bay until then. Call me when you arrive."

"Okay, and Guy, how are you making out with Clare St. Denis?"

"I had some more tea with her yesterday. My kidneys need a day to recover. She is terrified, but I think she wants to talk."

"*Merci*, Guy, *salut*," said Jack.

Kate looked back to see Dr. Beretta sound asleep. "That's good. We won't be getting much sleep when we arrive in Ottawa."

The border crossing through the town of Stanstead was

quiet, and both sides were expecting Jack and Kate. They checked Giorgio's passport then waved them through. Kate and Jack reminisced about the days when this was an open border; people in the town moved about freely without much thought the border was even there. Then 9/11 changed all of that — citizens of the twenty-eight countries of the EU moved about freely and easily, yet two countries on the North American continent were building a modern-day Berlin Wall. No wonder Canada was steadily forging closer ties with the European Union. It was becoming easier for business to traverse the ocean than to cross the forty-ninth parallel. But today … the Canada-US border crossing was good.

The sleek new Land Cruiser pulled into the underground parking on Rue Parthenais, where Dr. Bosum's office and labs were located. She met them in the lobby and arranged ID for Kate and Dr. Beretta. She greeted him warmly and asked how he was feeling. He thanked her then remarked, "You Canadians are a team, aren't you?"

She smiled. "At least on this case we are, and I hope you will come to play a key role on that team." She turned and studied him carefully. "It is my role to tell your friend's story. That is what pathologists do, Dr. Beretta — speak for the dead who cannot speak for themselves. I understand your role in your profession is to improve the quality of life for the living."

"Yes it is," said Giorgio.

They went into a small boardroom, crowded and spartan, and took seats. Kate noted it was nothing like the boardrooms of the British Intelligence Service. There was, however, a pitcher of water with real glasses on a tray in the middle of the table.

"Help yourself," said Dr. Bosum. "That which we feared has arrived — the various levels of intelligence service in Canada and the US are entering the fray. We gathered the Brits were already in the melée. What we have to do is capitalize on this manpower and momentum and not lose any energy fighting it. Kate, you must focus on the IP trail — there is no one else out there with your expertise and experience on this case. Dr. Beretta, we expect you to earn your bread and butter here, so you are hereby deputized you to work with Kate." Jack looked at her quizzically. "No, of course, I don't have that authority, but it must be so."

"Consider it so, Dr. Bosum," said Dr. Beretta.

"Good, then let's go." She got up and grabbed a rolly carry-on bag and her light spring and fall coat.

Jack said, "Where are we going?"

"To Ottawa to drop off Kate and Dr. Beretta at her house, then we are meeting with CSIS, CBSA, CSEC, and the RCMP at our Gatineau headquarters. You are in charge of Operation Chipdown."

Jack burst into laughter. "I love you, Dr. Bosum."

"You can't marry me. I think you are already spoken for." She smiled at Kate and headed for the door.

"Wow, a new car with an old CD player — that's unusual, car manufacturers stopped putting CD players in vehicles more than a decade ago." Jack popped the CD Daggy had given him into the player as he pulled out of the parking slot. He stopped as he heard his daughter's voice singing out through the sound system.

"Jack?" said Dr. Bosum.

Jack turned toward her with tear-filled eyes. "I guess the Boston police recovered the only thing I cared about from the wreckage of my car after the explosion. Elizabeth and I made this CD together. We always listened to it on our road trips."

They had exited the building seventeen minutes after they entered it. Dr. Bosum reached ahead and squeezed Jack's shoulder as he switched the sound system to a Sirius soft jazz station.

Kate outlined her IP chase plan to Dr. Bosum. "I like it, Kate. Let me work with the intelligence battalions to use them when we need them. When we need to talk, I will come to you, so you do not lose any time. I am afraid you two are under house arrest at Kate's place until we bring this thing down, and we will bring it down. I will stay in Gatineau with my sister and her family. They have a spare room, and it's walking distance from the SQ headquarters. Yes indeed, Jack, all those big boys are coming to us. It's our case. It was the only way to prevent them from squabbling among themselves over the power podium. The Americans will arrive tomorrow afternoon. I gather the Brits have already been here for a while. CBSA will want a word about that. Thank god the French aren't involved — that would be enough to send me scurrying back to my cadavers. Oh, and Kate, we have arranged for you to be able to swim at Canterbury pool. The pool will be closed for an hour each day from 1:00 to 2:00 p.m. You can swim alone with security. If you wish to join her, Dr. Beretta, you may."

He smiled. "Perhaps I will."

"One of SQ rookies is at your house now, filling the fridge with fresh fruit, vegetables, juice, milk, coffee, etc. They were going to pick up some of those Farmboy meals from that big new store up at the Trainyards. I understand that fare isn't too bad." Kate was amazed. From cadaver to cuisine, this little woman was a powerhouse.

"Oh, a dedicated, secure, super-high-speed cable is being installed at your house. It is yours to keep after all of this is over. There will be a CSEC tech there to show you the ropes when you arrive."

They pulled up in front of Kate's house one and a half

hours later. Kate looked at her watch in amazement. They had left Boston a mere seven hours ago, and they still had a healthy workday ahead of them. She said to Dr. Beretta, "My home is at the eastern edge of the city, so entering it from this way doesn't pass through the beauty that has kept me here for so long. After we finish this job, I hope we can stroll along our canal, view the autumn colours across the massive Ottawa River, and picnic along the smaller, tumbling Rideau River. Ottawa is an outdoors city filled with bike paths, walking trails, and many beautiful historic structures tastefully interspersed with grand edifices of modern architecture. While every season displays its splendour, this is a particularly beautiful season. There are only days of open-water swimming left before the autumn cools as it careens toward winter. The city of Gatineau and the Gatineau Hills reach eastward across the Ottawa River in a larger region known as the National Capital Commission. Administratively, it's similar to Washington, D.C."

Dr. Bosum went in to check that the rookies had done their job right. Indeed they had, including making up the bed in the guest room for Dr. Beretta. Kate showed Giorgio up to the guest room and dropped her bags in her own room.

When she came down the stairs, Big Ben mowed her down. He squealed, wiggled, whimpered, and lapped her face wet in short order. Francine was behind him. "Ben! Where are your manners?"

Kate rolled on the floor, wrestling with him like she was a second Golden Retriever. "At some point I guess we'll send them both off to obedience training," laughed Francine.

Dr. Bosum said, "Francine will come around once a day and take him on a long walk, then Raymond over there with the RCMP can do the rest. I don't think you will have time to go with Francine, but if you need out for air, take Ben for a walk, accompanied by Raymond."

"Okay!" Kate saluted.

"Oh, and we put in a large coffee pot. That little thing you have won't cut it. Yes, you can keep that too afterward. The small one is in the cupboard." She turned to Dr. Beretta. "Since we are giving you the benefit of the doubt that you are a good guy, we need your help to figure out Claude Mason. Did he get in bed with CCTech and bring British Intelligence into that fold, or visa versa, with the same result?"

"I too am trying to figure that out, Dr. Bosum. You will be the first to know when a definitive answer presents itself. All I can tell you is that he has a brilliant mind; he was a fine scientist and I, all of us — the lads, that is — remain perplexed that he chose to go the route he did. We keep thinking something is missing — there must be something we don't know. Maybe Vincent knew what it was, but obviously he can't tell us."

Dr. Bosum replied, "Don't be so sure about that. Those that have passed on tell us a great deal. The form of communication is different, that's all. If Dr. Taylor was trying to tell the story, then we'll piece it together. In the meantime, your job is to help take CCTech and their network out of action."

Kate accompanied Dr. Bosum to the door. "Thank you for doing so much to make this job possible. I have a cadre of invisible cyber geeks out there who assist me."

Before she could continue, Dr. Bosum said, "Kate, if we succeed, all of the freelancers who assisted in blowing this mess open will be handsomely remunerated. If we fail, all of us will be washing a lot of dishes."

Kate smiled. "We won't fail." Dr. Bosum nodded and left. Kate lingered for a moment at the door. She liked this tiny, amazing woman very much.

She turned and said to Dr. Beretta, "Let me show you the command centre." They descended into the basement. "I still call it the studio. It has a beautiful Swedish dance floor that I installed for my son, who dazzled the dance world at the time. He hardly used it. It sat empty for a few years until my IP tracking took off, and I realized that I needed to create a secure area. I still do whatever work is safe to do aboveground. I have never been keen on basements, but as they go, this one is pretty good."

Dr. Beretta looked around a large room painted a soft green — Vietnamese Lily Pad, Kate said it was called — with abundant ambient lighting, servers humming away off in one corner, and screens galore. There were several fixed desktops and laptops — all state-of-the-art — a high-speed printer that could print odd sizes like blueprints, a replicator for prototypes, and a small kitchenette with food and drinks in the fridge and on the counter. In addition to the three other bathrooms in this smallish house, there was a fourth bathroom just outside the studio. Framed photos of Kate's two adult children could be found everywhere throughout the room. There was also an ample distribution of firm, comfortable chairs and a stand-up workbench set at a comfortable height.

"Wow, very nice, Mrs. Roarty."

"The bonus cheques from my first three contracts paid for all of this," Kate remarked as she fanned the room with her hand. "Luckily, my clients were happy, so they paid well."

It was early in the day to connect with Bryant, but if he had worked through the night, as was his habit, there would likely be some messages in their secure site dropbox.

She checked. The first message read:

> Kate, we are rolling? Brought in two other guys. We are all fluid in every aspect of IP. One guy is bang-on in trade secrets and industrial design theft. The other in copyright, patents and trademarks. Will not reveal their paths or identities in case this whole thing goes south. Their work will come through me to you through lots of

firewalls. Rates same as mine. Good to go?

Examining all CCTech technologies then ferreting out those that went forward to snatch the iBrain platforms. These cowboys engaged in IP theft right from the beginning. They used their intelligence to copy, modify, integrate — steal and corrupt the medical therapeutic objectives of the designs. If we can, we will pin the theft to CCTech researchers, that is to individuals rather than the company. It is always easier to get convictions on charges against individuals. Suggest you not restrict to three technologies but as many as we can identify.

We need a scientist who knows this stuff working with us.

Kate sent a reply: Yes, yes, Dr. Beretta/iBrain now in the studio.

They worked around the clock, taking only swim, food, and toilet breaks. Dr. Beretta was a half-decent swimmer. He laughed and said, "By accompanying you to the pool, I not only get a break, some exercise, but a shower as well. This is more gruelling than working on a thesis."

Dr. Bosum and Jack were skilfully bringing the army of Intelligence services into the fold. All were wary of the Brits, so they kept them at bay. The documentation on the CCTech IP transgressions poured in from Kate and her team. The volume was staggering, and the implications were mind-boggling.

The original network at CCTech had reeled in more than one hundred researchers who were working in CCTech labs, various iBrain labs, and the labs of the National Defense R&D for the US, UK, India, Finland, and Canada. Dr. Beretta was doing yeoman's work in verification, but he needed help. Kate brought in her young scientist, Dr. Chad Jones, who was only too anxious to help, and as long as he was fed, he was tireless and exacting.

While Kate had no time to follow up, it seemed that Claude Mason had vanished. Nobody had heard from him since the dinner at the Charles Hotel in Cambridge. They had never reconvened for part two, as was originally planned. Suspicion concerning the British Intelligence Service held them back from contacting anyone there. Kate finally reached out to Graham Burke, who was only too happy to find out what he could.

While the CCTech team had attracted scientists working in many labs, it appeared they had not corrupted any members of the various secret services. Nothing untoward pointed at Claude Mason. The IP signatures on Dr. Taylor's and Big Ben's microchips were perplexing. They were not found on Dr. Beretta's chip.

By the end of day three, it felt like they had been working on it for three months. The intelligence services were clamouring to move in. Jack was keeping them coordinated, poised, and ready to take action. Dr. Bosum was mollifying egos. Most of them were men — big men, but whether Dr. Isabel Bosum was dealing with them in person or on FaceTime video link, they deferred to her counsel. CTEC, CSIS, and the RCMP were obstreperous, while CBSA was playing it cool. Without telling anyone, they were quietly looking for Claude Mason. Both Bryant and Graham Burke confirmed that Karen Palmer was trustworthy and had not been compromised. She had to be brought in, and it was decided that Kate and Dr. Bosum would do it rather than her counterparts in related organizations. The Canadian equivalent would, however, be present on the FaceTime screen.

Karen Palmer confirmed that Claude Mason had been missing for four days. "He last reported in after having dinner with you Kate and three others." Otherwise, she listened to the description of the entire Operation Chipdown, the documentation process of the IP, and the take-out plan. When Kate explained the initial reluctance to bring in MI5, MI6, and GCHQ, she said nothing but simply nodded. "About Claude Mason, we are aware that he is caught in the middle. We put him there. We are hoping that he wasn't corrupted. You were right to be wary of our intelligence service. We ourselves were cautious. That is why we tried to recruit you, Kate. We thought you could navigate the investigation in a way that we could not. The seam ruptured when some of our agents identified the defense R&D scientists who had been compromised by CCTech. CCTech initially bought them off then disappeared them. Three agents that vanished — Claude was working on it — now he is gone. We have a small cadre of highly trustworthy agents that can pull off our end of this operation. We hope Claude has not become collateral damage. While we can never say one hundred percent of anyone, we are certain that Claude was incorruptible. He gave up his personal and professional life to come with us. He did it to protect Dr. Vincent Bernard Taylor and iBrain. It is unlikely that after all that, CCTech would get to him unless it was to kill him."

Kate added, "Or use him." Her comment was left hanging.

"Kate, Dr. Bosum I will be your sole contact for the UK portion of Operation Chipdown."

Kate and her team amassed enough concrete IP documentation to put all of the CCTech principals away for several lifetimes. Depending upon the legal jurisdictions where their recruits were operating and what they had done, scientific research careers would be brought to a halt. In some cases, not only were numerous criminal charges laid, but conspiracy to commit treason also applied. Even with the wizardry of the best lawyers, few of those arrested would see the outside of a prison for a very long time, if ever. The five-country operation proceeded with exacting precision, resulting in the arrest of all CCTech partners and employees, as well as all of the scientists that CCTech had managed to corrupt. The covert operation took out a total of 121 PhD scientists and a number en route to attaining those credentials. The raids yielded up documentation on the targets for the implants. The list was a who's who among world leaders, rulers, and others in power positions. It appeared that only four prototypes had been launched. Dr. Taylor and Big Ben had been the first two, and Dr. Beretta was the fourth. It seemed that some more perfecting work was required to activate the chip remotely, although the science for taking control of various brain functions was exacting. The two Canadian scientists in the CCTech fold revealed that the systematic launch had been delayed to address the activation problem. As well, the recall technology required a great deal more work. They were probably six months away from going operational.

News of the operation barely hit the media. A small inside-page article made it into many major news channels. A devastating hurricane hit the Philippines at the same time. The world's media preoccupation turned there, so nothing more was broadcast about Operation Chipdown.

Scientists Arrested on Two Continents

Scientists were arrested in five countries for stealing and modifying the intellectual property of neuro medical innovations. While theft of inventions, trademarks, copyright, and industrial design has become more widespread in the modern cyber-tech world, the tolerance for theft and corrupt applications is diminishing in the high-stakes game of who gets to the bioscience platform first.

Everyone took a dozen hours off to rest weary bodies. There would be a lot of mop-up to destroy the sinister technologies developed by iBrain. The Saudi and Qatari financial backers scurried back to the Gulf and kept their heads down and billfolds shut.

Dr. Bosum and Jack showed up at Kate's house laden with food, coffee, juice, and fruit. Guy Archambault accompanied them. Chad was asleep on the sofa. They commiserated a bit about the entire operation. It was an anticlimax to the adrenaline high they had been running on for days.

Dr. Bosum spoke. "Kate, as far as we are concerned, you have done what we hired you to do. Of course, your work went way beyond anything we could have imagined when we first contracted you. All of the intelligence services are going to kick in to cover the costs. However, as far as I am concerned, the case remains wide open. Although we can readily surmise, we do not know who killed Dr. Taylor, and we need to find Claude Mason, even if he isn't in this country. He may be hosting chip number three, and if he isn't, we have to locate it and destroy it."

Guy said, "Maybe I can help. Kate, are you and Big Ben up for a visit to your beloved Meech Lake? We can stop in on Clare St. Denis."

Giorgio piped up. "Can I come too?"

"Okay, let's take my car so we are not too conspicuous. Oh, and I am bringing my bathing suit. No protests from anyone," said Kate.

"I'm on duty — regulation. How about if I follow you?" said Guy.

Jack said, "What am I, chopped liver?"

Kate smiled. "Jack, you just directed the most successful

international roundup in recorded history without any injury, death, or mishap of any kind."

Dr. Bosum locked her arm in Jack's and said, "Come on, big guy, we have some mopping up to do back at Gatineau HQ, not to mention the massive amount of reporting that you have to do. If Guy, Kate, and Giorgio can help tell Dr. Taylor's story, let them go do it."

Kate and Giorgio climbed into her SUV while Big Ben leapt into the back seat. She navigated them through the labyrinth of tree-lined residential streets down onto Main Street and across the Rideau River, where geese were assembling for the autumn migration. Ducks and paddlers were luxuriating in the warm breezes and sunshine sparkling across the water. They sped up past St. Paul University, a liberal arts institution enjoying a strong reputation in social work and theological studies. Main Street yielded onto Colonel By Drive that snaked along the Rideau Canal. University of Ottawa students scurried across the pedestrian bridge to classes or lingered playing Frisbee on the grounds that lined the canal. Kate pointed out the majestic Parliament buildings and the Chateau Laurier, one of Canada's oldest fine hotels, now under foreign ownership.

They sped past the imposing, austere, grey-block stone American Embassy that presided at the head of the ByWard Market, a popular neighbourhood of eateries, local shops, and farm produce sold from open stalls. The SUV swung north across the old steel interprovincial bridge, the subject of erudite award-winning humour in the hands of author Terry Fallis. Giorgio saw the mighty Ottawa River filled with sightseeing boats, cruisers, and rowers from the local yacht clubs. The spectacular glass-domed National Art Gallery and the soft curving lines of the Museum of Civilization celebrated the shoreline of the vast river. Parks, docks, cafés terrasses and the prime minister's residence were all visible from this narrow two-lane bridge crossing the river that historically united English and French Canada. The clackity-clack of vehicles crossing it spilled onto Boulevard des Allumettières.

Kate said, "I always consider this bridge Ottawa's touch of San Francisco. The boardwalk on the west side is a very popular crossing that affords spectacular views." From there, they meandered through a series of roundabouts, finally dumping onto Highway 5N as they followed the route that climbed up into the Gatineau Hills. "It isn't Tuscany, but we think these hills are pretty special."

Giorgio said, "I feel like a kid let out of school for the summer holiday."

They continued to climb another several hundred metres, where the air was fresher and cleaner and the changing autumn leaves stunning in their brilliant reds, oranges, and yellows layered against the deep coniferous greens. Kate turned the SUV onto the dense, bush-lined Gatineau parkway, where she slowed right down, watching for snapping turtles and cyclists. Giorgio shrieked with delight when he saw a beaver in the pond near the top of the parkway.

22

As they swung back out onto the park road that hugged the shoreline of Meech Lake, Giorgio asked, "Kate, is this where Vincent grew up?"

"Yes."

They let silence yield to the beauty of the fiord-like lake until Kate pulled the SUV onto the edge of the property, where a white, squared-timber cottage sat perched in a clearing overlooking the water. An old woman sat at a picnic table, cleaning a basket of blueberries. Giorgio asked, "That's her?"

"Yes."

They got out, and Big Ben charged for the old woman, wiggling and squealing in much the same manner as he had with Kate when she saw her at home after arriving back from Boston.

"*Bonjour*, Madame St. Denis," said Guy.

"*Bonjour mon fils, ça va?*"

Guy introduced Giorgio. Clare St. Denis looked at him while Big Ben vied for her attention. "You were a friend of my boy. Big Ben is my boy's dog."

Guy sat down, and Clare St. Denis motioned to the others

to sit as well. Kate pulled a wooden lawn chair closer to her.

"Madame St. Denis, we came here to tell you that all of those bad men have been arrested. I think you can feel safer now."

"I killed him."

"Pardon?" said Guy.

"I killed my son."

She continued cleaning the blueberries.

Guy, Kate, and Giorgio looked at one another. This was not what any of them had expected to hear.

They remained silent, digesting what the old woman had said.

Kate breathed in and looked up, seemingly asking for guidance from a higher power. "Madame St. Denis, can you tell us about it?" She paused. "In English or French or a mix of both languages, whatever is easiest for you."

For some minutes, Clare continued to clean the blueberries. Even Big Ben became calm lying under the picnic table. They all waited quietly, enjoying the warm breeze blowing across the lake and the quiet beauty of the surroundings.

"Vincent preferred English, but he spoke French so beautifully. He came home and stayed for a long time. He did a lot of fixing and painting. He swam in the lake every day and built that new dock. We went for some dinners in the village, played cards and chess at night like we did when he was a boy. I deeply enjoyed having him here. He hadn't come home in many years. He was angry with me, but I never understood why. Whatever it was, I guess he got over it. He was troubled about something — deeply troubled, but I knew it wasn't anything to do with our home or me. The phone rang a few times for him, but he just waved the calls away. Then one day Claude Mason came. He stayed for a couple of days. I could tell Claude loved my Vincent very much. Vincent was very angry with him. Down by the lake, where they thought I couldn't hear, Vincent yelled at him, and then I heard my boy weeping. Claude left after that argument, and Vincent left the next day. He went back to Boston. I missed him and Big Ben very much."

She stopped and cleaned more berries, then went in the house and returned with bowls, maple syrup, and mineral water. "Vincent liked mineral water. He said I drank too much tea." Her eyes were filled with tears.

She dished out bowls of berries for all of them and poured mineral water into each glass, dropping lime slices at the same time so the water released the fruity fragrance, then handed around spoons and serviettes. The three ate the blueberries, sipped the mineral water, and waited patiently in silence.

The old woman cleaned more berries, then resumed speaking. "One day two men came to my door. They were looking for Vincent. They were Americans — big fellows. I told them Vincent had gone back to Boston. They gave me a card and asked me to call them if Vincent showed up. I took the card, but I had no intention of calling them. I put it away and forgot about it. Vincent came back. He had Big Ben with him. He was anxious and agitated, and so was the dog.

"He went off in the boat across the lake to see a childhood friend who was visiting with her family on the lake. When he was gone, those two men came back in one car, and a second car pulled on to the property. The first two men came in while the other two stayed out. I could see they had guns.

"They asked if Vincent was here, and I said no, he had gone back to Boston. I was frightened for Vincent. They got angry and pushed past me into the house, where they could see that in fact there was lots of evidence that Vincent was here. They sat me down forcefully and asked again if he was here. I said yes, but he had gone off for a couple of days to visit friends. I don't think they believed me. I am not a good liar.

"They told me that Vincent and the dog were part of a

neurological experiment that had gone wrong. They had injected a chip into the brain of Vincent and another into the dog. They had to find both of them, because they would soon become quite violent and probably go on a murderous rampage. I didn't believe them, but I thought something very bad was going to happen to Vincent. They waited for a few hours, becoming more and more angry — giving more and more frightening details about how he and the dog would behave. They finally left, warning me they would kill me if I didn't call them to tell them when Vincent came back."

She stopped talking and ate some blueberries. "Vincent loved blueberries in pies, muffins, in pancakes, and fresh with cream. He even sprinkled them on his breakfast eggs and dinner potatoes then smothered it all with maple syrup. He was such a gentle, fun-loving boy, curious about everything."

Kate asked quietly, "Did Vincent come back?"

"Yes, he did. He was calm. He had enjoyed a fun visit with his friend Jenny. He said Jenny loved Big Ben. He seemed happier, so I didn't tell him about the visit of the angry men that evening. I told him over breakfast the next morning. He turned into a madman, shoving the breakfast dishes off the table, upturning chairs, shouting and crying at the same time. I had never seen my boy behave like that in his life. I thought maybe what those men said would happen to him was really happening. I was crying, and he was so angry that I couldn't tell him everything the men had said.

"I heard the cars pull up. It was the men from before. Vincent seemed to know the big guys. He wasn't afraid of them. They argued outside, then Vincent jumped in the boat and took off. The other fellows raised their guns, fired at him, and Big Ben leapt on the one who was shooting and knocked him down. He wanted to kill the dog, but the big guy wouldn't let him. He said he was too valuable.

"One of the big guys asked where Vincent would go. I said I didn't know. He asked if there was a road on the other side of the lake. I told him no.

"They waited, watching the lake for a while, then came in the cottage. The big guy spoke quietly and said they had to capture Vincent for his safety and the safety of everybody else. He would get worse quickly. They gave me this device and told me when Vincent came back to squeeze it when he got close, then call them. They said it wouldn't hurt him, but it would subdue him — make him go to sleep. Then Vincent burst into the cottage. To save him, I squeezed the thing. It killed him. They threw his body in the boat — drove him out in the lake and dumped him.

"Even though it was nighttime, I knew that is what they did. When they came back, they said I shouldn't worry, just feel proud that I had saved humanity, and they left.

"You know the rest of the story. I killed my own son — my beautiful Vincent."

Epilogue

The funeral for Dr. Vincent Bernard Taylor took place during the last traces of Indian summer. He was buried in the old Meech Lake cemetery that hadn't seen an internment in sixty years. The local Meech Lake Community Association cleared the brush, trimming it back from the forest that had overtaken it. They spruced up the existing stones and wooden grave markers, mowed the vegetation cover to make it look something like grass, and planted autumn blooming flowers. The clearing offered a vantage point to survey the lake and commune with its inhabitants.

Henry (Henri) Taylor's remains were reinterred in the adjacent gravesite, where his spirit could rest with his son and be readily available to his wife. Clare would be able to visit this nearby gravesite whenever she wished. Jack Johnson navigated his Land Cruiser up the rugged road to the old cemetery carrying a precious cargo — Michael Pepper, who had made the journey from the UK to be with his lads for the funeral. There was Giorgio Beretta, of course, who had remained in Ottawa/Gatineau to continue to work with Kate and the SQ. Matti Toivenen came from Finland. He connected through London to meet Michael Pepper, whose son Andrew had brought him to Heathrow. Matti accompanied him on the remainder of the journey, and Kate and Giorgio met them at the Ottawa airport.

Kiran Patel came from India, and Claude Mason came from Boston, accompanied by Officer Daigle and his wife Marny. Claude had just been released from the Boston General Hospital. One of the American scientists arrested in the roundup did a plea bargain for the whereabouts of Mason. Claude was in pretty bad shape, but they got to him in time. It would be slow, but he was expected to make a full recovery.

The official death certificate for Dr. Vincent Bernard Taylor listed the cause of death as heart and lung failure. The record about his death would be locked away for twenty-five years — and that could be extended, if necessary. The Ottawa Mind and Brain Institute at the general campus of the Ottawa Hospital agreed to do the microsurgery to remove all three bioengineered neuro-microchips from Giorgio and Claude — yes, Claude had been implanted with the third microchip when CCTech personnel in Boston kidnapped him. The neurosurgeons took some convincing to agree to remove the microchip from Big Ben as well. They finally consented to do it on grounds of national security. Kate Roarty and Clare St. Denis assumed joint custody of Big Ben. They would all gather again in June in Boston when MIT conferred a PhD on Claude Mason for his thesis on detecting corruption in neuroscience research.

Kate Roarty took one last late-autumn swim at Meech Lake. Superintendent Jack Johnson paddled a canoe alongside as she swam. Big Ben sat in the bow for ballast. He would be allowed to honour the skills of his breed with a plunge into the water to swim alongside Kate as she made her way toward the dock at the white, squared-timber cottage.

Acknowledgements

This debut novel in the Kate Roarty, P.I. series has been made possible by many people who inspired, believed, read, commented, and dared to challenge and push my boundaries. I owe a debt of gratitude to Karan Maguire, who read them all and hung in there for many subsequent discussions. Simon Griffith, who took time out of a busy schedule to read my wretched first draft, provide tons of feedback, and accept the presence of the world's largest swimming pool in a most incongruous place, albeit in 2026. Loretta Craig Taylor, who instilled in me the efficacy of the semi-colon. Ingrid Hibbard, who read and said yes, then read again. Robin Tilsworth, who whiled away summer cottage hours reading, commenting, and supporting. Gina Matesic, who rendered university library resources accessible. To Karen Adele Shave who makes the best breakfasts in the UK. They launched me into authenticating my Cheltenham experience. To MOND, Alex, Angeline, Keith, Ken, Raeanne, and Victor for answering the call on establishing a technologically consistent environment in 2026. To Jordan Mitchell of One Owl Creative and Raeanne Pearce at Tellwell for a collaborative and rewarding design experience. To Allister Thompson, my editor, I wish to express my deep appreciation for his enthusiasm to engage in the debate and work with me to communicate my story with energy and clarity to make *Vantage Point* accessible to the rest of the reading world.

To those who have passed on but continue to give this experience so very much because I carry you in my heart and mind forever. Katherine Roarty, my paternal grandmother and the inspiration for the name of my protagonist — I would love to have known her. Elizabeth (Shepherd) Filteau, my mother, Charles Filteau, my father, and Jessie Culligan, mentor, teacher, confidante, and best friend, who was always just a phone call away to talk about literature, history, politics, poetry, the human condition and the vagaries of life. I miss her very much. And finally, to all of those unnamed scientists whose singular and collective passion to innovate infused me with an inspiration to experience the wonders of science becoming technology.

Coming Next
in the Kate Roarty, P.I. Series by Patricia Filteau

Looking for more from Kate Roarty, P.I.? You won't have to wait long to dive into Kate's next action-filled investigative pursuit.

She continues to run ahead of culprits, international intelligence, drones, bullets, and bombs to restore technology to the rightful innovators.

Traces (coming in 2017)

Fresh from the success of a multi-country takedown that unfolded in *Vantage Point*, Kate is primed to take on the titans of the mining business. *Traces* takes her to South Africa, the UK, Kazakhstan, and beyond. The technological innovation she is seeking to restore to its rightful innovators is worth billions on a continent rapidly running out of the rare earth minerals required to fuel its digital growth. Kate is good at what she does; she knows too much. Her fierce independence and open water swimming put her at risk of demise as her detractors relentlessly seek to eliminate her. Her advocates remain vigilant in extending the arm of protection and collaboration. Her clients emerge from her home base in Canada where her lover, a few friends, and a faithful canine diligently strive to compromise her independence.

Steps (coming in 2018)

Kate tries to back away from the risk of death. Her love life is becoming more entwined and dashes her into unexpected intrigue. Her respite from danger is short-lived, as she is lured into a seemingly innocuous investigation involving the world of dance choreography. She is once again off and running, following the thread of stolen intellectual property. Little does she know that the world of leading-edge international dance involves big money, corruption, and culprits willing to employ whatever high-tech means to keep and profit by what is not rightfully theirs. Will Kate survive this one?

CPSIA information can be obtained
at www.ICGtesting.com
Printed in the USA
LVOW12s0030070516
487105LV00001B/10/P

9 781773 020686